little reef
and other stories

MICHAEL CARROLL

TERRACE BOOKS
A TRADE IMPRINT OF THE UNIVERSITY OF WISCONSIN PRESS

Terrace Books
A trade imprint of the University of Wisconsin Press
1930 Monroe Street, 3rd Floor
Madison, Wisconsin 53711-2059
uwpress.wisc.edu

3 Henrietta Street
London WC2E 8LU, England
eurospanbookstore.com

Printed in the United States of America

Library of Congress Cataloging-in-Publication Data

Carroll, Michael (Writer), author.
[Short stories. Selections]
Little Reef and other stories / Michael Carroll.
pages   cm
ISBN 978-0-299-29740-4 (cloth: alk. paper)
ISBN 978-0-299-29743-5 (e-book)
I. Carroll, Michael (Writer), author After Dallas.   II. Title.
PS3603.A774588A6   2014
813′.6—dc23
2013038687

These stories have appeared in slightly different form in the following places: "Pascagoula," *Jonathan*; "Referred Pain," *The Yale Review*; "Her Biographers," *Southwest Review*; "Unsticking," *Animal Shelter*; "From the Desk of . . . Hunter B. Gwathmey," *Open City*; "Werewolf," *With: New Gay Fiction*.

to
EDMUND VALENTINE WHITE III

"Do you live here all alone?" she asked of Olive.

"I shouldn't if you would come and live with me!"

Even this really passionate rejoinder failed to make Verena shrink; she thought it so possible that in the wealthy class people made each other such easy proposals. It was a part of the romance, the luxury, of wealth; it belonged to the world of invitations, in which she had had so little share. But it seemed almost a mockery when she thought of the little house in Cambridge, where the boards were loose in the steps of the porch.

"I must stay with my mother and father," she said. "And then I have my work, you know. That's the way I must live now."

"Your work?" Olive repeated, not quite understanding.

"My gift," said Verena, smiling.

"Oh yes, you must use it. That's what I mean; you must move the world with it; it's divine."

HENRY JAMES, *The Bostonians*

"They're just Baptists," Miss Jenny said. "What about the money?"

WILLIAM FAULKNER, *Sanctuary*

CONTENTS

PART ONE

AFTER DALLAS

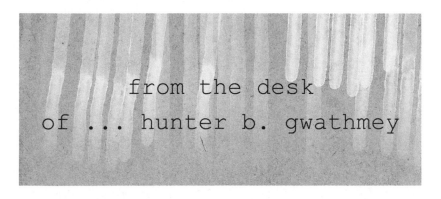

from the desk
of ... hunter b. gwathmey

to
REBECCA BOWEN CRAIG

You young people are the crème de la crème of Timucua County. I
hope I'm not boring you. I look out and I see intelligence in
every one of your faces. I see readers, but smart, bright young folks
with futures. One day, and sooner than you think, you'll go off to
college with your grades and the help of this countywide gifted program and this marvelous series of seminars, the Joe Berg Seminars. I
envy you. I wish I'd had a Joe Berg. I had a different education growing
up in the Midwest—sleepy stuff. But then I had the fortune of partici-
pating in World War Two," Gwathmey said, pausing pensively and
then blinking down at his notes.

It was an awkward moment. We were silent, junior high kids unsure how to react.

"And as schooling goes," the man went on and chuckled, "well, the
army ain't bad . . ."

And he waited for us to laugh. I wanted him to skip the army,
ahead to the part about becoming a writer. I was falling asleep in
my auditorium seat. I focused on his deep tan and broad, friendly
grin. We'd come from all over the county to see and hear Hunter B.

Gwathmey, an author we'd never heard of, and be inspired by him. He'd brought a sheaf of notes up to the podium after his introduction by the head of the gifted program, but he never seemed to refer to them, except for effect. Gwathmey sort of reminded me of an unusually pensive preacher.

He wanted us to feel proud and he started talking about local history. A lot of our Joe Berg speakers would do this. He said, "Imagine!" He poked at and molded the air. "Same year William Shakespeare's born, the French come to town. *Here*, right at our doorstep!"

We began tittering before we got what he was talking about. We'd covered this episode in fifth grade, then again in seventh (with more of the injustices the Indians had suffered thrown in—disease, dishonest deals, language problems). We'd just never heard it all so jazzily put.

He cooled the gesticulations for an instant, perfecting his dry comic timing. "The French were looking for gold. They could've asked us first. We would've told them . . ."

An underscore of giggles from us, yet Gwathmey pushed past it with a wave of his hand to shame us when he said, "And as you probably heard, those French were starving and dying."

I turned to Vickie, who was sitting next to me. Vickie wore the same continuous and pleasant smile she always got whenever we were allowed to leave school for half a day. I didn't know where I was with her. She and I had a private language. Every morning before gifted class we'd go over last night's Monty Python on PBS together. We'd do parts of the skits, accents and all, then reduce them to their essential gestures, signaling with those to each other for the rest of the day while working out our proofs, not always sitting together but still signaling. We twitched our noses and imaginary mustaches, raising circumspect eyebrows, mouthing: "Right!"

Reacting to Gwathmey's graveness, Vickie pursed her lips expectantly, staring up at the podium while trusting that I was watching her.

"Didn't wanna work. Lower and lesser nobles. They didn't know how," Gwathmey was saying, and so on, up until the point where

4

the Spanish sailed up from Havana hating the fact that Protestants were in their backyard and wiped them out. "Which as you know was the end of the French Huguenots," he said—pronouncing it *HUGH-guh-KNOTS*—"in Florida." He panned the room through his glinting windshield glasses. "*La Florida*," he said in a rat-a-tat Spanish accent. "Or as I like to call it," he then said in his regular purple-plush speaker's voice, before switching to a powder-puff Frenchy Pepé Le Pew: "*La Floride . . .*"

I'd done a little research at the library the week before.

A long time ago, Gwathmey had written a spy novel called *A Shadow at Midnight* about a German U-boat patrolling the northern Florida coast, and it was based on real events. The Nazi spies had rowed ashore from their submarine, just a few miles from where we were sitting, in an inflatable raft. They were hoping to pose as locals, infiltrate navy bases, and gather intelligence, but then they were caught and sent to a camp. The movie version was black and white—I'd seen some of it on TV one Saturday afternoon—and it starred the young, blond, and handsome George Peppard playing one of the Nazis. I knew George Peppard from *Breakfast at Tiffany's*, which I'd seen on another Saturday, an okay movie but I preferred the original novella by Truman Capote.

"I'd like to say a few words about that time," said Gwathmey, "that bloody, awful, and glorious time, which I won't describe to you, not all of it, but just to say how odd life is. Now, you're familiar as gifted students with the concepts of literary and dramatic irony, but I suppose it wasn't so ironic that I would one day write about that war, using some of the war experiences I'd myself had. Not directly, but as—I suppose you might say—*background* human research."

Gwathmey went into the ironies that his red-green blindness had saved him from entering the infantry and getting shipped off to be shot and killed on D-day, and that his grandmother had spoken German in Ohio and taught him some, so he was sent to Europe to work in intelligence.

Vickie seemed more interested in this part than I was. She was probably going to ask him a question at the end about Germany. She was mad that our school didn't offer German. Vickie was good at math and wanted to be a physicist and already planned to go to Cornell. I wondered if we were ever going to become boyfriend and girlfriend. I wanted to hold her hand. She was a few inches taller than me, though I tried not to think about it. I tried not to think about college. I didn't want to go to college at all, only to become a writer. Gwathmey had left the war topic and started talking about meeting his wife in Chicago, flashing his dentures to show his happiness.

I turned to Vickie and rolled my eyes and she smiled uneasily. I mouthed, "*Bor*-ing."

She cupped her pink-glossed lips and mouthed, "*Shhh . . .*" I pled with one hand. I had embarrassed myself and this wasn't comedy hour. I stared affectionately at her. I took her hand and she let me hold it and squeezed mine back a few times, and I felt peaceful.

Gwathmey lived in the area and wrote a column about politics and current events in the evening paper, the *Jacksonville Journal*, entitled "From the Desk of . . . Hunter B. Gwathmey," and lately he'd spent a lot of time in it complaining about Jimmy Carter.

We'd released hands—her idea—but whenever Gwathmey flash-forwarded and alluded to his later becoming a writer, Vickie nudged me in the ribs with her elbow, and I was following his thread now. Here was this successful man who seemed content. He was still in the northern Florida area, or no he'd landed here somehow, and he was happy to announce that in fact he was writing a trilogy—the *Matanzas* trilogy as he called it. That was the Spanish word for slaughter. Where he lived, just south of here in St. Augustine, there was a river called the Matanzas dubbed that by the Spanish after they'd killed the French Protestants, to commemorate their reclaiming of Catholic, Spanish-held land. And this fact of religious bigotry throughout history seemed to aggrieve Gwathmey especially. He said that his trilogy was meant to show that all throughout history bigotry, whether in the misguided Nazi ideology or the wars of religion that tore Europe apart back during the Reformation, had also been visited upon American soil. His last volume in the *Matanzas* trilogy, he announced, was going to be about the American Indians, focusing on the Florida Seminoles. The Seminoles, he said, were the most cosmopolitan grouping of folks, black and white (because they had runaway slaves, "half-breeds," and Native Americans from different Indian tribes) in the history of North America. He detailed this raising his nose like the prow of a ship defying an onslaught of crashing, foaming waves as it rocked on and bound forward.

I'd never paid much attention to any history, local or otherwise, to tell the truth.

Still, he must have known that he was losing us, and so he said, "Anyway, maybe you'll pick up one of my books and drop me a note sometime and tell me what you think about it, but what matters is that you keep learning, kind young ladies and gentlemen. And I thank you."

Gwathmey waited for his applause. And then that done, he called for questions.

Vickie and I both raised our hands.

"The fellow right here," he pointed at me, "this handsome, promising-looking dude."

I stood up. I said, "I wondered if you could say more about how you became a writer."

The room was politely quiet, wanting to hear more about Nazis and also Hollywood.

I sat back down and he gathered his thoughts, blinking. He said, "A funny person," and he scratched his chin, "a successful musician was asked on a street in New York how you get to Carnegie Hall, and that fellow replied, 'Practice, practice!' Guess that fella knew, all right."

"Was it hard?" I said, not standing back up but hollering it so that Vickie hooted a titter.

"Hell yeah it was hard," he said, and he chuckled, looking off. As though the murky, aquarium-wattage fluorescence of the auditorium were too bright, like flashbulbs at a press conference, he shaded his eyes and peered down at the end of the front row—where the gifted teachers were perched—and he grinned sheepishly and said, "I can say 'hell,' I hope?"

I craned my neck, straining to see, and watched our teacher, Mrs. Argonopoulos, nod her solid iron helmet of hair with dignified approval.

But I wanted to hear about passionately involved late nights of creativity at the typewriter under a burning lamp. I already thought I might trouble him with a typed letter later.

Gwathmey got the nostalgic look again and pursed his lips. He waited then said, grinning back the heaviness of a recalled feeling, "I never could have done it without the help of my wife, Dina. Dina—well, she couldn't be here today. She wanted to come, you see, but that's my Dina. Back in the day, I did something foolish I'd never recommend. I quit my job in the final months of writing *A Shadow at Midnight*. And sweet Dina went to work, two jobs, one as a waitress in a greasy spoon and the other, at night, as a hatcheck girl in a Chicago supper club. We were young and when nobody else believed in me, she'd come home tired after two shifts of work—and what did she do? She sat down and typed my book. My *manuscript*. You'll see if you ever pick it up, it's dedicated to Dina. That supper club, by the way, was full of old-time, old-school mobsters."

Just his mention of the word *manuscript* sent me into private fits of longing and envy.

Gwathmey pointed at Vickie and said, "Yes, the pretty lady next to that young man."

"Do you ever go back to Germany?" Vickie said loudly. "And what's it like now?"

A while later we filed out of the school board building, heading to a Wendy's for lunch before returning to class on our side of town. The mother of one of the other gifted kids was the second driver. But Vickie and I rode with Mrs. Argonopoulos in her station wagon, sitting in the front bench seat scrunched together so she could hear our reactions, and Vickie said, "I liked his joke about the French, how they should've asked us first. Gold in Florida, now that's a laugh!"

"But wasn't he the coolest?" I said, wondering if Vickie would ever type a book for me.

"You should write him a letter," she said, "and I'll help if you want. Collaborate."

"I'm going to," I said, squinting out at the hazy downtown skyline, "but all by myself."

Hunter B. Gwathmey had said that for reasons of privacy and security he never gave out his St. Augustine address and that he kept an unlisted phone number. At some point during the question-and-answer session he'd also mentioned that for an office he rented a room up in the Pelican Hotel near the newspaper building, just across the river from the school board building where he spoke. I hated Jacksonville, but then it occurred to me, in a sickening, sneak-preview-of-real-life type of revelation, that not everybody could live in New York, and that even some smart, talented people ended up having to make do in the provinces—as Holly Golightly called them. Easy to have your character say such a thing, however, if you lived in New York.

On a trip to the mall, I found a dinky paperback of *A Shadow at Midnight*. It had a sloppily painted cover depicting a tall, hunky blond man in dark sailor gear embracing a sluttily attired hayseed woman at well-built chest level. I opened it and read the first few lines. I had never gotten into suspense, and it seemed that the beginning of Gwathmey's novel was trying to make me sweat, get all hot and bothered just to get interested in reading it. Something about a wristwatch loudly, paranoically ticking, and the swashing of waves in chill moonlight.

"An icy night off the shores of Hades," it began, and I didn't buy its initial melodrama.

I put the book back on the shelf. The story was set here, and no one I knew would care.

I wanted to write good, honest stuff, what Truman Capote wrote. I worked on my father's college portable Royal but was saving up to buy myself a Smith Corona electric. I was a little ashamed of the uneven, herky-jerky alignment of letters the Royal's keys made, but at the same time I imagined myself tapping out my first book on it, a masterpiece that would get me to New York in time for cocktails with Tennessee Williams and others, and decided that it was good enough for my letter to Gwathmey. I had to write this author Hunter B. Gwathmey a little letter.

I began by reminding him of who I was and saying how much I enjoyed his talk. Then, swept up by emotion, I went on to tell him what a privilege it was to know that a real writer of successful books was living near me. I had gotten so much motivation and inspiration from his entertaining, informative talk. Again I thanked him for answering my question and my friend's question and said that of course I was planning to become a writer and I'd be grateful for any tips he could offer. Did I really need to go to college, I asked near the end—and if so, what types of courses should I take? Study what major? Finally, I hoped that he and his wife were doing well.

Gwathmey wrote back on a sheet of thick stationery, in slanted longhand flourishes:

Dear Matt,

What a pleasure and a delight to hear from you. Of course I remember you asking a question. As an icebreaker, it was ideal. I'm hot into a novel right now and hope you won't mind the brevity. Yes, college. My other tips are to read as many books as you can get your hands on. A famous classical musician was once stopped on the streets in New York by someone wanting to know how to get to Carnegie Hall. And this fellow replied, "Practice, practice!" The first novel I published was not my first novel. To get better and to learn to create suspense, I filled up on the masters like Graham Greene, an excellent mentor and to my mind good enough for any aspiring young writer hoping to learn many important points of style from.

Make discipline your maiden, and remember to stay in the saddle.

Thank you for asking about my wife, Dina. She's better and better lately. I've been working and staying in the Pelican Hotel a lot recently, but as soon as I return permanently to our home in St. Augustine, I'll dig up a book and sign it and send it to you. Then you can let me know what you think.

                  Ever yours, young sir, and thanks for your great letter …

"Where did you send it to?" said Vickie.

"The newspaper," I said. "I don't know, can you send things to people in hotels?"

"Look at the signature!" she gasped. "It's so old-fashioned and flamboyant. *H. Gwa.*"

"Have you ever read Graham Greene?" I asked her suddenly.

"I'm going to now, that's for sure."

"I was kind of annoyed how he kept talking about suspense. I don't write like that. I like good literature, period. I'm not into that hope-I-don't-get-killed-by-another-spy crap."

"But isn't that just what he writes? Isn't that his whole deal?"

"J. D. Salinger. Why didn't he say anything about F. Scott Fitzgerald? F. Scott Fitzgerald could write circles around him, I bet. I wonder if Gwathmey's actually squandered his talents."

Vickie wrinkled her nose and said, "What Gwathmey writes is just more commercial."

"But spies, who cares?"

"I know, but why did he write that part about his wife? Did you ask him about his wife?"

"Yeah, but to be polite. I'd feel like a jerk if I didn't . . ."

"I wonder. And what does he mean about her getting better and better? It's weird."

"Maybe she's been sick."

Vickie fretted, annoying me, and said, "I must've missed that when he was talking."

"You didn't miss anything," I said, thinking about her and me. "He has special feelings for Dina. You heard what he said about her working two jobs, coming home, typing for him."

"Yeah."

"No, I was the one falling asleep during the crap on the war in Germany. Pathetic."

"But I think I get it," she said.

"Get what?"

"You don't see it? That maybe she feels used? I could see myself as a wife in a similar situation—and I can tell you, I don't think it's any fun for the wife."

"I don't think we should make any conjectures about it. He wrote to me, not you."

This was tense and I didn't know why, although I should have. I was so moody.

When I showed the letter to my mother, she began reading and drew a breath. "Hey!"

For her, it was material proof that I was going to be a successful writer. And when she handed it back to me she arched her eyebrows and whistled and added, "Wow."

We stood in the kitchen with the sun going down and the oven ticking—waiting for my father to get home. She had a beer in its foam cozy and lit a cigarette. It was her smoking hour.

My father came home from the plant and put down the Tupperware container he carried the lunch my mother made him in every morning. Dad choogled a bit in his steel-toe boots on the linoleum. "Carolina, Carolina," he sang, "you're always on my mina!"

My mother handed him a cozied beer and the letter and said, "Well, our Truman!"

I was smaller when she and I would watch Capote's appearances on Merv Griffin.

"Truman?" Dad said. "You mean that funny little writer on TV, Truman Capote?"

I was embarrassed and went to my room. I sat at the Sears office desk they'd bought me and stared at the Royal. Beyond *Linda Goodman's Sun Signs*, her paperback book on horoscopes decorated with blue and green bubbles on a celestial field, my mother did not read much. I was a Libra and no matter what I said or did, Mom ascribed it to Libran behavior. When I was sick and had to stay home, she and I would eat Campbell's soup and cheese and crackers and watch Merv, where sometimes Truman Capote would appear as a spooky, garrulous guest—and no matter how drunk or weird he seemed to act, she'd cackle (a trademark of hers) and cry, "Love that guy!"

So I wrote Gwathmey one more letter. I told him that I had almost bought that copy of A Shadow at Midnight but didn't know if this was the book he planned to send me. Then I thanked him, in advance, for sending it to me. I wrote that I wondered if Gwathmey would read a story I was working on, which was getting long, but that—I thought—might actually end up as a novel.

Gwathmey didn't write back, and I never received the book he'd promised me.

Things changed when Vickie and I reached senior high and started tenth grade. Jimmy Carter was no longer president. I entered a countywide writing contest. It was being judged by George Trailer, the arts columnist for the Florida Times-Union, the morning paper that had just absorbed the Jacksonville Journal, which was about to put it out of business. In his column George Trailer covered everything artistic for the Florida Times-Union but the rock concerts.

My parents and I had driven to the World's Fair in Knoxville the summer before, taking a triangular route home while I lay in the backseat reading Music for Chameleons. We stopped in New Orleans to stay in the Holiday Inn on Bourbon Street. Our first night there, returning with them to the hotel from a restaurant, I asked if it was okay if I went off and had a look around the French Quarter on my own. Wasn't fifteen old enough for that? My parents looked at each other and consulted behind the noises of the pushing, shoving crowd. We moved onto the sidewalk, to get away from the drunks running into us in the street. I'd put them on the spot—no time for a real private conference. Finally my father gave me a curfew and said, "Man, we might just find ourselves someplace to go jukin', your mama and me."

Dad liked rednecking out with the speech when the chance served him, and New Orleans was famous, and neither of them wanted to look like clinging parents. I peeled away at the first chance and at

13

Jackson Square a man in his twenties stared at me from the far curb. I crossed and he called out to me in an English accent, "Hello, I've just noticed you. I'm Mark."

I got tentatively closer to him and smiled queasily and said, "Hi, Mark."

He offered me his hand to shake and I took it, then he said, "What are you up to?"

He wouldn't let go of my hand. It felt nice, but I looked around, checking all about.

"Just hanging out before going back to be with my parents. What are you up to?"

"Same, except no parents. You're really cute. How old are you?"

"About to turn sixteen. But wow, thanks for that compliment."

"I wouldn't have guessed sixteen. You seem more mature to me than that."

"Lots of people tell me that. Not tonight, but in the past."

"Because I'd really like to fuck you. Take you up to my room in the Marriott, fuck you."

Hands now in his pockets, he nodded toward the Marriott, the tallest building in sight.

"What street's that on?" I said.

"Canal. So what do you say? It's under five minutes' walk from here."

My face was burning. I wished I could quit smiling. He stared, smirking, I thought.

"Would you like that?" he added.

"I don't think so. God. So are you from London?"

"I'm more from the north originally, but I live in London. I'm from Blyth."

"Blyth! That's hilarious, but no. I've never heard of that before."

"Have you heard of the guitarist and singer Mark Knopfler?"

"I don't think so."

"Have you ever heard of Dire Straits?"

"I'm not living in a cave. I mean sure, obviously I've heard of them. That's so cool."

"What's your name?" he said. "We're just talking. No need to get defensive."

He had a look of disgust, like from some burning irritation I'd just caused him.

"I'm not getting defensive," I said. I looked around, then back at him. "What?"

"I've got a really big fat cock," he said, "and I bet you've got a really tight hole."

"My parents are waiting for me back at the hotel," I said. "I think I should go."

"Fine then, darling, but you still haven't told me your name. What's your name?"

I thought of my parents, wandering around trying to keep a distant eye on me.

"'What?' Oh come on, you're not going to disappoint me like that. 'What?' indeed!"

"Don't imitate me," I said and started away, looking back to ward him off I thought.

"Don't be scared," he said, his tone shifting to neutral. "Don't be a little puritan."

I wasn't afraid of him. He had a nice face and wasn't too tall.

"Daft little queen. Tease!"

"I'm not," I said, then turned again as I yelled, "and who are you calling little?"

I wanted to go back but he was treating me like a kid. That's what I was to my parents. I hurried toward the Holiday Inn, my face hot and pulsing. I thought about Mark up in his room at the Marriott and felt horny and miserable knowing I was sharing the room with them, and when I got to the corner and looked back I was relieved not to see them. The only one I could tell about this was Vickie, and even that would take me time to work up to, though strangely I wanted to. I wanted to write about this stuff, what I really thought and put myself through. I wanted to write, so I chose what I thought were pretty safe, shopworn topics, and I started a new story in time for the countywide contest, and I spent hours writing it each night, typing slowly, getting unsatisfied and using Wite-Out to change lines until I realized the whole page was wrong and started it over.

My story was about a teenage girl waiting for her boyfriend to get back to the motel room with their dinner the evening before her abortion. In the story, I never say why, but the boyfriend never returns. Lying under the covers, she goes over the story in her head of how she got there.

Somehow I was that girl waiting all through writing the thing, and when I was done I was pretty sure I was a genius on the order of Truman Capote.

I'd taken the Pinto wagon out with Vickie when George Trailer called to say that I'd won a writing contest. "Who's George Trailer?" my mother said when I got in. A pinched smile and arched eyebrows. "He said you'd won this Timucua County Young High School Writers thing."

"What the hell?" I said, starting to dance.

"Well you won a contest I didn't know you'd entered. Now, is it a writing contest?"

"Oh, Mom. *Think.* You just said that he told you I'd won a *writing* contest."

"And that I didn't know anything about your having entered, G. d. it."

My father dragged in. We were in the kitchen again. When we were together we were always in the kitchen. He put his hand on his hip. "What the hell's going on here?"

"Asshole wins a writing contest, gets an award, and didn't tell me he'd entered."

"Didn't tell me, either. 'Jambalaya, crawfish pie!'" he holler-sang. "This is splendid."

We kept a novelty notepad next to the phone. Each sheet of paper was headed:

You better get on this
RIGHT FUCKING NOW:

My mother had written Trailer's home number on it and said he expected me to call him.

Trailer, I had deduced, knew about everything from classical music to books and would be a sort of ticket to important taste for me—and I didn't want him to think I came from a home where we tackily Christmas-shopped for my parents' fishing buddies at Spencer Gifts. Before I could dial him, my English teacher, who by the contest's rules had submitted my story, called to congratulate me. She was originally from Massachusetts and I badly wanted to impress her, too.

"My darling!" said Mrs. Waddington. "What a wonderful, creative young man!"

"Ma'am, I want to thank you and tell you how grateful I am for nominating me."

"No one else tried. You were the only one who gave me a story, and such a story! But I will tell you, I've a hunch yours likely would have been the finest, if he or she had. I *knew.*"

I felt relieved, but then complained, "I'm so ambitious. I want to be the best."

"Oh, I know. Believe me, I see it. I saw it on that very first day of class."

She spoke lyrically and matter-of-factly, with a measured delirium in her voice.

I exulted to her, "I can't believe George Trailer was the judge and he picked me."

"He certainly did pick you. But I do have to go make dinner now. I'll see you in class tomorrow, Matthew." I'd forgotten that teachers had housework to do, too, like everyone else. In class when we were discussing a book, she looked at me a lot, pretending not to wait for me to raise my hand. "Tell your mom I want to meet her soon, all right, Matthew?"

"Okay, that'd be great. Good night, Mrs. Waddington. Thank you again."

"Not at all, Matt."

I tried George Trailer, but each time the line was busy. I tried again after dinner but there was no answer. He'd already lost interest in me. Around ten, my father told me to stop trying.

A week went by. Mrs. Waddington read my story aloud in class before we got back to *Tom Jones*, and at the end, when the girl about to have an abortion sadly and quietly sings "Que Sera, Sera" to herself, my classmates clapped politely. I hovered above them, I thought, briefly.

My mother volunteered at a hospital. When I got home that afternoon I found her note saying Trailer had called that morning and apologized for before, but that his mother had died. Could I try him again? I paced the diamond-designed kitchen linoleum catching my breath.

"A pistol, that mama of yours," he said when I got him. "I want you to hold her in your heart and love her as dearly as you might," he went on. "That lady is looking *out for you*."

"Well, Mr. Trailer—"

"*George*."

"Ha ha. That feels odd to me. But I was going to say, it's almost like a dream."

"That's it, that's it. It is a complete dream. Enjoy it, the way I've really enjoyed my two talks with—Barbara? Is that her name? I know she thinks the world of you."

"It is Barbara, and we're very, very close, or always have been," I said, trying to sound suddenly tired and disabused. "People in the mall think we're brother and sister."

"And she *sounds* so young. She's a big booster of one Matthew Hammer I know of. I want to tell everything, hear from you everything, learn it all. Unfortunately, I am on deadline just now and have to sit down right this instant and write-write-write my next review."

I heard him sigh and asked him what was the matter. He sounded rather old.

"I'm afraid I will have to disappoint the Rialto Little Players, regarding their tepid little *Cabaret*. I have friends in the cast, as well as the director, and oh! it is a tepid little, treacherous and lackluster, bloodless, uninspired, utterly boring little mess of a thing."

I said, "I love, love that movie. I watch it every time it comes on Cinemax."

"*Ugh!* Why take a show so originally, deliciously abject and turn it into *Oliver!*?"

I giggled and George Trailer said, "*Although.* My friend Renny Quinn as Cliff is pretty good. I'll give him one thing, he's a talented singer. He doesn't know of the calamity about to befall his production, but I suspect he's counting on me to be present at the anniversary."

"The tenth anniversary of the theater."

"You're pretty with-it, son. How on earth did you get to be so smart?"

"You announced it in your 'Out and About' column a while ago."

"That's right, so I did. Have you ever attended any of the shows at the Rialto?"

"No, sir, but I do like plays and musicals. We've read a lot of drama in English."

"What are your favorites?"

"*Pygmalion.* Last year in gifted we saw *My Fair Lady* out at the dinner theater."

"They had an interesting idea with the minimal sets. But please, an old sitcom star?"

"He was no Rex Harrison, I agree."

"An out-of-work sitcom star? Let me have your address, so I can stay in touch."

"Sure."

"And Matt? Congratulations. Your story . . . oh, we'll talk. I promise you that."

I called Vickie and she laughed and hooted and said, "But what's he want from you?"

Trailer lived in a fancy part of town where rich people lit their lawns and houses like theme parks. Since I'd gotten my license Vickie and I would sometimes go to a movie at the mall then take the expressway and drive around San Marco talking about owning one of these places. She liked the ones with columns, tall porches, and magnolias, the Taras, and I liked the mock Tudors with carefully trimmed firs.

The only trees we agreed on were the grandly spreading live oaks lit from beneath to show the joint-like gnarls of their shinily leafed, massively shouldered branches.

George Trailer lived in an old-fashioned apartment complex resembling a Spanish castle with stucco walls and a slot-windowed turret topping each of the four corners of the building, the skinny pane in each of the turrets dark and blind. You entered El Morro through an iron gate that led to a courtyard full of shabby shrubs and bushes, then up a few cracked steps into a tiled open-air hallway, like a dim tunnel of pointed arches (where only one of the lantern-shaped lamps was working and glowing a watery amber)—and then through to the back where Trailer lived.

"Who've I been dying to see and meet?" Trailer said when he answered the door.

His place wasn't small, but it was crammed with enough antiques for a mansion.

We started in the salon, he called it. He'd been sending me his clippings, a couple at a time, always what I had already read in the paper, each with a funny note clipped on. "Like to know what you think of *this*," it said on a lined sheet torn from a small spiral notebook. I had learned the ironic use of the word "inexplicably" from a theater review of his: "Inexplicably, Ms. Mann's Annie Oakley resembles a rather bedraggled, chiffon-bedizened Cyndi Lauper."

He was holding a tall glass of black liquid and said, "Can I get you a cold Coca-Cola?"

"Oh God, thank you. Can I help? I meant, may I?"

"You may not. You are in fact strictly, and under pain of lashings, expressly forbidden."

He took his drink to the kitchen and carried it back, refreshed, along with my iced Coke.

I said, "I'd like to thank you for the clippings. I don't know a lot about classical music."

He said carefully, "You simply expose yourself, bit by bit, is merely all."

"Go and listen, absorb?"

"That's it. It's the only way we learn anything, by going back and back into it."

"Obviously. We did go to a lot of symphonies—well, not a lot—back in gifted."

"What is this 'gifted'?" he said, narrowing his eyes, as though he'd heard about it but never had it fully and properly and satisfactorily explained to him.

"Oh," I said, trying to sound sophisticated, "this thing where we learned cultural stuff."

"Have made available to you all of the cultural outlets Jacksonville has to offer?"

He smacked his lips getting me stiffly in his sights and pursed his mouth tartly.

"Yes. And like in ninth grade, we made this movie, to learn how to collaborate."

I was embarrassed about it and wished I'd shut up sooner. I was nervous. The phone rang and he reached for the princess extension next to the wicker rocker he sat in.

He picked it up but before replying into it asked me, "Do you like hamburgers?"

"Absolutely. Are we having hamburgers?"

He nodded rapidly with a boyish flare in his eyes.

"Hello, dear heart?" he greeted the party.

I studied the wall, thinking it would be rude if it looked like I was eavesdropping. In the corner was a bust of a woman on its own dark wooden stand with half of her face gone.

He glanced at me and said, "Add cheese?"

"Cheese, please."

"Cheese all around." He winked at me. "Oh, those are yummy. Coupla those, too."

When he hung up he said, "I can't wait for you to meet my friend Maxy."

"Was that Maxy?"

"That was my friend Carl, about the burgers. Carl's sometimes wont to fetch supper."

We heard a key in the door and in came Maxy. She was redheaded with a wavy perm and was in a stylish yellow tracksuit and clean white sneakers. We both stood up.

"Matthew. Matthew," she said. "I hope you don't mind, but I read your story and loved it. But how did you do it? Get into that girl's head, know what she was thinking?"

"It was that good?" I said.

She got an appalled look, panning it around at Trailer. "More than that, but George!"

I thanked her and said to her shoulder, "I just sort of got inspired and wrote it."

"Meaning you didn't plagiarize?" Trailer said, mugging theatrically, a hand on a hip.

Still with the look, she turned back. "'Just sort of wrote it.' What was your inspiration?"

"I'm not sure. People get abortions and nobody wants to talk about them."

Trailer said, "And they're not getting any more talkative about them—the way things are headed. No, I can nearly guarantee you that. But darling, just before you came in Matthew was telling me about a movie he and his gifted classmates made in, what was it, ninth grade? Junior high, and making a movie. Be honest, Maxy, have you ever heard of the gifted track?"

Maxy fretted, saying, "What rock have you been living under, George? Everyone on the entire planet's heard of gifted. My niece is in gifted, in Spartanburg—it's extremely common."

"Which niece?"

"Brittany, my brother Barney's girl."

"How is Barney?"

"Well, recall you've met him. Barney'll never reach his full potential, not with *her*."

Trailer looked back at me and said, "Cream o' Wheat's my lifeline, my rock. We share all but blood cells. But let's move now. I'm afraid the dining room is impractical for eating in. You can't see the top of the table, what with these stacks of papers and boxes and books: half a ton of reference volumes alone. But I work constantly, which is why I'm so foolishly out of touch with the wider world. I haven't offered you a thing to imbibe, Cream-o."

"I noticed that, too, Jingles."

"Would you like a cold Co'-Cola? Doesn't that sound lip-smacking?"

"I would expire without one."

"I'm afraid, Matthew, that in order to relocate we have to pass through the kitchen in its miserable, hovel-like shape. There's no alternative. Thus it would behoove you not to cast your eyes about, neither left nor right, as we quickly traverse. Eyes ever forward . . ."

Passing through, I glimpsed on the right the liquor bottles gleaming under the concealed fluorescent strip. To the left next to the sink was a half-drunk bottle of dark Bacardi rum.

"Matt, go in there and look at my Schiavelli drawing—and tell me is it not exquisite, and let me know if I should move it to where we might behold the thing to even greater advantage."

It was a woman's hand, the pencil lines half-faded. The light was dim. You had to look closely. It tilted slightly up, languidly reaching, each finger fanned at a slightly different angle.

"It's beautiful," I said, getting closer and squinting at the details.

Trailer called from the kitchen, "Oh Matt, I was just acting silly and thick a while ago."

"We tease a lot," said Maxy, coming and standing next to me. "George's people have been passing this down forever. Now, I love how she holds her finger out for her ring. It's just a sketch, a study. For a detail, I gather. I don't know a lot about art, either, Matthew."

Trailer came in and said, "Don't do it, lady! You'll regret it till the day you die!"

"Did you get that part?" said Maxy to me. "I didn't. I just thought it was a nice hand."

"Plain old garden-variety Renaissance-era bride's paw," Trailer announced. He went to a love seat on the far end of the room and fluffed a throw pillow for back support and eased down.

I waited for Maxy to sit on the bigger sofa, then joined her, and she touched my knee and smiled, blinking, and said, "George is from a very prominent family in Charleston."

"From my mother's side, yet with nothing in the world but what you behold here, now."

"Are taste and comportment so absolute zero?" said Maxy. "Well, for my part that is not what I've been hearing for the longest time. We're from just up the road from each other."

"My father, on the other hand, was from nothing and clawed his way up using only the sweat off his brow—stop me if you've heard this one—and I do believe I quite favor him."

"Jingles, come on now. *Lord.* And nothing whatsoever from Nadine's line?"

"Wrong side of the tracks, I've always felt to be," he said, nose in the air. "Despite all."

Maxy laughed wickedly: "And with only that much, and yet thank God for me!"

They leaned out to each other from their separate places, trying not to splosh their drinks, and clenched hands firmly then shook them mightily, once, twice, covertly like old teammates.

"Thank you, baby Jesus!" Maxy said, addressing the ceiling.

"Cream o' Wheat."

"Jingles."

I heard Bach piano music tinkling and cascading low a room away. I said, "Working in the same building and writing for the newspaper, you must know Hunter B. Gwathmey?"

About to take a sip, Trailer quickly said, "Oh, her!"

Maxy cautioned, "George."

"Okay, not another word about Miz Hunter B. But just to say, what an awful pity, what a distinct and terrible shame, the way they've let that Pelican Hotel go to seed, accepting trash. It's become a boarding-house, and you know what they'll do with the woodwork and plaster, all those murals and frescoes, every bit of it peeling and dying—well, they will tear it down. They do that here, to people and things. They let everyone and everything fall apart, then draw the curtain."

Carl came with our cheeseburgers. Rugged, athletic, good-looking, youngish, he flushed red when we were introduced and made to bow at me but without making eye contact. He wore a knit cap that looked squashed on, like from New England or Canada, with woolly pom-pom tassels hanging by each ear touching his neck in the Florida heat when he glanced robotically about.

We sat around with our burgers on china. I wadded up my wrappings, putting them in the paper bag by my feet. I opened little packets of ketchup and squirted it on my onion rings, trying to concentrate on the piano solo, then a symphony coming in or something else orchestral.

We discussed the currently playing *Annie Get Your Gun*. Already it seemed that my time here was about to run out. I waited for my chance to bolt. Carl asked Trailer about his Saturday, and Trailer said that he had to run out to the beach that night for *The Merchant of Venice*.

"I normally wouldn't bother. Del Bixby has been doing the most boffo, insane inanities with costumes—fascist military uniforms—and laying this punk music over on top of it. *Yuck.*"

Carl licked the last bits of juicy burger from his palm and pronounced, "But it's chic."

"Whatever you call it," said Trailer and guffawed, eyes not straying from Carl.

"George," I said, "do you think I should go to journalism school? Did you?"

"Not on your life, on either count," he replied. "What can they teach you? How to run the photocopier? If you can type and have half a brain, you can do what I do. But don't do what I do, it's a dying form. I promise thee. Go into computers—whatever else floats your boat."

I said what I'd rehearsed: "But to me, nothing *made* is as good as something *created*."

It got quiet except for the twiddly-hop, twiddly-hop of woodwinds and strings.

"Amen," said Maxy.

Trailer said, "That's pretty good, isn't it? Is that from something, a text, Matthew?"

"Not that I know of," I said. "I don't think I unconsciously stole it from anyone."

"Well, it's pretty good. Wouldn't you say that's well put, Cream o' Wheat?"

"It's lovely," said Maxy, smiling at me like before: a sad smile, it occurred to me.

We surrendered our china and greasy wrappings, then Trailer and Carl took it all into the kitchen. I didn't like being alone with Maxy now. I wanted to fall asleep on the sofa, knowing I might look cute to Carl and Trailer if they came in and found me later.

"Are your folks and all of your people originally from around here?" Maxy asked.

In the kitchen, Carl screamed, "All right, all right already. Jesus Fucking Christ."

We could just hear Trailer hissing, "Don't get that tone with me, *you.*"

I cleared my throat and replied to Maxy, "We're from Tennessee originally."

"Tennessee, half my family's from Nashville! But which part of Tennessee's yours?"

"Of all the nitwittedness," yelled Trailer, "I have flat forgotten about dessert!"

"Oh honey, who cares?" Maxy hollered back in to him. "Next time. No big deal."

"Well," he then said, reappearing, hands clasped in front like a deacon's itching for the collection plate to home back. "Dear heart, before you have to run I have a gift for you."

"Oh." I stood up. "This has been so much fun, folks—so interesting, and a lot of fun!"

He took me back through the kitchen, where Carl was leaning over the sink with a sponge scrubbing at the china under a steaming tap, wool beanie still on. Carl got me in the corner of his eye, stood upright, and turned to me holding up his sudsy, reddened hands without drying them.

"Sorry, Matt. Good to meet you, man, anyway."

In the front salon, Trailer took a book from the top of the piano and said, "For you."

It was *Music for Chameleons*, with the original metallic-lavender cover.

I said, "Oh, how nice. Thanks. But hey, I've already read this, actually."

"This is a first edition, kid. Hang on to it and it'll be worth something to you someday."

We went outside together and he said, "Put it in your car then we'll take a little walk."

It had been a humid day and there was a chill in the air and fog was forming. He led me onto a street I didn't know and I said, "Those oaks look like crouching old men."

He said, "A quick, excellent description. Bravo."

"They look livid and wild, with their arms in the air, ready to scream."

"Let's not go overboard."

We walked on a ways and I wondered about everything. Would I be famous?

Trailer took his time and finally said, "You know, Matthew, we cannot be friends."

I wanted to hug him and thank him, but part of me was too proud. I was confused.

"The world is fiercely stupid," he said. "Folks get the wrong idea, really so stupid . . ."

"I know," I said emptily, "they're so stupid. People are morons."

"You're not listening," he said. "I feel like you could become a better listener, Matthew."

He put his arm around my shoulders and turned me a hundred and eighty degrees toward him, and I said, "Sorry, rewind. What did you mean just now? I was off in my own world."

"I know, dear heart," he said, frowning, then laughed like an old friend saying good-bye.

But it was true. I never saw George Trailer again, either.

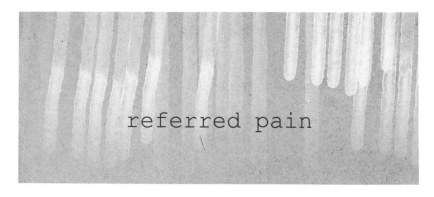

referred pain

She was married to a man who was extremely popular with his students. The English department had even allowed Gary to choose the title for his own chair, which he'd named after an antiquarian bookseller in Gary's native New York who'd closed his doors a while ago. Gary collected all the old avant-garde editions, mostly mealy paperbacks smelling of must and mold, the old Grove and New Directions and Olympia Press originals, and stored them in glass cases in a room that in other households might have been reserved for baby's nursery. Gary had been inspired by Beckett, Ionesco, and his mentor John Hawkes, and in his own writing was content to frustrate readers with lyrical repetitions, lack of scene-setting detail, and characters he called "X."

People didn't read Gary's novels so much as talk about them. He brought them in at the rate of one every two or three years. They were brief and he did most of his work on them in the farmhouse they rented for a couple months every summer in the South of France. It was her idea to have his grad students over a few times a semester. Gary was so self-contained that he didn't seem to need them or Diane or anyone else around, although Gary never seemed rattled by their company, either. Diane kept the house clean and cooked for him, and when he came home from the university Gary smiled at the neatness of things, and when he sat down to one of her meals he thanked her pleasantly and complimented whatever she'd bothered making, his fond, far-off look never wavering. She remembered the shy Gary she'd met at Columbia thirty years ago, compact and smooth-skinned, his well-formed body an unblemished envelope of unimposing masculinity. After only a year of dating she'd inadvertently proposed to him in his room one night when she'd said, "Do you think this is leading to anything permanent? But if that's dumb, you can just say."

"Well for goodness sake, Di," Gary had then said, getting an alarmed look that he quickly swapped for a clever, sage gleam, "and how long has this been going through your mind?"

She'd read all of Trollope, then all of Dickens, and by now all of nearly everyone, trying to find distractions. She kept the garden going and mowed the lawn herself. The only thing she wouldn't paint was exterior trim. For a long time she had felt like she owed Gary this much, but she didn't find any of the work she did around the house too great a challenge. She didn't have a job, and this had been a mistake, and sometimes while he slept without snoring too loudly she sat up in the living room, like a Joni Mitchell persona, she thought, the speaker or narrator in a Joni Mitchell song from the mid-seventies specifically, and drank wine and wished she could ask one of Gary's students how to get ahold of some grass. She'd liked smoking grass, only having lied to Gary when she was helping him through grad school up at Brown by telling him she didn't see the point of grass. She'd always wanted to be alert for him. At any minute he'd ask her to listen to something he'd written—not his own creative work, just the dull seminar papers he didn't care anything about. He'd usually liked her suggestions. His main thing was to be clear and go for a decent grade, though he didn't really care about his literature courses. Gary was confident about his fiction, and she left that alone. Once, here, trimming the ivy that had gotten shaggy along the front of the house, she'd fallen off the ladder. He'd heard her impact on the lawn—somehow she managed to fall flat and not break anything—and Gary had come running outside then driven her to the emergency room. When she was released after a couple of hours, the X-rays a thumbs-up, he'd put her to bed and stayed close to her the entire weekend, returning regularly to her from the desk in his study and darting in and out of their room to heat up soup and fix sandwiches and administer Tylenol.

He needed her to need him, she'd decided. "To need to be needed," she was saying now to Taylor, a pretty, very promising-seeming girl from Maine with sunny features.

"Right?" said Taylor, gasping and waiting for Diane to finish her idea. "Oh, and? And?"

Taylor was often on the verge of overdoing it in the felicity department.

"It was a long time ago when Gary and I met," Diane said, "and I don't know if anybody needs to hear that old shpiel," and started to laugh. "I mean, who needs to hear that old shpiel?"

"Oh but they might!" said Taylor, turning her face full-on expectantly to Diane, who had a weirdly special thing for Taylor. Diane rooted for Taylor—though she still could not say why.

Taylor was more talented than Gary. You even got the sense that Taylor knew it already, but Taylor had *come* to North Carolina to study with Gary. Her father revered him. There were those families, Diane knew, where everybody loved books, and they talked about them nonstop, but Diane hadn't come from one of those. "It's all right," Diane wanted to say to the girl, reach across, and touch her. Taylor's fiction was full of agony—whether lived or not it was hard to tell, since it was vivid but took place in settings where Taylor had probably never been, in trailers and boardinghouses (and how did Taylor know about boardinghouses? but she obviously read a great deal). What an imagination. Taylor was affectionate. Now as Diane had taco night, going to the trouble to serve beef and tofu fillings separately, Taylor wanted to sit on the couch for hours, and drink wine and talk. "We should go to the movies," the girl had once proposed, "or shopping."

Taylor wouldn't expect any special favors with her grades—she didn't need help with her grades. But a few years ago, one of the girls in Gary's fiction workshop was obsessed and would ring the front door while he and Diane were in bed. She left things she'd baked at the front door and rang and got in her car and drove off, Gary swearing that he'd received no love notes. Diane believed him since young people always needed extra attention. They'd lavish it on you to get a tiny part of it back. Joni always found a way to show this without saying it. Gary disliked Joni Mitchell, though he'd never said it outright. First Diane had stopped playing her whenever he was around—then she'd stopped playing her altogether. Joni, admittedly, was a depressive influence, but in her prime Joni's finest thoughts had rhymed with Diane's most painful views of humanity.

I met a redneck on a Grecian isle . . . He cooked good omelets and stews.

But Gary didn't cook. Gary acted as though he were incapable of anything but thoughts.

Every year brought a Taylor (or a Josh, a young man she'd felt great kinship with), but at the end of the second year, she knew, the bond was broken. Josh had been a beautiful boy. Josh was a name you heard a lot now, so that not every Josh was special, but Diane had felt something for the one from Atlanta. The warm, intelligent ones never stayed. It was too small a town, and there were no local opportunities for a graduate from this program. Yet with a recommendation from Gary, they could go anywhere in the world. They got teaching fellowships in California or New England. They were invited to colonies in Italy. They found agents and editors; they ended up publishing their books and became professors themselves. The ones who stayed didn't have a big future, anyway, not right away. They stuck around and taught lower-level courses. They got married and stayed and asked for full-time positions teaching those lower-level courses then never had their books published. There wasn't anything wrong with that, but they lost their ambitions. The creative sparkle went out of them as they settled into parenthood, some of them changing careers and going into carpentry or landscaping. They managed video stores, until the video stores went out of business. They helped open restaurants. Gary didn't seem to judge them harshly. He was happy teaching and encouraging them. Not everyone was going to be successful and it was cruel to ask them to try to be—as cruel as it would be to ask Gary to write a bestseller.

Diane switched gears on the couch with Taylor and tried not to get too maternal a look in her eyes and said, "You're almost done here, and so what are your plans? You've obviously been thinking about them. Have you been applying to all that good stuff, filling out applications?"

Taylor smoked, something Diane wished she wouldn't do. It was a mild evening. Diane had opened all the windows and lit some candles. Out on the screened-in porch Gary was doing doubles in Ping-Pong with a couple of boys and another girl. Only half of Gary's workshop had showed up. It was that time of year, when the numbers began dropping off. Diane imagined this happened for good reasons and some terrible ones, too, like envy in the ranks. Some people had been handed goodies already, and the others were waiting and wondering and starting to worry.

"I'm going back to Maine for a summer," Taylor said, "probably work for my neighbor's lobster-pot type deal—it's a shack right on the Union River Bay where they ready-make the rolls and dinners, and you can go out on the water, on the dock I mean, and sit at a picnic table and eat your dinner. They don't sell beer or anything, but you can bring your own. It's so, *so* pretty."

"I bet, but are you going back and doing that because you feel like you have to, Taylor?"

"No, no, Diane, Steve, my neighbor, and his wife Jane—they could sort of use my help."

It came back to Diane, that she'd read a story by Taylor about this. The man got cancer and for a summer was unable to work at the shack when summer was their big season, and they couldn't afford to close. It must have given Taylor a sense of accomplishment. If Diane could go back and do something like that for someone who really needed it, she would. What a stupid thought, though. Diane was already on her third glass of malbec. She'd be on the purple pill for her reflux again by morning. Gary didn't take any medications, but Diane was on three different prescriptions. Gary ran in the morning, played tennis with the department chair (whom he didn't especially like), and watched what he ate. Two beers and he was ready for a good night's sleep, and woke up ready to do it all over again, never complaining.

He left his students' stories on the breakfast bar when he was done making his comments, as though Diane should have a skim, too.

"I remember that one," Diane said, knowing that Taylor understood that she was referring to the lobster-shack story. "I hope you don't mind, but I was curious." She stopped, wishing that for this one idea she wanted to express she had a cigarette to handle for help. "I'm curious about all of Gary's students," she went on, arching her eyebrows vaguely. "And I'm often amazed."

"Thanks, Diane."

"By quite a lot of you," said Diane, then winking at the girl, added, "or some of you."

"You caught me," said Taylor. "He doesn't say it but I think Gary thinks I'm just a bit too confident and cocky. That's why I want to go back to Maine and just be quiet a while, regroup."

It hit her again there was a chance that Taylor and Gary were having an affair, or fucking on the side, meaninglessly. Whenever this possibility hit her, it seemed too absurd. Confronting this distant possibility with Taylor always comforted Diane; Gary *should* have fun with someone. But he wasn't, of course. Gary was too fucking disorganized to bring something like that off.

"And after—do you know what you'll do after?" said Diane, watching Taylor steadily as Taylor imbibed, more than sipped, her smelly, fragrant cigarette—courting death, as we all did.

"I might go to a family friend's fish camp in the Keys and work—maybe get on a boat or do some housekeeping or cooking or waiting on tables. I'm not scared of hard work. And in the end, I suppose I think I need something like that. I'm really not afraid of menial tasks."

Diane gazed at her and they both laughed, at what Diane couldn't be sure. Pretty Taylor!

"You're so humble," said Diane. She would have liked to be this humble at that age: the things she might have seen, and not just from the closed window of an air-conditioned car or the purview of a farmhouse in a part of a Europe hours from where menacing stuff happened. Even going to Columbia had been a safe move and made her parents proud. Anyway, the city had lost its edge by then, people said. Not even telling them she planned to marry a writer had fazed her folks. Before Josh, Gary was the only man she'd ever slept with. Josh was a man. She'd let him fuck her because she'd thought of him as a boy, and he'd been tender. But he was nearly twenty-five when he'd said good-bye and he never wrote, not even when it was so easy now with email. Nor was he going to at this point. He had his own website and had published a novel and a book of stories already, and a deal for his next book, a sailing travelogue, had just been announced and God only knew but he'd sail into Taylor's port one morning and bed her. Then Taylor would find out about Diane, which didn't matter either. Diane had sex with Josh maybe a dozen times in his apartment, which was underfurnished but not dirty. When he pushed into her his back undulated, and she held his buttocks and her palms rode in along on them toward her. When his motions got faster she squeezed, pulling; when Josh came, she smoothed them. She smoothed the soft brown hairs. He dropped his head next to hers and drove the side of his face into the pillow looking the other way. Her hand motions got wider and she felt his thighs relaxing and when he rose up she kissed his chest, too desperately, she thought. You didn't do anything too desperate, so then she cooled off, tried to make a joke, yet keeping her hands near him. She liked the way his nipples felt between her lips, which she tried not to tense too hard. She liked his smell. It didn't matter if it was sweet or something more mixed but was lovely. And he was lovely but not a boy. And she'd never been a girl. Everything had happened too late, and she wanted to mention this with Taylor. She had a feeling if things weren't about to wind down, and she knew they soon would be, she'd ease into it and confess that all with Taylor—for no reason except that it would be nice to confess something for once in her life. And to have a friend from one of these groups. She'd gotten this idea from the way Taylor could sit still, without saying anything, just waiting for a topic to suggest itself, the two of them listening to each other's silences, watching each other's features, and apparently both enjoying sitting here. She thought Taylor could have been her friend.

But in a few weeks the girl would be gone, and Diane would be alone again, so nope—no confessions.

From out on the porch came a ruckus, all of the Ping-Pong players crying "Oh!" together.

There was a striking-down of paddles onto the table, but Diane could hear the ball still in metrically clacking motion. One of the boys was tapping it back up and up with his paddle.

"No no no," Gary was saying, shouting actually, "don't let me stop the big tournament!"

That was Gary's signal, though, that it *should* stop. Evenings always ended far too early.

Taylor turned to Diane, waited, and said, "Hey, girl. Let me help you clean up?"

"Absolutely not."

"Please! But Diane, *please*. You never let me and yet I always *want* to."

Taylor was nice but her language could edge toward the pretentious, so middle-class. At times, Diane had actually heard Taylor make the construction "between you and I." *So realtor.*

"We have a rule about that," said Diane, "and that rule is absolutely not. There's nothing to clean up. All I have to do is turn on the dishwasher. It's all set to go, I'll just flick the switch."

"But help pick up glasses and take them in?"

"Don't bother. Machine's nearly full and they won't fit. You've helped enough already."

"Okay." Taylor reached across squeezing Diane's hand. "All right crazy, sweet you."

She hadn't fought too hard, but then all of Gary's students had a sense of entitlement. It was cool, forbidding Gary. But it was also Diane. She'd just dump the remaining opened wine.

Gary was seeing them to the door when she went around blowing out candles, getting the lights, pressing the dishwasher button. She was careful not to rattle the recyclables around in the container on the side porch. It was too friendly a neighborhood for something as impersonal as a note about her rattling things around outside when it was late. People came over and started with an opening line about the weather: but make no mistake, nothing out of line went unnoticed.

Upstairs, Gary ducked into the bathroom in his T-shirt and shorts, saying, "I missed you."

They were calling back and forth as she pulled back the covers on the carefully made bed.

"Me, too," she said. "I was with Taylor the whole time. Those boys adore you."

"They're friendly guys, those nutty, rascally boys. And Jill-Ann. I'll miss her, too."

She was in one of her short nighties, but she was starting to wonder if she should still be showing her knees so frankly, the last thing or almost the last thing he'd see before he closed his eyes. Dirt from the garden smeared on them below the frayed bottoms of her cut-offs, fine. She couldn't see herself in pajama pants and a tee, the way the catalogs were suggesting she do.

"But honey, just curious," she called kindly, "where do you think Taylor will end up?"

"Are you suddenly worried about Taylor? *Vous?*" he said, appearing in the doorway with his toothbrush pasted. He put the other hand on his hip, a bit effeminately yet appealingly so.

"Watch it now, darling," she said. "Just asking, do you think Taylor has any direction?"

Gary mugged, and before he began brushing his teeth said, "Does any of us?"

Now in all of history, young peoples' lives seemed most delicate. The wars in the Middle East, the banks, the jobs situation. It was a terrible time. Like before, in a way, but much worse.

"Your students are grateful," said Diane, "and the French act like you invented the baguette."

Gary went up and down on his toes as he brushed, flexing and scrubbing machinelike.

"You always had direction," she said as he was ducking out. She heard him spit, rinse.

Gary had never solicited her critical thoughts of him, so self-confident was he always.

"Taylor's a free soul," he said, wiping his mouth. "I don't force them, no one forced me. I'm always glad to write recommendations. Some say I'm indiscriminate with them. There's no deadline with me. If Taylor wants one later, I'll certainly write it, but why take on extra work?"

These application processes were ruthlessly officious and both of them knew it, and here Gary was choosing to be coy and obscure. What it boiled down to was Gary hating paperwork.

Diane narrowed her eyes at him and said, "Really, Taylor's not applying for *anything*?"

"Or she is and she doesn't want my recommendation. She went to a good undergrad."

"You're amazing," Diane said, shaking her head and sliding under the covers.

"I'm Ludner the Amaze-O," he said with the grin of some character out of his beloved childhood comic books, his first collectible passion—as though his words were suspended in a speech balloon hooked to the side of his mouth with its cheerful check-mark shape. He turned out the lights and got into bed with the same punctilious cheer, sighing for effect in the dark. (*SIGH!*)

He turned on his side away from her, curled his legs, and pushed his butt against her, and she lay on her back and her hand gravitated there. She reached under the waistband. I'm an ass woman, she thought, and always was. She thought of Taylor's absurdly pleasant face. The baby softness of Gary's skin against her dry palm and roughly worked fingers soothed her. Of course, she'd forgotten to lotion her hands again. But she wasn't getting up now. Then sometime in the middle of the night she thought the phone was ringing—her mother again, from assisted living.

"Di honey, is it you? I've misplaced your father again. My hearing's terribly degraded."

Before she'd died, Diane had given her mother a cell and the woman, whose real problem was losing her sense of time, would use it to call her in the middle of the night when she couldn't sleep and was thinking about the past and wanted to go over it again. More than once her mother would say, "Was I any good to you? I was good to your father, which wasn't easy. But to you?"

This time a SWAT team rappelled from the ceiling's attic door shouting that it was time to go, there was no time to get dressed: they were coming to escort her to see her mother in assisted living down in Florida—it came to her in the confusion. "But I'm on the line with her now," she wanted to say. "Ask her yourself. I'm not due to see her for weeks!" In her throat was caught a makeup-removing sponge soaked in a pH-balanced clarifying lotion made with pricey botanicals, but already the ninja-attired men had disappeared. There was no one to talk to if only she could. She tasted the preciously derived essence of a rare African fruit gagging her, and she whimpered, and then she was alone and already starting to feel foolish, but she wasn't sure, wasn't at all sure.

A Black Hawk with its rotors churning was waiting out on the lawn, shining its lights. It was the neighbor's kid pulling into the drive next door, thunderous rock just dying as the boy got out of the car and slammed its door. Once her mother sat up bolt-erect in their settee across from the bed, and yet Gary's light wheezing snores didn't interrupt their oddly calm conversation.

"You were wonderful," her mother had said. "Did you pray for me, like I taught you?"

Usually she knew it was a dream and would sleep right through it. For a year before she died, her mother was racking up incredibly high charges on the cell, calling numbers in states the woman had never visited—and it was Diane's idea to pay them, billing herself for her own guilt. Gary had been nice about it, nodding forbearingly since nothing flustered the Amaze-O. Nothing could block Gary's sleep. He awoke refreshed and tied on his running shoes, stealthily exiting.

She was making the plans for Provence. She'd gotten proficient on the computer. Gary liked to pretend he was hopeless about paying online.

Instructions and prompts made him visibly tetchy. His antsiness allowed him to stay in character, encouraging in him a trait her friend Holly called learned helplessness. Holly was recently divorced for the third time and would occasionally call to say she'd done two hours of cardio at the gym—an hour on the elliptical and another hour on the StairMaster, which she set for what she called Zermatt Bergsteiger Intensity. She'd achieved a tight, feral midlife angularity and a hungry cougar regard and said that when she looked in the mirror she asked herself why she had ever needed a man to tell her what was glaringly obvious to someone as discerning as herself. During Holly's Zumba class, aping the snaky festive moves of the fetchingly mic'd gay Brazilian, Holly experienced the first intimations of cascading orgasms.

Diane shopped the sites pricing rental cars and monitoring ticket prices every day or two, waiting for rates to drop a couple hundred dollars. Today, a Tuesday, Diane found her airfare and pounced. It gave her a sense of accomplishment better than Holly's so-called cascading orgasms.

Then she got the email from Taylor—though she never gave her email to Gary's students. Gary's handiwork, thought Diane. Taylor had written: "Thinking about you. Can I come over?"

Diane was frightened by impromptu visits. She was frightened by insurance companies, by state troopers on the interstate when she drove to the mall four miles over the limit. An hour before the mail came she worried an exorbitant gynecologist's bill would arrive marked "Patient Responsibility." When it didn't, but brought only more junk, she was relieved. She attacked her next task with this foolish-feeling satisfaction. She confessed her folly to Gary, hoping he might make something fictional out of it, something that said yes, she was along for the same ride with him, but Gary was not that kind of writer. Lately, he flirted with genre, trying to dull it down and show it for the dopey entertainment it was. Reading should be mentally aerobic, a strenuous and daunting activity. Readers who might complain that he confused them were not his ideal readers.

Diane stared at Taylor's email. It made her uncomfortable but strangely galvanized.

"Hi. Give me an hour," she typed. She took out the caps and punctuation and hit Send.

She cleaned a little. She knew she could have been a Taylor. At Taylor's age, she'd had the means. Diane's father had made a fortune in construction by helping turn central Florida into a gaudy vacationland. The big doughy English children she saw in the Orlando airport each time did look happy to be there. Their sunburnt parents in their shell suits seemed to be having a good time, too. Nothing about the hawking of this nonsense bothered her. People did what they chose to do—until, according to her mother, there wouldn't be any more choosing left to do: fire or ice, one. "Those orange groves they tore down," her mother had said, "they weren't the first Eden."

Satisfied, you stopped noticing that you were only surrounded by other satisfied people.

She was glad she'd escaped Florida, all expressways and interstates. Gary might want to try Maine some year, its curving two-lane roads and rustic countryside. They both found boring *restful*, but the trip across the Atlantic each way was exhausting and disorienting. After they got over the jet lag (Gary was better at that), they slipped into the same quietly busy roles as the ones they took during the regular school year. She drove down to the market with just enough French to ask for what she needed and pay and say good-bye. Gary's French, which he only practiced in museums and restaurants, astounded her. The French translated every word by Gary; the reviews he got for his short, experimental novels also astounded her, if she comprehended them correctly. She shopped in the cheerfully businesslike market, and he worked up in his room all through the bucolic, radiant mornings—and in the afternoons they took sightseeing trips, Diane at the wheel.

At the door, Taylor arranged her cute face into a mortified mug, saying, "Don't be mad at Gary, please? I begged him for your email. Anyway, I'd've called, but email's more personal."

An odd thought, but then what was writing except a direct line into someone's head? No irony, no pauses. Emails had a flattening, innocent, persuasive effect, and Diane said, "Don't be silly, sweetheart. Now, we're going to have lunch in a while. Are tuna sandwiches okay?"

"I shouldn't cheat like that," said Taylor, "but it's so fun. Fun to be bad with *you*."

"Oh, darling. I completely forgot!" said Diane. "Well, I still have tofu in the fridge . . ."

"Give me a hug," the girl said, and Diane hugged her. Taylor whimpered: "Oh my God!"

"What?" Diane said, freezing in midsqueeze. It was as though the girl had flatlined.

"Nothing. It just feels good, like something I can totally honestly trust, I can count on."

The girl smelled like tea roses, her shampoo or soap. It was stronger than that, a perfume.

"Come on in. Would you like some iced tea?"

"I'd *love* some iced tea. No dead animals involved in that, right?"

"I left them out," Diane said, thinking happily about her clean kitchen.

"I wanted to bring you something."

"Oh, that wasn't necessary. But how thoughtful of you."

"But they didn't have it. Aren't tropical fruits always supposed to be in season? Jeez."

"Well, I happen to be sensitive to fruit sugars. Berries not so much."

"I wanted to bring papayas and mangos, but all they had were bananas, prosaic bananas."

They stood on either side of the breakfast bar, Diane loading up her woven bamboo tray.

"What perfume is that?" Diane said, now reminded of her mother's room freshener.

"It's from Paris by somebody called Annick Goutal, some dude or chick. Annick Goutal, is that a guy or a girl's name? A good, dear friend bought it then brought it back to me. The fuck knows. Are you ready? It's *Ce soir ou jamais*."

"Your pronunciation's a lot better than mine, that's for sure. I remember it from a shop in the village near where Gary and I rent. Oh and look, what's this? Is it a nice, clean ashtray?"

"You're so awesome. Yes, an ashtray for me and my filthy habit, cute, wonderful Diane."

Gary had folded and rolled the Ping-Pong table to the side of the porch. They had a good view from the padded wicker couch. Autumn bulb plantings still bursting, bushes neatly pruned.

"Taylor, you have something on your mind."

"You're perfect," the girl said. "My mother is perfect, but not like you. Lainie's weirdly perfect. Meanwhile she doesn't *need* to be. If I were in her shoes, I wouldn't try to be perfect."

"Your mother, Lainie did you say, should not try to be perfect in what way?"

"Just for example, how it's not necessary to be best friends with your daughter? Jeez."

At least Taylor seemed to be saying that she didn't think of Diane as maternal.

"Gary never really wanted kids," Diane sighed, "and I couldn't have cared either way."

Taylor laughed and started to smoke. In Diane's day around the Columbia library, it was cloves or Gitanes. Taylor's pack had an Indian-logo'd label, those new organic delivery systems of toxins and early death, but the smoke was fragrant. Diane's father's had smelled like clogged mufflers. Taylor blew it toward the line of hydrangea bushes just outside the screening. Nothing could kill hydrangeas, not even Diane's dad's Winston smog. Taylor inhaled, exhaled peacefully.

"Are you ready?" Taylor said. She had shiny hair striped bronze, black, and platinum, this new oblivious fashion, part ironical and part I-really-mean-it, I-own-this. Right? This is *me*.

"Is it news?" Diane then said, recomposing herself, "I mean, good news or bad news?"

"Diane, I'm—don't get mad or think I'm insane—but I'm thinking of getting married."

"Why would I get mad?" Diane said. "But you're still thinking? Taylor, are you sure?"

"Not a hundred percent."

"Do you have to—is it so urgent that you have to decide immediately?"

"Oh, it's not anything like that," said Taylor. "It's just this dude I know from back home, who's gay. Jesse. He summers in Bar Harbor with his rich-bitch relatives, but they're all great."

"I see," said Diane drolly, only she didn't see. "And do they know he's gay? He's *gay*?"

"Sure they know. Diane, you'd know right away! He's not femmy-like but you'd know."

"Is he cute? Why am I asking you that? Sweetheart, why would you marry a gay man?"

"We've just always known. We're actually in love, best friends. And yes, Jesse's *hot*."

"But have you ever slept with Jesse?"

"All the time. It's so much fun! He's so demonstrative, so there, so present. So verbal."

Someone had hit Diane with a ball-peen hammer, wham. That's what it felt like. Dizzy.

"Not to mention *oral*," Taylor then added. "Yeah, Jesse likes to keep it overall *oral*."

"Which you really didn't have to mention," Diane said. "But I asked for it, so go on . . ."

"Ha ha! Totally chill. You're so chill. Okay now Taylor, back up. Back to base, lady."

"You're completely serious," said Diane, feeling old and nervous and somehow afraid.

Taylor nodded and smudged out her cigarette.

"Okay, you really want to know? We're best friends and I don't really care what he does. As long as he plays safely. I might have my own fun, but it makes sense: we're *friends*. Most of the people I know don't really have true friends, just people they hang out with. Not people they trust. But Jesse and I talk in bed—we're always talking. Plus he *reads*, his whole family reads."

Judging from some of the people in that class she'd known, Diane seriously doubted this.

"Well, it must be interesting," said Diane, nodding meekly. "I think it must be different."

"Coming from my family? My dad and I are the only readers in the whole family tree."

Gary wasn't gay; if he had been, or if Diane had suspected he was, she never would have gotten engaged to him. That much she knew, she thought. Diane used to be so incredibly horny.

"But honestly," she said, "even if you say Jesse is cute, and the sex is good? *Good?*—"

"But the freedom. Oh, God. Guys I've dated. Boys. They're such prats, and brats, they want you all to themselves. Look at me, I'm not something for up on the shelf. I'm adorable but let's get real, a trophy wife? Not Taylor. It needs to be more chill than that. I want my liberty."

"Honey, freedom isn't exactly the first word I think of when I hear the word marriage."

"But isn't freedom what you have with Gary? I mean, that's what I get from you guys."

"But you always compromise in the end," said Diane. "Almost always."

"One compromises in every situation in life," said Taylor, an Edith Wharton matron now.

"To be fair, you're talking to the wrong person. I barely even remember being single."

"What are you really thinking?" Taylor said, nodding importantly.

"I wonder about your future. Yours is particularly bright, Taylor."

"For which I will not apologize, and which I know and understand utterly."

"And—" Diane bit off the end of that word—she was flustered, and repeated, "And—"

Usually they had more humility, the talented ones. She'd seen them come and she'd seen them ride off bound for bigger things. Taylor put up the hood on her sleek cashmere hoodie top.

"I don't believe you gave up your freedom, Diane," she said, lighting up again.

"Well. Certainly not the freedom to choose. By the way, I'm worried you're about to set yourself on fire. Cashmere isn't exactly flame-retardant. But we should have lunch, Taylor."

Taylor said, "Let's have our net-caught tuna. Let's kill a few more dolphins."

Rising, Diane said, "Actually everything is line-caught and dead and ready to go. I don't use canned tuna. That might be the only nice thing about me. No no, no need to protest . . ."

In the kitchen, Taylor said, "We have the freshest line-caught fish all summer in Maine."

"So you've been holding out on me," said Diane cleverly. "You do cheat sometimes."

"Sure, just not lobster," Taylor said, scooping Diane's salad onto her bread, then stacking on top of it the complementing tomato and avocado Diane had carefully sliced. *Immigrant labor*, the girl might have added. "You and Gary should come to Maine this summer. You'd love it."

"I'm afraid Gary doesn't like varying his summer writing routine by much."

"You could stay at the Bunches' family compound—where they have all these houses? It wouldn't be any problem, and Jesse would love it. In the old days, they had their own railcars to bring them up for the summer. They don't have them now, of course, just these cool old houses."

"It sounds lovely, with the wild blueberries and seafood you hear so much about."

"Diane, oh. It's so beautiful! Hate to be a booster, but Maine in the summer . . ."

"What I wanted to say," Diane began, "is it's not so much freedom you give up as the will to try new things that require you to go away. Last night you mentioned your Key West idea."

"Jesse and I cooked that one up together. It's where a lot of his family go in the winter."

"Gary and I have been there for a conference," said Diane without mentioning the gays.

"I'm ambitious," Taylor said, "and Jesse wants kids, too—*has* to have kids, really, to pass everything on to, not least the Bunch name. But I'd also want to work, not just write."

"How will you write, waitressing for sports fishermen and dropping Bunches, and what if you have to have four Bunches before you get a boy? The old conundrum of the Salic Laws . . ."

"The what?"

"That's why the French never had queens on the throne," said Diane. "They were around for mating purposes, to give the king his male heirs—since only men know how to do whatever."

"I don't know what to do with that," Taylor said, talking with her mouth full. She did not seem hurt but charged forward. "See Jesse and I are different. It's not just about love—although love is a huge part of it. In our generation we don't see differences of orientation, just like we try not to see color. I'd go so far as to say we just don't see it. A lot of us in this generation question whether there are any gay-straight differences. We don't subscribe to labels, is what I'm saying."

"'We don't subscribe to labels.'" said Diane. "'Don't pin labels on us, we're special.'"

"Are you mimicking me, Diane?"

"You're mimicking us," Diane said. "That was us. We said that about no labels first, and it wasn't true then and just by dint of time and civil rights it isn't any truer now. It's a myth."

She wanted to throw her lunch in the trash and go upstairs until this silly child left.

"Time for lunch with the Bunches," Gary'd probably say, "lunch with the Bunch bunch."

"That's bitchy," Taylor said, dropping her gaze. "And I think unfair and wrongheaded."

"Taylor," said Diane, rinsing the mayonnaise knife under the tap to use it for the hummus spread she liked, "we used to say that sentence exactly back in the eighties. MTV, David Bowie, Flock of Seagulls, it was this amazing, brand-new concept called Androgyny. 'Hey big corporate guy, don't tell us how to live! Don't label us for your marketing strategies, old man!' *Gahh!*"

"But maybe we're the first to mean it. Did you ever think of it that way? Maybe you're just bitter. Maybe you feel like you missed out on something, I dunno. Diane! *Please.*"

"I need a break," said Diane. "Could somebody just give me a fucking break?"

Diane wasn't even going to wish her luck. Minutes ago she'd been thinking of opening a bottle of chardonnay to relax the mood a little, but now she wouldn't waste it. She drummed her fingers restlessly on the breakfast bar. Her sandwich was ready, but how to enjoy it now? It was too perfect not to enjoy under optimal circumstances. She'd *grilled* the tuna. She looked at it—a perfect thing she'd made. She looked at it wanly. She couldn't stop looking at it, hating herself.

Taylor said, "Wow. I mean, wow."

"I'm going to go upstairs and lie down now," Diane said rustily, making a good move.

From her bed Diane listened for the front door, and when she heard it gently close a few minutes later, a little relief came to her. Just a little. It didn't pay, and she'd never do it again, to entertain these obnoxious, self-loving kids. She was getting the burning again, a little in from the left side of her groin. The bladder or the kidneys, something shooting down from the kidneys and expressing itself closer to where everything had an outlet—a referred pain. Back to the doctor. She'd dilute pure cranberry juice, gulping that for the rest of the day. Brewer's Yeast tablets, acidophilus, no citrus, no coffee. To bed early, then Gary'd come in from bowling. He and some of the faculty bowled on Tuesdays.

A little time passed. She'd napped. Diane woke up refreshed but in a state of uncertainty.

She had hidden her Bible. She didn't believe in its myths—just the essential wisdom of yearning expressed especially in the Twenty-third Psalm. Gary had liked it, too, and once she'd asked him what he thought it meant by that one line about the rod and the staff: "They comfort me," it went.

"Is that patriarchal Old Testament might on the one hand and peace or love on the other?" she'd said, waiting. He'd come in from the bathroom into the center of the bedroom then put his hands on his hips and stared at her like she was this complete stranger suddenly. "Well. Is it?"

"I don't know, Di. It's just language. All it is is incredible, noble imagery and poetry."

"Just language?" she had said, thinking that he was indeed a stranger to her then. "Is it?"

It twinged under her ribs, first the left, then the right, trading sides. Too much to look out for, the liver, the pancreas. In the twinkling of an eye, her body's blinking, freezing spiritual eye.

Sometime past midnight she turned away from Gary. Across the blinds in the window that overlooked the street the lights of a patrol car prowled past and the car's intricate security system issued a bleep of disapproval, a smart-technology vote of no confidence. This light could detect the subtle odor of a potentially epidemic disease inside a domicile, borne by Diane Ludner. Even then she knew she was dreaming, but then the dream continued vividly, captivating her: Diane, its bewildered and physically uncomfortable captive. The light reversed course and Diane knew she was had—just like in some old early seventies movie, *Omega Man* or *Soylent Green*.

But it wasn't her fault. Nothing could be her fault, only her responsibility.

barracuda

She'd failed at everything in her past so it surprised her that she was making it in New York. And not that she was in love with her job. The PR biz kept getting crazier. Becca was just ripped that their star client Adonis had come in at lunchtime—without his usual entourage. He'd stopped to chat with her at her desk and at one point even told her that he *never* lunched. Used to seeing him in spike heel boots in videos, you might not have guessed it, but he was tiny—five feet high at the most. He was about six inches wide and had an amazing waist, almost no waist, a waist more like a wrist, and perfect little features bunched prettily to the center of his face with a trim, skinny black mustache. His hair was pulled into a lamé turban and he was well groomed and smelled of tuberose. She'd asked him what his scent was, and Adonis had giggled. Then he had told Becca it was in fact tuberose, as though imparting the great secret of his own immortal, unstoppable pop allure. Adonis was sex condensed into five feet by six inches, period. Becca's father, the dead rector, would have made a meal out of the mustache. It was the star's style, and her father thought he was the funniest man he knew, the subtlest, picking out one feature of somebody's looks and running with it. "Get Little Richard," he'd probably say behind Adonis's back. *As if.*

Adonis had come off as fascinating to Becca and she was trying to say just how, although she was having trouble fusing her ideas while perched on a stool in her green fog of margaritas.

"He's a fruitarian," Becca explained about Adonis, "and a Seventh-day Adventist."

"What the blab's that mean?" said Hunter, the dumber one of her two close gay friends.

Imagine coming from Miami, from Cuban Americans, and being called Hunter.

"It means he only eats fruit. If fruit doesn't get picked, it falls off the plant. It's good for the plant, our taking the fruit, and doesn't hurt it at all—so fruitarians think it's more humane."

"No," said Hunter, "I mean Seventh-day Adventist. What the hay's that mean?"

If you weren't Catholic or Jewish, she knew, Hunter couldn't place you. Not possible to be a lapsed Episcopalian, Becca thought—not that she'd ever get Hunter to understand what she had gone through. Already Hunter and Jesse were ahead of her in the drinks department tonight.

The smarter and cuter Jesse said, "It's a cult, right, Seventh-day Adventism?"

"Sort of," Becca explained, "I guess more of a denomination. I don't know. But I think they're one of those that don't drink alcohol or caffeine and are pretty strict about their diets."

"That puts me out," said Jesse, who was from Maine and called himself a hunter-gatherer.

"Me, too," said Hunter.

"But they're a brand of Christian, I know," Jesse said. "Whatever. Christian."

This made Becca laugh. How come all of the cute guys had names that started with a J?

The bartender came over and said, "Anybody need anything?"

"No thank you," Becca said. "We were just laughing about something interesting."

The bartender closed his mouth, as though suddenly remembering what he'd forgotten to do all the way across town. She wasn't ready for her free second drink yet. She trilled laughter. Still, the bartender didn't move. He stayed in Becca's headlights, a captive audience, poor guy.

Already she was tipsy (what was wrong with her!) and she said, regretting it immediately, "It's just been such an amazing day. So, I've been at my firm over a year and never once has any star client of ours come in, like just to say hi? But one finally did today, a really important one."

"Amazing," said the bartender, fluttering his pretty lashes knowing they were pretty-ass.

"Right?" said Becca.

It wasn't that crowded. She liked it this way. There was always the anticipation of more things to come, more crazy jibes to overhear and laugh about, chill videos, more new customers she might turn and talk to. The bartender wiped up a little spill in front of her and began moving away from them. When it was dead like this, the bartender stayed close to the bar back, who was always in a tank top, the two chatting at the end. The bar back was adorably young, with an arch and innocent demeanor. Left alone down there, he'd stand staring and sing along to the divas.

A new video began. Before the first note was sung, Hunter said, "One of her best *ever.*"

"Please," said Jesse, "it's so recherché and already her voice was completely shredded."

"It's not as bad as it eventually got," said Becca knowingly. "I'd hate to hear her now."

This was meant as a joke, as the diva in question had recently died by perhaps suicide, a detail that was not mentioned because it was too boring or unnecessary or something, whatever.

Hunter stirred his drink and languidly said, "*Now,* forget it," and Jesse pinched a smile.

Jesse was the handsomer of the two boys, so the more conservative of demeanor. Hunter was the prettier, about-to-go-off sex freak. If both were straight Becca would've had a hard time choosing, *as if.* She felt fat, but not as fat as she'd felt a couple months ago. She'd worked on it.

It was early, the beginning of happy hour, giving them good stools near the main screen. She secretly hoped Adonis would come on, the one where he played the heart-shaped guitar and that featured Baby Scrimp. She wanted to tell them about the rose, but Hunter would probably just make a crack about that, too. Coming in, he'd cracked that he liked her short, *baggy* dress.

"It really suits you," he'd said neutrally, "in a classic-rock, Stevie Nicks kind of way."

It hurt, but she loved him and felt that in his cracked perverse way he loved her as well.

Adonis had given her this gorgeous coral rose. He had given her the rose and said that he liked her dress. Hunter was bitchier, more demanding. Adonis, a soulful man, a great performer.

She wasn't going to mention it. She sometimes stopped to ask herself why she bothered coming to gay bars so much, but it wasn't like they only went to bars. They stayed and hung out in Queens in one of their apartments and smoked a bowl. Actually, that was her favorite thing to do. Jesse and Hunter could be friendlier there, appreciating her cooking and baking. And being from Bucks County, a simpler place she missed, though the time wasn't right to go back, she felt at home in the kitchen. It was like doing something nice for a lover or family member. With gay friends it was the best of both worlds. But too much weed and Hunter would begin making more jokes. "Jeez, Bec," he said one night, "have some of your own dang banana bread—you made it, remember?"

"I'm *going* to," she said and paused, "when I'm good and ready, you big heinous bitch."

The word *heinous* was popular just then. It was hard to keep up, but Becca tried.

And she went out on the fire escape to smoke. Jesse joined her, asking for a ciggy and consoling her, saying she was right to call him a bitch. Jesse would make someone a great lover.

Lover. She liked this word. Becca's last lover was black, but not all gay men were color-blind: a myth about homosexuals she would no longer kid herself about. They could be as mean and intolerant as the next guy—as, say, the rector, who'd put himself at the right hand of Jesus.

"Disgusting, filthy habit, both of you," Hunter called, eating, not putting on an ounce.

An older guy at the end of the bar, but closer to the door, with big bronze hair like a noble Roman helmet, was studying the slick glossy full-color bar rags. He came in from the foyer with a stack and sat down and took out his reading glasses. He studied these gay reports on what was going on in New York gay life for their gossip and toward the back the personal websites and cell numbers of hustlers and massage therapists. He was a professor close to retirement, she thought, who kept thin not because he had to but because he had the natural discipline. The readers he put on were drugstore half-moons. Becca knew that the very backs of the magazines featured photo spreads of guys at huge parties in various states of publishable near undress. She'd peeked in on this life, too. With Hunter she had done Halloween, the whole crawl, accompanying him to bars and the after-parties. Hunter would leave her hanging toward the end then peel off so she'd have to get back to Astoria whichever way she could. He'd make her swear this was fine—pretending to care for her safety but just hoping to get laid. Jesse swam in different waters. He worked at a magazine styling photo shoots of modern-chic or antique-filled rooms, the owners of these rooms posed defiantly on couches resembling cloth-covered concrete slabs, or silk-upholstered canapés. So queerly, Jesse would insist on a word like canapé. The subjects were dignifiedly aged, or else dazzlingly forced with enormous effort into a false perpetual youth. Some clients he called "near royalty." Nor did it bother Becca that she'd never meet these people ever, Hunter's chosen tribe.

"Please, royalty?" he'd said. "I think what he means is nouveau riche—while I'm related to Castellano *dukes*. Havana? Boatloads more aristocracy than with any Hollywood trash."

"Darling," Becca had countered that time, "I think all Jesse said was *near* royalty."

The nice geezer kept studying the rags, making notes, typing info into his smartphone.

The next few videos were retro and she was back in high school in Bensalem. She'd like to see some of those assholes now. Hot jocks, slut cheerleaders, or fly girls who didn't cheerlead but who would ridicu-lously overtreat their hair. The worst were the frumpy girls sneering at her because they were like her, and dumpy weird Aaron in forensics trying to discuss the Epicureans with her, quoting Lucretius, or quoting Epictetus, who'd said, "If you desire to be good then start by believing you're bad." Aaron was sweet but didn't know her father called him the Dolt when, yeah, she'd let him take her to the prom. "Live! It's a mistake not to," he kept quoting, then got sick on forties so that he had to stop saying it. He tried to get her bra off when they parked—and she wanted it off, it wasn't that, it's just that he didn't know how to do it. Poor guy, he just didn't *have* what Becca wanted. Better the memories of her neighbor who did well in basketball whose parents were very Presbyterian and snob. They were at church when he had a cold and she snuck in through his window and they got into bed and it was lovely, from the first insertion to the time when he yelled "Oh, crap!" and had a fast-erupting orgasm, his mass and weight big all over her. After that, she was ready for Penn, ready to get the hell out, though her grades weren't great. No one would ever ask about them, which was the dirty secret. All you needed was those references.

In the center of one rag you could undo a map of Manhattan, gay bars all marked. When he was done typing the addresses into his phone, the man returned the rags to the foyer and came back inside, settled on his stool again with his light-brown drink, and patiently began finishing it.

And the pretty Latin guy in the stocking cap and nerdy eye frames, complexion unflawed: straight Latin men were mad about her but she wouldn't marry one. When she finally moved on, she narrated to herself—marrying somebody who need not be rich—she'd just be "Rebecca."

The bartender was monitoring their levels and loped back casually, and Hunter began to flirt with him by asking him about his Halloween costume for this year. The bartender said that he'd been thinking about it and wanted to go as an MIA in Nam, if the weather stayed like this.

Jesse, as though framing himself in a movie, suddenly slammed his glass on the bar and some of the ice came hopping out and spilled

over the counter and he yelped and flung his arms around and pretended to flail haplessly. It was too early for this and it got on Becca's
nerves.

"Did I do that?" Jesse said and laughed at himself, showing his
white and straight teeth.

Really, Jesse had one of two choices: become like her father, the
handsome devil who's sliding through, just getting by, or break out
and get sober and become his full, wonderful self.

Hunter, looking steadily at the bartender, said, "Opens her mouth
and her purse falls out."

Bitch. Hunter was wonderful but was always there to say the
wrong thing, bitch. Bitch!

The bartender scooped up the spilled ice. "No worries. Another
round, guys?"

"God yes," Becca said, like a secondary female character in a
coming-out film. "Please."

Hunter, playing the charmer and thinking he might get the bartender, said, "This one and me, we go back," and threw his arm around
Jesse, who pretended to bristle and be put-out. What was Hunter
doing, whom was he trying to make jealous? The bartender rapidly
filled his shaker.

But the first taste of that next one, *amazing*—"Just what the doctor
ordered," as the rector would have said and said every damn time.
The first taste of the next one and she'd be content.

Hunter and Jesse had met at NYU, friends pre-Becca—before
Hunter's Time of Doubt.

She'd met Hunter at a pre-party. These things in New York had
levels and stratifications. You were invited to the pre-party but not
the after-, say, but either way, you wouldn't go to *both*.

She could remember back when she was lighthearted, when she
could still be hilarious.

More coming into the bar. A fifty-plus guy asking for a manhattan.
The bartender carded him, like really? The guy acted flattered but
obviously didn't know it was just a formality. Then the bartender
served it and the man clarified, he wanted it on the rocks, and the

bartender obeyed, he hadn't heard. He poured it over a glass of ice. Becca's father before he died, and it was grisly, a gnarly thing to watch, liked manhattans. He was the rector by then, about to die. The people of the congregation came from miles around. They'd loved him for his liberal bent. He'd asked for a manhattan the night he died. The congregants formed a ring around the bed as he sipped it, and he said the *thing* and they laughed. They didn't stick around, though, moving on to supper clubs.

Becca supposed he'd had a kind of dry, effective humor, and that she'd learned hers from him. Nor was it like Daddy would have disapproved of the company she was keeping. He'd had plenty of gays milling through, taking communion. Once she'd thought Daddy was gay—but no. He'd described himself as a fellow traveler in his parish, and his many indiscretions with women had proved him straight, she'd only ultimately learned. Flamier ones, like Hunter, he'd despised.

So they were at this pre-party, and she didn't remember what it was for. A book of photos or some project. *Project* she'd learned, meant anything involving giving a party at the end. Also no one *organized* anything, they were *curators* of it, whatever. New York only had curators.

That night, Hunter had been a really good lover, attentive—like a little brother, actually.

In the morning, he'd told her about Jesse. He'd wanted her to meet Jesse. Obviously, he was in love with this guy Jesse. Even then she got it—that Hunter and Jesse were never to be.

The boys went out for a cigarette, leaving her alone. Even that, Hunter's new smoking.

One day he hated, looking down on something, and the next day he loved, was hooked.

She'd never gotten the full story. Hunter kept changing the story, but she knew one thing. He'd known about himself before taking her home, and weirdly the sex had been good, soft then hard in all the right proportions and she wasn't face-down for it. She wished she knew what was genuine about Hunter. There was going to be a time of reckoning for the boy. He could not play around with others' feelings forever. It took every scrap of Becca's Christian charity at times. It wasn't all his fault. Hunter had too many people to please, didn't know what he truly wanted.

He had to make his family proud. This seemed weird to the indifferent Protestant Becca, raised coolly, ambivalently. Yet incredible Jesse was under no illusions about himself, and he'd never been. Looking at him sitting there calmly soaking up the bar's ambient red-filtered light to breathtaking advantage. He forthrightly wanted the same things and never changed his story. He wanted a husband as soon as it was legal, two yellow lab dogs, children eventually. He loved life and nature, all the undefended creatures of the biosphere. Jesse was admirably, covertly spiritual and could tell you how many whales and polar bears there were left in the world, week by week.

A very pretty man. Where did they come from? These giants in down-to-earth sizes, the princes? Walking among us, but rare, were the princes. Philosophers, poets of Gaia. He hadn't asked about Adonis, but he was a reserved one, a cool customer. He was going to ask, she knew. It was Jesse's style to ignore her for a while then hone in with this mad, killing empathy of his.

Once recently when Jesse had said something about it, and Becca had replied that yes she was losing weight, twenty pounds in three months all told, Hunter had scowled and said, "It's not good for you to lose it so fast, Becca. Jiminy Crickets, be careful. Don't expire on us."

And then and there Jesse had taken her hand, kissed it, and said, "I'm proud of you."

Right now the boys were outside gossiping, and Becca thought, I'm already tipsy. Hunter was right, though. She had to watch. And go easy on the alcohol, lady. Those hidden sugars.

She stared down into her swampy cocktail. Guys liked her. She needed to speak up more at work. Adonis had come in and there she was at her desk, and he was shy, offering her a coral-colored rose with his black-lace-gloved hand, demurring when she thanked him, saying shyly, "I always like to surprise the ladies." A gentleman somewhat effeminate: that word, *androgyny*.

"Not one of yours," she wanted to mutter into her glass. "Sorry but that one's hetero."

Disingenuous Hunter, she'd heard him that time she was out alone on the fire escape, and when Hunter drank or baked he got loud. He was a kid, with no self-awareness. His voice raised in the kitchen, not twenty feet away, he'd said to Jesse, "You know she eats *sometime*. Seriously, have you seen lately that chopper pad she calls an ass? Just attach a vacuum hose to her mouth."

Home in the last round before going off to hospice never to return, her father had said to her, "You understand what I've taught you and what the Gospels decree about forgiveness, don't you, since it's important even to yourself to forgive?"—and she thought she'd forgiven him. She felt a little chunk of ice growing and accreting in her aorta threatening to choke it in the end. But even that would be a relief. It must have been for him. He was cold; loved coldly, then forgotten.

The boys came back, talking their goofy baby talk. "We're hungry! Becca hungry too?"

One day this would all be over, and she'd have to be fine with it; she could just move on.

Ditch the bitch. Isn't that what they'd probably finally say to each other, full of zingers?

No round of shots for the road on Jesse tonight, it turned out. Poor, overworked Jesse.

How could she break up with them? No, they'd leave *her*. Hunter ditched nice guys left and right, getting bored, finding little failings in their personalities, or getting wasted then waking up in some new guy's bed while Hunter's other, current boyfriend was out of town on business. How could you break up with a nice older guy who'd taken you to Paris and sprung for it all?

"You guys leaving already?" the bartender said and began snatching up their glasses.

It was a lovely early October evening, the sky blue ink seeping into orange sherbet, clear, bright. Her second winter coming on. Out on the sidewalk she smelled wood smoke and then *it*.

She said, "*Eww*, who wears patchouli anymore?"

What did it interest her to try keeping up with them and acting bitchy on their same level?

barracuda

"No kidding," said Jesse, "seriously. Patchouli. Seriously?"

"It's making a comeback," said Hunter, who was stylish, no questioning that, but still just an intern and at a kind of pseudo magazine that was purely paid for by some Gulf States emir.

"Becca," said Jesse, "you didn't finish about Adonis. But what do you feel like eating?"

She laughed and wished she had a cigarette for a prop and said, "Is that one question?"

She didn't know why she teased him. Jesse shined and could be unpredictably gallant.

Then a bum came up to Hunter and said, "Pardon me, but could I trouble you for a butt?"

Hunter brought out his cigarette pack, doing it automatically and cheerfully—like a little proud nephew in a tiny tux lofting the wedding ring on its eency ceremonial satin pillow, just so.

Then the bum asked him for a light and Hunter, saying "Sure," was again gracious. From emotional midgets—too beautiful to live inside their awfully conflicted selves—sometimes came great, kind gestures, and perhaps they, too, would be saved. Despite their sweet bastard selves.

Hunter's parents had died together in a car crash on the Julia Tuttle Causeway, which was supposed to be hard to do since usually traffic on the way to Miami Beach (they were headed to a fundraiser) went at a snail's pace. She remembered it. He'd come over to her apartment, the old one on Roosevelt Avenue, not the new one on 69th Street, and said he had no one else. She'd let him sleep in the bed with her, and he'd snuggled close to her crying through the night, waking up periodically, his hand a moist paw on her neck, his wet cheek against her boob. Tender, grateful.

Then again, people like Hunter were more common than not. There had to be more guys out there like Hunter than there weren't. At least Becca hoped so—with a yearning like starving.

Imagine being this hungry and feeling sated, just like this, at the same time.

59

her biographers

H is days were all the same, weather his only variety—and not much variety at that.

He'd fallen for the island immediately, and she had taken to its eccentricity. Tolerance for eccentricity, he knew, had never been his strong suit. He'd been the one to edit it out when it had appeared in Marion's work apparently for its own sake. He had thought that the palette of human nature, manifestations of the spirit, did not range over a broad spectrum; that aberration could not explain the species, only obviate itself as a dead end. In Westchester County, Leo hadn't seen so much variety in the people he'd grown up around. It wasn't a town to stay in all your life; they'd erred on the side of conformity, but later it was comforting to be with a woman who'd known the same geography and natural features in her girlhood. (Coincidences being mystical forges.) The spring lilacs with their deep odor of evening, a matronly odor, aware of death. Spinsters recalled their youths and what might have been. They sighed in the houses they'd inherited. A long time ago, a boy had a pattern of bicycling past—but each time kept going. Harbinger March crocuses, a more hopeful sign going up and spreading out across the sunny lawn. Marion had shared some of the same galvanic tropes: Lenten tulips and Easter lilies. She was drawn to hyacinths but said their scent was so strong it suggested entire lives. She would remove a potted one from the room to give herself peace, quiet down her creative imagination: a little going a long way. On Martha's Vineyard each year, the homely hydrangea would touch her more subtly, like grandmothers' lace. Hydrangeas lasted into September, when slowly and finally the fatly massed heads of purple and sky-blue petals would fade and go papery, crisp up, curl, and die. Things at the beach were more evergreen. She would take long walks. Time to pack up. Another summer was come and gone.

He'd met her all that time ago when she was thirty-one—when Leo was already fifty-six, just divorced. (In the spring, a hint of June. Deep into August, an annual knowledge of frailty, the bitter drying grasses a warning of fall, russet, gold, a flat powder gray, a moldy newsprint mole.)

Rare was the word he'd used for her, but she hadn't liked it, laughing it off with each use.

How many more summers now, here where it was almost always summer? Where before they'd both always believed she would of course see him into winter . . . ?

If he'd had kids with Marion, the children would be adults and they might resemble these two polite, overall presentable young people he'd let into the house, just now, without getting up.

He sent the girl, Andi, into the kitchen to make coffee, but she wasn't acting put-out. She had sprung into action instantly, saying, "No, it would be my pleasure, Leo."

He was especially taken with Andi. The boyfriend, Josh, he was a little less impressed by.

Answering Andi's first question, Leo said, "No, it was up in Massachusetts. I was staying with friends who had Marion along, whom of course I'd heard of. By then Marion was a comer."

"And here you are, man," said Josh from the sofa—smirking, Leo thought. "So cool."

Though he didn't particularly like the sight of them, in the intervening pause Leo checked the nails on both of his hands—hands anymore like parchment-slipcovered claws.

The kitchen did not have a wall to divide itself off. Andi called, "Do you like Key West?"

He went terse, felt his neck stiffen, and he called out painfully, "Tolerably enough."

Talking was such a strain. And his gravelly *haute voix*, he knew, could be frightening.

Andi came with the three cups on a tray. She'd found Marion's pottery service (the sugar bowl and little milk pitcher and matching cups and saucers), and Leo said, "Wonderful, my dear. I can see you're clever enough to get top military secrets out of me . . . would that I had any."

She giggled at that last phrasing. He sounded, he realized, like the old magazine articles he'd started his career penciling up— genteel, bumptious, and with titles like "The Ideal Gimlet." A glint of Eisenhower-era titillation. Breasts heaving almost clear of their red-velvet bustiers.

He saw the little recorder on the coffee table and said, "Have you turned that thing on?"

"It's voice-activated," said Josh. "Thing is, when it turns on, it cuts off your first word."

"It's digital," said Andi, handing Leo his cup and saucer. "I don't understand it, either."

"Technology, man," Josh added. "I think all it does is further enslave us, build walls."

Leo leaned forward with creaky difficulty to pour milk into his coffee, then took a spoon.

Stirring, ignoring Josh a bit, he said, "So it's on. What would you like to hear about?"

"Mm," said Andi, settling next to Josh on the sofa and opening her notes. "What did you think of Marion the first time you met her? This was in, what again, Martha's Vineyard?"

"Correct," he said, knowing print no longer held an iconic finality. "A brunette vision."

"You said you already knew who Marion was. It's what you meant by a 'comer,' right?"

"I was editing at this one house, but the job wasn't going to last. They liked me less than I liked them. I'm happy to report the company is no longer in business. They ran fresh out of dirty crossword puzzle ideas, I guess. I was keeping my eyes out for names to take with me.

An author of mine who'd been at Iowa with her kept telling me, Marion Jillsen, Marion Jillsen . . . I was a tad—I didn't know what to believe. He wasn't one of those I was planning on taking with me."

"Not naming names," Andi said amusedly. "But, so, you didn't take him seriously?"

"He could have been in love with her, had rose-colored goggles strapped to his great head of yellow hair, slept with her for all I knew. Never got the full story on that. Female mysteries."

"Which basically knocked her down on your scale, initially."

"Only until I got around to reading the samples, by which I was more or less impressed."

Andi hazarded, "Not bowled over."

"Not until I met her, but then I was impressed. Utterly impressed. A talented storyteller, whose work had somehow escaped me, smuggled into the safety of little journals and lit mags."

"What had you read of hers by then?"

"I had read Xeroxes of a couple of her stories."

"You seem rather hard to impress, but you detected a little spark in the Xeroxes."

"I took them seriously. Xeroxes from respectable journals I had missed. In the old days, that's how we got wind of things, like some kind of screen test. You know about screen tests . . ."

"When a young actor or actress went to Hollywood trying to break into the movies."

"You got it," said Leo. "It's callous to say, perhaps, but look at it from a New York point of view. More than books we were looking for authors to publish. There was a sense of bringing an author forward, but gradually. Publishers used to be in it with their writers for the long haul."

"And Marion was the real deal. A strong female voice, not to say feminine necessarily."

"Anybody with taste could see it, and everyone I knew and associated with had taste."

"Books meant more then, didn't they?" said Josh. "We're philistines nowadays, I think."

It was as though there was an unnecessary echo. Josh should go get pizzas or something.

Leo didn't need help, was the deal. But here was this clueless kid, pretty stupid boy Josh.

All he wanted was to feel the little click. Leo could draw that click out for hours now. His liver needed just the slight tickling and away he went. He could make two drinks last to bedtime.

"Well, let's put it this way," Leo said. "What does a book mean to young folks like you?"

For her part, Andi felt immense goofy vibrations of mad talent under this roof, orgasmic.

She thought about her most joyous reading experiences, which of course were when she was small—before she had found out how awful the world was because of a few key people in it. How wonderful it had been then, believing a mouse might have his own car to drive and have his adventures in. Her father had given her *Stuart Little*, his very boyhood copy, an irony not lost on Andi—an irony that for a while made her bitter until finally it lacked all flavor.

Leo smacked his dry lips and said, "Got any favorite memories of opening a book?"

He should drink more water, he knew. Old people forgot to hydrate consistently.

"Easy," said Josh. "For me it would have to be *Ramona the Pest* by Beverly Cleary."

"I think I was a little too old for that one," said Leo, propping his chin on his palm. The leather on the sweatiest days was too slick; his elbow would slide off. The chair was a gift from old friends who couldn't be bothered to come down anymore, marking a monumental birthday. It was called the Papa Fauteuil, ordered from a catalog featuring the Hemingway Collection.

"One thing's for sure," said Josh eagerly, "we ignore books and authors at our peril."

"Do we need something stronger?" said Leo. "I have all sorts of drink, no smoke. I don't inhale anything since cancer. Situation scared the bejesus out of me. I've got beer and liquor."

"Ah," said Andi, blinking around at Josh, "we have that plane to catch in a few hours."

"And we still have to get back to the hostel for our bags," Josh elaborated.

"I see. Presently I might want to indulge a bit myself, if you don't mind."

Andi shook her head, saying, "This is an amazing moment for Josh and I, both big fans of Marion's. Sorry, but we just really want to get this right. I guess the elephant in the room is—"

"Why she left me," said Leo.

"Not what I was going to say! No, no. Just to ask what her personal appeal for you was, that first time you met—after that writer you don't want to name brought you two together?"

"He didn't bring us together. The first thing I liked about Marion was when she indicated she didn't care for him any more than I did. Or that was the third thing. It was pure chance."

"Serendipity."

Leo shrugged.

He was thinking about that object of a preposition, "for Josh and I." Leo had not finished college, but he had had a good high school education in Triermont. In those days, you could learn enough in high school to break into New York and start on the bottom rung right out of Korea. In no time they were handing you a blue pencil and getting you started marking up pages, judging.

Leo said, "She was two worlds merged. Marion had a foot in each."

"You mean the old gentlemen's world of publishing and the newer, crasser—"

"Vulgar and debased and corporate publishing world—yes, I think it's safe to call it that."

"Before literature became more of a commodity, right?" said Josh.

Leo hadn't had a conversation like this in years. When he got together once a week with the other fellows, to play Latin Scrabble, they moaned about their backs, arthritis, hemorrhoids, acid reflux. Their flesh hung like slack crepe from brittle bones. They remembered the old days without talking much about books anymore. They ought to play Seniors Scrabble: *heating pad.*

"We did believe in literature as something unique. That it had a power to help us . . ."

"See things?" she said and formed an adorable moue with her pertly lipped mouth.

There was some of the eager beaver about Andi.

"It was written entertainment. Whatever else it was doing, it had to entertain."

"But smarter, more intelligently written than regular entertainment?" she said brightly.

"Not always. I wouldn't want to be too romantic about what we might call my *era* . . ."

And she laughed.

That morning, in the diaries of Thomas Mann, Leo had read about Weimar winking itself out from twilight to darkness. A kid on a scooter working for Episcopal Services had been good enough to pick the book up for Leo from the public library and deliver it, along with Leo's daily-allowance tuna fish sandwich, flavorless scoop-sized garden salad, and boxed grape juice. Mann was Leo's youthful idol, a multi-tasker whose intelligence seemed as big as the Fatherland's, and yet as Leo settled into the Hemingway chair and snacked on the pale slices of cantaloupe women volunteers had packed in Tupperware and sent off with the boy on his loudly buzzing rounds, his attention had begun wandering—as Mann's own attention seemed never to have. Between meals with his forbearing wife, Katia, and their countless eccentric, neurasthenic offspring, Mann would scribe off more warnings to himself about the shadowy, ever-nigh-drawing reach of the Führer—each entry exquisitely phrased in highly figurative terms of foreboding—then note with reserved pleasure that the Festschrift edition being printed in his honor had made it safely across the Alps.

Leo had set the book down on the arm of the Hemingway chair and it stayed there for hours.

"Son, if you don't mind, go reach up into the cabinet over the kitchen sink and grab down that bourbon. You'll find the glasses a cabinet over. And throw a little ice in mine, would you?"

"Now you're talking," said Josh, looking nervously over at Andi. "Honey?"

"Sure," she said, but raised an unsure eyebrow. "This is fun!"

Josh moved sluggishly but was built long and lithe. Young males these days, so indolent. Kid was like a noir slattern slotted into a skinny hippie's body. Andi must have liked unwrapping the smelly layers. Sex was past Leo, and to feel in any wise potent he could at least run the show.

"Just the one," Leo said, winking at her as they sat waiting. "Indulge an oldie, my dear?"

"What's it like being you, Leo?" she said, studying him with her stare. "You're a legend."

This was too much. He could imagine kissing her neck from behind, her bare shoulders.

"Editors aren't legends. Three in all of history are legends—and I haven't worked on any manuscripts in fifteen years except when friends ask for an opinion. I don't softball them, either. I tell them what I think, old friends, established authors. They in turn are indulging me."

"I would bet my last dime, sir, that they respect every comment."

"I used to keep track. One or maybe two suggestions in the end, they'd take. They were being good eggs, trying to keep me from feeling too obsolete. Even that they've stopped doing. First Marion gone, then the bottom fell out. Writers stick together. Editors are . . . expendable."

"But I'd also bet Marion did all of her best work with you at her side. At least nearby."

"You shouldn't sentimentalize me," said Leo. "What we're talking about is just a curtain of social manners. Boil us all down, we have the same concerns and doubts. We're cliquish, too, hopelessly tribal. Sociologists used to define us largely in terms of our reference groups."

Andi did a double take. "Editors?"

"Leo, dude, give me hope!" Josh said returning with the glasses. "Throw me a bone."

Josh had pubic-looking whiskers. Was that considered rakish, comely, sloppily fetching?

Leo said, "Editors more than any other. Do sociologists still talk about reference groups?"

Josh took his first hissing sip of bourbon and said hoarsely, "You're asking me?"

"For instance. You're an educated guy, obviously."

"You're talking about Merton," said Andi, "who was at Columbia. All those latent versus manifest functions, right? Good stuff. Yeah, I think he's still considered foundational."

With a withering burble Leo said, "That does sound rather like my period, my *epoch*."

Leo thought of cigars and liquor and the gone, past ways of doing things, martini lunches and gentlemen's agreements. He used to bow down before authors, considering them oracles if the writers were any good at all. He'd wanted to write at one early point, do his James Jones—if truth be known, his Hemingway. Only to Marion had he belatedly confessed the goal, as gone as bebop, and she had said that she was glad he hadn't gotten his hands dirty. Only *she* was the star.

He thought of girls in the summer on Park Avenue in their light dresses, the chivalry of an old, war-tired world, before the spectacle of a homosexual riding off with his wife. He'd stopped understanding anything, including himself, on that day. He thought of the army. A corporal in his unit in Yongsan had heard his mother was dead and that night come to Leo in his bunk and asked if he could lie next to Leo and have his arm around him. The boy was in pieces. They were away from all the action at their garrison, but you didn't know where Truman was going to take things next in the "conflict," the "police action." Suddenly it was the Chinese, those Chinese. A warrant officer, Leo was two or three years older than most of the enlisted men, who went around calling each other sweetheart and wolf-whistling at each other's backs, but it was all show—that talk of skirt men and legs and, oh boy, what they wouldn't do to get Marilyn down off that pinup.

You had to be tender with a kid like that. You treated him like your little brother.

"Don't worry," said Andi, taking bird-sips, "we're not being *socio-logical* with Marion."

"What's this book about?" he said. "What's your angle? Don't be too slavish over her."

"I want to be true to her," said Andi. "I never met Marion. I almost got the chance, but it didn't happen, a reading when I think she was already sick. I wouldn't have wanted to see her in that state. Tell me who she is, not just who she was. What do you think is still her essence?"

More corniness but he recognized the kindness and felicity of it, the gesture of it.

The bourbon went to work. There was nothing better than the first three or four tastes.

He said, "Well, you want to know about my wife? Part of me still considers her my wife. She never remarried, so that might tell you something. Marriages wear out; they get old. We all get old. But they don't die. I left another woman for her. She didn't want me to but she couldn't stay away. That sounds egotistical, and I don't mean it to. But you talking to the other guy?"

"Actually, we already have. Dan's here in town now. You knew that, right?"

"I might have heard something. And presently I will try to forget it once again . . ."

Poor Corporal Maynard. Funny thing, he got killed in a silly accident. Some requisitions being craned off a transport dropped on him and crushed him, but the last memory of him was of the kid digging into Leo's armpit and bawling, soaking his undershirt. Had a screw loose, maybe was queer. Or the mother messed him up, smothering him. Unresolved conflicts. Shitty shame.

More and more, people misunderstood the word tragedy.

"Do you think you'll ever speak to Dan again?" said Andi, leaning forward, her notepad hanging out from the clutch of her pretty white hand, the wrist sweetly limp. She fretted, waiting.

"Not a chance. I don't have anything to say to the guy. What's the common ground?"

"*Well*—for one—*Marion* . . ."

(That sly smile of hers could turn on you, go from complicity to subtle condescension.)

"When she decided to leave," he said, "I made sure I was sitting out back by the pool."

The boy cocked his chin and blinked toward the back of the house, spotting the pool. Leo thought of Marion, ready to go, bags ready for the driver to take out, spotting him out there, too.

"I had a cup of coffee and the paper, the Sunday *Times*, to make my way through."

Andi felt sorry for him. She'd known men like this, starting with her father. Men without apparent feelings, but get them a little tippled and they might let loose. She'd watched her father fall apart during his toast at her sister Cara's wedding. You were supposed to congratulate males for expressing themselves, but the one she admired was Cara—for not expressing herself. Cara avoided making a hell of a scene. She could have accused him in front of everyone important to the family: "You abused me for years, and *that's* what you're blubbering about." But she hadn't. Cara and her nice, poor husband got married a month out of college and moved to Seattle. Their parents never heard from them; their mother pretended not to notice. Andi only blamed Cara for taking the money and letting them pay for the wedding—didn't that just feed into the cycle? You couldn't trust family. Had Marion hesitated at the front door? Had Leo not tried to stop her? She had left this man for a much younger, gay man, an intelligent fan who became her helpmeet and final nurse. The hangovers, the manuscripts (she didn't use a computer), her ultimate cancer.

"Did you think of her leaving as completely personal?"

"Did I think of it as what?"

"Sorry. That came out wrong."

"Yes, it surely must have."

They were at an impasse. He wasn't going to softball these kids. He'd rather be alone.

Carefully, Andi said, "When I read Marion, I think, what a strong, strong woman."

"Sure you do."

"And I think, here's somebody who knows what she's about, what she wants . . ."

"There's truth in that."

"But at the same time, would you say Marion was emotionally needy? But we all are."

"She was a human being, was she not?"

Josh fretted into his half-drunk drink. "That came out as maybe sexist, Piglet."

"Honey," said Andi, "Pooh Bear."

"But Piglet, you're just hooking into worn-out, male-centered stereotypes of women."

He was too pretty for her, too passive and fey. That was their problem.

No. Leo thought he could see it now. The pricey liberal arts college Josh attended on his rich folks' dime, the jargony mind-bending they were no doubt still putting kids through there.

Andi smushed her mouth around and moaned to Josh, "Remember what Lily said."

Leo said, "Ah!" The click felt good and festive. "What did Lily say?"

"Hmm, I'll just go ahead and tell you. Lily said she'd always considered Marion as being rather, quote, 'fractious.' 'Frangible.' She had all these funky, I thought, harsh, words about her."

He felt resentment and the contradictory impulse to protect Lily, all in a headachy tangle.

"Lily's my friend, but she's quite old, remember, and she's always held singular opinions about people, curious and eccentric ways of looking at the world. This is the same woman who wrote a children's novel that doesn't just kill Santa and the Easter bunny, but takes away a child's idea of heaven. The mom dies and Lily parachutes in with a dose of grim, stern reality. Now I'm as nonbelieving as anyone. But aren't some youthful illusions, y'know, fine for kids to hang on to? Shouldn't we just let them entertain certain ideas for the better duration of childhood? Jesus."

"I read that when I was a kid," Josh noted. "Really did a number on me. Well, actually, I wasn't such a kid anymore. I was, like, sixteen. But I remember being depressed for, like, ever."

"Sometimes we're a kid at heart for a while longer than others are," Leo said. "I applaud this in some people. The point is, Lily can be crisp and a touch self-righteous. Didn't ring true."

"Real buzz-killer," said Josh.

"Won the Caldecott and the Newbery, too," Leo added.

"I don't think Lily meant her words treacherously," said Andi. "She admired Marion."

"I sure as hell hope so," said Leo. "Marion admired her back."

Josh said, "Just to say, meeting Lily didn't depress me in the same way her book did."

Leo said, "Josh brings up a good point, about the author as distinct from her characters."

"Do you think I'd be disappointed if I met Marion and she were sitting here now?" Andi said, having thought of Marion for so long as almost a lover. "Lily said she was charismatic."

"Piglet, didn't Lily say Marion was shy?" said Josh, stoned already, was Leo's thought.

"We can't have both," Leo said, laughing. "You won't find a single page that came out of her real life. Tell your readers autobiography was one of the temptations I warned her against."

This was right about when—in the past—Leo would have reached for another cigarette.

And if they ever offer it to you, he also thought to tell them, don't take the chemo. No one should have to live through that. They didn't apparently smoke but perhaps he should warn them.

(His third or fourth, it would have been already, because time was so dull and heavy.)

Andi put down her hardly touched drink and panned the room saying, "I just love the idea of the two of you working together in this place. She wrote a lot of her fiction here, right?"

"In this room above us. You'd know what kind of mood she was in depending on whether you heard her typewriter going. You didn't even have to see her face to know. A lot of fast racket and it was thumbs-up. It was like miniature workmen up there with all the clacking and racket."

"Thrived on productivity," suggested Andi.

"But when it wasn't all systems go, then look out."

"Moody."

"Moody as hell," he said.

"What did you do when it was like that, when Marion wasn't so productive?"

"Got out of the way. I did a lot of getting out of the way, come to think of it. Somewhere down the line it occurred to me that some people are not outfitted for a lot of maintenance in the form of affection. They don't need it or want it—offer it at the wrong time, and they'll thank you to mind your own business." He coughed. "Puritanical desire to be punished for not working."

"And yet she was plagued with crippling anxiety every time she sat down to work."

Now he couldn't stop coughing. But when he stopped, he hesitated, looking at the girl.

"Did Lily tell you that?" he said, through strangled sounds.

"Yes, Lily—and Dan, too."

"The first because Marion confided and the second because they were shacked-up. I had better get my two cents in here. I don't know what he went through with Marion. I don't care."

"He"—Andi began—"*he* confided in me that a day didn't go by that he didn't feel guilty about the part he'd played in her leaving you. He still carries that. He said there were days when he felt like a eunuch, almost—no, exactly like a eunuch—before and after she got sick."

"The man said that?" said Leo, though it hurt his throat to say the damn "gay" word.

Josh said, "That must have been with me out of the room."

"Dan wasn't proud of it," Andi said. "I think he wanted to confide in just me about that."

Leo waited. It hurt to keep talking, but the ice numbed his throat some as he chewed.

"And do you suppose he was there for her all through the end? Do you have witnesses?"

He felt bad for saying that, but he was curious. Only the one answer would do for his ego.

She sighed. "Everyone says so. That's the story. That he barely left her side on the Cape."

Josh laid his head against the sofa back giggling, the edges of his white teeth flashing.

The Cape, how pretty. Scenic. Literary. Snug. Treacherous. He'd been there with her, too.

Andi nodded saying, "We'll be talking to some of the New York people real soon."

"What's New York like now? Is it as conventionally bourgeois as everybody says it is?"

He said this knowing he'd never been anything but bourgeois, in his way, and was fine with it.

"Oh, man," said Josh. "Parts of it, sure. Do you get back up there anymore, Leo?"

"Because we'd love to have you over sometime," added Andi. "We're out in Bushwick."

Leo said, "The next time I leave here, it won't be by car or plane."

"Harsh," said Josh, "but good one, anyway. Hilarious, actually."

And then he was tired. Outside, the afternoon was full-on. He kept the blinds lowered and pulled three-quarters shut and yet the sun hammered at the house. The interior glowed with just that bit seeping in. Reliable subtropical sunshine was the one thing that kept him from being too depressed or self-involved here. He often wondered what life, their lives, might have been like if they hadn't left New York. It was for *her*, he'd thought at the time. This would make her happy and she'd never leave him because of her "blue tendencies." Leo remembered how his hand had trembled as he signed the mortgage, which he had only paid off two years before her departure. Along the way, they'd had some luck—an inheritance, a few windfalls—so they'd thrown down chunks of cash to clobber away at the debt. Time had a way of passing. *Debt, you shall die, too!*

Over time Marion had become dimmer to him—a concept, a presence, Leo could less and less discern through the fog of these young strangers' grasping, even misplaced, pleasantries.

"I'm pooped," he said, "and I'm afraid I have to wrap this up. I don't sleep well at night. I start to fade about this time. *Summa summarum,* we were good for such a long time, but it was a surprise when she came home and told me. And then not much later she was sick. And you're not supposed to find out things like that third-hand, from a landscaper who heard it from a friend."

"You found out Marion had cancer from a gardener? Dude!"

"And in awfully broken English. I almost didn't believe him. Does that make me racist?"

"Wait," Josh said, "I'm still just trying to get used to the first thing you said."

Then again, in Key West you usually found things out through your gardener. Gardeners pollinated the ecosystem, exploiting its prosperity and disease, the little town of sublime ill ease.

How to get rid of these two? Andi and Josh didn't seem in a hurry to make a damn move.

"But hey, listen," he said, "you two. As long as she was happy, I was supremely content. When she got that way, and I could get that way, too, I told her, 'You do what you have to do.'"

"That is really touching," said Josh, but Leo seemed to leave him stricken. Leo's gift.

"I was nuts about her. When you're enough nuts about someone, you'll say anything."

He directed this at Josh, an admonishment. The light changed and Josh was a silhouette.

People thought Josh was dumb, a stoner, but no, Josh did know about loneliness.

When they left and started walking back to the hostel, he said, "I feel sorry for the guy."

"But something doesn't smell right," said Andi, off on another one of her scent-trails.

"Must be humiliating for him," said Josh. "This time of the day here, it's a little sinister."

"You know what I mean. What's the first thing everybody says about her, about Marion?"

"How much they loved her," he said, taking out a cigarette to cope with the pretty tedium of it all. They walked along, past all the color-fully painted wood and bursting-out-bright flowers. Andi reached for the American Spirit to get the first puff. "Whole deal's depressing," he added.

"But we have to go beyond and ask exactly why. If we got that New York State grant we could come back. There are still so many people to talk to, not just other writers."

"Like who, landscapers from El Salvador? Andi, Honey Bunch, what's left to cover?"

"Like the people running the nature conservancy where she volunteered, the bird refuge."

"You think the same people are still around running that stuff? Marion left a while ago."

"She did return. Everybody's so old, maybe they forgot some things they could say later."

"Uh-huh."

They were at the corner waiting to cross over to the gas station, then over to another one.

A middle-aged Latin on a bike festooned with holiday garland crossed with the traffic. He pulled a little trailer with a plastic crate that held a boom box issuing a hectic, high-volume salsa.

"Marion had to leave," he said. "She was too smart to stay in what's basically a suburb."

"I get why they came down. You can still see vestiges of what it had to be like then."

"But it changed and got too homogenized, I bet. That's how we should open, at least the Key West section. Don't you think? Pan down, like when we landed, what we first saw . . ."

The lights changed.

"Sure, Pooh Bear. I'd need to get more quotes on what the old version of here was like."

Andi had a fetish for face time. You could cover half this stuff through emails.

"But you know what I mean, write it as a sort of ghost story?" Josh said, feeling that was lame. He was no intellectual, he'd admit—if there were anyone he knew he could admit this to.

She made a tight frown and Josh thought he knew what she was

doing. The not having sex more than once or twice a month anymore—
that was his idea. Where had that come from?

"I mean, I know you don't want to hurry into anything," he said,
covertly panicking.

"I just want it to be the best book it can be."

And if he said, "Relax, it will be," he'd just get that back in his face:
"Relax—open a bag of weed maybe—get stoned, talk about it? No,
Joshua. That's your solution to things, not mine."

He loved weed! Weed was your buddy. You didn't have to do any
explaining to the bong.

"What sucks," Andi said at the next corner, "is I don't think I even
like Marion anymore."

Uh-oh.

"Why's that?"

"Joshua," she said, nodding along to each shaken-out syllable,
"marriage is a *covenant.*"

He agreed. He'd been holding back proposing. Marriage wasn't
supposed to work after five years or so of only living together, and
they'd nearly reached the six-year mark. Before that, he'd adored his
freedom, those seven or eight precious months of living with a bunch
of guys in Greenpoint. He'd tried to talk her out of quitting her M.A.
program and moving down. Then he'd had to apologize. "You don't
talk to me," she'd said, and he'd said, "Sorry, not wired like that."

The lights changed and Andi continued, "I think of that poor man,
literally ruined by her. Look at him, a husk of a human being—I'm
sure a mere shell and a shadow of his former self."

"He's an old man, Andi. He's had cancer. He probably drinks all
day. It was one p.m."

"Oh-ho," she said, "we excuse the intoxicated while the oppressed
suffer. Or did. Suffer."

Marion was in glory, as they said, her career soon to rise phoenix-
like after their book. A hit or two and he could believe this shit—it
was true, when you were lit. Just get high. The world is better then,
enlightened, fun. Loosen up, don't be mom and dad. Squirm with hot,
wet love.

"Seriously, baby. Just write what we saw. I remember the day you came to my dorm room from reading one of her books. You were so alive, on fire. You were this crazy burning bush."

"I was in trouble at the time. I needed guidance and I thought I'd found it in Marion."

"She's your personal record. You spent a year reading her stuff. You got that essay prize writing about her. She means more to you than most people do. We've got to follow through."

She didn't say anything. She was still tender, confused. She had gone around talking the line about art and art's power to transform and transmogrify and transcend mere us. She'd gotten drunk at parties in Brooklyn and said, "You don't understand, dude." Even girls she called dude. She'd jabbed the chests of older, better-established men and said, "No, what you're talking about is master narrative, dude. What I'm talking about's visceral, intellectually challenging, mad-hot visionary—*visionariness*. The bitch had a vision, but now everybody's ignoring Marion Jillsen."

Andi could make Marion sound almost like Madonna, but who cared about writers now? Leo was right, or somebody back there was. Maybe it was Josh himself. End of a fucking era. A new species was called for: this writing thing, even this pop star thing—dinosaur material, man.

She had not come from a reticent family, but Josh had. All he had was his short, humble poems to attend to. They were about nature and the lightly churning epiphanies of a life quietly felt, like a butterfly quickly perceived on the fleet, in the peripheral, before it was gone again. It was fucking gone, but Andi crazily persisted. His favorite Bible verse finished something like

faith, hope, and love, these three; but the greatest of these is love.

And that's what he wanted to give her, if he still could. She didn't care for his religious side, and she was right. Every rational facet of Josh's soul and his mind said so, but Josh loved his God.

He said, "Baby, when we get the hell out of here we can think more clearly about stuff."

She liked that. They passed a house where the front door was open and this guy paced the weathered porch. She could hardly see a second guy inside yelling out at him, "I know what you do, you think I don't know? You're going down to the beach every day looking for that pootie!"

She and Josh stopped on the next corner and flat-out laughed. They did have fun together. At the topless bar the other night, she'd tried to get up on stage. Busted hangover the next day.

The hostel was in a better neighborhood. They still weren't convinced that their itches in the middle of the night weren't caused by bed bugs, and the staff was one sourpuss after another.

They had paid full price, but the pale dreadlocked girl working the night shift had tried to sneak an unbathed European onto a cot in their room one evening while they were out at dinner.

"This way I won't charge you the same," the girl had said when they'd complained. Even with the overhead light on, Euro Boy had stayed sacked-out: "This way is better for everyone."

The windows were transom windows they had to get on a chair to crank open. They had him booted, making the girl wake him up and explain it to him in their mutual language. But the smell hovered near their faces in bed and there was no fan and the screens had holes in them, and they'd lain awake laughing, remembering their trip to Europe and the continent's irritable service.

A major surprise now to see Dreads again—as they'd started calling the girl—behind the front desk so early in the day. Josh did the honors of explaining the situation, their stored bags.

She wouldn't let him get behind the desk and go into the closet himself.

"Okay, take your shit," she said once she'd retrieved them. "I hope you enjoyed your all-important privacy. My friend was very tired. He traveled for two days, sleeping in airports. Two whole days! I hope you get rich so you never have to stay here again. I want to leave the

United States, where money is so prized—where the world's *resources* and *space*, they are so *prized*."

"Surprised?" said Josh.

Andi said, "Tell your friend thank you for leaving his scent behind, so we could savor it. Is that one of the amenities included here, free BO? All-night armpit and garlicky anal stink?"

Dreads stood behind the bunkering desk, smiling, not blinking, out the window. She said with rich, moist Carpathian consonants, "You know the number for a taxi to the airport, I trust?"

Leaving the office, they met her friend coming from the unisex washroom in a sarong.

"Have a nice trip," the now obviously clean traveler said, not uncheerfully—and glad to be completely through with airports for a spell, it was safe to say. "This is good-bye, correct?"

Feeling a bit foolish, Andi said, "That's right. Well, have a nice stay. Nice meeting you!"

A sarong, Josh thought. A really nice sarong.

The ride out to the airport was lovely, down the highway lined with quivering palms. The driver listened to something ethnic and draggy on the radio clamoring ebulliently. He reached to turn down the radio and said, "Hey, look at that front coming in, might be your lucky day! Might not have to leave after all. Yep, might just get to hang out another night on old Cayo Hueso!"

Up ahead, the front was clearly defined and dark, an anvil of purple-gray-black swirling at its outer edges with fog or whatever, a condensing or evaporating moisture, whichever stage was relevant. The top of the anvil head gathered and expanded outward, leering forth it seemed.

Andi dropped her jaw and was hushed for an instant, then said, "But we can't afford it."

Not another night with Dreads! She wanted to wake up and go to their own coffee shop.

"Anything bad like that coming from the mainland, they shut her down. Puddle jumpers."

But an hour and a half later, they were up in the air. The front had dissolved, going from a deep bruise to a bright platinum gray and veering right then moving out to sea before it could hit.

She had given him the window, and when he looked down saying bye-bye to the island of Key West, Josh believed that Andi felt his sadness, too—the one they shared whenever they left a place together, as they'd done many times from many places. A sort of going-away-from-but-not-moving-toward-anything-especially-important sadness.

little reef

Jo's looked small from the street, but go inside and you'd be amazed how spacious it was. Nets covered the walls, electric-bulbed paper lanterns were swagged along the ceiling, and behind the bar, tropical fish hung luridly in a tank the size of a picture window filled with eyeball-achingly bright saltwater.

Jeanette had come in by herself and sat at the booth near the front door. At nearly eighty, she was well preserved, with convincingly auburn hair still and a cream complexion and flaring green eyes, an "Irish" look. It was early, and she probably wouldn't need to vacate the booth for a smaller table before she and Wesley left for dinner at one of their chains. Jeanette had stopped watching the door by the time Buster mixed and delivered her margarita before she'd even had to order it. Not for hours would it swing into boogie at Jo's. Buster had the itchy, poached eyes of every chain-smoker Jeanette ever knew. He was friendly, a little *too*. He set her drink down and hovered, smiling. He wore a shiny teal and gold and black Jaguars jersey and denim short shorts, his legs dark and hairy. His face as well, though not the baby-smooth top of his fireplug head so pinkly flushed from high blood pressure going purple by his slightest exertion. He always asked after Wesley. Buster was eager, kind, chatty, and lonely. It was un-imaginable what communities like this did to men like Buster. Buster scratched his shoulder, then his right tit, blinking rapidly.

Jeanette ignored the simian bit of nervous grooming and dipped her forehead toward him and said, "Thank you, Buster," reaching in to dig around in her bag and soon finding her wallet.

"If you're staying a while," he ventured wryly, as always, "I could run you a tab."

A tab wasn't her style, as by now he should've deduced, and she said, "I don't think so."

She handed him a ten—she wasn't one of those demure biddies—and he took it instantly.

Closing his lips and drawing them forth, Buster said, "Wes coming in, Miz Blake?"

"He'll be along directly, I expect. At least I hope. How are things for you, Buster?"

"Had a nasty cold last week, but I'm on the mend now. Nice day out there, you'll note."

"Real pretty day," she said, nodding, waiting for him to skedaddle.

"Be right back with your change," he said, and his heart seemed to be bursting bright.

Jo's was a bar for women, but Buster ran the day shift. He opened at an unthinkable two in the afternoon. While in her thirties, Jeanette had left inland Jacksonville to be closer to her job and after retiring stayed out here. The beaches had a more bohemian feel, which did not disturb her enough to make a fuss over. In general people minded their own business, Buster and Alison being the only two exceptions. Alison, as usual, was at the bar and had been leaning over it with one of her cocktails, something concocted of juices and hard liquor, when Jeanette had first come in. Alison had also been in love with Wesley, who'd lived with Jeanette since he was a tot, since before that—since he was born and after Jeanette's only daughter, Lisa, had passed away. Alison had eventually gotten over her crush for Wesley, unlike Buster. She was young still, living with her father, and as far as Jeanette could tell she'd never worked a day in her life. She called her father the Bastard. You got used to stories like this. Jeanette reckoned by now she'd heard them all and most of them here at Jo's Little Reef. In her agnostic way, she prayed that her Wes would meet a nice boyfriend (not here, God almighty, no!) and thus have no further use for Jo's. At times she'd try to see what this man looked like in her imagination, playing her game of mental slot machine. He was a tad older than Wes, gainfully employed, something of a father figure, and very sensible with money—in short, a male role model. Shouldn't be any harder than hooking a bride, and yet meeting your grandson habitually in bars on Friday nights hardened you not just about gays. Her only husband, all that time ago—well, people were people. She liked the salt crystals around the cool sweaty rim of the curvaceous glass. The first few sips, like breaths drawn in the cool depths of a cavernous rainforest. She wanted to go to Brazil someday alone, ensconced in a tour group.

The electric-blue and uncannily gilt fish flicked bigly with their self-possessed dignity off to one side of the tank, hovering unblinking. Buster's hemorrhoids were killing him. He'd done a sugar reading just before and it topped off at 80, a triumph. Everything was medical. Get after the age of thirty in life and it was just numbers, stats you filed with medical authorities. He lived alone. Buster wanted a lover, but not as much as he needed tips. To live, he served.

He turned and wiped the counter, and Alison straightened up from her slump. *His* slump.

Alison was becoming Alex and so now Alex said, "Shit, I forgot to bring my STP."

Stand To Pee: a plastic funnel and little hose gadget Buster hoped he'd soon not have to hear about again. He hummed, saying, "I'll watch your drink. You want to run home and get it?"

He'd been sipping beer and went to the register to make Mrs. Blake's change, thinking of Wes. Have Wesley Blake and he'd be calm like sipping watery Jack, intoxicated. But he'd never have Wesley, not with Mrs. Blake as gatekeeper. Life got you in its tickling reaches and laughed.

Alison/Alex slumped again and Buster felt a certain love for her, wild beaten-down thing.

"No," Alison/Alex said, touch of the drama queen, "I'm fine," tittering to herself. "Fine."

Kid was a quiz, messed up some at home then shoved out the door to hang out in bars.

Buster came around with three and a half dollars' change, thinking, nice lady, you do not know. How I'm on the edge, how we're all on the edge, and I need affection as much as you do.

Tall, fine, bony, lanky Wesley, his Wes. Unable to admit his own tenderness, sweet boy.

"Oh!" said Jeanette, as though surprised by her due, and suddenly bright. "Keep two."

She taught him to be generous, is where the Blake generosity came from, he thought.

Jeanette *wanted* to be generous. She had money, the only thing she didn't have was time.

Buster said, "Well, you know where to find me," and returned to his spot behind the bar.

"I'll give a holler, Buster."

Jeanette wasn't always sure why she came into Jo's, except that Wesley liked it so much. She was uncomfortable at times with how inexplicably she allured some of the women, even the much younger ones. A long time ago, when she'd dare to go into one, at any other bar men often hit on her—given to blind-drunk states or hoping to have her soothe their battered egos. Flirting and fishing for compliments. "You're a good-looking fellow," they wanted her to tell them, "and believe me, mister, if only I were just a few years younger . . ." But she'd never been that young.

The beaches were all-or-nothing, a free-for-all, pick-your-rock-music way of putting it.

The "mores" at the beaches could be funkier with so many aging ex-hippies; you took the good with the bad. She knew what pot smelled like. Jeanette would leave the house, if walking, and pass rows of carports. Under the concrete roofs of the big open airy carports, bearded, long-haired grays listened to loud music hunched over the open engines of their vintage automobiles, tinkering and wailing along. In the air, wafting along to the rock, was the smell of burning sage, she'd thought, and it had taken Wesley at nine to explain to her what this really was: "A *sausage* smell, Nanna?" he'd said. "No, Nanna. That's grass, ganja, Mary Jane!" Jeanette walked to the beach to stroll on a windy afternoon. Now always on Fridays she walked to Jo's to meet Wesley.

She just wanted to have a margarita in peace, or two margaritas. Sometimes she had two.

Here came Alison, Tugboat Annie. Only Jeanette, Buster, and Alison were around yet.

"Can I just come over, say hey?" Alison said, puffing her lips but not lowering her head, a movie-screen timidity that still must "play." She had lovely eyes, needed to learn about manners. Jeanette loathed poor manners. The violation of others' personal space was—but Alison dropped her voice to a deep mauve and whimpered, keeping her distance, saying, "Ma'am, it's just hey!"

"Why, of course," said Jeanette. "How are things treating you, Alison?"

She made no indication for the child to sit. She valued peace, and even dreamed about a little of it on her own somewhere sometime. But she couldn't be anything but instantly friendly, being a silly Southerner. The manners to her were a language, not rule of law. A minute passed.

"Oh, Miz Blake."

"Alison?" said Jeanette, and nodded—her mistake. Manners, perfunctory and invasive.

The girl, what Jeanette supposed they still called a baby butch, made a baby-talk goo-goo sound and dropped her bulk onto the padded bench opposite Jeanette with impressive impact.

"Shit, I have to go into the Center and inject myself the first time. I'm scared, ma'am."

She presented Jeanette with another fat, exaggerated pout. Even as the smallest little boy, Wesley had never acted the brat like this. He was an even-tempered, sweet-natured little soldier, acting unaware of the tragedy that had happened to him. Jeanette would come home from work, excuse the sitter with a small tip, and get down on the floor next to him and his Legos or Tinkertoys. Pretty soon she would be thinking about dinner and announce the menu. "Oh, delicious!" he said, his head inclined to the floor and caught in a cloud of building plans. It seemed apparent to Jeanette that in her childhood Alison had not often been called upon to use her imagination for much except perhaps how she was going to feed herself. (Jeanette imagined a jar of peanut butter almost empty, the two heels of the stale loaf of sliced white sandwich bread pressed together like praying hands.) Alison was not just languid, self-pitying, she was lifeless—and too pale usually.

Now Jeanette said, singing the irritation from her voice, "Out with it, what in the world?"

Alison kept with the pout, nearly intolerable. Nothing would straighten *her* out. It wasn't going well between them; it never would. Jeanette should stop frequenting Jo's Little Reef—and she'd tell Wesley they needed to develop new habits, new traditions. They were each older now.

"Alison, it can't be as bad as that," Jeanette said confidently. "Have you been diabetic a long time? I mean, is it the juvenile kind, or the adult type 2 that you develop later on in life?"

Alison looked at her incredulously. She was a girl, a young woman, who if she'd just lost a little weight and let her hair grow would be almost lovely or lovely enough. Alison had pierced her nose and lips and whatever other parts of her body. She had a range of tattoos, mostly on her chubby arms, what the girl called sleeves. Jeanette imagined that she was putting herself through a series of African tribal scarification ceremonies. Alison's girlfriends, her lovers, never worked out. The most dramatic failure—briefly but widely broadcast scuttlebutt—was the time when an older lady in black leather named Rita rode into town from way up north on a slung-back Harley sweeping Alison off her feet and onto the back of her bike for an intense, theatrical few weeks of bar storming, suspenseful knife-wielding jealousy fits, and at least one police arrest during happy hour, which Jeanette and Wesley had witnessed. Rita had never lived at a fixed address, although she'd worn clipped to her belt a ring loaded with shiny keys, and according to gossip had pushed on in the middle of the night suddenly, aiming her obsidian hog down at some place on the Gulf Coast. It was all too sordid to inquire about, yet Alison had come begging Jeanette for sympathy. Alison had *hung the moon for Rita*. Rita had told her this repeatedly. Plus it had been Alison's sincere understanding that the two of them would ride off together to Pensacola and open a B&B on Santa Rosa Island or along the East Bay. With what money, Jeanette had no idea. Pensionless dreams. They got you into trouble. It only meant other people would have to clean up after you.

"Honey, first and foremost," Jeanette had told her that time, "just take care of yourself."

She'd said some variation of this every time she'd seen Alison for the next several weeks. Jeanette had been very lucky with Wesley. But at a certain age—if you weren't careful—the stuffing went out of you. If Wes himself didn't find more direction, he'd end up alone, lost, lost.

"You're young, so let's just see how strong you can be. It's a test, and we'll see how well you pass it—I bet with flying colors," she'd said, secretly without much confidence in Alison.

Jeanette had almost opened up to Alison about her husband, whom she remembered quite vividly, and who'd left Jeanette and baby Lisa early on. Marrying him, she'd known it was only for his name. No child of hers would be a bastard—at the time it was still quite the stigmatizing, cruel fate for any kid around here—and she'd always seen through Edwin. Edwin was handsome, but she had never quite believed his routine, his false Dale Carnegie act. He'd go three days and no drink, then come spectacularly crashing down off the wagon. He could not hold onto a job. It wasn't the right environment for raising a child, and even then Jeanette had known that if she had to, she could go it alone. And one night as she sat up worrying, while little Lisa slept in oblivion, the decision ended up making itself. Edwin had called from his office at Prudential to say he was taking clients out to the Post and King Lounge and promised to drink ginger ale. It was the last time she'd ever hear from him. No one taking her calls at Prudential had caught sight of him in weeks. In fact, he'd been let go or walked out a while back—it was unclear which, and no one was saying, especially not his boss, who'd calmly registered his categorical wishes to her that all should work out well. He'd inquired about the baby, then said he had to take a call. Jeanette had needed someone to talk to, she'd realized only much later. Women back then had had no reliable confidantes. All the women she knew even vaguely were churchgoers. They'd sooner sell you a Brooklyn Bridge in Jerusalem than try easing your mind, assign you the blame as the nice lady.

Now to Alison she said, "I had a boss at the law firm where I worked before I retired, one of the attorneys, and he was diabetic and had to inject himself twice a day. But I'd thought folks with it now didn't have to use needles anymore. I mean, isn't there an oral medication you could take, or stick yourself with one of those new pen doohickeys? I'd heard there was, anyway."

Jeanette had always taken care of herself more or less. She felt less sure of what she was attempting to say, and the way Alison was looking at her suggested Jeanette was mistaken.

"No, ma'am," Alison said, her eyes big and pathetic. She sighed, looking away, and said earnestly, patiently, and rather condescendingly, "Ma'am, it's *hormones* for my *reassignment.*"

She said this and her interlocutor felt shaken, but it was a slow epiphany as to why. She laughed at herself, or would later. Jeanette Deirdre Blake, you are truly behind the times, lady!

Jeanette was still caught up in the pleasantly advancing spring afternoon. Earlier she had walked on the beach south of the Holiday Inn. And now the sun that the front door of Jo's Little Reef—a glass door—emitted was a poignant, nostalgic hammered gold, going into a bloodied bronze any minute. She wanted to feel good about her life, about this day. She'd lived it through and it wasn't bad. She had enough money between her pension from the law firm and her Social Security to see her through and exit gracefully and leave some to Wesley. She felt slapped by her own insensitivity and ignorance. Had Wesley said something to her about this sex change? They didn't say sex change anymore—it implied all the wrong things. *Gender reassignment* it went.

"Oh," said Jeanette, "how foolish of me," and she touched Alison's chubby clammy hand.

Now she decided she might, a slight fascination sparked in her, come to like her. Him.

"It's really hard," Alison said and she watched Jeanette. "I have to go out for a cigarette."

"Go and do that," said Jeanette, without adding what they'd discuss later. *Sex.* Having it and being one, possessing gender and using that to mate—the world's horny hubris . . .

Alison got up. Jeanette wondered about all the chemicals, the hormones and nicotine and alcohol, swimming through Alison's system, all of this constantly introduced foreign matter. She might survive it, but she might not. Jeanette remembered worrying that a Tylenol she'd taken for a sore ankle after a day's running about the firm when she still worked would mix unpropitiously with a glass of wine, which she felt guilty enough about—*drinking*, in front of an impressionable boy with some drinking issues already in his family history. She wanted a glass to help her wash down their Salisbury steak TV dinner, which she hated to serve a growing boy, all that salt, those chemicals they added. Wesley got a glass of milk to allay her fears. What a hysteric she still was in those days, completely unable yet to quit foolishly focusing on the feckless, gone-gone Edwin.

The sun went down over and beyond the Intracoastal, and it made Alison's shadow faint, watery. Then Alison moved to the side of the door with her cigarette and the sun hit Jeanette's face full-on and she winced. Wesley had his last day of driver's safety. The accident was not his fault, except on paper, a light bumper-bash he'd caused from behind, but still he had to complete this duty, and it never hurt to learn something new. Jeanette herself had never been involved in a fender bender that was legally her fault. She still drove her Ciera when she had to run to the post office or bank or the CVS. That was about it. She didn't want to push it—her reflexes no longer what they were. She nearly tasted that baby stack at St. Louis Grill. Wesley behind the wheel of his Toyota, his pride and toy. She worried about his consumerism, his yen for pricey goods when he should be concentrating on his MBA, maybe increase his course load and get done faster. She wanted to see him in something better than managing the breakfast shift at Wagon Wheel. Truck drivers and Yankee tourists zooming through and stopping for pancakes and sausage on their way south, to points down along the coast or to Sea World and Disney World. As a pubescent Wesley was obsessed by all things Disney and said he planned to be what he'd explained to Jeanette was called an Imagineer by the Walt Disney Company. He checked out books from the library. With his allowance, when they went to Disney, he bought souvenir editions with mind-opening photos of the planning and building of the theme park. "An Imagineer," he explained to Jeanette, "is the man who dreams up, he *imagines*, a ride. He draws it out and he makes up the story, and it's the best, most wonderful job." Wesley was captivated by what were called the audio-animatronics, the robots like Abraham Lincoln in the Hall of Presidents or a ghoul in the Haunted Mansion, the only trouble being that Wesley was bad in math. She'd tried to get him to take his algebra a great deal more seriously, but Wesley's head was full of dreams—he wasn't practical. His impractical nature, too, may have been her fault. That sort of thing wasn't genetic, was it? It was built into a way of upbringing, and she could never have given him enough attention. Curiously, she'd never blamed his sexuality— what was the right, usable word, *identity*?—on herself. They were finding out all sorts of wonderful scientific things now, which she wouldn't live to see being proved over and over again in the faces of the redneck local right-wingers who were so self-satisfied and sure of themselves. Jeanette remembered thinking how people in that last church she'd ever attended in downtown Jacksonville, First Baptist, had looked at her with pity and a false-approval smirk—it was so obvious what they were truly thinking—heading up the aisle, holding little Lisa's hand. She remembered the last time. She pushed right past the pastor in the after-service receiving line and Lisa said, "Mom, aren't you supposed to shake his hand?" Sure, dear, if you're a big sucker.

Outside, two voices semaphored back and forth, light into sound. Jeanette was tipsy.

A second silhouette, flaming at the edges with orange sunset, slid across the glass pausing in the dully gleaming aluminum frame. The cowbell trip-wired above the frame gonged, then the shadow spread dissipating through the interior as the man causing it entered and became the kind of hefty local-yokel species of dude you saw a lot of, many of whom ran things. He slid into the place opposite hers, and numbed by the tequila and triple sec, she heard her name calmly said.

"Jeanette?"

He removed his mirrored shades and exhaled garlic, scooting and settling himself daintily into Alison's abandoned place and causing the vinyl-encased foam to emit a high, thin fart sound.

Needing time to collect herself, before she gave herself away, she smiled lightly, quickly.

"Hidey, Jeanette," said Sam Garth, as though he thought she hadn't yet noticed him.

Tartly, Jeanette squirmed slightly and said, touching herself lightly, "Well hi, I reckon."

This was too much. Put it on TV and—no, not if you'd seen TV lately, "reality shows."

She wouldn't look at him except in snatches. He'd left so long ago. She'd barely caught sight of his face back then before he'd become a blur in her and Lisa's life. Wesley had not even been born, it was that urgent, though in memory the exchange had seemed so slow, such a blur.

"Had no idea you'd stick to the same neighborhood," said Sam. He looked good, his hair the same coal dark. His beard was kept trimmed, though the hair was buzzed too close—making the lantern jaw and flaring dark eyebrows too familiar. It was no wonder she knew him right off. He had the same careful way of adding phrases, suspenseful phrases building one upon the other, and Sam said, as she noticed a few stubbly strands of silver catching the light, "I missed y'all."

"Really. Missed us."

Her blouse had shoulder pads and she huffed one up. She remembered sending a letter to Wilmington, his last known address, to tell him about Lisa. She'd stewed so long before writing that. He hadn't replied. She had Wesley, already enjoying his tricycle and full of life— and there was no time to look back. The past was too preoccupying: go into the now, think about what was coming up. The future could be more interesting, anyway, than yesterday. She'd thought of Sam as a disappointment from the moment he'd come home with Lisa. It wasn't that he was a loser; it was too early then to tell. Smart, nice-looking, yet the environment didn't offer much for anyone not raised on golf. All any Garth boy had was killing looks, perpetual dark hair, silver-ice eyes.

"Just gonna sit there ignoring me," he said, chuckling. How she'd loathed that chuckle.

"I can be civil," Jeanette said and panned her gaze closer toward him, unblinking still.

"Look always scared the bejesus out of me."

"What look? Either you do or you don't want me looking at you. Which is it, Samuel?"

"You remember my friend Royce?" he said. "That was so good with plants and things?"

"Who opened the Cedar Branch Gardening Center off of Butler? Used to see him lots."

"Yes, ma'am," he said. "When I left, Butler was just a strip to near nowhere." He wrinkled his brow and it was spooky. Wesley had taken his name, of course. One day, was Wesley going to have this same tired, post-handsome look that was just seductive enough? "Well, so," he said, snickering wetly, "back then I didn't know what that green thumb indicated. Now I don't care."

Jeanette slid her drink aside. Wanting another taste, now she wouldn't touch it again.

"So y'all've stayed in touch. The two of you, you and Royce. Interesting, I'd say."

"That's right," he said, but didn't bow his head in shame. Even more interesting. She'd always liked bold-faced honesty, an antidote to mealy-mouthed Southern demurral. But *this*.

He did something odd. With his balled fist he thumped around the left side of his chest. Heart pain, palpating around for echoes of a twinge? A rattle to knock back in place? Disease?

She said, "Mr. Garth, are you all right?" and his yellow-white smile flashed and he quit.

"To answer the other, I'd get in touch with Royce coming through from time to time. You know how we used to run around. It was the three of us, Lisa and me and him, the Fletcher Trio, *ha*—and it riled me having to let go. I did start driving trucks, and I liked Wilmington and had a girlfriend, but she wanted me to marry her. Naturally, no way—but why blame her for asking?"

Impatient with his meandering, wanting to tell him they were almost done, she pursed her lips and said, "I'm sorry about your father, I'm sorry about your brother. But Sam, come on get a grip. This is pretty late in the game now. Want to see your kin, fine, but you and I aren't blood."

Buster had taken his time coming over, sensing the awkwardness and sensitivity between them. He approached with his jaw wryly set and said to Sam, "Howdy, anything I can get you?"

Nor did the denim hot pants seem to unsettle Sam, who nodded saying, "I'd like a Coke, if you wouldn't mind." Jeanette enjoyed watching him "not" be disgusted. "Easy on the ice?"

"Maybe charge that to me, Buster," Jeanette said.

"A tab lady," said Sam. "I like it but *good night*, I can manage to pay for my own Coke."

"Suit yourself."

All that time ago she'd decided the legal drinking age should be set at thirty. Wesley had escaped the evils overall, she thought, but what if you had just this one law in place? What was left of their conversation consisted of his AA story. Of course, AA. What else? All these good old boys went into AA, had they any sense at all. And she was glad for him. If only he'd had the sense to do it thirty-some-odd years ago, they wouldn't be here now. She wouldn't be here now.

They'd given Wes a breathalyzer and it was negative, Wes had said. Had said.

He needed a lot of love and he was crazy with this need for it. He was crazy about sex. He was nearly six feet tall, like his daddy it was said, although he'd never met the man. His height made an impression with males and females alike. He was worried about his baldness. He wasn't bald yet but his temples were receding. There wasn't a lot of time. He was in a hurry just now, trying to get to Anastasia Island. Royce had a forty-five-minute window. Oh, what was the point!

There was a girl in his statistics he'd liked, Shauna, so funny. She undercut what went on in class, texting him from two feet away. If he were straight, and though she'd had a big butt and wasn't conventionally pretty, Wesley would go for her. One day he'd gone into class but Shauna wasn't there. That following Monday not there either, then not the Wednesday after. He went to see the lecturer, hot Blaylock getting on in years. Wes had kind of a thing for Blaylock, who was paunchy from disappointment but had this alive face. Later Wes felt crappy about thinking about Blaylock sexually, in light of what he'd learned. Life was designed to make you feel guilty. The subject, too: he couldn't concentrate on business, on figures, numbers. Wes was a people guy. It made him feel alive out on the floor of the Wagon Wheel, scooting in to help his girls pick up the dirty dishes, nod hi to the folks, make a few one-liners, and wink at the wives. Folks took you as you took them. They were nice when you gave them a chance. They saw the swish in your step, they drew their lips forth in a cheesy Hollywood gesture, but that didn't mean much. Everybody wanted regard. They liked manners; they played along. Love was like that. Love wasn't perfect but it was patient, it was kind. And there was wisdom in the trying to be gentle. So many people and so little time to make an impression. And he liked the Wagon Wheel model, down-home. It was not a bad organization. It was owned by serious Christians in Nashville. Officially gay was not good with that bunch. But here they came, almost every day, he picked up on them. Turning in an application, wanting an interview. Oh, the world could change slowly, one face at a time!

Blaylock's office was just a slot in the department suite, with a door he would never shut.

Wesley smelled the oil off Blaylock's scalp—the essence of failure, disappointment. The cigarettes, maybe a little alcohol from the night before. Living on plastic-bottled Diet Pepsi.

Blaylock said that unfortunately Shauna had pancreatic cancer. She had a golf ball–sized pancreas, or actually a tumor in her pancreas the size of a golf ball, and she wouldn't live more than a year. She was sending her homework in by email attachment. Wesley was twenty-seven and felt eighteen. He wanted to drive into the night, farther south, keep going, maybe die in the knowledge that everyone would do the same. He'd never gone to church, ever.

What was your fucking pancreas, like your gallbladder or appendix, some hidden squirm?

He'd wanted to send her a card but didn't have her address and wouldn't ask Blaylock for it. He wanted the man with a burning like a tumor and was ashamed because he was already in it with another man already, and that wouldn't have been professional—and Shauna had since *died*.

He'd had a couple of manhattans at the Atlantic Beach Olive Garden. He needed an hour for a quick thing in the Crescent Beach house that Royce rented out but was empty now. He was woozy, though he could train his head to nod up and then it was fine, nodding, blinking brightly.

He entered St. Johns County and it was fine. Civilization was thinning out. On the right, the low bush of the natural preserve, on the left along the beach the developments of the rich, the whims and egos of people with money building up their gnarly jungles of local flora. He was so hungry, but never ate, wanting to be boy-beautiful for Royce. Everybody knew about Royce and his wife hating each other, and some knew about Royce and Wesley, none important. But forget it, Royce was leaving Candy like it was going to rain frogs, but Wesley needed to believe in shit. To believe, that was his religion from Walt Disney's example. You had to will dreams into being.

At Wagon Wheel, where he felt slender, their hugest customers commented that obviously he hadn't partaken of the restaurant's filling outlays, its starches and saturated fats. He wanted to deserve Royce, great complex Royce who tanked him up on happiness when they were apart and that was often. Royce texted horny shit constantly, fuck-ape Royce grooving, baby-Royce ape.

Up ahead there was a knot of traffic—along here where there was never a problem at all. He wanted to feel Royce big over his back. Royce was big but not quite fat. He ate and said he was fat and ate more. Big you became in the rush of success. And Wesley's job was prettiness.

Then the Candy drive. Royce kept threatening to pave it but Wesley said it was romantic, like they were going to move in there together. It was Royce's perfect place and he wouldn't let too much grow up around the cement-block, flat-roofed, and admittedly quite modest home since the first tropical storm would come in and bash everything through and insurance was high. Tree trunks were missiles. Royce said at these rents people expected asphalt, so they could keep their undercarriages clean and salt-free. It was easier to power-wash under there atop a hard surface.

The light was on and there'd be Maker's Mark, Gilbey's, Absolut, and Wesley's favorite, Skyy. Recently Wesley had tasted Boodles at one of Royce's clients' Ponte Vedra house and said it was the work of the devil, it was so clean. It was like floating in a boreal forest (Royce had told him a lot about trees and their native zones, what he read a lot about)—and breathing in deep and getting some of the little pink and purple flowers growing on the mossy green forest floor in your nostrils, which made up half your sense of taste. Royce was sensual and troubled. That Boodles.

"Another taste, one more taste of that and you'd have to drown me in a tub of that mess."

"Gladly," Royce then said, his blond-dyed hair glinting, "all that and more, Poodly-Boo."

When he talked, Royce was no Robert Frost. He wasn't a great lyricist like Sting even.

Royce was waiting for him in the front room. He was wearing his reading glasses with a glass of bourbon on ice resting upon the wood crate end table beside the fat padded chair with just the freestanding brass lamp turned on beside him facing, without looking up at, the drama of the Atlantic through the line of big picture windows as he turned the pages of his *USA Today*.

They made love freely. Wesley liked having his kitty punched, what Royce called it.

"My little heaven," Royce said raspingly, poignantly, sweetly, filling his condom. In the middle of the sex he'd say, "You like that? Way up inside your whore pussy? You like it, slut?"

Wesley desired it bareback but Royce was protecting himself and said that he and Candy might have one more baby, another not-good sign. Only now would Royce look him in the eye mid-fuck, having worked up to it. "Tight hot little pussy," Royce said, "I'm plowing that skank."

Wesley had always liked and even desired Royce's filth. At Fletcher High School, where Wesley went a generation later, Royce had conquered cheerleaders, nerd chicks, big-titted babes desired by all kids, and the experience fifteen or so years later left Royce shrugging dry-mouthed or so he said. The mysteries folded into this guy. His favorite place was Australia, where Royce had his first boy. If he could be completely honest, he'd marry a tree then become one somehow. Royce was an alcoholic. Wesley looked down that tunnel trying to spot himself but just couldn't see himself. You pitied men with addictions, and what housewife didn't need a drink?

People desired a crazy, remote faith. Sunday morning TV. Housewives, all Christian.

When they were done Royce said, "We have to go now, baby. No whiny tears now . . ."

Before, Wesley had liked Royce's forthright honesty. A word like "forthright" was good.

Don't look at me like that lingeringly unless you're ready to do something about it, dig?

The sadness of going back. The ride so beautiful in the near dark, with the moon-clouds shining but the land below black, the trees and structures on the ground dark. The emptiness. He wanted to ride away, just once, on the passenger side with Royce—lover and giver, quiet couple.

The clotted traffic right when you got to the disgorgement of J. Turner Butler Boulevard, all the cherry slashes of brake lights ahead and the flashing gauzes of oncoming headlights.

And you know what else? The dream between the living we were all doing and the dying everyone eventually would do. It was constant. It hid itself, making itself known in drowses.

The verge was Candy and he pulled over where some low, salt-blasted oaks could conceal him in the Toyota, unless Royce turned his head and looked around as he passed. In the tortured cave of branches twisted like witch's hair away from the ocean, he could just see the strip of road behind him out his side-view mirror. Royce's Lexus had Xenons, bluish headlamps. Headlights, in the parlance of auto brochures, were called headlamps. Wes's Toyota still smelled new inside.

In his side-view Wesley saw a regular pale-yellow pair of head-lights drawing forth at the speed limit. He panned right a little and looked ahead. A truck was headed his way faster. The two opposing vehicles would pass each other right about where Wesley was parked. Then an SUV speeding up and gaining the oncoming lane tried passing the truck, which was wrong, overtaking it too late.

He bolted in the seat of the Toyota Royce had helped him buy checking the side-view, but it was late, a bit offbeat. Light all in his face. Light everywhere then darkness. Claustrophobia, car folding neatly around him and crumpling in, no crushing sensation yet, neck and back pain slow to bloom.

The Imagineer had tried talking her into a cell phone—but she was always at home and her only contacts were Wes and Sadie. Sadie was ninety and had been married to one of the partners, one of Jeanette's bosses—Tom, the one she'd liked *too* much—who had died listening to a speech on investments at the Sea Turtle Inn. Sadie lived in a condo in Neptune Beach and was going gaga already probably. Jeanette hadn't heard from her in a while. And after Sadie there would just be Wes. Jeanette had gotten comfortable, relatively, being by herself a while ago. Wes had to work and get his life together, which he just might. Anyway, Jeanette was old now. She'd die soon.

She had been born in Green Cove Springs. Her father had been a bank clerk up until the Crash, when he'd gotten work feeding logs into a pulper at a paper mill—dying young of a heart attack. She didn't remember one iota of this man's personality or aura. Actually, Jeanette didn't believe in auras. She knew customers at Jo's Reef often believed in such. She had lived through the Pork Chop Gang period in Florida. People believed in anything, "No Taxes!" They believed in stuff no rational being could believe in, nonsense. Florida was a nutty business.

She believed it would be better hanging out with the Jews in South Florida than these rope-swinger nut-jobs.

Her mother had then moved them up to Jacksonville to live with her relatives, working as a secretary in the insurance industry: a widowed mother, living with her sister and sister's family. These should not have been important things, but Jeanette had been aware that she was looked at in church pityingly as a little girl. Not much later, Jeanette had been "taken up." All a blur, truly.

After she was grown she would never know her cousins because, as she'd realized slowly, they hadn't *wanted* to know her. All Jeanette had done was be a victim and no one liked or could account for victims. She'd been told only later about her mother's alcoholism: a disease that had isolated her mother and that had been presented to Jeanette—when she was told she was ready to hear—as something practical, medical, and scientific. They at least had been good enough not to mention sin or Satan or any of that. The father of the First Methodist family who'd taken her up, as Jeanette was turning five, after all was a doctor. He'd explained everything to her in his office when Jeanette reached her majority, as a cautionary tale before she went out on her own never to come back to them. And the world did work best that way, when it managed to work, because of reason and compassion. Faith was one thing, what you whimpered over in the middle of a really dark, terrible night, while the daytime mechanics of the human animal, subject to the decisions it had to make, the hundreds of choices it grappled with and fluttered its fingertips graspingly at in order to bring to fruition some semblance of dignity and independence—the unflinching mode of survival it had to assume merely to eat and move on, in order to wake the next day and start all of itself over—well, real life didn't have anything to do with ideas. She hated to sound un-idealistic or idealistic in an unorthodox way. She'd found it hard to believe in anything intangible but then who was the one who walked always beside you? At noon with no shadow at absolute meridian, which one was there to prick your conscience, the Lord or the Devil? Jeanette's mother had been a believer. Striding beside you all through the day—this rasping-voice thing, whispering yes, no.

She'd known she was the only person to keep stride with little Wesley, aim him straight.

She'd wondered about this walking home from Jo's later after the blood-boiling encounter with Sam Garth. Jeanette had never left the Little Reef without Wesley and it worried her. Sam had tried to hug her. Tried. She'd shrugged a shoulder pad and said, "Give Wes a call then. I'm sure he'll be interested to hear from his father. You look good, Sam Garth. Good night, now."

It wasn't like Wesley, at all, not to call or show up. There was this gnawing in her, maybe it was some disease. More and more she thought about disease. It naturally happened to folks as they got older. Her waking each morning after a spotty night's sleep could be timed to a sense of doom that would progress toward morning. But after she got up it would abate. She had heard that depression lifted like a cloud as the day ripened into fullness and suggested evening as a nice alternative to death, just. Her phone didn't ring. She waited drinking chamomile tea and still the thing didn't ring. And then at midnight it rang. It stopped. A moment later it was ringing again.

Of course she did not believe in visions, but later she would say that for an instant before picking up the receiver she'd thought she was having one. At least when it began to ring she had imagined the worst, then chased it from her thoughts when she finally picked it up, and it turned out to be the worst possible thing she could imagine. *Oh Miz Blake, Miz Blake, I'm just so sorry.*

pascagoula

There the mood was coy and fey, and the crowd followed the mood like the sun as it yearned toward the horizon outside the door. Now the bar was in a particularly tender phase. It was near the end of summer when expectations had either been dashed or were suddenly waning.

A boy entered and became the fulcrum of frustrations. He was sturdy with a long torso: a nice back to serve as support, strong shoulders. The guys paid attention, trying to figure out how to get an *in*. An *in* was a smile back: a joke was hollered from across the way, but unfortunately deflected. This was a hard boy. He was a hot one, but at some point they just gave up. Because some things just weren't worth it. You had to get your drunk on. You had to retain your dignity. Then in came the drag queens, precious species. They livened things up a bit. They said, "How are you, girl? Honey, big sturdy man, could you spot me a *drank*?" These were hard days.

The nights bled dark, they were vampires of a swollen, precious reality. The nights told on us all. They began with sundown, syrupy honey-like sundown when all things were possible. It was an illusion, and illusion was what made things possible. Just wish and it might be so, but the boy's presence was a reminder, not all things might be so. I was thinking about my mother. Let me start again. My mother would cry. She'd had a good start, Miss Kumquat of 1973. Her future husband mowed my grandfather's lawn, a not-quite-emerald expanse. My grandfather was incredibly rich but the house was of no such indication. Apparently he would say that, not being a Puritan but an Anglican, he wasn't bound up in appearances. That old manse was something of a dump by the time I ever laid eyes on it, but I occasionally long for it now that it's lost. I dream of hanging out in its abandoned, crumbling, drop-clothed rooms reading William Faulkner. This is an old, tired, typical, Southern gay story. My father was poor. His only distinction in life was being voted as having the best facial hair in junior high. He'd started at Auburn but dropped out of the aviation engineering program, and owned a plane for a while until we'd had to sell it. My father was vaguer to me than my mother—it was all the perfume tonight reminding me of her.

When I was six my mother calmly put me to bed—just as outside a party was igniting in our yard, a yard in West Tennessee outside of Memphis—and said, "If I'm not here tomorrow, if I can't report to you in the morning because I'm gone, what of it? Would it wreck your world?"

I was naturally nervous and I remember looking at her expectantly, trying not to cry. At some point she'd made things like crying and expressing myself incrementally too competitive.

"If I'm gone and lit out for other parts," she clarified, "would you think it bad of me?"

"I'm a child."

"Exactly," she said confidently, then her thoughts dragged her gaze away from me.

And she was there the next morning, boiling my oatmeal and stirring my chocolate milk.

In the bar, the show was about to start. Several of the drag queens hung back flirting and waiting for gentlemen to buy them drinks. They went for straight vodka, nothing flamboyant.

"Okay bitches," said the hostess, picking her way about the narrow stage holding the mic as though her nails were drying. "Shut up, bitches, shut on up! Respect, respect—as this is some damn-sure top-drawer serious entertainment about to roll before your baby blues. Yes yours, and yours too! So now that you know what kind of mood I'm in, how are the rest of y'all tonight?"

103

I'd drifted into the lounge to watch and the incredible boy took the place next to me. He introduced himself as Trevor. This was an old neighborhood in downtown Memphis. Up to then I'd never gotten out. I wasn't so much bored as fascinated by watching Trevor watch Suzee.

He reminded me of my cousin Darby from my family's more redneck, Tuscaloosa wing.

"There's a raffle, you know about the Sunday raffle," said Suzee. "It's all for charity, it's all for the Horton Bridgeways House, so get out your goddamn tickets because I am on the *rag*."

I got out my ticket.

While Suzee delayed things with a few of her scandalous, faintly racist, and sexist jokes, I watched Trevor, who laughed a beat behind the rest then turned saying to me, "What'll we win?"

"Probably dinner at Praline's," I said.

"Winner gets free dinner for two at Praline's. One complimentary drink, period, splat."

"You were right," said Trevor, and I wondered if this wasn't his first gay bar. He watched her as though watching a twisted nature special, something on the La Cage aux Folles channel.

Suzee called out the number and Trevor said, "Shit, I won! That's me! I'm the winner!"

Just like that. We hadn't been there long. Usually Suzee dragged it painfully out forever.

"We have a winner. Come forth, native son. Or are you not? Are you a damn Yankee?"

"Hell, no!" and the crowd yelled and clapped, indulging Trevor.

Trevor went up to the stage, looking happy, acting the shy part. A few looked around at me, watching me, waiting for me to fail with him, which it seemed inevitable that I would do.

The music was loud and on stage Suzee and Trevor spoke into each other's ears.

Suzee said, "Y'all, this is Trevor. Who wants dinner with Trevor at Praline's? This is a raffle within a raffle. Just say something, give a holler. Hie thee to Trevor's side pronto."

I was trying not to drink too much. Trevor held the envelope up as he stepped down off the narrow stage and got his applause. Soon I realized I was losing that battle with the alcohol, and then the show began and all I wanted to do was parcel out my last drink for the next hour. A cocktail waiter came and took my order before I was done with what I was holding but I was too gone to resist, and then I began to feel fine, surrendering. Too, I had the hunger for young flesh.

I sat watching only the stage, not looking around, not thinking about anything.

The show was about the death of Donna Summer. Trevor was no longer sitting with me, which was all right. He made me nervous. Let him make some others nervous. I was too busy remembering Donna Summer and the boy I was before I'd become the wreck of a man. It was a delicious evening. Trevor pranced about to the songs of Donna Summer, who herself was a great role model or something. She was a life force. All alone next to the wall, Trevor danced.

Our townhouse was something of a dream given the town. Memphis always felt small, but I'd managed to make the place my personal heaven. The main room had a cathedral ceiling and I'd decorated the scenically crumbling brick walls. Carnival masks, silk banners, some of the usual corny stuff sure, but the key was the indirect lighting. The main room was my introduction and I introduced myself well, I thought. Trevor wanted to come home with me, why I cannot tell you, and before I'd gotten him his drink he looked around and nodded approvingly. He said his father would be disgusted, which he liked the notion of. His mother would be amused. She'd "get it," he said. I spotted right away that he was too drunk really for social or sexual consumption, and he was eaten up by his neediness or something worse I'd rather not hear about, but he was too pretty and too *here* to ignore—and I was who I was at the time. So I watched him, didn't touch him.

He nodded and announced that he liked where he was now and then without my inquiring judged the guys back at the bar by saying, "Bunch of dumbasses trying to climb all over me."

I agreed too quickly, standing too close to him, and he said, "You're a dumbass, too."

I went off and put on some Boz Scaggs and he said, "What's that white-boy ofay mess?"

I'd forgotten that even the redneck boys nowadays thought of themselves as hip and beat and liked to use black slang, or liked talking in a way they'd heard in songs or read about.

"This some kind of cracker smooth jazz?"

"You don't know what you're talking about," I said. "You're too young. But if you'd like to go, I'd understand. I'm a lot older than you. I know, I looked younger in the bar lights."

"I know how old you are. You work with my mom."

A woman I worked with, Eileen, I knew had a son named Trevor. But there, who did not?

Once I'd returned from the bathroom and Eileen had said, "You just missed my boy!"

I had a state job, and not a bad one. I wouldn't want to put that position down. I got a good salary but yeah, it was boring. I was boring. I was a pencil pusher, a drudge, a drone. A lot of these younger kids were unironic Republicans. My older lover was asleep in the back.

"Is she Eileen?"

"Eileen, that's right. Has me call her that. She likes you, she's even kind of hot for you."

I said, "She's really sweet. She always covers for me. I'm not my best in the morning."

"She said. But she likes you, man. She hates the higher-ups. For her you're a victim."

"That's part of my silly act," I said. "So she knows."

"Knows what?"

"Never mind," I said, because he seemed nervous to me now, certainly not all there.

Such small towns—you still couldn't be too careful. What was, wasn't. What could be, you'd never speak of. I'd learned to live there. I didn't want to be there but it was my home. It was a while ago, of course, and things have started to change even there. I've since moved out.

He flung up his arms and grinned wildly, saying, "Hey look, the stars, infinity!"

I'd painted the cathedral navy blue and stenciled on gold stars like those homework stars back in elementary school. Did teachers still stick those on kids' homework papers and quizzes?

"Good job, good job," he said, swaying then catching himself before falling. "I like it."

I nodded, smiling, and said, "What would you like?"

"Everything."

"What would you like to drink?"

"What've you got?"

My older lover woke up and came in. The kitchen was separate from the main room by only a breakfast bar. George didn't seem fully awake and didn't even blink. He didn't seem to register anything, just wanting a drink of cold water. He pushed across the linoleum in his sock feet to the fridge and I opened it for him, like the woman opening door number three on the game show. Trevor moved away from us, awkwardly gavotting, knowing the drill somehow.

"Good night," said George.

"Good night, darling," I said, deciding to hide nothing. I was in control, or not. Nothing mattered. I was in control and part of being in control was knowing I couldn't control it all. And I knew it didn't matter. I lived in a small town where nothing mattered, not even me. And I was alone here, with George, where nothing mattered except us and me. My mother had approved of George tacitly not long before she died. He was rich and that was all she cared about, truly, and I had watched him get old, having met him when we both seemed young and my parents not.

The boy, Trevor, stirred. We were alone together and I said, "What can I get you now?"

"What've you got?"

"Everything."

He pointed at me and ordered, "Make me a gimlet. Now, motherfucker."

"Done," I said, feeling an old odd cheer. "Gimlet then."

This reminded me: we'd done our best work as father, mother, and son on the Gulf Coast. We'd covered the full reach and done it in style. Maxing out the cards, eating, drinking it all up.

Then for an instant it was as though something drunkenly cosmic was going on, uncanny.

Trevor said, "My dad used to whale on me, just blistering. Times I couldn't walk. Got to school all right but then he'd do it again. I couldn't keep up! He hated me then died, thank God. Fucker died. Still curse his shitty bastard memory but I'm here! My mom and I, we're still here and I thank my stars. The stars. The stars are so forgiving where I can't be. That was tasty."

"Would you like another?"

"Please."

My father was gentle, never raised a hand. He was passive that way. He'd gotten his money yet did seem to believe, rightly, it would slip out of his grip if only he looked the other way—and he had. Not his fault. Dad was an all right man, just foolish. Naïve you'd say. My mother died and then—nothing. Not a sound. Her folks would not report their misgivings but then they had the lawyers on their side and everything went over, scooted to mom's side of the family, the part of her life she'd despised although she'd liked the money okay, but she was gone. And then not long after, my father died, dissipated in unbelieving, unforgiving forgetfulness, and now I get it. I get the whole thing about liquidity, but still I romanticize our brief sovereign trio.

I got Trevor his second drink and he said, "Let's go out on the deck."

"Okay."

We went out onto the deck into darkness and he said, "Do you believe there's anything?"

"Anything at all?" I said, feeling I could follow him but no longer in a forbearing mood.

"Yeah. Like, do you think anything out there exists?"

"No."

"But there has to be! There's all this! And it's beautiful," the last phrase added lightly.

As he said this his voice got progressively dimmer, dimmer as the tree frogs shrieked and seemed to pulse louder. He started down the stairs of the deck, swerved, and came back up.

There was another room where I wanted to take him, but I didn't think we'd get there.

He said, "I don't think despite all that stuff my father was evil. Do you believe in evil?"

"No."

"Then what? You've been saying all this crap, this mess, but what do you believe?"

"I believe we're here not for any purpose but to enjoy."

"No you don't."

"I do."

"Do you want to enjoy me?"

"I do."

"I'm nothing."

"You're not nothing."

"I was never anything. Can't make my way. My mother says I just need time. Moron!"

"Don't listen to her or bother trying to interpret anything. Go. Get out as far as you can."

"But you didn't."

"I didn't have to."

"You're a fake."

"Yes."

"And you're saying go."

"I'm saying go, just get out. You're young."

"And what?"

"Take what you have, use it, and get out."

He started crying. He said, "You're a fake."

"Yeah."

He turned and kissed me painfully hard, that second drink a mistake but an exciting one.

And then we went upstairs to the room. The room was nothing. Something I'd done in a day with a paintbrush and some mail-ordering online.

He said, "And what about George?"

I said, "He doesn't care."

"You're going to die."

"I know."

"And I'm going to die. Does that bother you?"

"It bothers me more about you than about me, to tell you the truth. You're young."

"That's sad."

"It's not," I said. "Don't you want someone to mourn for you?"

He waited then said, "But you'll be dead."

"Rub it in, but that's not what I meant."

Already this sounded inane to me, but I felt as though I had the moral upper hand anyway.

We were in near-complete darkness but I could see the shine of his eyes looking at me.

"Oh come on," he said. "You'll have lots besides me mourning for you."

"I won't."

"You're full of self-pity."

"That I am."

"You should be."

And then we did it. It wasn't much. I'm not slighting him. I'm just saying it wasn't much for him—and he didn't even stay till morning. I felt worse for him than for me though later I did feel sorry for myself. It seemed typical. Life was like that, typical.

Later I saw him in a mall in Pascagoula, where I had moved, when he was with someone better suited for him. They looked marvelous together, and I mourned for myself and for George, too. But then I thought things weren't all that bad.

He winked at me while the other guy wasn't looking. We had both moved on. Life.

werewolf

to
THOMAS ERIC JACKSON (1965–2013)

After a while, I got so tired of going back to Florida not because I didn't miss it but because each time I returned I got more and more disappointed by my life, and by myself. Plus I couldn't afford it. I'm not talking about the disappointment of the suburban nature of it. I missed driving around the old places but even renting a car for a week was way out of my budget. In New York I was getting poorer just staying alive, while my friends who'd had the good sense to stay behind owned houses; they had pension funds and investments, as grown-ups were supposed to. They'd thought that my living in New York, where the rents are obviously insane, meant I was rich. And I was single and gay and you know what that meant. Champagne cocktails before the opera. I'd lost touch with most of them. I just assumed they were all flourishing down in the palmy 'burbs.

Then my best friend from high school got sick. He was living in a boxy apartment off the expressway not long after his second divorce. His kids, one from each of his two marriages, had been living with him, and it sounded happy until he'd gotten the diagnosis about his liver, and so they'd gone back to their mothers. He had insurance from his job, but it didn't cover everything. He'd had to take a leave of absence and go on disability. When the insurance ran out and he was scheduled to go into hospice, he would be depending on Medicaid. And I think there were debts, although before I left New York to see Phil I asked a friend who'd been on disability for twenty-plus years with AIDS if anyone would be liable for paying the debts and he said he believed not.

"But who knows," this friend of mine in New York said with his patent kooky, wild-eyed foreboding (since New York bred just as many kooks as suburbia had), "between all the different dumb laws in all the different fucked-up states, and what the Republicans are planning to do . . ."

Still, Drew, with AIDS, appeared to flourish. He swam five miles a day at the Fourteenth Street Y in Chelsea and traveled a lot. He was a good saver. He had a BlackBerry full of friends who took him out regularly and bought him dinner, gave him tickets to see the sold-out shows at BAM, and let him stay in their country houses in upstate New York or out in the Hamptons while they were in Europe or Southeast Asia or India (they were all Buddhists, it seemed)—and they'd leave him "expense" money so he could buy himself groceries and the food for their pets he was sitting. In May, just ahead of tourist season, he somehow scraped together enough cash to fly to Spain, where Drew had more friends. He'd had his Paris and Berlin periods and he spoke French and German and was working on his Spanish. He was from Houston and had the withering habit of making fun of Texas and the big-haired rich ladies he'd grown up around, wearing the prestige of knowing it top-to-bottom while beaming an assurance that he'd been smart to get out. He was a snob—and I took it as a moral failing, in his eyes at least, that I should want to return to Florida at all. He had a sense of entitlement all the more devastating and annoying to me because he had nearly died three times, which should have made him more empathetic but didn't—since, I guess was his reasoning, as an eternal patient he had a spiritual outlook that didn't punish him for being apathetic to the point of offensive preachiness. He'd had every opportunistic disease in the book: viral and bacterial meningitis, pancreatitis, kidney failure, a heart attack, gout, bloody-puke bouts with severe ulcerous reflux . . . and the list went on. Given his two decades of living with HIV, I suppose I thought of him as something of a testament to modern medicine, an inspiration capable of shaming me out of my own silly hypochondria. Around Drew I swung violently, but covertly, between admiration and a perhaps slightly misplaced pity. Drew was intelligent and had wowed them briefly as a student of classics at Columbia before dropping out. He knew everybody—from his stories that I didn't necessarily trust—and he had slept with most of them. Cosmopolitan Drew.

With Drew, the world was imperfect except for wherever he was at the moment or was headed next. Drew was always in a good mood. But with my old friend Phil, who did not have rent control in Florida, and who'd been told he had only a few more months to live, there wasn't going to be any world by the end of the year. Phil and I were both agnostics and didn't have the comfort of a poetic, onion-layered nothingness. Our neither believing nor disbelieving but being sure of a horrible nothingness had kept us loosely in touch for more than thirty years—and meant that I had no idea what to do when I finally saw him again after maybe two decades. Only that I had to leave New York right away to see him, wet-eyed, nostalgic, and with even greater self-pity.

The day before I flew off, I was meeting Drew for lunch and told him about the situation, giving him the background of my friendship with Phil then shading in some of the finer nuances.

"Oh no question about it," he said with a tenderness that was unlike him (and all the more frustrating because I'd always had a crush on Drew, those flashing blue eyes): "You *have* to go."

My anecdote took up most of the meal—at the end of which I hastily grabbed the check, despite my personal financial straits. Nor did my volunteering to pay the tab disarrange Drew's usual Zen composure. He smiled handsomely and nodded semibrightly. How I hated him then!

It went like this, and despite the fact that Drew was into Eastern medicine and loved to use disease horror stories to spank Western doctors and form object lessons out of them as quick, hard-to-follow advertisements for nontraditional practices (starting with acupuncture, which had helped relieve me of a nasty few months of GERD), he sat by and listened, drawing me out at the right moments, touching my hand when I almost blubbered, and telling me it would be okay. (A rather different Drew, I was seeing. And stupidly I wondered if we could still be lovers after all.)

I knew it wasn't going to be "okay," but I took comfort from Drew saying my loyalty was sweet. "It really goes to show how important old friends are," he said, but I also noticed a glazed look in his eyes that made me think he was really just trying to contain himself and not show that he was getting a tad revved up for his trip to a private island off St. Martin, paid for by a designer friend. Drew was getting on a plane the next day, too: "No, darling, it's a sweet, sweet story."

At the door of the bistro he kissed and hugged me, saying, "Best of luck to Phil, okay?"

Which wasn't much like Drew, either. I felt jealous, envious, and, as always, unsatisfied.

I went home to pack, and as usually happens I completely forgot about Drew within a few hours. I wondered if this was generally the case with foul-weather friends. Was I one of those to my old flame Phil? It occurred to me that time got behind the best and the least of friends—that only in times of crisis did we rise to the occasion and remember ourselves as loving familiars.

For a long time Phil and I had only exchanged a few scant emails to stay in touch—until, of course, those recent, terrible back-and-forths by email between us. I hadn't directly spoken to Phil in years. But we'd been talking a little in the last week or so. I was ripped by the news, and suddenly I was back in his life, and he was back in my mind. So I flew the fuck back to Florida.

Although he was basically straight, Phil and I had slept together in high school two or three times. One night when most of our classmates were at junior prom and my parents had driven up to the St. Marys for the weekend to fish, I asked Phil to stay over. He confessed that he was part werewolf and said that he believed this meant he was a bisexual. He was open to trying it out. I blew him and at first I thought it was going to take too long. We went to sleep in my bed holding each other. The next morning I scrambled him some eggs while he colored a sketch of a satanic-looking superhero he'd created in his sketchpad. We didn't kiss; he didn't talk. I looked at what he was doing and touched his shoulder as I was serving him. He growled, ate, then went home.

And I hated myself for that stupidity of having touched him like a lover, like a girlfriend.

Someone, not our friend Cindy, told me that Phil was getting into drugs with some of the other kids in gifted, the ones he played Dungeons and Dragons with, and I seethed inside. I was a priss who would never finish even one beer at a pool party if the teen host's parents were not at home. In fact, I disliked the taste of that stuff, so who was I? Since the night of the blow job we spoke less, and I was hurt—and before school was out for the year and summer began I told him in the hall in front of our lockers that I couldn't be his friend if he kept on getting high.

"That's your old tomato?" he said, sniffing, sneering. *Old tomato* was one of our jokes.

"That's my ultimatum," I said steadily, nodding, then waited and watched as he slunk off.

That summer I went to Memphis for a couple of months to be with relatives and to avoid growing up, I think. I helped out in my grand-mothers' gardens and read books in the AC. I was not homosexual. I kept telling myself that. But I knew I was the gayest person I'd ever met—so in love.

I got my second chance with him during our senior year. Phil lived in my neighborhood, and one night while my parents were in bed he scratched on my screen and I opened my window and helped him wriggle over the sill into my room. We whispered. He said he'd missed me. I think I was crying, but in any event I told him I'd missed him and could we start over. I was a snob and an idiot, I said, and then he quietly growled and we kissed for the first time, deeply. We took off each other's clothes and kept kissing and also for the first time he went down on me. I wanted to keep the lights on and he settled for a desk lamp. He asked me if I had any Vaseline. I put a robe on and crept into the hall, stopping to hear my father's snores. Then I hurried to the bathroom, opened the cabinet carefully, and found the Vaseline. In the bedroom he kissed and licked and bit me some more, quietly growling, then he put the Vaseline on both of us and I crouched on my bed in front of him on all fours and he slowly entered me, which didn't hurt at all, only at the beginning and then exquisitely as my head went numb and white noise bristled in the canals of my ears and my vision went blank. Somehow he knew to tell me to take deep breaths. I pushed back against him and it was over in two or three minutes. He pulled out and let himself into the hallway. He was dirty and needed to wash up. I held my breath and led him through the den and let him out through the French doors. He sprinted across the backyard and scaled the fence. There I was in my sweatpants, shirtless and feeling delicious, my naked arms folded across my chest, taking in the night air. I must have smelled the air carefully. I must have thought, now just let me sleep.

The next morning I got out of bed forgetting about the bites and my mother said to me in the kitchen, "Did you have a date last night that you failed to mention to me? My God, you have hickeys. Hickeys! You sneak out and see some girl? You're all marked up with hickeys!"

"I was scratching at these mosquito bites and I guess bruised myself," I said, yawning.

"Bullshit. That's a hickey, that's a hickey, and that's a hickey. Can't fool me on hickeys."

I just mostly miss my sweet little Gretchen and my big cool Pops," he was saying. He looked cadaverous yet pinkish, and I could see some of Phil's old contours. "My big sweet Pops."

I smiled encouragingly and said, chuckling foolishly, "Why do you call Derek Pops?"

His daughter was the senior in high school, I remembered, and his son, the oversized gay kid everyone picked on because of his effeminacy and his autism, was a sophomore. Derek was half-Asian; Phil's second wife was Cambodian. He'd met the first while they were both working at the Walmart out on Beach Boulevard—when Phil was working as a pharmacist's assistant and "between things" as he put it, finishing his degree, getting sober, about to get his first divorce, as it turned out. I was trying to keep the chronology straight. It seemed clear, Phil preferred Derek.

Phil was sitting up in his crushed velvet swivel La-Z-Boy in his robe and sweats and said, "I call him Pops because he's more mature than me in some ways—except when other people are around. He can laugh at me in a way I take fine, but only from Pops. Kid's really hilarious when he wants to be, so I give him that—figure it's his due. Those bratty fucks give him enough shit."

In school, Phil had never bullied anybody, even after tenth grade, when he'd gotten taller and had more muscle. It was his father who was the bully. But when we had first met, in middle school, Phil still looked chunky in his dark cords and Black Sabbath T-shirt and gray hoodie with drawstrings—the hoodie even on warm days to help hide what he called back then his blub.

I said, "Does Pops come over a lot? Does your mom or Pops's mother bring him over?"

"He's too scared. We're close, and if I'm not with him I guess in some ways he can miss me less, not think about me. But I'll have him come see me in the—y'know—when I'm . . ."

Phil must have been determined to be the dad, but with a lot less money, that his own dad had never been to him. Phil had been artistically talented. He drew series of comic books when no one else I knew was into reading them even. He worked on the covers he'd like them to have with oil crayons with far more dense detail than the frames on the pages inside. He read Tolkien and played Dungeons and Dragons with the gifted druggies. The only thing we did together was go to the movies or swim in his pool. His father snickered and said flat out that if Phil wanted to go to college and wanted him to pay for it, Phil wasn't studying anything artsy, he was going into a practical area. Which luckily my father had never said to me, just wanting me to go to college.

"What do you want Pops to do?" I said. "I mean, what's he interested in doing in life?"

"Anything he wants. Look, he's got long, black painted nails. He says he's going to be a dress designer and do everything for Madonna, from her apartment to her clothes. Pops plans on *marrying* Madonna. He can't decide if he's going into architecture, fashion, or musical theater."

"That's great. Jesus, Phil, you're the best father he could possibly have. So incredible."

He half closed his eyes and said, "It's nice of you to say that. It's really cool, so thank you."

He was evidently tired. I imagined he was like that all day, of course. I'd dropped over by appointment, texting him. He'd said he was too tired to talk. We'd talk when I came over.

The apartment had clean walls and overall clean but flattened-down tan carpet, and there was very little furniture in it. In the living room, just our two crushed velvet swivel La-Z-Boys. Mine was wobbly on its axis. I had to sit still not to pitch left or buck suddenly forward. He was already getting rid of most of his stuff, parceling it out to his younger brothers, keeping a dresser and the bed in the bedroom, minimum kitchen utensils, towels, linens. The fridge held his meds, some uneaten fruit, and several individual-sized bottles of Ensure nutrition supplement drinks, like instant shakes. When I saw those, getting myself some cold distilled water, I prayed stupidly that he could get better and beat the cancer just from having a pure infusion of vitamins and minerals. Not even for the two kids, for me. Not because I was still in love with him. I wasn't. He wasn't yellow, and I thanked my stars for that. The last time I'd seen him he was a bit overweight again, tan, and vivid. This was back at Walmart when Phil was finishing night school after flunking out of college in Gainesville. His parents were helping to support him because of his DUIs, and his wife had to pick up their daughter, Gretchen, from daycare then pick Phil up at work and drive him to his AA meeting. Knowing none of this, I had come in to buy soap and toiletries, right there in front of the pharmacy counter, and he called down from his perch, calling me Mr.

West, and we'd stopped to talk, me dazzled, him full of "pressured speech" and epic confession. He knew, and I knew, that it was another brief encounter for us, and that we were about to say good-bye and not see each other again for a long while—the tendency of ours.

I remember feeling awkward, out of place, and not because I was in Walmart. I'd wanted to travel, be free. And I knew that he knew this about me, too. "Wow," I'd said, taking in his slightly beat-up appearance. "Wow!"

"Some fucking anecdote, right?" he'd then said, looking right at me, not looking off.

I had stood there and said he looked great, then wondered if this wasn't uncool, smiling at him longingly and not acting impressed or stricken by what had happened to him.

"Well, you look terrific," I said, and he frowned. "I'm glad you're getting it all together."

"You're the one who looks great," he said. "How do you do it? Clean living? Hope so."

"I'm just here for a little bit," I said, "passing through, actually. But you look and sound great. I'm still just so shocked. I didn't think you were in town. You were really the last person I'd expect to see for some reason. I mean, there's never any time. I just miss you, but you seem like you've got this one, like you've got it together, and I'm glad. Married! Child! So cool . . ."

I told him I was just in town between grad school years and was headed back to Ohio. I hated my graduate program and wondered why anyone should do anything but live a real life. I was lying, though: I wasn't going to finish grad school at all. I didn't want to teach, no way.

"No, man, I really fucked up," he said. "All I do's work and go to meetings and go home and fall in bed. But Laurie's a saint. I know it's bullshit to say that, but I'd be in jail without her. My asshole dad doesn't want to see me, he just writes checks and my mom brings 'em over."

"God, tell them hi for me then, okay?"

He made his way toward the counter, touching things along the way as though attending to them, accounting for them as a good employee, and I was making moves to go, too. I'd been surprised in my funk, hating the old home haunt, hating myself, wanting to chase the past away.

Worse, I had the self-loathing feeling that we never should have fooled around. We might still be friends if we hadn't fooled around, good friends, the kind who kept up with each other.

Finally I waved my purchases at him, and he said, "Stay in school, dude. You got that?"

Then I was mad at him. Jailhouse Joe wants to go avuncular, scare me straight, I thought.

I walked away knowing I'd misunderstood him. And I thought of Mr. Johnson bawling a great son out over the rim of his scotch glass, the old man's eyes looking boiled. I went overseas a year later, though, and heard that the old man had died suddenly of a heart attack. I thought of Mr. Johnson jiggling his scotch and ice and getting worked up over something Phil had said and keeling over, the way I'd actually imagined for years would happen. I'd seen too many movies, I thought when I heard about this from Cindy. Even more than for Phil I'd felt sorry for his mom.

Mrs. Johnson came in, first knocking on the hollow construction of the apartment door then unlocking and pushing the door right open. Of course she looked older, but not a whole lot older than Phil. She'd moved out to the beaches years ago, away from our neighborhood, and played a lot of golf and tennis, but she was carrying a lot of weight that I supposed was appropriate to her age, and she still had a girlish laugh and a bright smile. She set down her plastic shopping bags, in the middle of the carpet, managing not to seem embarrassed by the sparseness and sordidness of the room, and went to kiss Phil on the forehead. Phil smirked and didn't get out of his chair.

I got up and she said, "Well, well, always the gentleman. Always the gentleman and hey, looking so good. So handsome, like always. So what do they put in that Manhattan water?"

"We probably don't want to know!" I said hugging her, then we pecked on the cheek.

"Right you don't," she said, and she pinched my arm, and when I withdrew it she lunged in and got another snatch. "That's right you don't, mister. How are things in New York City?"

"They're fine, I just don't have any money is all."

"Hey, but you can't have everything," she said and winked. "Can't have everything, can you, Phillip? Phillip can't have everything, I can't have everything, but you've got Manhattan!"

They were originally from Ohio and Mrs. Johnson was too tanned to dream of New York. Once Phil and I had dreamed of getting out of Jacksonville together and heading to New York as writing partners. We were going to write sci-fi and horror books. Phil said, "Mike's a writer."

"That was always the dream, right?" she said, looking adoringly on.

We'd always had this flirty rapport, this quick flame to friendliness and intimacy, in their kitchen or on the screened-in porch next to their pool. Phil knotted and knotted a rubber band.

I said, "But hey, Candace. Take my chair. I've been sitting all day driving."

"Driving in this hellhound heat and traffic?" she said. "Thank you, I will. I bet you don't miss the Jacksonville traffic. That's one thing. Don't miss that. And Dick died, you knew that."

"I did," I said. "Cindy Cross told me. She wrote me a letter not long after it happened."

"Well, not a day goes by. Nothing changes; he's still sort of here. But I swear, the traffic. And how is she, Cindy? Phillip—I'd nearly forgotten all about her—you guys been in touch?"

Phil said blandly, "She came and saw me last week. I told you that, Mom. Jeez."

"That's right. I stay so busy, Mike. I'm all awhirl. I have five freaking grandkids!"

I was sitting on the floor to the side and I said, "It doesn't seem possible."

"Thank you, but should it seem possible that your best friend from high school has a pair of kids in high school, when you've hardly changed?" She pitched it to a holler: "Hardly at all!"

I felt this power again that I'd felt back then. I'd been a pretty boy, once I'd dropped a lot of weight from dieting and running, lost the zits with the help of the burning cream, and gotten the braces off. I had been sometimes happily in love with her son: did she have any idea? Moms of the world had to be as randy as the rest of us. We were now the age Candace had been then.

A moment of quiet passed, unnervously, wherein she and I kept smiling at each other.

Phil said, "Mom, did you remember Dickie's card?"

"Oh, damn it," she hissed, then smiled at me for sympathy. She rolled her eyes.

"I'd like to be able to describe it when I call Dickie up and thank him for making it."

"It's in the glove compartment," she said, clapping once, and hitched left in the chair.

I offered to go out and find it so she wouldn't have to get up out of the tricky chair yet. Her car was right out front. I opened the passenger-side front door and the inside smelled like cigarettes. I found a manila envelope curled and crammed in the glove compartment and undid the brass clasp and slipped out the homemade card. It was done in Magic Marker, which made me think of Phil's earliest colored drawings in sixth grade. It read, "Dear Uncle Phil, I'll come see you real soon, okay? Before that I hope you get better and better. Love, Dickie (the Third)."

It was a picture of a man and a boy in the basket of a hot-air balloon, a close-up, which I thought clever. (Whenever my father made photos of anyone, he backed up so that expanses of a brick-veneer side of a house dwarfed the human figures he'd shunted to the lower right corner of the picture, their faces obscured by shadow or erased in strong sunlight.) On the card, the man's spidery hand rested lightly on the boy's shoulder. Only the bottom section of the colorful striped balloon was shown. The sky was streaked a cloudless pale blue, banners flapped from the tethers attaching the basket to the balloon, and the boy waved at the viewer with a friendly, frozen howl.

Before I left I made Phil a pan of rice, which he said he'd take with a little parmesan. He said just to give him the Kraft container and he'd sprinkle it on. He called from his chair while I was lifting the lid to check the rice: "Hey, are you planning on seeing Cindy while you're here?"

I stirred the rice, waited, then replied, "I guess so. I thought I'd give her a call at least."

"Cool."

He asked me to bring him his meds in from the kitchen counter. And when I sat carefully down in the chair again and he swallowed the pills with wads of rice and distilled water, he told me things—not about his fears but about his kids, how he regretted that they didn't live together, even though they had two different mothers. I settled in for a while longer and enjoyed myself.

I'd already decided to wait her out, and you know how much I always liked Candace," I said.

Phil's and my friend Cindy was a married mom of two, and I wanted to give the moms of the world a shout-out, although since I'd realized I was gay I'd never wanted to be a parent.

"That was your time to be alone together," said Cindy. "Candace is sweet, she probably thinks it's partly her fault—or more than partly. Moms just naturally will. I feel sorry for her."

I said, "I told him you and I would come together one time. You know what he told me?"

I didn't tell her about when Phil had said of Candace, "I kept wishing the bitch'd *go*."

Cindy and I were sitting on the deck of the top floor I'd rented of a beach house, which had fallen into my lap at the last minute, and it felt propitious. We were drinking riesling.

"So what did Phil say?"

"Well, that his mom was an alcoholic. That it was all over the family, all of his brothers, his mom, and that it was what killed his dad. That and the Kents. And then just before I left, he was mixing his rice around and dropped this bomb. Maybe it's not a bomb. You never left; you were the one who always gave me the updates. He had hepatitis twice, from using needles."

"Habitually? Like a lot?"

"I didn't ask. See, I made a vow never to ask him questions like that ever again."

Phil had mentioned trying everything once and, according to the Oscar Wilde dictum or whatever, giving it a second try just to be sure. Smoked crack, injected things. My puritanism I'd had to push into the back of my mind. Maybe it was Mae West who'd said that.

She fretted her brow and the frets stayed up there a bit. I smiled at her and lit a cigarette.

She said, "God, can I have one of those? I could get myself into so much trouble."

She did an imitation of her daughters mewling judgmentally, "Mom, Mom! God, Mom!"

I slid the pack her way across the glass of the little outdoor table, its wicker frame starting to rot and wobble on the deck. None of our families had come from here, we'd all migrated from different cities, hers from Atlanta. This was a clear, windy March day. The owner had rented the three floors to people planning to go to the races at Daytona, but those weren't happening, they'd been violently stormed-out. The bad weather had passed, but I was alone and spent the evenings when I wasn't running to the pharmacy or grocery for Phil driving back down the coast, stopping at Publix for supplies, then heading home and out to the deck to see the moon squat on the ocean.

My father had called Phil and me the Gruesome Twosome, and when Cindy came into the picture, the Gleesome Threesome, then more and more the Three Caballeros. It was Phil who not long after Cindy and I started dating in tenth grade told her that I'd already confessed to him that I thought I was gay—but that I was in love with her and another guy I hadn't specified. Now she was a mother who was probably grateful that she didn't have to pretend not to be glad she didn't have boys. In time, she'd learned everything. We weren't the Three Caballeros for nothing. She had asked me, around graduation, just before we all went our separate ways, if I thought Phil was jealous of her and me, and I'd acted angry and asked her why in the hell he should be, Jesus.

I'd told her, "It's all right if you want to date him instead of me, I'll be fine. Honest."

"I like him but I don't want to be with him," she'd said. "I like being with you."

"I like it, too."

"But who are you more in love with, Phil or me?"

"Neither. I love you both the same," I said.

And she'd made a fart sound with her mouth and looked evenly at me, saying, "Bullshit!"

Which was one of the reasons I'd loved her. This and the fact that she had liked being a virgin and never had any qualms about not having sex. I'd told her I wasn't great at it, anyway.

It was agreed that next time, a Saturday, she'd pull a shift with Phil at his apartment then drive him down to the beach and we'd sit out on the deck and I'd cook. Then she'd drive him home.

"Only it pisses me off," she said, "that we shouldn't drink in front of him. You have no idea, how good you have to be as a mom! It's bull-shit, acting the role model. It's restricting. It's like a slow suffocation. Since you told me that about Candace, I've thought a lot, good for her."

I thought not wholly tragically about the aging of our childish generation—gone youths.

"I can refrain," I said. "I can tie one on while I'm cooking then chew breath mints. I can smoke, can't I? I mean, I'll shower before you guys get here, then sneak one surreptitiously . . ."

Cindy was an OR nurse and she said, "Not such a hot idea, actually. Not the secondhand smoke part, but what if he gets tempted and begs us? There's liver portal hypertension and Phil's vulnerable to a sudden complete organ shutdown. We'll just have to be good little bunnies."

"Then I guess I can wait until after y'all go," I said, "and all the good bunnies are in bed."

125

We held hands watching the moon that was partially melted down tonight. I was glad she and I had this time together. I thought we'd never have it again, though we said we would.

"Now that the kids are in middle school and junior high, thank God," Cindy said, "I can swing it so I've got afternoons and evenings while they're doing all their extracurricular junk."

She and Todd had considered getting a divorce, but recently he'd gotten promoted and his workload eased up. He was good about taking turns with her watching the kids on weekends.

"This is just so nice," she added, a little slurry on only her second glass, and I nodded.

I said, "You know, it won't ever be often enough, me coming. I'm just way too poor."

"Where'd you get the money this time?"

"I told my parents, and they'd always loved Phil, always loved the sight of the three of us together actually, so they fronted me. But I hated taking it, even though now they have more."

My parents had retired comfortably and had no debts, no mortgage, but I'd been raised to be independent once I'd gotten through college. I had a problem with debts. But at least I didn't have a family to bankroll. Secretly I had my first book on contract to edit: stories of growing up. The debts I'd incurred to people for providing me with my material for it bristled uncomfortably all through me.

Cindy said, "If I got sick, would you do the same and ask your folks for the money?"

"Absolutely and unequivocally yes," I said and hated myself for sounding so literary.

She didn't say anything, and I was proud of her for that, too. We had to deal with this, I thought, as honestly as possible. By my next trip Phil would be long gone. She expected me to take off before Saturday, the way I'd run from my "bisexuality"—the issue less important at the time than how much you loved someone, or what your HIV status was, back when the virus was raging uncheckable. There was one question I'd previously evaded over the years, but Cindy had asked it of me over and over: "Did you ever think you were really bisexual?"

Inevitably it was followed by, "Did you ever want to sleep with me? I mean, did you ever want to, out of sheer physical lust?"

She'd put that last part different ways, sometimes drolly, during a bunch of long-distance calls and with a hint of falsely shared conspiracy, of queasy complicity.

You didn't ask those questions then, not when you were eighteen, nineteen, twenty. But I was still evading them when I was thirty-five. She'd stopped asking around my fortieth birthday.

She said now, "My mom told me to tell you hi, and that she'd like to see you."

"Why don't you invite her out on Saturday," I said. "Is she doing anything Saturday?"

She was trying to finish her cigarette without gagging or coughing. She tamped it out in a way that reminded me of noir movies, those films we'd gone to see sometimes with Phil in the museum's vintage movie series. She said, "But wouldn't Candace say she was being excluded?"

Her voice was squeaky and I nodded and we laughed, and I said, "Good point."

I lifted her hand and kissed it. She'd always been so real to me, the way my mom had.

"There's never enough time," she said, and I knew she needed to get ready to motor out.

My parents had hoped I would marry her, and she knew this. She'd married the guy who in college had gotten her pregnant and derailed her education for a while. They'd stayed together and she'd gone to night school, then she'd started her career and now they had this nice family. I couldn't fathom it but I'd started to see the point of it while knowing I didn't have the stuff for it.

She mashed the butt out in the crock ashtray, extinguishing just some evidence of her sin.

Later that evening, when I was comfortably tipsy reading Stevenson, my New York friend Drew called having returned from the Caribbean and said, "How's tricks, sweetness, you good?"

"Sure."

"You don't sound that all right. That would make two of us, bloody fucking hell!"

He liked to make fun of Brits while co-opting their idioms.

I said, "If you want to know the truth, I'd like to be life-flighted out of this entire deal."

"Your buddy Phil, if he wants to get better—and look, I'm not saying he doesn't want to get better—but if he wants to, he needs to get off those meds. His liver qi's in a rage. That's the story on his liver. It's shot. The drugs and pharmaceuticals, they're only making things worse."

He sounded like he was well into the malbec, like he was giving his own liver qi a zap.

I waited and then said, "How was St. Martin? All tropical paradise and great splendor?"

"Oh you know," he said, "those freaking airlines, they have us where they want us in this corporate-hostage country. All the corporations have us. Listen, I know of some herbals . . ."

Drew was a coddled, welfare-aided brat, I flattered myself, but right now I was a victim.

I listened, lying in my bed, holding my book open and pages down on my chest.

"You need to get him to an acupuncturist, get him some Chinese herbs. The acupuncture is one thing, the Chinese herbalist another. But go online and look, you might be surprised . . ."

We hung up finally, leaving the topic at nothing, and I went back to *Treasure Island*.

I can't do this," Cindy called and said into the phone on Saturday morning.

I was just having my coffee on the deck and steeling myself up. I couldn't do it, either.

She said, "Todd thinks I've gotten obsessed, and the girls all have colds. It's cold and flu season and they're all sick and Todd has to go into work all of a sudden. But I called Phil."

"Uh-huh?"

"He got it. He just hopes you'll come up and see him."

"Obviously. Hey sweetie, no problem. It'll be all right. Double-pinky promise, okay?"

She said, "My mom's mad."

"At whom?"

"I couldn't tell."

"Will you tell her I miss her, and that I'll see her, like, really soon? Promise?"

"Are you mad at me, Mike?"

"Not in the least. I couldn't possibly love you more. I never could."

I drove up. I'd been up too late the night before on the deck drinking and smoking and thinking. Adolescence had been just an embarrassment and it locked you into making too many romantic, silly statements you lived with forever if you thought about it. You couldn't overthink it. That way you'd go crazy. You'd had no idea you'd live to feel tired and defeated all the time.

He came to the door and seemed energetic. He said, "Man, all I can think about's pussy."

"I get it," I said, stepping past him. He was wild-eyed from the meds, I guessed.

"I'm supposed to be sick and I'm not supposed to last, but that's all I can think of. All I ever think about is hard, horny sex, doing nasty things with girls mostly. I never did it with her."

"You didn't?"

"Because of you, asshole, and because she was never in love with me."

"But she was. Cindy was always in love with you."

"But not like she was with you, man. You were my best fucking friend for a long time."

They had him on mood elevators, and maybe they counteracted the opioid dosages.

He said, "And it's not your fault that I'm dying. Obviously. No fucking shit there, too."

"I didn't say that. I hate this. I hate knowing it. I loved you more than I did myself."

"We were a team," he said.

I nodded and said, "We were."

After a while, sitting there with him, thinking about the sex, and thinking tenderly of him in bed with Cindy, should that have ever happened, I said, "Who says you can't beat this, man?"

He'd been crying but now he got quiet, smiling, then said, "And I thought *I'd* lost my mind."

There were only so many extra livers, so many motorcycle casualties to provide livers.

Finally, no laughing, no crying, just faint, twitchy smiles between us.

I said, "And I always loved *you*."

Then he wouldn't look at me, though after a time he gave me the thumbs-up.

"I hear you," he said.

Later, after he'd been moved to hospice and I learned he'd passed after a botched excision, I had some more things to say, but he was gone finally, and there was no reason to say them, and no one to say them to.

PART TWO

AFTER MEMPHIS

first responder

My brother Jeff called. I'm not even sure why I answered, seeing on the landline's display who it was, or at least recognizing the area code and the prefix of the number, though of course I was expecting him to call any day, any week, since I had heard from our mother that he'd broken up with his new girlfriend, after getting cold feet about divorcing his wife Deanne. I had not met the new girlfriend, Terri, now the new ex-girlfriend. Jeff still had a touch of the guilt, I could hear in his voice, but I could also discern a gratifying exasperation with Deanne. She had taken thirty hard years out of Jeff, bankrupted him, and was now daring him to follow through by hiring a second, more aggressive lawyer—whose services he was paying for. To top it off, the case was complicated by the fact that before he could finally be cut loose, my brother first had to settle up with the banks. I didn't know much else except that he wasn't expected to pay every cent of debt she'd rung up on the credit cards, just a big chunk of it. No doubt, Deanne's pride had been hurt, because after all *she* was the one being *left*. Oh yes, Jeff said, Deanne was now officially pissed.

"But after the hundred and ten thousand," he said, "how the fuck could she question it?"

That was new, the f-word. I hadn't heard that or any other cussing out of Jeff's mouth in thirty years. Of course I sympathized, but I couldn't let on too strongly, not yet. I'd been highly supportive of their union then the shotgun wedding when we were in high school. But Deanne, really, over time she'd taken the cake. She'd raised and homeschooled three kids, but when you don't work and your husband's a firefighter, you really had to rein in the indulgences, and she had been quite indulgent, denying those kids nothing in the way of clothes and gadgets and meals out at Wagon Wheel and TGI Friday's. I was finishing the cold coffee left in my Grumpy mug from Disneyland Paris and feeling seized upon and getting low on blood sugar as he dived right into all this and told me something none of us had ever known: that he'd always put Deanne in charge of the monthly bill paying. He was still getting to the bottom of how many cards were involved.

"But this," he said, "I take partial, no, the lion's share of responsibility for. I was an idiot, so I guess that's what I get for my willful ignorance. Having to work three jobs to get untangled from responsibilities I take very seriously. I'll be under the fucking water for a long-ass time."

"Uh-huh," I said, allowing myself a chuckle.

"The woman thinks money happens *magically*," he said, his voice cracking incredulously.

He was driving around Jacksonville in the Jeep he was about to lose, doing errands.

"Well, that's horrible," I warbled. Myself, I was only about five thousand in debt.

Barely drawing a breath, he traced the pattern back to their earliest born-again days, when he and Deanne would respond to Jimmy Swaggart's TV appeals to donate money in order to help spread the Gospel to Africa and help feed the hearts and souls and stomachs of the poor children.

"Yep, *before*, I was in on it," he said. "The woman had me convinced that any gifts we'd send in, and let me tell you, bro, we sent in a shitload, would come back to us as blessings, and I wanted to believe this. *I* wasn't starving. We had the house. We had the family safe and secure. I felt a responsibility, a guilt for not having it hard enough—and there were those African kids."

Guilt wasn't a blood thing, it came to me. Ours was a family-borne infection.

Perry was giving a lucrative talk in Minneapolis. I was alone in New York, trying not to think about Jeff or anybody but myself, loving my privacy. It was two in the afternoon and I was going to open a bottle of red and sip it covertly to get through this in style. I hated talking on the phone, and already I was moving about the apartment finger-dusting the bookshelf edges, sponge-wiping the kitchen counters, opening the bottle of wine and letting it breathe ten minutes, lowering the toilet seat in a darkened bathroom and quietly sitting down to urinate. In the dark, I somehow recalled Sugar Pie, the beagle mutt we'd basically neglected as kids. Jeff took his time, which was fine except that we hardly knew how to talk, for decades having barely been brothers.

"But you're doing it," I said, "you're going through with it."

"Yes. Shit!" he said, and it was as though I'd thrown cold water on him from a thousand miles away. "I guess you hadn't heard. That just started to happen again. I don't know if you've talked to Mom and Dad. I guess you haven't. But I'm just so angry. I go in every week for these weekly arbitrations, negotiations really is what they are, and all over again I'm just so fucked-up about the sums. Target *alone*, twenty-three thousand. She had a *Target* card I didn't even know about, but again that's a great deal my fault. Visa, MasterCard . . . I wouldn't let her take out an American Express, and hell I'm not even sure they would've given us one, given how much debt we had that, again, I knew nothing about. But see, half that plastic, I was none the wiser—"

"You have to stop flagellating yourself," I said. "You have to try not to self-flagellate."

"I get you. I'm not going to keep you on forever, don't worry."

"No, no."

I'd stopped hearing the road noises. He had said he was on his way to Walmart. Maybe he was in the parking lot, negotiating the traffic there. I was going to pour a glass and settle in. I was performing the service of talk therapy, which I'd benefited from myself, crossing Chelsea to Gramercy Park once a week for my expensive sessions during which I'd range anecdotally over every topic related to my family and relationships. I had very good insurance through Perry and my co-pay was only fifteen dollars. My therapist, an older man I'd only slowly deduced was gay too, had said that he thought I had what was called an "observing ego," meaning I worried about what others might be thinking and themselves going through—that I tried to see their side, which had been my role as the younger brother caught in the family situation when I was sixteen. I had tried to see every side, was my problem, and Bob, my shrink, was never too hard on me. He said that he trusted me as an "accurate historian," and begged me to proceed, nodding, waiting for me to get it all off my chest, not just family stuff but stuff related to Perry—groping my way toward my next, and next, breakthrough. And it had helped. I can't say why, except that I'd paid a man to listen to me and paid money to listen to myself and take myself seriously, so now all of these issues were old hat to me, dead and buried in effect. But here *we* were again. I was the younger brother. As a kid I'd taken it as my job to stay out of Jeff's way but snicker at his jokes, listen to him talk about his taste in music, which at the time I didn't get. I hadn't liked alcohol, either, but to curb the boredom I started toward the kitchen—and ramped up the tough love a notch or two.

"And whatever else happens," I said, "I guess it's no good being bitter. You're getting a divorce—right?—so you can cut things cleanly and get the past behind you so you can move on and try to be happy, right? You say *everybody* made mistakes. Everybody makes mistakes. And to be honest, I'll just admit this right now, don't know how you're going to react but I'm going to go ahead and say it, man—I'm looking forward to your being legally single. I think this is what you need, what you want, and what you're looking forward to. But it's really happening, right?"

"It is happening," said Jeff, "for damn sure."

I could see him nodding in the earnest, vigorous way I'd readily recognize. I'd seen him nod like that in Memphis, where our parents had retired, when Jeff had first opened up about the divorce idea, and when we were talking about our father's hospitalization, the "eventualities"—because Jeff was big on euphemisms, while at the same time talking turkey post-evangelical style.

I said, "So then it's all right if I'm happy for you, right?"

"Well, *I'm* happy. I'm not exactly over the moon. I'm going to be paying for this shit for the rest of my life, but it's happening. I'm making like a hockey stick and getting the puck out."

I waited cleverly and then I said, "What's going on with, what's her name, Terri?"

"Oh, Terri. Well, that was another situation. I felt like she was moving in too fast. You know, when Dad got sick she started this sympathy-card campaign. She was busting a *move*."

Our father had been diagnosed roughly two years ago with lung cancer, and in the middle of his first year of recovery Jeff had met Terri. She would send my parents cards, sympathy and just-saying-hi-type cards. *Can't wait to meet ya'll.* Most people using y'all can't spell y'all. I didn't want to think of Terri as cynical or calculating—and my mother had appreciated the cards, although I suspect Mom wanted Jeff to have a magnet pulling him away from Deanne for good.

"Terri just wanted to move things along at a different rate than I did," he went on.

"Well, I'm sorry to hear that. Mom appreciated her cards. She did sound sweet."

"Oh, she was," he said. "I don't know what happened there. I got claustrophobic."

"You have to do what's right for you. That's what you're doing."

"Anyway," he said, sounding infuriatingly distracted, "she was angling to get married."

So things were moving forward and I hoped that the conversation would end soon, except that there was one more little matter, the visit he'd been promising me, and this was stressful to a degree. Jeff had been a born-again for God only knows how many years, and in my heart I'd said good-bye to him a while ago. Once while I lived in Paris with Perry, a card showed up signed ostensibly by Jeff, telling me to change my ways and including Bible quotes—as though I hadn't already memorized those as a secret little junior high queer. I tore up the note, and for the next few days on the rue Saint-Martin, Perry would regard me tenderly as though I were on suicide watch—yet I'd only been wondering what had taken my brother so long to pull a stunt like that.

"Married?" I said to him now. "Wait, forget I said that. I never even met Terri—and I try to mind my own business. She doesn't always stick to it herself, but Mom taught us to do that."

"Yes, she did," he said, taking his time between transitions. "And it's a good policy."

I'd begun drinking my wine, noting its cherry notes. I said, "Anyway, end of an era . . ."

We laughed, though I daresay mine felt and tasted more delicious. I ideated a heart attack but knew that the phytochemicals and antioxidants in red wine should only prevent one of those.

I removed a cigarette from the pack and rolled it between my thumb and forefinger.

"Deanne was a good mother," said Jeff. I heard in the background a jangling of keys, his great ring of uncountable keys, which guys like him always had, then I heard solid metal making contact with more solid metal, *fwump!* I took this as Jeff closing his Jeep's door in the Walmart parking lot. "I will give her that. I leave that alone," he went on, and I could picture him nodding along to what he was saying. "She raised three more or less levelheaded kids, all three of whom I'm proud to be called their progenitor, their father, and so for that, sure, I will be eternally grateful."

You know we have this thing in the South called gab, the more words the better. Jeff had long called our father the progenitor, and I'd forgotten about it until we were in Memphis for my dad's lung cancer surgery. (By now I'd moved into the living room, settling into one of the club chairs, a hulk of disintegrating leather and a heavy oak frame Perry and I had brought back from Paris. I'd tried not to smoke in the house after my first evening alone. I was lighting up now.)

"But yeah, Deanne did a bang-up job of homeschooling them," he said.

"Sure," I said, remembering when I'd tried to give one of the boys *Treasure Island*, which Deanne had taken back to Borders, and I suppose traded in for some teen Christian saga.

"She tried to teach them cleanliness and politeness and personal comportment, what have you, but you know what?"

"What?"

"She fell down on one essential duty, to my mind."

"Uh-huh."

I remembered my Dad once saying, "Smoke 'em if you got 'em!"

"She didn't work very hard to instill in them the value of a dollar, and now I pray it's not too late for them to learn. I have taken them each individually aside and tried to explain to them what happened financially. Man, I am telling you I am just so completely wrecked, fucked-up or what have you about this death sentence the woman has passed on my credit history. I will be in this shit for what I'm sure will feel like forever—and that is what cheeses me off so badly on this otherwise nice afternoon. Is it nice there? I'm actually in the habit of checking the weather up in New York on basically a daily basis. Forgot to look at the app on my iPhone. Yeah, definitely. I am so screwed but you know what? I've just decided, I've tried to look at this situation like from the end of a telescope, you know? Just imagining? Projecting forward into the future? And I've tried to look at it from the other end, and I know, I know, I'm going to get through this somehow."

"Of course you are, man."

"I've already started making my adjustments, cutting my expenses. I've found a situation where I can live for next to nothing rent-wise. I got some advice from a financial consultant, and he was utterly and frankly helpful, and so now with the position I'm in, bro, yeah I'm determined to find my way out of this conundrum, you know? Since that's what it is, a *conundrum*. I have a set of goals as my financial man said to have. He helped me draw up a plan but not without fees, but it was worth it, and I've—okay, I've been going on. Is the weather nice there in New York?"

"Not a problem but yes, it's nice. I should probably go out soon, do some shopping, too."

It was a perfect spring day. The pears growing along Twenty-Second Street were in full leaf, the skies, if I looked out the window, were clear and blue. Today it was everything I loved about New York: solitude,

139

peace, fresh perfect weather. Now that I was smoking in the house—
Perry had quit in the early eighties, along with the drinking—I'd open
every window and turn on the fans, light some candles, spray some
room freshener about. I just needed to get through these next few
minutes, then I could go outside into the immaculate day, maybe
head over to the bar.

I was enjoying that second glass, a little more relaxedly. Which
was the good thing about talking on the phone, I realized. Nobody
could see you and judge you on your coping strategies.

He waited on the line then said, "So, have you talked to Mom and
Dad anytime lately?"

I could have killed him," my mother had said a couple weeks back, on
the line in Memphis. Jeff and I were born there, but I had no memories
of then. I was eight months old when we left, Jeff a couple of years old.
Our parents couldn't wait to leave. They were raised Baptists and had
grown up told never to drink or dance, and as soon as my father had
graduated from college he'd looked for a job to take him away. Bumper
sticker from back then:

IF THE VAN IS ROCKIN'
DON'T BOTHER KNOCKIN'

And our folks had had parties. I don't know of any sexual tom-
foolery going on between them, I'd be surprised—but maybe the
children are always the last to know. They'd played their CCR and
Linda Ronstadt, and I remember seeing that bumper sticker out on
the highway and my father and mother laughing and calling into the
back seat, "What do y'all think that means?"

We'd had some laughs, but somewhere in there I'd learned to keep
secrets, the family spy and double agent, not so much out of mistrust
but maybe amusement. I wanted to write early on.

"I got a sad-ass card from her," my mother was saying, "and it just
tore my G.d. heart up."

Yes, Mom was upset that Jeff had broken up with Terri, but she'd had a lot of shit going on recently. Dad was two years into his recovery, and they said that if it came back the window was two to five years, which sounds like a prison sentence—and for her it was. They'd sucked his right middle lobe out, and then had begun the hell for them both of his chemo and radiation. When he had survived the first year, Jeff and I had flown "home" to Memphis for Dad's surprise seventieth birthday party. We'd grown up in Jacksonville, but we all knew what was meant by "going home." It was hard not to be proud of Jacksonville, Florida, even though it was so very horrible and wrong. And it was where we'd left Jeff behind. And where we went to high school and where Jeff was working at Albertsons grocery store when he'd met Deanne, the woman my mother had nearly lost her mind over. Deanne was five years older than Jeff, who was a bag boy while she was a checkout girl ringing up groceries. Messed up with Deanne, and now with Terri.

"I could've kicked his ass all over town, if only I'd been there to do it when he told me."

Mom had a stream-of-consciousness style of talking, another Southernism. You interrupt yourself when you were saying something else. You begin to narrate a story and another thought occurs to you suddenly, and then your listener is a little confused and gets a little exhausted. The telephone. You can't read gestural irony, but if I'd been there as Mom's interlocutor I could have looked around and gathered context clues. The cigarette, the freshly mixed wine spritzer of Diet 7UP and her horribly sweet California muscat, the dinner she was stirring on the stove. Actually whenever I flew to Memphis to visit, she'd already premade everything, so there was not a stove involved. She let the food thaw in its freezer-safe Tupperware or Corningware dish, then while I stood at the expensive black granite-topped kitchen island nearby, she heaped individual portions into separate bowls, covered them with Saran Wrap, and one by one zapped them in the microwave.

"I never met Terri," I said.

"Do you know what I said to him? I said, 'And what about my seven thousand dollars?' Like, was I ever going to see that again? Because I bet not. I told him, I said, 'Your father and I volunteered to give you this money for the lawyer.' I stood in the post office. I waited. I got up to the counter and insured the damn package. I sent it all certified mail and I said, 'And now you come to tell me this shit?' Now Terri. I could kick his sorry ass from here to kingdom come."

Perry was in the next room. He was getting his talk ready for Minneapolis. He'd started dinner and I felt a little stress of obligation. When he began yelling my name, "Scott, Scott!" to get me to the table, I'd be in the middle of all this—mostly commentary and throat-clearings and my mother's bravado and ire and rage—I'd learned through therapy to reason my anger away but *just.* Just give me the facts, I wanted to say to her. I said, "And you say Terri wrote you a note?"

"Why did I have to get a note?" she bawled over the line. "Why was it my problem all of a sudden? I hope he's happy. The note would break your heart. I have it right here, if I can find the damn thing. But why would he do this? I mean, he's your brother, why would Jeff do this?"

"I don't know, Mom," I said, "we were never very close. I've told you this, I don't know how many times. We were never particularly close. Just because he's my brother . . ."

"And I've said to Doug, I've told your father, that makes me sad, it really does, depresses me to tell the truth. But you're a writer, an author—"

"To call me an author . . ." I began.

"But you know what I mean, thinking into people's minds. Why would he decide to call off his divorce from a woman who's given him nothing but grief for I don't know how long, and break it off with a girl, a woman, he said over and over he liked? She was the one, that's what he told Doug and me. I stood here on the phone with him and he said that, he said as far as he could tell he liked her and that she was the one. Treated him right. Didn't hurry him along. Didn't act anxious, just gave him his space. The asshole *said* he liked her because she gave him his space!"

In New York it seemed incredible to some of my friends whenever I reported the vulgar speech of my family members, but at some point, again owing to the seventies I suppose, we began using cuss words—it seemed incredible how nasty my mother could sound. But I think it was our fault, my brother's and mine. We were boys and came home and reported our classmates' speech and this I think unleashed the freeing vulgarity in my parents, who'd had a history of that, too. It became unsurprising hearing the f-word from either Mom or Dad, and Jeff and I were never too embarrassed to say it, either. My partner Perry, for example, thought this incredible. He was my parents' age and had grown up in the Midwest and expected better comportment out of women. I liked shocking him. He could be a pain in the ass about this, but he liked my mother. She spoke the way she wanted around him. Perry had helped break down barriers of sexual comportment in American life, and whenever he got too prissy about female social behavior, I'd remind him he'd been celebrated for writing books about sex in back rooms, on the West Side docks. Of course as you have already deduced, I worked from the vantage of guilt. I wasn't handed a sense of shame from my parents, though we'd gone to church. Numerous times I can remember Mom telling me not to be ashamed of my body. We were, to others, unreasonably close. She had raised me to be a gentleman, which in the context of mother-son closeness, I think now, meant that I ended up as something of a male Southern belle—an accurate historian as Bob my shrink had called me, and as I'd strived to be, an observant ego—and so I said to her, "I don't know, Mom, maybe Jeff was just freaked out about Dad. Maybe with Dad's health problems Jeff got cold feet, or something."

"And why do you say that? How does that work?" she said, a bit defensively, I thought.

I replied, "I don't know," as though I were a tad uncertain, but strictly out of politeness of course, still just reaching for something at this point, "but maybe looking at Dad got him worried that if he got sick he might end up alone and maybe that freaked him out. I never met Terri and I don't know what she was like, but maybe he was worried that he'd up alone a second time. You said before that it all happened so fast with Terri," I added, treading the surface of my chatter.

"I never thought of it like that," she said, as though considering my words unsteadily, and as though they still hadn't quite penetrated. "But what do you mean exactly? Why's that worse? What's worse than living in hell with a lunatic, who's manipulative, who manipulated him so?"

"Mom, Jesus Fucking Christ. I don't know. I'm just speculating. I've told you we were never particularly close, Jeff and me. Remember, I get most of my information from you. I got used to not having a brother, honestly. I have friends who are like my brothers and sisters."

"I'm glad about the last thing but not the other. I hate to hear you say that. I hate it that you and Jeff are not close, and I always did. I hate to think a family isn't like a family to you."

"It honestly stopped bothering me after a point, Mom."

"But your *brother*. You see what it's like between one of my brothers and myself?"

"Uh-huh."

"And so are you saying that he might have pulled out of the divorce then got rid of Terri because otherwise he'd be alone? How does that work? That's terrible if it's true, just awful."

"Maybe it's not true, though."

"So what is it, then? If it's not that then what else could it be? Why would he pull a stunt like that? He sat here in this kitchen and talked to your dad and me over a year ago and told us it was over between him and Deanne and that he was happy with Terri . . ."

Mom had the often infuriating habit of digging into something until she got a satisfactory answer but rarely got one. For years after Perry and I moved back from Europe, she would stop me in the house in Memphis when I was visiting and say, "I want to know what your father and I did to make you so distant. Did we say or do anything? Just what the hell happened?"

And I would have to tell her, again and again, nothing had happened at all really. I'd just gotten older and changed. I couldn't explain it. I was more withdrawn, I'd learned to rely more on myself, and then too

I had Perry. I'd stopped talking about my problems with them. I'd gone to a shrink, for another thing. Finally, around the time that my father got sick and Jeff and I went to Memphis for the surgery the year before, she'd backed off. And then when the following year Jeff and I returned to Memphis for Dad's surprise seventieth birthday party, she'd said, "It's good to see you and your brother talking and laughing again, like when you were younger . . ."

It occurred to me that I'd never get certain points through to her—and this, according to Bob, was going to have to be okay. And so now I said, "Don't worry about it. I'm not worried."

"I can't find that note from Terri," she said, "but I'm telling you it'd just break your heart. He'd led her to believe she was the one, and she obviously thought *he* was the one."

"Maybe he'll change his mind again," I said. "Who knows?"

"You think? Maybe. I could just kill his ass. How are you on your smoking, do you get weak at times? Tell me the truth, I want to know."

"I have my weak moments," I said, without telling her how many of them I had per day.

"In the middle of it, and now with this shit with Jeff I do again now too, but in the middle of your dad's cancer, all that treatment and his getting sick from the chemo? I won't lie to you. I had to stop in the middle of everything and go outside and sneak me a ciggy, one or two and then I was fine. I'm telling you, there were times I couldn't deal with it. I told him, I said, 'This is on you, I can't,' and I'd make him drive himself to the hospital for the treatment. And then I'd be in the house thinking about him and break down and go outside and sneak one. He knew. I wasn't going to lie to him or anything. But you do? Sometimes? Get weak and then go and light up?"

"I go in waves," I continued to lie, and was probably into the wine by then, too.

After a time she said, "Well, I could kill that boy's ass—and that fucking bitch's, too."

She laughed girlishly, though she cackled when really cracked up: "I am fit to be tied!"

But what finally did it," he said, "I came home and she had all my tools out on the lawn, doing a yard sale. *All* my shit, my clothes, my power saw, every damn electric tool and Craftsman tool, socket wrenches, screwdrivers, what have you, and a sign that said Tool Sale, and she was sitting right there at a card table with a cigar box taking money, hand over fist—and what the fuck?"

He *still* has not entered Walmart, I thought.

"Had she sold it all?" I asked.

"Had to wrestle my power saw from a man's hands, and he wasn't letting go. I got really close to popping him one upside the head and almost knocking his lights out but then didn't have to. Fucker saw the look in my eyes and said, 'Man, you're just crazy enough!' and let go, but by then I'd lost a good half of everything, and that's when I decided, fuck you bitch, I'm doing it."

I heard voices from his end. He'd gotten into Walmart and I could hear the crash of metal mesh and bars, his removing a cart from a line of shopping carts. I only went to Walmart now up in Maine. Walmart was one of the few reliable places in that small resort town for groceries and everything from underwear to toiletries. When I went to Walmart I was acutely aware I ought to be ashamed of myself, because of their low wages and even lower benefits, their flouting of labor laws, but when I went the people working there didn't seem unhappy; on the contrary, they acted happy to see me, another customer who kept them in business. I still felt guilty, but with Perry I was the only one to curb expenses. When I'd first met Perry and decided to move to Paris to live with him, he'd said, "Maybe you can help me with my budget. After I seroconverted I started to throw my money out the window at practically any passing stranger." I'd lived with Perry there in Paris for three years, and there weren't a lot of ways to save money. In Paris, food is good but it's also very pricey—precisely because they don't have places like Walmart. Not that the French were any happier for it. In the realm of unhappiness, they gave Americans a run for their money.

Jeff said to the Walmart greeter, "Hey, how are you today? I like your hair like that!"

I heard the hoot and drawl of the greeter but couldn't understand what she was saying.

I said, "Hey, Jeff. Can you smell popcorn? I always liked that smell."

"I don't smell any popcorn. I think you're thinking of Kmart, bro."

"Right," I said, and I remembered my grandfather buying me Polaroid film at Kmart.

He said, "Now, Deanne didn't know my schedule. She thought I was pulling a shift at the station, but she got the day wrong. And then I pulled up and there she was trying to sell my shit. Caught her red-handed, and all she did was get more pissed. Am I boring you? I realize I might be taking things too far. But hey, know what? I'm coming to see you, man, I'm finally coming."

We'd talked about this in Memphis, both years. Pity the Southerner who has to extend an invitation repeatedly, even when he dreads the actual visit. The visit my mother was referring to, the one where Jeff and I were laughing and generally hanging out, on the occasion of my father's seventieth birthday party, my brother and I would sit up late watching DISH TV, raiding the liquor cabinet, and eating snacks in the entertainment room. We'd gotten to a channel playing a concert movie, Led Zeppelin's *The Song Remains the Same*. It was still a terrible movie. We'd first seen it together in high school, when Jeff was first dating Deanne, and when Jeff let me tag along with him and a friend to a midnight showing of the movie at the Regency Twin, where all the midnight shows played. I had fallen asleep during "Dazed and Confused," still a boring song, too long and ponderous and psyche-delic. It was the drum solo by John Bonham, God rest his soul, that did it, all that cymbal-splashing and tom-tom-thrumping. I'd felt guilty about falling asleep in front of Jeff and his friend, and I remem-bered avoiding him all the next day. I still wasn't impressed by it, though since I'd cottoned to Led Zeppelin. *I* was the Zep fan now. I'd bought everything on CD. I'd made a conversion, late on the heels of his religious conversion with Deanne. And then at the airport at the end of that Memphis trip I'd said, "You should come see me in New York."

I got nearly through security when he hollered, "Hey, I'll do that! Come see you, okay?"

"Okay!"

"Just got to do a little math, take a look at my budget."

"Come, come!" I had called back, thinking of my first cigarette at the end of my flight.

I was going to have to open all the windows, turn on the fans, light some scented candles, get the smoke smell out before Perry returned from Minneapolis. Here I was lighting up again.

From in Walmart now, he said, "Good-ass deal on Cheerios, and Folger's coffee—but in humongous containers, and two-for-one. Get me some of that. Now that's a deal if ever I've seen one."

I said, "Do you and Darby split the expenses down the middle?"

"Not always."

Jeff said this sotto voce. I could picture him studying and marveling at the giant family-size packaging. Our mother had always been the ultimate bargain hunter. She and her sister, our Aunt Joyce, would head out for an afternoon of driving from store to store, buying canned goods here and meat and produce there, in the process burning God knows how much gas—back during the seventies oil crisis—and armed with stacks of variously labeled rubberbanded envelopes full of coupons they'd sat up late on previous nights clipping and sorting, *Breakfast Cereals, Roll and Bread Mixes, Canned Rolls and Biscuits,* the craft of their executive-homemaker generation. My father would come home and stand in the kitchen in his gypsum-encrusted work boots (he wasn't allowed to go on the carpet without pulling them off in the garage), sip his can of Old Milwaukee Light, and open the Amoco card statement and mug heart-attack shock, eyes agog, bill trembling in his hands, and say, "Well lady, you saved a bundle on pork chops but sunk us on fuel!"

"Fuck you. You try and make a go of this shit," my mother would say.

For the moment, Jeff was living with a friend from his old church called Darby, who had a house but had started living on disability. Darby had a degenerative eye disease and was going slowly blind. He couldn't work, and without an expensive operation—which his welfare doctors were putting off—he would never recover his eyesight. Jeff called him the forty-year-old virgin. Darby needed Jeff to drive him to the doctor, take him shopping, help him with his bills, and Jeff said, "Between him and Deanne, I'm frankly at a loss for words how to describe it. Both of them need me and at ridiculous, unpredictable hours. Deanne, for example, whom I'd already told she should get her oil changed, just last week the woman calls me from the side of the road in a rage. She'd half burned the engine out. And as long as we're still married, it's on me. I'm on the way to work, but no. She's been to Target and she's angry at me. And Darby, well, he's just my other son, my third son. But I leave that alone. He actually truly really needs me, but if he could meet a girl. Guy's not *bad*-looking. Blind as a bat but presentable. Needs someone to tell his troubles to, not just me. Relies on me a bit too much. Holy shit, a tower of Charmin bathroom tissue, for what? $9.99? That could last us three entire months. When should I come? June?"

"June sounds good," I said, doing a quick calculation. "Second weekend of June, bro."

I knew that Perry was going to Italy for most of June, and I'd been looking forward to the time alone in the apartment. This would have been six months before Perry's first stroke. I still had a romantic view of living, the optimistic Protestant. I wanted the party to go on, and for now it was continuing. Perry was still traveling around the world making appearances by himself and leaving me to take care of things in New York. Perry was overweight, and his solution for getting out of breath was taking a taxi even when he was only going three blocks. My solution for a few years had been to sit up at night drinking wine and smoking. What am I going to do, I thought, if it really happens? I worried when he was gone, but I would also have peace of mind. Perry was only getting more famous but he was a literary author, meaning readers recognized his name but didn't buy many of his books. Perry had to fly coach to collect an overseas honor or attend some festival, and you know how uncomfortable those seats must have felt. His doctor was after him to lose sixty pounds, but I'd grown up in the seventies and resented body fascism and knew from watching my friends and their parents that nagging was not an effective inducement to change. It only made things worse. I had wanted my June in New York to myself but at the same time I was intrigued. I'd never really had a chance to get to know my brother. It's not that we were never, ever close. For maybe a year when he was a high school senior and was working at a grocery store and began seeing Deanne, we talked. Once I went to the kitchen around midnight and saw my mother in the foyer standing on tiptoes peeping through the front door's small slot window. Double doors, so I crept up to the other small slot window and looked out. Jeff was standing on the driver's side of Deanne's MG—the top was up—standing still but staring back at the house as though he saw us. I think she was giving him a blow job, but it hadn't occurred to me until much later—when I was sitting in Deanne's car which was parked in our driveway. She was about to become persona non grata, then not much later family—it felt coolly rebellious to be sitting in her MG passenger seat while Deanne sat behind the wheel listening to Fleetwood Mac's *Rumours*. I nodded and smiled along to the music saying, "Great, cool," and when the whole album was through Deanne ejected the eight-track and handed it to me in the dark and said, "Gift." So I'd defended her all that time, in the early years. I had stopped when I got home from college after my first semester and they began talking to me about God, quite earnestly.

In the foyer, my mother had screamed, "Go to bed! Get out of here! Go to your room!"

She was desperate, full of gnashed-teeth rage. She saw the future. But later when I came home from college all those fate-done years later, Mom was calm, composed and not a little arch.

She said, "So here's the juice. Deanne said that when you came in from Tallahassee, she felt the presence of Satan in her living room. *Her* living room! What a—"

I wasn't used to hearing my mother say the c-word. The f-word, okay.

So it was imagining him in Walmart hunting for a bargain that brought all that back.

It fascinated me while I was talking to him to consider, I do have a brother! His name is Jeff! To think I lived in New York. It seemed almost mystical to him now, as it once had for me.

He said, "To be honest, I just want to walk around a lot, just look at everything. If I could come for a long weekend and we could hang out and chill—you say Perry's going to be away?"

"He travels a lot," I said.

I wasn't ashamed to have Jeff around my lover. But Perry and I had an open relationship, and I didn't want anybody coming over to fool around with Perry while Jeff was in the apartment, and I didn't feel like explaining the arrangement. The arrangement was, Perry hooked up online from a "daddy" site and usually hosted, since the guys he met there were younger and didn't live alone and not all of them were out. Most of the guys, incredibly, even though it was anonymous, were jealous and would have freaked out or walked out if there was a guy in the next room while he and Perry were having sex. When a date was announced, I'd go to the movies, or if there was nothing playing at the movies, my neighborhood bar. It didn't bother me in the least but some of our friends pitied Perry and me both. My parents adored Perry but wouldn't have understood. It would have run like this: my mother would ask me over and over to explain, and I doubted there could ever be an explanation on the planet that would satisfy her. I wasn't *proud* of my attitude; I just thought it was the best arrangement for everyone. So no, Perry needed to be *gone*.

"Well," said Jeff, "I was hoping to meet him, but next time, I guess."

"Sure. Some other time. He just stays in motion," I went on. "He's curious about *you*."

"Mom and Dad adore him," he said, and I smiled at that verb. "They say he's one of the nicest people they've ever met. They wanted to meet Terri. What did Mom say about Terri?"

"Not much. You know how she never wants to appear nosy."

I'd almost let it slip, but I could keep my wits about me even on my third glass.

"Yeah," he said, "whatever. I know that's one of Mom's ideas about herself. You know what I'd like to do when I come up? Go out dancing.

Is that something we could do? Because I love dancing, and this is my time. It's so freeing, you know, just to get your ass out there on the floor and shake your ass and boogie. I've got places I'm starting to go to at the beach. One time I took the forty-year-old virgin. Darby didn't dance. He's just such a shy kid and pretty easily abashed, plus he's self-conscious about his eyesight—the noise and the dark and not knowing what's going on around him. That night girls were giving me tips, because I'm always the first out there getting the party started, and I don't care. I don't care how I look. I get extra points, too, for it. But is there someplace you know of where we could dance?"

"There has to be," I said vaguely. This was going to be even more work than I'd thought. Now I had extra homework and was already losing my precious free time. "I will look into it."

"That'd be much appreciated. But hey, I'll call you again when I look into flights. I'm headed to the register now. I need to get out of here. I've got somebody's well I have to go over and look at. I won't buy a ticket until after talking to you—but can't wait to see you, Bubba."

That's something guys hadn't done in high school: dance. Nobody wanted to look like a fag, so the girls had danced with each other. To this day I had to be in a foreign country to dance.

I'd let Jeff chew my ear off and I talked to Mom one more time before his visit. She was thrilled he was going through with the divorce, and there wasn't any more talk about Terri. Jeff needed a little recreation, she said. He deserved it, and she cackled. I told her about Jeff's dancing idea.

"Sounds fun," she said and repeated, "The boy could definitely use some recreation."

The boy who was going to be fifty before long.

To pay off the debts so he could finalize the divorce, Jeff was working as a fire lieutenant downtown and earning extra money as an EMT reviving heart-attack and pool-drowning victims, and he was also digging shallow wells for people who wanted to water their thirsty Florida lawns off the grid of the expensive municipal utilities. His voice sounded calmer and he said, "I'm ready to do it, and I'm ready to come see you. I know I've been a sob-sister, but I really want to spend some time with you, find out how you are. And I'm curious about your life up there, I'm curious about the city, I'm just generally curious, ready to have some fun, go out for long walks, see shit."

All those years, it had been easy to take for granted how different our lives were because I'd taught myself not to think about him. He'd naturally slipped out of my mind. It came home to me that I would never know work and life travails nearly as hard as he had, and I told myself now that I owed this visit to him. I was spoiled, a housewife in a Joni Mitchell song, and he was more a country and western persona singing from the end of a bar. I'd begun to respect that. He had opened his life to me, the way those singers did, but I was covert, saving myself as a writer.

His mediation was scheduled for the week before his projected visit. I congratulated him and gave him directions from the airport and said I looked forward to seeing him, too. Perry left town but before he left said, "You're going to have a good time. I'm going to feel fat around all the Europeans. I love our life but I was talking to somebody the other day and it just came out of my mouth. I said, 'Everything's great. I have a wonderful lover. But it can't last forever.'"

I was not a great lover, but we had understandings that I could only discuss with friends.

And that was the frame of mind I remained in that summer. Life with Perry—who was a year older than my father—was privileged but could be hectic, a real adventure. Anyone, family, friend, or colleague, who met him could easily understand our connection. But our arrangement, no. That wasn't for the Baptists I'd left behind in Florida. Some of those Southern Baptists had gone nuts on drugs and drink in college but eventually returned to the fold. My brother had done it all and was just now coming out the other end, and in a way I envied him.

Either I was just learning about him or the guy had the power to surprise.

By the time he came to New York Jeff had already met somebody new: the mother of a younger colleague at the fire station back home. From emergency-crew reality shows, I knew that first responders talked in carefully composed euphemisms. In court they might call a homicidal crack fiend "a gentleman approaching with a potentially lethal weapon." To reality cameras they said, "The gentleman approached at a rate and in a fashion I considered menacing, and I could see that he was carrying what I knew from fishing avocationally to be a Rapala fish-gutting knife. When he got within an uncomfortable and, as I was able to ascertain, a dangerous range of more or less a yard, I was then able to make out in the adequate overhead lights of the parking lot the handle of a partially concealed pistol projecting from the front pocket of his hoodie. From there I quickly decided, judging not to mention from the wildness of aspect in his eyes, to draw my sidearm."

Divorced several times, Michelle had grown kids. I liked the sound of her. No-nonsense, unspiritual. Jeff said that Michelle just always wanted to have a good time. Also promising. He had barely set down his nylon carry-on duffel and backpack on the dining table, looking around.

"And man, we *fuck*," he said freely. "Last night we stayed up fucking like bunnies."

"Well, well," I said, "and good for you, bro. No, great!"

"No question," he said, on a roll. "We're pretty much compatible, in bed and out."

"I was sorry to hear about the Jeep. Yeah, your reward for being good and playing by the rules is to end up driving a vehicle Deanne did her best to run to hell and back and *destroy*."

"And you know what?" he said. "I don't even give a bald rat's ass. We are *done*."

I wondered if I'd overstepped by interpolating motive in that awful woman.

"I'm sorry I haven't been too available," I said. "I've been busy getting ready to see you, finishing up some work on Perry's papers, getting them ready to sell."

"What does that mean, getting them ready to sell? You mean publish?"

"It means a university wants to buy them but first they have to be organized, cataloged."

"Uh-huh," he said, stepping into the photo-lined hall, "so this is a New York apartment."

"This is my New York apartment," I said. When Perry and I moved in I'd said I was tired of wandering the planet and that I planned to be taken out of here for the last time on a gurney. I had since begun to daydream about living on the Carolina shore, gardening in upstate New York.

"Not exactly like in Woody Allen," he said, hands on his hips. "But I like it. Roomy."

We had not shared Woody Allen. We had not shared reading. In high school, he'd taken late shifts at Albertsons, or he'd lied about some of his shifts to go out with Deanne. My father went to bed by ten and was up by five to get to the plant by seven. On Cinemax I watched slow foreign movies full of sex, or took advantage of the quiet to read when nothing good was on.

"I noticed on my way down from Penn Station," he said, "and you were right, it was easy taking that train from Newark—I noticed some buildings I might have seen on *Law and Order*? Interesting. A guy I know from the department's from here, Queens, Brooklyn, the Bronx, I don't remember, and when I said I was coming up he told me I could *have* New York, for all he gave a shit."

"He doesn't ever want to come back, your colleague?"

"I think he still has an aunt and cousins here, but he couldn't wait to get the hell out. I'm going to walk, that's my plan. Walk, see stuff." He nodded vigorously. "Want to go out now?"

On the subway, which was crowded, we had to stand. He watched the people but kept his expression poker. We got off at Columbus Circle and waited at the light to enter Central Park.

"Man, I'll tell you one thing," he said. "I don't think I could live around so many people. That was interesting, that train experience just now. A real menagerie," he said and laughed, and he went into an impersonation of our mother and her old pet idioms. "Menagerie" was one. Jeff and I, when we were about to get close in high school, before the disaster struck, used to imitate her constantly, and not only behind her back. I cringed at the possible damage we'd done to her ego.

We slipped right back into it now, though, impersonating her mincing, eye-raising style.

It was a beautiful day and when we got away from the Indians trying to rent us bikes, and he'd remarked on that—"Boy, they sure didn't want to let us go, without first taking some of our money!"—I steered him into Strawberry Fields. He shook his head at the piles of dead bouquets left for John Lennon. Since I'd gotten tired of New York, emotionally detached from it, I was no longer embarrassed by the tourists, pilgrims, and mourners. He wanted a look at the plaque in the sidewalk, but too many people were bumping his shoulders trying to get at it, see the artifact.

"First dead Beatle," said Jeff.

"And already forever ago," I said nodding. This wasn't hard at all.

"I remember when I found out," he said. "I was in sociology."

"I was in AP chemistry," I said, then wished I hadn't mentioned advanced anything.

The trails were packed and we made our way to the lake filled with rowers in rowboats.

I said, "Do you want me to take a picture of you on your phone in front of the lake?"

"Now that'd be good to send Michelle. I need to tell her I made it here safely anyhow."

I took the picture then handed the phone back to him, and he said, "Michelle does worry."

Already to me, while hardly knowing him at all, he seemed dead drunk in love, eaten-up.

We crossed the bridge and entered the Ramble. I didn't say it was an old cruising ground.

We topped a hill and his phone went off, and he stopped to check it. He giggled—a teen, I thought, musing on the excitement of just starting dating. I'd dated girls in high school, too.

He was red in the face and he said, "I asked her if she was taking good care of my pussy."

"Ah."

He read out loud, "'Pussy misses you. Have fun but you stay away from other pussies.'"

This went on back and forth as we crossed the park then reached Park Avenue, a deserted canyon just then. I said I thought the rich people would all be in the Hamptons for the weekend.

"I've heard of the Hamptons," he said. "I do notice it's appreciably cleaner along here."

After a while, a walk of twenty-five city blocks past the buildings and Russian doormen, we entered Grand Central and went down to the food court for Chinese and took it to a table.

"For one thing," he said, "they sure don't stint on the noodles and rice. It wasn't clear to me at first they understood what I was ordering. Guy just looked at me, but he got it right."

A man shabbily overdressed for the season rooted through a nearby trash barrel.

"Is that usual?" he said, grimacing sheepishly. "I mean, is that typical for around here?"

His phone chimed and he got it out. The screen's bluish light seeped into his wrinkles.

"Deanne," he sighed, "wanting to know if I got here all right," then powered it back off.

I said nothing. I was going to maintain a cool ambiguity. He nodded. That was it.

Before we left he said that he couldn't finish his meal and that he wanted to give some of his food to the homeless man—who'd moved farther away from us, on to the other trash barrels.

"What would be the protocol for that?" he said. "Just leave it somewhere he can see it?"

"I couldn't tell you," I said. "I've never done anything like that before."

Then I worried that my ambivalence meant I was a terrible person. I did now respect true Christians, the ones who cared about others and made such gestures. But New York had allowed me to indulge the hardness in me. It was a city for the rich, young, or famous, or all three.

After a time, he got up, carried the closed Styrofoam container to the trash barrel and left it on the top, where if the man turned around he could clearly see it.

Jeff turned, red in the face, and giggled. He said, "Let's get out of here!"

We went to my neighborhood bar, the local queer Cheers as I described it. We got in early, right at the start of happy hour. The bartender, Mark, was playing one of his mixes. Happy hour there was Mark's show—his personal taste the same music my brother had liked, that I now liked.

Mark was tall and leaned over the bar, offering his hand, and asked Jeff what he wanted.

"You know what I recently just tried and liked," said Jeff, "was a white russian."

"I don't have any cream," Mark said. "But tell me what kind of liquors you like."

"You know what I really like is Kahlua. What can you make me that has Kahlua in it?"

"How about a mind eraser, that's Kahlua and soda. Try it and tell me if you like it."

Gym-built, Mark wore a flattop, like a pump boy at a fifties filling station. He made a sample of the mind eraser. My brother tasted it and said, "I like it. I'll have one of those."

Recently they'd installed video monitors over the main bar. Mark would do things on his computer, compile clips of old movies he got off the internet. And some were ancient homemade porns, black and white, often explicit. Mark would bring them in and play them in a great mash-up with old TV commercials and safety demonstration spots, eroticizing the vintage past I guess.

We were sitting at the corner of the bar near the door. On the screen, two guys fucked.

"Anyway," Jeff said and turned to me stoically. "Tell me what else. Tell me about you."

I said, "Well, this is where I hang out. This is my social life. I guess it's weird for you?"

"Not really," he said, "but what do you call Mark's haircut, a flat-top? Is that a flattop?"

"I think so. I can't imagine Mark without one now."

The Kahlua and soda did seem to relax him, and he said, "I think I said already, but we've got these great places at the beach where they have live rock bands and you can dance along . . ."

"You said. I wish I could be there, I just don't have the money to come down right now."

"Michelle likes going. I hope she and I'll get into this thing where we go regularly, since she likes to dance, too. She gets wild—the girl gets wild. I end up the designated driver."

After a while, Mark came over and pointed at Jeff and said, "Same thing?"

"This shit's starting to grow on me," said Jeff. "Thanks for hooking me up, man."

On the screen, a guy in a posing strap was spanking a guy in a posing strap, too. A close-up of the guy being spanked: mugging pain, he bit into the heel of his hand, eyes swimming. An old Cascade dish-washing commercial, then two naked beefcakes mounted like horse and knight.

In front of Mark I said to Jeff, "But you're getting the house back."

I wanted him to know that I was caught up on everything, this time through Mom.

"Five thousand dollars for a new roof," he said, sipping. "Yeah, I'll be rolling out dough for the next five years just to bring her up to speed. And it's in terrible shape. I'll just say that."

I didn't want to talk about any of it, not the time I'd come home from my first semester of college and they'd gotten saved, and not the time I was in Paris and got the letter purporting to be from Jeff reminding me of any injunction against homosexuality in Romans and Corinthians. I'd been working my way up to discussing it with him before he arrived, then thrown that idea away just as I had the letter. I'd decided that it probably wasn't his handwriting, and that I didn't care.

I hadn't smoked all day and had a hankering. I said, "Be right back."

I went out to have a cigarette—and then Mark joined me. Mark would sometimes do this if there weren't too many customers inside. It was too early still for the much younger guys who came in toward the end of Mark's shift, but I was always sure to be long gone by then, buzzed.

"He's nice, your brother," said Mark. "I could see the resemblance when you walked in."

I said, "He is nice, right? I just barely know him. But here we are. How are you?"

He laughed and inhaled. "I could see his discomfort when he looked up at the screen."

The little bit of alcohol swam through me and I said, "Yeah, I forgot about the videos."

"But he's straight, right?" said Mark.

"Yes. Straight and getting a divorce. How are you doing, man? How's your writing?"

Mark had been writing a novel for a while. I romanticized guys like Mark, with his skill serving drinks but also his dream. To me he was New York; I was suburbia still. I loved hearing about his life, but whose life did any of us envy? I was just glad I wasn't in my brother's place.

Mark gasped and inhaled and said, "My writing would be fine if I was doing any. All I ever do's worry about money, but I want to show some of it to you, later, when you have time."

"I always have time. You know that. You see how I spend my after hours."

"Thanks, babe. I've just got to take care of some things first. How's your visit going?"

I said, "Before, New York had nothing to do with my family when I still romanticized it."

"Uh-huh."

"Then Perry and I moved here and it was great, a climax. But you're always yourself."

"That's true," he said and put out his cigarette as people entered the bar. "See ya, babe."

I was alone for those two or three minutes, enjoying those puffs. I'd given myself away to my brother by saying I was going out for a smoke. I trusted him not to say anything to Mom and Dad the way I'd given him a pass when we were teenagers and he snuck out in the middle of the night to see Deanne. I felt guilty and finished up and went back inside. Jeff looked content.

He sipped from the thin red straw and propped his elbow on the bar and leaned against it.

He said, "Some of my colleagues have flattops like Mark. Well, they do look practical."

"I don't know how it would look on you," I said, and then I remembered once when I was in college having lunch with him at Wagon Wheel, and Jeff asking me if there were any "militant homosexuals" on my campus trying to "recruit" young guys. I didn't indulge him that particular line of inquiry. I had never met a militant homosexual and wouldn't have known how to identify one, but I was sure there probably weren't any in Tallahassee, Florida. Since no one at the time, who wasn't on MTV, had worn a flattop, I decided he must have thought of flattops for starters.

Mark made his way down to us from the gay guys and their girlfriends at the other end. I was aware of how hard it was to make a living in New York, anywhere. Jeff nodded at him. Jeff was friendlier than I was, I then realized. I just hadn't known that before now, when we'd ended up in New York together. I started thinking about this, not feeling guilty but self-conscious.

Mark said, "You guys all right?" and Jeff said, "Man, I am just starting to feel all right."

I nodded at Mark as though I hadn't just seen him and said, "How's Danny doing?"

Mark's lover Danny had ALS, Lou Gehrig's disease. Danny was already in his fifth year with the disease, according to Mark outstripping his doctor's expectations. He should have been dead two years ago, but Danny had opted for alternative therapies, acupuncture and massage.

"Oh, you know," said Mark, and then he stopped and filled my brother in on the situation.

Jeff told him, "As an EMT, I had a client with that whose heart stopped."

"A client," said Mark and laughed. "So you work as an EMT. So does my sister-in-law."

Before long they were into it like two old old friends catching up after a long separation.

"We brought him around, he was fine," my brother said. "I was amazed how long he said he'd had it, seven years. I think the record we know of's that famous physicist, Hawking?"

"Ten years after *diagnosis*," said Mark. "But the record is either thirty-two or thirty-nine years, depending on how you define onset. But lots of people have it more than seven years. It's controversial, between the ALS community and the medical community. Another round, boys?"

About the Sister Sledge we were listening to, Jeff said, "An oldie but a goodie."

I decided not to ask him if he'd hung on to his "Disco Sucks" T-shirt from back in the day.

It didn't matter because we were getting sloppy.

I took him to a Thai restaurant I thought was all right, though he said it was the best food he'd eaten in New York so far. I was happy that he was happy. I should be happier, I thought. I had made it to New York. I wasn't who I'd wanted to be, but I wasn't the cowering gay kid back in a redneck 'ville. I didn't want to hate them anymore. I didn't feel like bothering to hate.

We were eating cake back at the apartment when he began talking about his job. By far it was the most interesting part of our time together. He was describing one call to a house fire.

"Most calls have to do with cooking fires, grease. The lady was frying something and her clothes, a housedress made out of polyester or nylon, caught on fire and wham! We get this call from a neighbor seeing the smoke. We know it's domestic and we ascertain from the description that it's probably from cooking, thick and black. So we arrive and I go in ahead, and as soon as I enter I can hardly see a thing. Right at the front door, I fall into a hole. I'm wondering what I'm on top of. It's her, only now she's a greasy charred skeleton. Obese, fuel for fire, and before she could get out of the house she burned right through the wood floor. And I'm *sitting* on this shit."

We laughed, and I recalled the gross sense of humor that kids, especially boys, shared. He and I had shared that humor a few times, but I reached through into my memory. Nothing.

Firefighting was what he'd always wanted to do. His other story had to do with a woman who was a former porn star, who occasionally came by the fire station and said, "Is Charlie here?"

For three dollars the captain could take her behind the station and feel up her bare breasts.

"With three dollars," said Jeff, "she can buy a couple of forties. A forty's a buck-fifty."

We laughed, and Jeff said the fire captain had later told him, "Man, her tits are so hairy!"

We started talking about our father—and at first I wasn't comfortable with that, either.

He said, "Dad is seventy and at seventy the body starts breaking down. Shouldn't be any big surprise to any of us, things start happening then. He's lived a full life, worked hard—and, as should be the case, Dad's been amply rewarded. And for everything, man, there is a season."

He spent the next few days wandering around Manhattan on his own, seeing Ground Zero and crossing the Brooklyn Bridge on foot. He wasn't interested in museums. He had tried to get a conversation going with some of the local firefighters, but they'd had to hurry out on a fire call.

"Overall, I find the people here nice," he said, "just always in a hurry. Constant hustle."

He was staying in the bedroom where I normally stayed with Perry sleeping in the bigger room. Jeff was in there with everything I owned in the world, my books, my CDs. Jeff was now me for a few days. I hoped I hadn't left any evidence of my weird arrangement with Perry.

He asked, "Would it be all right if I took some of these CDs back home to download?"

"Sure," I said, "but keep them as long as you like. Take as many as you want. Really."

He took some of the ones I'd been buying in the last twenty years when we did not speak.

A month later the CDs came back to me Express Mail, insured. It was all the same music he had bought on vinyl with his Albertsons pay while he was dating Deanne then destroyed after getting saved: music he'd listened to on his pricey Realistic turntable when I was still listening to bubblegum on my cheapie—when I was giving my first blow jobs and living in my own world. I was my own kid then, too—dreamy, frightened, and, I'd thought, self-contained. Only much later had something led me to buying and collecting and listening to my brother's high school music.

Led Zeppelin, my favorite now, and the Stones, and the Who. Hard, resentful rock.

admissions

All through these horrible weeks—in the cath lab where their journey had begun, in ICU, then on the so-called stroke step-down floor, and now finally in Perry's physical rehab facility just off Stuyvesant Square—Scott would invariably be asked what his exact relationship to the older Perry was, and each time the younger Scott would have to stop and consider. He was raised in demure politeness, but his anger would rise, then he'd tamp it back down again because Scott didn't want to make a fuss. Still, in each case, Perry's situation was a fucking *emergency*.

"Sorry, sir, I have to ask," he heard. "But are you Mr. Knight's son?"

Then he'd have to correct them. Admissions people, nurses, whoever at the moment was attending them: understandably, each needed to know. With quick, efficient, flashing concern, or else with a rueful officiousness, they looked at Scott amid some emergency or another transfer of Perry's tired, afflicted self, and said, "I'm sorry, sir, but who are you again? Friend or family?"

And each time it still surprised Scott to stop and reply, "His partner. His fiancé, actually."

"Oh, hey!" they inevitably said, but every time. "When's the big day?"

This was New York, after all.

The whole thing was disconcerting, from Perry's sudden medical reversal to the recently passed fact of gay marriage. Imagine, in the

165

state of New York now, a man could marry another man. Meanwhile, as a teen a long time ago coming to terms with the fact that he preferred men, Scott had thought, well at least I'll never have to get married. He'd grown up in the evangelical South, right at the historical intersection of religion and politics, Reagan pandering to the Moral Majority, the now non-Eisenhower Republicans in bed with the Jerry Falwells. It was enough to make Scott flinch back then, reading Romans and Corinthians, that terrifying sentence *Man shall not lie with another man as with a woman*—and he flinched now when hospital workers reacted so generously and even ecstatically to his frank reply: "Congratulations! Holy cow! Awesome!"

Jesus, Joseph, and Mary, here they were, looking for rest and finding no rest.

"Congratulations," said the female EMT, grinning. "So what are you guys planning?"

Perry was being transferred to a facility for his recovery and to be taught how to walk and talk and pick up the smallest objects again. A semifamous writer, Perry could barely hold a pen. Partially paralyzed, and once stubbornly independent, Perry had become a compliant weight (his phrase), a hopeful burden, a ward of the country's spotty insurance industry. Without complaint, he settled stiffly into his new situation, wanting to get better, terrified of becoming a vegetable.

Meanwhile Scott's heart was breaking, a moist bloody mess. Everyone was so *nice*. He wanted to follow orders, do everything he could, whatever that might entail, and he was grateful to everyone. They'd just had the ambulance ride downtown from Columbia Presbyterian, where Perry's simple diagnostic procedure had gone terribly wrong. Scott was in the mood to sue, rail and rant, but the EMTs were being so cheerful and patient, waiting with Perry on the gurney and Scott standing by waiting for more orders. Actually it was an *ambulette*. In this situation, Scott was learning a lot, and one of the things he was learning was patience amid tedium. Meanwhile, Perry didn't fuss. Of all things Perry became a model of behavior, but at the same time was not Perry. His eyes bugged, or else shut for a quick infant's slumber. He had a sweet, sloppy smile.

admissions

They were standing on the first floor of the rehab center waiting
for the paperwork to go through. Scott had presented the chirpily
administrative woman on duty with Perry's photo ID and the docu-
ment designating Scott as health-care proxy. The EMT who had
driven them from Columbia Presbyterian down to the building
opposite Beth Israel east of Gramercy Park was an obese Queens
Puerto Rican. As she and her quiet colleague—a small and well-knit
black man—were wheeling Perry in on the gurney, she and Perry
began discussing diets. Perry had just asked her how Weight Watchers
was working out for her, tending to believe obese people would always
be obese—as Perry had been for a while, starting the climb to over
three hundred pounds back in Paris, the city of the famously thin
French. The driver was still pretty hefty herself, although she said
she'd lost forty pounds and was losing still at a rate of three or four a
week: the ideal. They didn't want you losing it too fast. Too fast and
you'd just start putting it back on. Lifting her end of Perry's gurney
she didn't let out a single grunt. Perry gazed up at her like a cribbed
infant and spoke, and when he spoke his speech was more or less still
panting and slurry, still stricken.

"And—you're—you're—so—so—struh—struh—*strong*," he said
to the young woman.

"Weight Watchers is awesome," she said confidently in the hallway, raising the gurney or cot's back to help Perry sit up and looking
to Scott as though she might want a sandwich or at the very least a
cigarette. The ambulette, Scott recalled, had reeked of tobacco smoke.
"See, I can eat what I want," she went on, nodding. "Eating's not the
issue. *Food*'s not the issue at all."

"Oh?" said Perry, though it came out more as a Santa Claus *Ho!*

Every behavior control system was a mind control system and had
mottos like, "Food is not the issue. Drugs weren't the issue. Alcohol,
not an issue. It was all in the head, see?"

Scott had come from religious territory, and everything in America
was religion anymore.

"Portion control?" said Scott hopefully, encouragingly. Perry
needed portion control.

"Doesh Hweight Hwatchersh deliver huh-mealsh?" said Perry, smiling lopsidedly.

"It's mainly portion control," she said. "I go to the gym two hours a day, which is great. My daughter notices the difference. And they teach you little tricks, like, they say if you're not hungry enough for an apple, you're just not hungry. You guys going to get dressed up or what?"

"You mean for the wedding," said Scott.

Perry grinned and said, "Ish been put off, hyou shee?" and chuckled hoarsely.

The other EMT smiled at Scott. He said, "I can swear I've seen you someplace before."

He was handsome and appealingly small and tightly knit; Scott would have noticed him.

"I bet we don't hang out at any of the same bars," Scott told him. "Or maybe we do?"

The elevator bell went *ding*. At the time, Scott had no idea he'd be returning here for the next several weeks. He just went with it. He was terrified but tired, yet how selfish of him. The little black EMT winked at him. Hospitalization posited a different time zone—a far dimension.

The nurses on the ninth floor were all from the Caribbean or African countries. Claudette took them in and told Scott, "Listen, we're liberal. This is not like those others. Here, we are *open*."

"But visiting hours?" said Scott.

"It's not *like* that, I'm saying. See? We're not like other facilities. We're not like *them*."

"I have health-care proxy."

"That's not what I'm saying. I know you're the proxy. You gave a sheet. Now there's no staying overnight, but listen. Come anytime—*don't* come at nine in the morning." She regarded Scott earnestly but with a code-like grin. "He'll be busy see, and you can sleep. Sleep as long as you like, *then* come in. Nobody's checking—it's just in the morning, he's busy with things . . ."

The second nurse, who came in then, and whose name Scott had not gotten, was tinier but broader and said, as Claudette was undressing and washing Perry on his new bed, "Here we are!"

Claudette said, "Girl, you don't even know."

"Now don't even start."

"This is my man, and you don't even know yourself with this man. This man is mine."

Perry laughed even as he was presented fully naked and looking yellowish. His skin was dry and shiny, and the main shining was like lemon rind. He looked haplessly at Scott, and Scott wanted to go out into the hall and choke. Just since Tuesday his Perry had been through a lot.

"Now girlsh," Perry muttered, smiling proudly, gamely, being a good boy.

"Don't even listen to him," said Claudette, "because he needs me and he knows it."

"He don't need you."

"You get away from him now, I said."

Scott received Perry's balled dirty boxers from Claudette. She soaked a cloth in a plastic basin of soapy water and squeezed it out and began scrubbing Perry gently, starting on his legs.

"Does that feel good?"

Perry said, "It *nuzh*, ackshly."

"Stop looking at him, girl. Now you just deceive yourself."

"You need to drive that demon of self-deception out of yourself."

Before he was getting ready to go home, late that night, Scott saw Claudette in the hall.

"I'm leaving," she said, her stylish bag strapped over her shoulder. "Lord, listen to me. I won't see you for a while. I'm normally at night, when you'll be at home in bed. Anything—but anything—you just ask. Don't worry, they take good care of folks here. He is in *good hands.*"

"I just wanted to thank you."

"Don't. That's why we're here. I've got to go. I'm tired. And you take care of yourself."

Scott went back into Perry's room. Perry was sharing it with a Korean man who was sat up for part of the day in an orthopedic chair wearing a neck brace, his spine inclined back just so. Mr. Park stared at the ceiling. Mr. Park had the window side of the room. His wife and daughter talked to him in Korean, encouraging him. Then there'd be a moment or two of reflective quiet.

Perry's own bed was slightly inclined up. He looked so tired. Scott pulled up a chair and put his arms over the guardrail. Perry was in a minutely patterned gown. He took Scott's hand.

"That poor *hman*," said Perry, gasping. "I heard them talking, just a little, in Henglish."

Perry's articulation came and went, but he had no idea of modulating his voice.

Scott tried to suggest a lower tone for them by muttering, "Yes, darling. I understand."

Perry said throatily, groggily, "He can hardly talk, but—he—said, 'Cold, cold!'"

"Room's too cold for him?"

"Hi guess." Perry sighed, relaxing back a little. "Hi'm—I'm—worried about you."

"Don't be, sweetie, I'm fine. The important thing is for you to get better. All right?"

"Hi was thinking," said Perry, swallowing, Adam's apple bobbing, eyes revolving. "Hin a couple days, not tomorrow, bring hin the bills hand the checkbook, hand hwe'll go over them."

"Not yet. There's not a lot yet," said Scott, thinking about the apartment, their home.

"Hokay. But watch it for me, hokay? Hi want hyou to go soon—darling—hall right?"

Scott squeezed his hand. Scott said, "Are you comfortable, sweetheart?"

"I—*ham*!"

After Scott had left, Perry lay there thinking a lot of things. Finally Mr. Park's wife and daughter—Perry had learned the man's name from the nurses—had left, and Mr. Park was lifted out of the chair and eased back into his bed. Why wouldn't they draw the divider curtain at such a tenderly vulnerable moment? It seemed Koreans were not as embarrassed as Perry would have felt. Every few minutes or so, Mr. Park barked up phlegm. The divider had been drawn, finally, by the nurses, and it was night outside. The room got dark and Perry couldn't see the window; it was like an aquarium in here now with just the fluorescent lights going at a low visual hum. Mr. Park was watching a sports network. The *hish* and sudden cheering wildness of a crowd at some soccer match intermittently erupted. There was nothing now from Mr. Park but phlegm-barking.

Hearing the barked phlegm, Perry wondered about his own functions. He had no control.

Perry was exhausted remembering the ride in the ambulance, quite peaceful. It had been a beautiful day and much of the ride was down Park Avenue, sunny and leafy out the two narrow vertical windows of the ambulance's twin back doors. He remembered something the lady EMT had shared with Scott as they were wheeling him out on the cot—gurney—what did they call it?

They were leaving Columbia Presbyterian and Scott had said to the driver, "My brother's an EMT, part-time. His regular job's firefighting, but for extra money he drives an ambulance."

"*Fires* rock," she'd said, swiveling a bit of her heft and nodding fast. "We like *fires*."

At first Perry had thought she was saying that the fires firefighters put out rocked. He'd only recently learned that "rock" as a verb was a Thing—and that a Thing was a phenomenon.

In the room now, he waited to be alone, but people kept coming in, waking him up.

"Mr. Knight? I need to take your blood pressure now. We need a stool sample."

A while later he'd fallen asleep without reaching around to pull the long cord of the light switch, which was extended by a length of gauze tied at the near end to one of the handles on his heavily handle-outfitted bed. He fell asleep dreaming he was in court as the defendant about his driving record. He hadn't driven in years and didn't generally need to drive in New York, but he wanted this power back, without which he felt old and useless—as whenever he and Scott rented a vacation house. The year before he'd had his cataracts out. He thought that he was exonerated of all possible driving offenses. He wanted a license; he had medical proof of his worthiness. The judge in the dream with his powdered wig said that of course there were *other* considerations.

"You're old," the fat-faced, periwigged duffer said. "Go home and consider this hard!"

Sometimes when he was enamored of a pretty boy he'd met, Perry would believe himself to be much younger, at an age that still made him presentable, and yet mirrors frightened him and he avoided them or else laughed at the image staring back at him. He felt his eyes getting wet, so he was still alive, still human. He could use this as part of his appeal. Perry wanted his freedom.

He was in the court, and then he wasn't, and then he woke up crying in court again.

The judge banged his gavel and dismissed proceedings for the night. Perry imagined he could feel the thick atherosclerosis clogging his carotid arteries and wished he'd never smoked. He'd been a young writer, hopeful. Cigarettes had pushed him along, but he hadn't counted on a culture that vilified bohemian excess. Art was nothing now—the death of civilization instead of a harbinger of vision. The great visionaries now were the budget cutters. They ran for president hatefully and spitefully. Now he was just a client, infantilized, looking forward to being washed and patted dry, then lotioned. He liked the babying too much but he'd earned it—except no one noticed anymore how hard he'd worked to earn it. Only Scott was there to notice, but even Scott could be punitive. Getting older sucked, he thought. The floor was quiet. He looked forward to getting better, determined to. He had to show folks, even those not paying attention, and soon he was moving on his walker with its spindly aluminum supports like a crippled metal spider, clack, clack. Clack. Insurance companies, right-wingers. And his bladder always felt full.

It bothered him that he should have to do it in his diaper. No one came. He rang again.

What time was it? What day? Sometimes he woke thinking he needed to make dinner, he'd let the evening go after too long a nap. But he was too heavy and stiff to get out of bed. He did this every night for a while but when he woke these wonderful therapists came, and they got him up and out of bed and they put him on the walker and he was a great aluminum spider again.

He came home and did laundry. That's what he began to do every evening for the next couple of weeks and it gave him a rhythm. At Columbia Presbyterian he'd slept in his own clothes the first night, pulling two chairs together and grabbing a pillow to lay over a chair arm and drop his head against in ICU. Perry had gone in for a cardio cath, a routine procedure. They'd wanted to make sure he had no blockages. There weren't any, was the outrage. Perry had a smaller, more minor stroke a few months before, and they'd just wanted to be sure. Once at a cocktail party, a doctor had said to Scott, swilling booze and laughing, saying it smugly, "Tests only breed more tests."

There was a certain calm among doctors, Scott observed. It seemed to be holding back a scream, a howl of impotence that masked a confession that would never happen, neither that nor the scream, because it was a calm edging funnily into a whimper that wouldn't resolve into truth, and the truth was that though they were scientists, which they certainly were, medically trained, a later element came into play which had to do with the unknowable. They were still exploring. It was a pattern, this constant exploring when Scott felt he knew what was wrong, Perry's diet. His steamrolling appetite, his need to get things *into* him, and the calm that came over him after that.

During recovery in the cath lab after the cardio catheterization procedure, Perry had been ecstatic that the chambers of his heart were clear, proud that the Lipitor had done its job keeping them from clogging. "There's nothing wrong," he'd tittered, and Scott had been relieved, too.

This guy is indestructible, he'd thought. Here we are, and we'll be going home soon.

"You haven't eaten anything since seven this morning," said Scott. "Aren't you hungry?"

Perry raised his brow expectantly as though suddenly realizing that, yes, he was hungry. He'd never forgotten hunger before, but here he was in bed, coming out of the logy drug haze.

Scott went to the cath lab team and asked for some food and said, "I'll feed him myself."

The cath lab had a row of prep/recovery cubicles on either side of a hallway, made more private by curtains you could whish around and snap shut. Most of them were occupied still, but gradually the outpatients in each were emptying out. They'd been there since noon and already it was six. A nurse said she'd bring Perry a sandwich and ginger ale, and Scott went back to Perry's cubicle and before long the food came and Scott tore off the wrappings and began feeding Perry.

And this was when it was obvious something had gone wrong with the routine procedure.

"*Hi* can hardly swallow," said Perry, and Scott got up, put down the food, and stepped out.

The leader of the team liked to joke, jovial, asinine: "What's wrong, Professor, tired?"

"Can't. Swallow."

"Stick out your tongue, Professor. Okay, good. Now follow my finger with your eyes? I need a light. Somebody? Now try to resist here where I push, Professor. And here? And here?"

A nurse came in with a penlight and it was flashed into each of Perry's eyes.

Scott said, "His pupils are huge."

"They're not so big. It's only the light in here. The eyes haven't had time to react."

And it was true, thought Scott, always the same dim, aquatic-dim light.

"It's the sedative. We see this all the time, patients coming out of the sedative."

Then Perry calmed down. No more food. But by then the cath lab had emptied out. The team excused themselves to go make notes or sit on their thumbs when they were supposed to be finding their doctor, who'd vanished after the procedure. There wasn't a real doctor around. The members of the lab team were off in a corner eating their takeout. Scott let his mind go blank.

Perry said, his eyes bugging for the first time, "Where—the—doctor?"

Scott held his hand, trying not to look worried, and said, "I don't know, sweetheart."

"*Hask*, please?"

Scott peeked out. Some of them were texting, doing their emails, finishing their takeout.

It was authority. Perry had been at Stonewall, helping smash parking meters, screaming at the police. Scott had grown up a Me, narcotized by junk food, game shows, sitcoms.

Perry began touching the leads on his chest linked to his vitals and said, "Let's ket houtta here—the—fuck—*hout*. I hwant—go—home. This, r'diculous—*less*—houtta here!"

Scott went back and said, "He wants to go and he will, I warn you. He's stubborn."

"He can't go until the doctor comes and first walks him. The doctor has to walk him."

"Well you better call the doctor to walk him, because I'm warning you, he'll just leave."

"Call the doctor."

"The doctor's still in a case. I just frigging called. It's a family matter, consultation . . ."

Scott checked his watch. After nine. He said, "I'm warning you, something's wrong."

Another member of the team came quickly and then calmly said, "Doctor's on his way."

Then it was another half hour. The doctor came in his suit, looking ready to head out to a fancy restaurant, a clothes horse, a popinjay, silk pocket hanky, his hair all aswirl with gel.

"How are you, Professor?"

Perry gasped out his words, smacking at them like globs of paste caught on his lips.

"Well, Professor, before you can go we have to walk you. Can't walk, can't go. So!"

Perry prowed his chin, looking desperately up, his eyes yellow-ishly boiled. The doctor blinked interestedly, a pomaded animal trying to comprehend the nature of his opposite beast.

The team was called to help Perry out of bed. A walker was rolled up to his bedside. He got upright with difficulty, gripped the handles, pushing the walker forward. Scott paced, halted.

"Good, Professor, good!" said the doctor, motioning his hands flamboyantly, and backing away with these conductor-like hand motions. "And a little more and a little more, please, yes?"

They got Perry clear of the cubicle with guidance and he began to push at the handles and walk, but he was weak and hunched. He veered woozily and the surgeon said, "Keep going."

Perry shrank under the command and stopped, panting. He hung his head, waiting.

"A man like this should be on a walker or at the very least a cane."

Scott said, "He hasn't needed one since two weeks after the first stroke. Not once."

"Look at him! A man like this has no business—"

"I'm telling you, he wasn't like this before he came in today."

"Call neurology!" The doctor tugged and straightened his wide lapels. "We need tests!"

The surgeon waited for the neurology resident who came in her white coat and took notes then moments later he excused himself to go home after a long day. He shook Perry's hand.

"Don't worry, you're in different hands now," and he vanished in his expensive suit.

"When was the first stroke?" said the resident, a very obese young woman. "And you say you could walk? Left side or right side? Stick out your tongue. Try to resist my hand. Resist?"

The neurology fellow came. He was handsome and blond, tall and difficult to age. The legs of his aqua-green scrubs were narrowly tailored, and when he smiled, Scott looked at Perry.

"He. Took too long. Coming. Why—did he take so long—coming?"

"How much time do we have?" said the fellow to the resident.

"From the first recorded symptoms of onset?" said the resident, checking her notes.

"That's right."

"That was three hours ago," said the resident, rechecking her notes. "So, another hour?"

"That's pushing it. Have you talked to them about the scan?"

"They're getting ready for him."

"We don't have much time, just under an hour." The fellow looked at his cell phone. "A scan in fifteen minutes, then put him on the floor. Do we have a bed for him?"

"We talked to the floor. They say they're ready for him. I'll call and ask about the scan."

"We're cutting it close but it should be just enough time. Mr. Knight, we're going to give you a scan then look at the results while you're on the floor resting, then decide about giving you the clot-buster injection. We call it the TPA, the clot-buster. You've had a stroke, most probably. I want you to know, I know who you are. I'm going to take care of you, I promise, Mr. Knight."

For whatever reason, at home now, drinking wine, Scott sat down at the dining table and made notes about what had happened next. Alone in the apartment, he got out a calendar. This was what writing was for nowadays—remembering, getting details down as exactly as possible, in case of lawsuit. The rehab facility was Shangri-la compared to that fucking Rube Goldberg cath lab days before, when and where the diagnostic and the cure had nearly killed his lover. It had almost been too late to get married. The first stroke, months ago, was nothing, two nights in the hospital and nothing. It was a tiny point of memory on a distant dark field next to this mess.

He felt guilty, Perry alone in rehab, sleeping next to his new roommate now—who knew how long a period of recovery Perry had ahead of him this time?

177

Scott recalled and wrote. He liked being alone in the apartment while he did it. He felt guilty, and feeling guilty made him angry, and feeling angry made him drink wine—wondering what Perry was thinking and feeling at that same moment. He remembered and wrote guiltily.

Perry was afraid for his life, but then he was used to this sensation. It came back to him every once in a while though each time it returned, its sting had a little less potency. Still, he was afraid of dying tonight—without any warning. After the first stroke, he'd wake up at four or five in the morning and go into Scott's room while Scott lay sleeping and ask Scott to get into bed with him.

He wanted to sleep but they wouldn't let him sleep. More tests and procedures, no sleep.

Time collapsed. Where was he now? At home, in his own bed? Home was better even if you were dying. And he might be. Dying. Better at home under familiar blankets, slipping. He didn't feel Scott in the next room. Institutionalized passing. He hadn't thought of that. He had a suspicion, he'd always had suspicions, but now he needed to trust. His roommate was Mr. Park.

Mr. Park—elevated, Perry imagined—barked up more phlegm.

Perry drew terrible comfort from knowing that Mr. Park's was a much worse case.

The injection was important. It was key because it could cut healing time. They were in stroke recovery now, the "floor," and the neurology fellow, Dr. Ryan, explained what could go wrong.

Dr. Ryan said, "In five percent of the cases roughly there may be significant bleeding. In one percent of the cases, given their vulnerability and histories, it could be fatal. Can you write? Your right side has been affected, so with this pen and paper could you give me your signature?"

Perry took the pen, novel device. Its tip wavered in the air and Dr. Ryan guided his hand toward the paper and Perry began to scribble, and Scott said, "It looks like ancient Phoenician."

Dr. Ryan said, "Give him the TPA."

An hour later Perry's gums began to bleed. The blood flowed freely and his lips turned a bright red. Dr. Ryan was called back and he nodded and said, "Yep, that's Joker mouth."

After a while the bleeding stopped, and Perry was still alive and still awake but groggy.

Another hour after that, he went to a bed in ICU, where Perry spent the next two nights.

ICU was a technocrat's dream, all emergency-ready equipment, soft lighting, and calm.

Scott wanted to sleep, but knew Perry was more desperate for sleep. The nurses cleaned Perry then dressed him in a cotton gown. They said, "We're waiting to send you for an MRI."

Scott stayed by him. He wanted to slip downstairs, light up, and enjoy a smoke.

Perry took Scott's hand, his speech temporarily better, and said, "I was so scared then."

"You came through."

"I know, but I was so scared."

"I understand. I'm here. Your voice is better. Your speaking's clearer, sweetheart."

Perry squeezed his hand, so tired. Everybody looked so tired, even the nurses and staff.

He pushed two chairs together and got a pillow and nested. They both fell asleep.

A nurse came in and said, "Mr. Knight? Mr. Knight, it's time for your MRI, honey."

Scott shook himself awake and straightened his body in the chair but was irrelevant.

The nurse was new and said to Scott, "And who are you? Could I ask you to step out?"

We were all of us waiting for the next thing, which might be the next worse, really bad thing. It might even be death. Scott hated concentrating on himself, but he remembered youthful worries about dying

179

from AIDS. His grandiose fantasies of doing himself in included jumping off a cliff in a beautiful Greek setting. Now he wouldn't die of AIDS, probably only a middle-age disease affecting his gastric system. He had a host of intestinal ailments that he'd inherited—big deal.

Perry was on the "floor," in step-down, the stroke unit. In his room were three others but he had a window bed. Out the glass, the magnificent silvery Hudson and the George Washington Bridge. Outside, spring was happening. The trees were green. It amazed him to know that three days had passed and he'd not smelled fresh air, but visually now he had fresh air and sunshine.

Across from him was an extremely old woman, withered and colorless. Her race was no longer distinguishable, though later her son, a tall and muscular black man, would drop in and he would stridently and holleringly address her: "I can't stay, Ma. I gotta get back to the family."

Perry could discern her reply, which was all throat-cracks and hisses.

She *was* family, thought Perry. But that was hours later. Time was weird here. Perry got into the rhythm of nurses' visits. Two nights in ICU, always on call as a patient hardly sleeping.

Scott came in as the breakfast was delivered. It was yogurt, toast, and nectar-grade juice. Because of his swallowing he couldn't take straight liquids. Everything was thick, nectar-grade. Scott opened the milk carton and the plastic-wrapped plastic silverware and arranged things for Perry. Across the way, the old woman asked her male nurse of Perry, "Can't he feed himself?"

"What's that, ma'am?"

"Can't that man feed himself? He ain't old, can't he feed himself?"

"I don't know his case, but maybe he can't. He's not my client, ma'am. Now, here . . ."

Already Perry looked better. He'd slept. His face seemed less putty-colored.

This is exhausting already, Scott thought. He wanted to go home and relax. Relaxing for him meant going home and before he got into the apartment, buying a liter and a half of wine. It was a citrus-flavored pinot grigio. He would drink the whole thing before bed. He knew he had a problem but for now it was a comfortable problem, no stumbling mostly. Just going easily off to bed after finishing the bottle. And cigarettes. The neurologist said that atherosclerosis was the main problem in Perry's case. For thirty years Perry had smoked three or four packs a day but he wouldn't ride Scott's ass about it. He tolerated it gracefully, the way he tolerated hospital care.

Before, Scott drank red wine but then needed something more like soda pop. His system, his gastrointestinal track, couldn't take red; the tannins, he supposed. The summer before he had gone in for tests and it seemed clear that he needed to lighten up, slow down. He had his father's reflux and diverticulitis, a hiatal hernia, and a spastic colon to boot. Scott had earned all that.

A bit more himself than before, Perry said, "And how are you, babycakes?"

Scott stirred Perry's applesauce and said tightly, "I'm fine, just worried about you."

In the bed next to the old woman was a young man, and who knew why he was here? He was big, a Latino who should not be in any stroke unit. In the late afternoon, he got someone on his cell phone. And when the person on the other end answered, he said, "Yo, what's up, dawg?"

Scott stood over Perry's bed. Perry was sneezing chunkily and violently, and Scott waited to hand him a bunch of tissues from Perry's miniature box, transfixed by the pretty young man.

"I was at home, dig, and I'm watching March Madness, dig? And I get this headache, it's like a nuclear-ass bomb going off in me and I'm like, what the hell? For the second time, there's that swelling in my brain. My mom calls the ambulance, so here I am—it's unreal, dawg, dig?"

Scott was distracted by the kid's youth, while thinking of himself at the age of forty-six.

"But I was just thinking about you and your family, your beautiful family, with your wife and beautiful children, and I was like, that's a beautiful thing when we were out at your party on your property, it was nice. It was nice, man. And she turns to me, Sheila, and says 'So wassup?' I was just like so resentful, like what's her right? What right's *she* got? So I was like, 'I'm young, I'm single, I'm hitting the shorties, and that's what's up . . .'" There was a headachy pause.

Scott looked at Perry and reached down to smooth the top of his arm. They were both so bored, waiting. Healing was waiting. Dr. Popinjay, the invasive cardiologist, pulled the edge of the curtain and sang, "Hello! Hello there! May I come in?" and Perry writhed on the bed.

The doctor didn't wait for an invitation but stepped around the curtain, leering brightly.

"How are you feeling? I'm not disturbing the professor? What happened to your hair?"

Scott said, "Well, he's been in the hospital for three nights and he hasn't *shampooed.*"

"Right. I've been going over your MRI and CT scans. When you've had a first, then the second is almost inevitable. You must get used to this idea of another occurring. It was inevitable, and so you must not think darkly of me. We did what we could. We were right to go in, and so it was a good thing, however unfortunate. It was a procedure they ordered—I cannot be liable!"

Pretty soon he'd retreated.

Just before Perry was taken down to the ambulette to be transferred to the rehab facility, the neurology fellow had come in to see him. He looked like a smart chevalier in his surgery-liveried tailored scrubs. He sat on the edge of the bed and took Perry's hand, and Scott watched as the two of them smiled at each other. Dr. Ryan handed Perry a copy of one of Perry's books.

He said, "I was wondering if I could ask you for your signature one more time."

Mr. Park had a crisis in the middle of the night. The machine monitoring his vitals went crazy and the nurse followed by other members of the team came in to check on then discreetly remove him. An hour later Claudette, the sassy nurse, came in saying, "And how are you, Mr. Knight?"

"I couldn't sleep."

"Mr. Park, he ain't coming back, so. Blood pressure, everything, no way. He's in ICU."

"Where I started," said Perry, chuckling through a dry cough. "Where I started, see."

"You're different now, you ain't going back! You want a second sleeping pill, darling?"

"Please."

"You're a big boy, you're my big boy. I know you can handle it. I'll be right back."

He kept thinking of Mr. Park's barking. Here was a man barely seventy, a tae kwon do master with his ninth belt since he was thirty, his daughter Olivia had said. He had run into bad luck when a spur growing from his spine into the spinal cord became dangerous and so he'd had a neck fusion, which caused a massive heart attack. Because he'd just had the fusion he couldn't take the blood thinners necessary for heart surgery. While he was waiting to heal he had another heart attack, this one a massive coronary, and while they were preparing him for surgery, a stroke.

Just like that, with Perry thinking he might slowly be on the mend, Mr. Park was gone.

Some got the shittiest breaks, but the shittiest break was just around the corner for us all.

Perry had gotten used to the daily rhythm. He pitied Mr. Park, and that felt therapeutic.

Poor Mr. Park. He'd only been around a few days, Perry thought. The daughter Olivia would come in bowing at the edge of the bed saying, "Father?" She would stay the entire day.

Time was sloshy. Mr. Park was gone now, but then he wasn't. Perry had him, just here.

Olivia was always there, taking care of her father. Her mother ran a bank and couldn't be there around the clock, although tonight Olivia had left earlier than usual, because her marketing job, which had given her a three-week leave of absence, needed her back. Olivia's brother, Perry thought, was useless. He would come sailing in around six or seven and tolerate the situation for an hour then yawn and apologize and leave. Once, though, he'd brought in several of Mr. Park's tae kwon do students, forming a queue. One by one the young men, lithe most of them, stepped up to the foot of Mr. Park's bed and bowed, eyes closed, as though praying, and Perry had wept.

The next morning Olivia came in to get the rest of her father's things. Perry drowsed but looked up just as she was leaving, head lowered, with the duffel bag. He said, "Is he all right?"

"My father is strong. But he doesn't want to live. He doesn't see the point. Plus here, he was always cold. He complained about the air conditioning. It was too cold for him, too drafty."

"Tell him good luck," said Perry. "I'll be thinking of him. Good luck to all of you."

"He'll like that. Bye-bye. Be strong. But hey, you look very good, really strong!"

"Thank you, but maybe I'm just lucky," Perry said and thought his voice was stronger.

"Maybe. Great wishes."

But then when she was gone he worried about having said that. Did that mean he said he thought her father wasn't so lucky? Which he wasn't, just look at Mr. Park. The hours unwound here slowly. Perry was getting used to the new pace. He rather liked it, and with the room all to himself he thought with the second sleeping pill he might get some rest, not thinking about sex at all. He'd gone two or three days not preoccupied by going online to find a younger usually Latin partner in search of a daddy. He didn't need to hear "Papí" during the throes of passion. Passion actually wasn't so important now. His body had failed him, and in turn he may have failed it. He wasn't being spiritual but practical. Without your body fully functioning how could you think of the sanctity of the orgasm? How many men, how many frittered afternoons? Not a concern now. For the first time in his life since infancy, he was rocked in an insurance-sponsored cradle of care and he was special. His life was dear and he hadn't felt that in a while. Oh sure, his work; it was something. He liked what he wrote all right. At least it was honest. It was about sex largely, and most writers shied from the subject. He felt special, that he was blessed to have the

Seventh-day Adventist nurses. He'd achieved something but was resting now: for full details go to Facebook.

Scott wrote on his Facebook page to concerned friends and readers: "Perry has good days and bad days but gradually, thanks to this incredible facility, he seems to be getting better. You'll understand if you don't hear from us in a while. Thank you, everyone, for your well wishes."

Well wishes. The cornier the better. The oldest sentiments were the truest, Perry saw. He had spent half his life seeking the mot juste, but all lives boiled down to the same in the end.

He could now put his laptop on his tray table and slide it toward him and read his emails.

People came by, concerned. There was no shortage of late-afternoon visitors—but who'd come exactly? It was hard to recall. Next time Scott came, he'd ask. But he'd felt them, surely.

Scott was equally moved by their expressions of love, their outpourings of sympathy: and Perry was probably going to die eventually, if not sooner, they thought. You could read it in their suddenly stricken facial expressions (meant to look inspiring, or else spiritually potent), or hear it in their tone of voice. "Just be sure to take care of yourself," they inevitably told Scott, then they patted his shoulder with a wan, frightened, droopy smile. "Will you do that for me, take care?"

Some friends came and visited, an older couple. The man was a neuroscientist with this pooty, lisping way of talking—like Sylvester the Cat's. He said, "Studies show"—unhappily he used a lot of *s*'s in his speech—"that stroke patients recover more strongly and rapidly next to a window. A view of the outside world—that's the important thing, these studies showed."

The wife said, "And also if they have a great, loving partner to be with them, like Scott."

The scientist shook his head with certitude: "No, just the window. That's all it said."

Later Scott got an email from the wife saying, "I think you two should get married sooner rather than later. Perry looks great! His voice is so strong! Do be sure to take care of yourself."

Two days after Mr. Park had vacated the space, Perry asked if he could move over next to the window. It was nothing. They unplugged his call console and wheeled him and his monitors across the room. There was the Empire State, that big beacon of old to Metropolis, to Gotham.

Every couple of days a neuropsychologist came in to discuss Perry's mental state.

"So tell me what you're going through, Perry, what are your thoughts and feelings?"

He liked the nurses to fuss over him addressing him informally as Perry. The shrink had a soft, friendly, "trustful" look, and he wore a clinical white coat even though he had no medical credentials. He was a shrink, and in his life of coming out trying to defeat midcentury Freudian ideas Perry had learned to despise trendy notions of mental health. Plus this shrink was touchy-feely, and Perry thought probably a big Buddhist, another road Perry had traveled without much success. He'd authored a text called *Many Ways, One Direction*. He sat at the end of the bed in a "casual," "observing" position. To be called Perry by this man was condescending, since Perry had written with difficulty twenty-five books, each of which had to be miles beyond *Many Ways, One Direction*. Perry thought the shrink was smirking "wisely" as he discussed his fear of losing touch with his old, adventurous sexual side. And maybe for the shrink, everything he heard from all of his broadly differing clients boiled down to the same delusional goo, jellified corpse-gunk.

"What are your fears? Your hopes? What things do you find yourself hanging onto?"

The shrink was referring to attachments, that Buddhist bugbear. Attachments only hung you up and left you clinging to the illusion of this life—a delusion so very few would let go of.

Perry, exhausted but recovering, learning things or just not giving a damn, went with it. He said, "I'm afraid of dying and leaving Scott. I'm afraid he'll survive me; he'll find someone else to be happy with and forget about me. I'm not, actually. I really want Scott to be happy."

The shrink fretted warmly, opening his mouth and preparing to ask a tender question.

"And what do you think Scott thinks? Have you discussed these fears with Scott?"

"He cares about me. He's human, he'll move on if he has to. Oh, why not just ask *him*?"

"Because you're afraid, unsure, to ask him yourself?"

"Because I'm tired and trying to heal and I don't want to think about it. To be honest."

The shrink inclined his head empathetically, blinking on. Oh, he desired to understand!

"That's perfectly valid. Let's talk about the things you miss while you're here, what else you're afraid of losing." The soft-faced, watery-haired man paused. "What are you tiredest of?"

"Tiredest" sounded purely out of Salinger, something a Glass family member would say.

"I get tired of typing or writing or reading," said Perry, "and I'm afraid I'll lose touch, but I kind of enjoy letting go at the same time. Lying here talking, I'm afraid of dying of boredom."

The shrink laughed gently, reminding Perry a little of the Dalai Lama—and before he left said that his book, *Many Ways, One Direction*, was also available as a series of video lectures, in case Perry would like him to order the set of DVDs for him, then charge it to Perry's insurance.

They joked that for that entire halcyon week, with no midnight interruptions of violent phlegm-barking from Mr. Park, it was rather like a country club here *except* for the food. Scott thought it smelled awful but was grateful to Perry for not complaining about it, which anyway he didn't eat much of. He seemed to be losing weight, the old goal. Looking up Second Avenue, Perry had a view of the shimmering Chrysler Building, all lit up and bejeweled at night. Perry's shrink from the post-Stonewall days chewed sunflower seeds and said with Borscht Belt timing that this part of Manhattan was informally called

Bed Pan Alley for all its hospitals and medical facilities. He had pointy incisors to crack the seeds and said languidly, "So what's up, toots? Tell me . . ."

They had Perry on Prozac and Provigil, a mood elevator. A week ago Perry had teared up and said to Scott, after arriving from his morning PT, "I walked thirteen steps on a walker today," then bit the heel of his hand and got hot in the face and felt all embarrassed, which would *not* do.

Now, with the Provigil, he said that he felt—at most moments—as high as a penthouse.

Then one day around noon Scott entered amid a crowd of bustling hospital workers. He'd been up late the night before drinking white wine, feeling the situation had turned a positive corner.

Now in Perry's old end of the room, a new man was being craned into bed by a Hoyer Lift. Scott entered just as the man was hanging, his legs drooping like raw drumsticks, in a cloth sling before, at the push of a button, he was articulated over to the bed then lowered into place looking clueless and exhausted. The sling was unhooked from the Hoyer Lift, then he was rolled onto his side and the sling was pulled out from under him—and he was rolled the other way and the sling was removed. One of the attendants worked the buttons on the side of the bed to get him upright, but the patient's glassy expression never changed. His limbs were repositioned like a cadaver's.

"How's that? Better?" said the nurse, observing and doing her part. "Better, Andy?"

Andy made a nasal grunt then mumbled the sentence the grunt had pushed into being, but it was hard to know what he was saying. He was tall with wide shoulders and with the flesh hanging slack on his cheek he looked as though until recently he'd been rather hefty. He was wearing a crash helmet and in the horseshoe-shaped opening for his face the expression was glazed like a Halloween cookie's. His mouth curved up in one corner, all four of his limbs shaking. His long, pinnate feet pushed into their no-skid hospital socks waggled like nervous windshield wipers and his hands were bound in plush padded white mittens so he couldn't tear the trach from his throat.

"What?" said the built-out male attendant, who leaned down to hear. "Whassat?"

"What, Andy?" said the nurse, and she leaned down as his sandy throat sifted sounds.

"Can't do, that, buddy," said the attendant with his gorilla-jock build. "Can't take it out."

"Andy, you need that in," the nurse explained. "Remember how you couldn't breathe?"

The second attendant stood in the doorframe, and Scott took his seat across from Perry.

Scott made a pitying face. Perry scrambled his eyes, not even making an effort to sound discreet when he said, his voice stronger than yesterday, "He's a pain in the ass—big baby."

To Scott's right, the quivering Andy with jerking limbs still looked surprised to be here.

Scott frowned at Perry but noticed that at least Perry was in bitchier, more fighting form.

"He's a tennis pro. I don't think I know what that means? Hit a tree and had a stroke."

Then Perry was sitting higher up in bed, alternately brightly grinning and then not: "Hi!"

A little more himself: around the apartment Perry would say "Hi!" several times a day.

"As opposed to a professional tennis player," said Scott, remembering being a teenager in Florida hoping against hope—he was too old already at thirteen to be seeded—to become Jimmy Connors or Björn Borg. "A tennis pro is basically somebody at a club who corrects your stroke."

Perry's eyes lit up and he said, "Today I did deep squats and went up and down stairs!"

"That's marvelous, sweetheart," said Scott, nearly choking the words, eyes wet and hot.

"Isn't that great?" said Perry, and he couldn't quit fucking with his bed's back elevation.

"You'll be back to normal in no time," said Scott, smiling beatifically. "It is great."

On the other side of the room the attendants were clearing out, removing the Hoyer Lift, backing out, and nodding. The nurse—one Scott had never seen before, at least he didn't think he had—said, "Now let me just get your helmet off, Mr. Andy. Somebody's here to see you."

Scott told Perry, "Lots of people have called the home phone concerned, like Francine."

"What did she say?"

"Apparently she hadn't heard. She wanted to confirm for dinner on Thursday, so I called her back and thank God she wasn't there. I left a quick exhaustive summary explaining. We had about seven bills I wrote checks for and forged your signature on. Nothing out of the ordinary."

The food people came and Scott got up and wrestled with the tray stand with its extension that was supposed to pop out at the mashing of a lever, but it always got stuck. Scott couldn't fit everything on the stand without releasing and rolling out the extension. Books, Perry's Mac, his boom box, earphones, plastic cups, the water pitcher—all kinds of cluttery shit, just like at home.

Andy called out from his side of the room: "Sir?"

Scott paused. The extension wouldn't fucking release. He turned and said, "Me?"

Yes, he must have been feeling better about Perry's situation— indulging in irritability.

"Sir?"

"Me?" Scott collected himself. "Is there something you need?" he said on a down beat.

The nurse had vanished. She'd removed Andy's helmet and he doddered his mitts in the air. He stared at the wall and said, "Just need you to do me a favor. Just one favor, don't mind?"

"And what's that?" Scott said, putting his hand on his hip and narrowing his eyes expectantly.

"I need you to go out to the bar. There's a guy, named Matthew. I need you to tell him to come help me get this guy off me. He's on me—big asshole. I'm going to kick his jerk-face in."

In came a young man who wasn't the other nurse, Matthew, but someone in street clothes carrying a bouquet of white roses. Scott sat down again and Perry shook his head unpityingly.

"Andy? It's Bobby. Remember me, Bobby? Yeah, I thought you did. You look freaking great, man. Awesome. How're you feeling, Andy? *Bobby.* It's *Bobby.* I'm psyched to see you, you know why? It's already been two weeks. And you know what? *World of difference . . ."*

Perry rolled his eyes at Scott. He looked better, Scott noticed, but was spending energy unnecessarily expressing the irritability factor. Relax, Scott telepathed, but Bobby was so loud.

"World of difference, between here and Stony Brook? *Awwe-some.* What's that? I can't do that, sweetie, okay? I don't think they'd be too happy if I took these mitts awffa-you."

Andy whimpered, gathering his anger and muttering to Bobby about his imaginary brute.

"I'll go ask, dude. I'll go ask Matthew. You say his name is Matthew. What? You want me to do it instead? Okay, *get awffa him, get awffa him now!* Done! You need anything, Andy? Anything from the outside world? Blondies? Blondies from the Golden Pear? Done. Done!"

Scott said to Perry, "How's the food?"

"It's all right," said Perry, eating methodically and not without some relish, "not shitty."

Lunch was tuna salad, mashed peas, whole-grain roll, and fruit cup. Perry ate it, and Scott was glad though he wondered if Perry wasn't just being brave. He could do that in a pinch. His courage could be unstoppable and clobber away at Scott's heart and even shame him. Everyone was so nice here, too. It was heartbreaking, it seemed so effortless as long as you had insurance.

Perry said, "I was talking to the physical and occupational therapists today, who said I'm doing a wonderful job, and they said I might not have to take the four weeks but could go home after three. I got a note from a fan today who's doing my bibliography. And he's offering to transcribe my Paris memoir. And I told him how much better, especially with the encouragement I get from you, I'm doing, and he said, 'Scott must be a really great guy.' I wrote back, 'Without Scott, nothing!' And I meant it, too. I cried. Sweetie, I wrote three pages today!"

Scott was not going whole-hog with the sentimental today. If Perry was coming home so soon, rather than on the originally projected date, he was not getting the cushy, sugary treatment.

"And didn't get tired?" he said.

"Tired, a little. But I'm really starting to get restless."

Then Perry quietly grinned at Scott. The curtain was drawn. The Long Islander prattled.

"But Andy, you know what? The stock's doing beautifully. And you know what's flying awff the shelves? You were right—it's the Vapor Sneakers." He said it *Vapah Sneakahs*. "They cannot stay on the shelves, I swear to God! My friend Georgie, you remember Georgie?—by the way, everyone says to tell you hello—Georgie came in and bought two pair. What, sweetie? No, I can't do that, they'll kick me out. *Get awffa him!* Done! But seriously, Andy, sales are *boffo*."

After Andy had been assured of sales in the pro shop, Bobby left. Scott could see around the curtain as Bobby got up—he was an attractive, youngish man—and leaned over the helpless-looking patient, who wheezed and prattled against the exhaustion and no doubt the drug doses.

"You want what, sweetheart?" Bobby lowered his ear to Andy's lips. "You want what?"

Andy's eyes gazed moribundly. With the helmet off, a deep dent that extended from his right forehead nearly back to his shaved crown shined with scar tissue as white as a fish's belly. Andy clutched a plush bunny that Bobby pulled from his grip and repositioned between the right side of Andy's head and the bed railing. Bobby kissed the un-dented side of Andy's shaved head.

That night, Andy startled Perry awake, calling, "Sir, where's Zach? Have you seen Zach, my boyfriend? Do you know if he came and went already? I miss Zach. He's my boyfriend."

"I haven't seen him, Andy."

"Sir, can I ask you a question? I have this boyfriend Zach. He was supposed to come see me, but I fell asleep. Did a guy named Zach come while I was asleep? Did he leave already?"

"I haven't seen him, Andy. No one's been in here but the nurses, okay? Try to sleep."

"But if you see Zach, tell him to wake me up, okay? Make sure he wakes me up?"

"If Zach comes, I promise I will not let him leave without first waking you up."

"I miss him. Do you think he'll come?"

"It's already late. It's four in the morning."

"Means the bar's closed. Fuck! Sir?"

"Good night, Andy. Good night. Good night."

Before Scott had left that evening, Andy had asked his friend Bobby for a Cap 'n' Coke.

"Can't do it, sweetie, but you know what? Amber and Ray and all those guys in the shop and club and around the courts, they all said to wish you the best, and tell you they're rooting for you. So you see, everybody's rooting for you, sweetie—and I think that's awesome, don't you?"

After Bobby was gone, Matthew the nurse came in and said, "So you're a tennis pro?"

"Fuck that," said Andy, his pronunciation coming and going. "Doesn't mean shit."

"Do you know how you got here, Andy?"

Andy waited. He smacked his lips, breathing hard as though his chest were collapsing.

"Hi had-huh car-haccident, hand-huh stroke. Hi-had three stroke—hin—three-hweek!"

The next day when Scott returned, Andy had just been hauled off for his swallowing test.

"I couldn't sleep," said Perry, keeping his voice low. "All night, he wouldn't shut up."

Scott wondered if Perry was refusing to modulate his voice or if it was another symptom.

"Should I be whispering?" said Scott. "I mean, should we be holding our voices down?"

"Is she out there?"

Scott looked into the hallway, and there was a woman he'd passed coming in. She was sitting in one of the wheelchairs they kept lined up near the elevator until they needed one. She looked fashionably soignée, on a course of Zumba or something. She had a bright, steady smile.

"That's his best friend."

Scott said, "So he's gay, like I said."

"But he has a daughter, I think, with some kind of weird name."

"*Coach*. That's his dog. He was asking Bobby to go check in on it. Well, we all say it too much, and it must mean less and less to you each time we say it—but you look great."

"I just hope you're taking care of yourself, getting enough sleep and eating enough."

"This is a vacation for me compared to the first time," said Scott. "It's not a country club for you, I know, but you're getting full service. I don't have to worry, just leave and go home."

"I did deep squats today, and some stairs with a cane. I walked a yard without a walker."

"You're kidding! And did they at least hold your hand?"

"They were on either side of me ready to catch me the instant I might start to fall."

The nurse whose name he couldn't remember came in and said, "You see how he looks?"

"I sure do," said Scott, always more cheerful here than at home. "Are you Molly?"

"No, that's my friend. You're confusing me with my girl Molly. Now Molly's my girl."

"And what island are *you* from?" he said, wondering if this sounded racist. "Aruba?"

"That's Molly," she said, staring theatrically away. "No way, I'm from T and T."

"Trinidad and Tobago. That's where they make the famous bitters, Angostura."

"You know that?" she said, readying the wheelchair for Perry. "That's exactly right."

She took Perry off for forty-five minutes of occupational therapy, and the woman who had been sitting in the hall saw Scott, got up, and came in with a tired smile and one raised eyebrow.

"You taking care of yourself?" she said. "It's important, it's what we have to do."

He didn't bother to get up. In fact, he couldn't sleep, so he sat up every night listening to Joni Mitchell and Al Stewart. He'd just started playing Seals & Crofts' *Greatest Hits* and he was nostalgic and weepy, but Perry was losing his weepiness. Some of those songs transported Scott.

"Hello," he said, already too friendly and too familiar—and she moved kittenishly farther into the room. For no reason, he winked at her. It was like he was flirting. He got so sweet here.

She said, "Perry's doing well, isn't he? Is he naturally hale?"

Scott wondered if "hale" wasn't a euphemism for what used to be called portly.

"He's amazingly strong, always has been. But how's Andy doing? Is he getting better?"

"Hard to say." She had her hands on her hips as though gearing up for a whole run-down.

"Have a seat," he said. "I'm sorry, what's your name?"

"I'm Marsha," she said—as though he must have heard already of this famous Marsha.

"I'm Scott, nice to meet you. *Marsha?*"

He pointed at her, as though they were at a class reunion, sending out gossamer signals.

"When do you two plan to tie the knot?" she said. "You guys planning a big one? I plan weddings. I'll be planning my daughter's, I'm sure. The thing is, simple invitations is what I've learned, simple Crane's plain cream stationery, nothing too cutesy-pie or cutting-edge or fancy."

"We haven't talked about it. He needs to get well. But what about Andy? Will he—?"

"You're asking the wrong person," she said, slumping into a chair on Andy's side of the room. "Four weeks ago, I said good-bye to my best friend. I knelt at the side of my friend's bed to tell him I loved him, to say good-bye to him." She shrugged one shoulder pad. "And now?"

"Amazing," said Scott. "Yesterday I noticed Andy's voice kept—wavering—good, bad."

"It's up and down, it's up and down. But I tell you, when he was at Stony Brook . . ."

"Where his dog Coach is now, right?"

"When he was at Stony Brook—night and day between here and there. I did not see how Andy could—well, if you'd just seen him. A piece of his skull's in a hospital basement freezer."

"In a freezer."

"Just the one part. It was a hemorrhagic stroke," she said quite insouciantly, with a touch of sparkle in her eyes. "You can't have pressure on your brain. Happens all the time, apparently. If they take a smaller piece, you know where they put it? In your abdomen, so it stays with you."

Perry's stroke hadn't been hemorrhagic, which is why they could give him the clot-buster and not have him bleed to death in his brain. Scott had already stopped writing it all down. He'd stopped being angry. Perry was getting better—the only important thing now. Perry would live.

Scott thought, I've never been less happy or hopeful, and I've never been calmer.

As a kid in Sunday school, Scott had had a favorite Bible verse that went something like, "When you pray, do not be ostentatious and pray so that others may see you praying, but go into your closet and pray by yourself," although he didn't know why he should recall this suddenly.

Perry didn't have afternoon therapies and Scott came in early. Marsha was already there with Andy. She sat on the other side of Andy's bed by the wall—comfy, as though she'd just enjoyed several peaceful hours of needlepoint. Andy and the plush bunny stared at the bathroom door.

"Get you some sleep, Scottie?" she said, stretching deliciously.

He knew he looked awful. He hadn't trimmed his beard since things had started up at the other hospital. He knew he needed to make more of an effort, but morally he was slumping. He was waiting, not so much in terror as in a state of loathing, slumming, vacationing even, before a predicted storm, a clear and present meteorological and inevitable danger, wiping them all away. Oh yes, he'd finished a bottle of the pinot the night before, and smoked a whole pack, dumbass.

"That's a face that hasn't slept," Marsha said as Scott glided by stupidly. "Am I right?"

Then she went back to cooing at Andy—telling him she'd like to cook him some lentils.

"Intolerable," Perry hissed as Scott came around the curtain. "'Nurse, nurse!' Big baby."

"They're right there, honey."

"You know what I miss?" said Perry. He was ready to check out, restless. "Bread. Oh, I get bread here, but the good bread, the deli across the street from Balthazar's? Yum-yum."

"Bread, and more bread, is part of what got us here, darling."

"Oh, I know."

The oppressiveness of the hospital atmosphere came home to them both. They were in a hospital, an institution that said you were either gravely ill, vulnerable, or dying. When Scott was in his twenties and had little infections, he thought he had AIDS, although he hadn't done enough to get infected, he'd hardly fucked around at all, and this in a small college town. No matter how much sex you'd had you were supposed to be leery. Later it turned out according to others you'd been scared into thinking you were vulnerable, you were a saint, acting out your natural instincts, and shouldn't people be worshipping you? Porn sometimes depicted pretty young men as angels with actual snowy-feathered wings. From gothic perches beside gargoyles the angels looked into the camera poetically, then turned to look out over the ancient city full of hidden possibilities.

My mother, he thought, used to say, "Never be ashamed of your body. Nude is natural."

She was coming out of the shower toweling off, and then she began powdering her pubes.

Perry pressed his call button and said into the handheld console's mic, "I have to go to the bathroom. I need to poop," and Scott got up and made maneuvers clearing the path of hurdles.

"Yes, Mr. Knight. Hold it a little, be right there."

"I can't, I swear I'll shit," said Perry, then to Scott: "It's all these fucking meds."

In came the team. Scott removed himself, not wanting to shame Perry or smell his shit.

In the hall Marsha said, "Have you met Andy's mom? This is Madame Sullivan."

Scott shook the hand of Andy's mom, a small woman who he now knew was French.

"Oh, hello! You are?"

"Hi, I'm Perry Knight's, the other guy's, partner. Actually his fiancé."

"I'm André's mom. Hi. He is doing well, no, Monsieur Knight?"

"Yes, I think he is. But what about your son?"

"We wait. It's all we can do. When the Lord decides, this is when we know."

"But you're from France?"

"I'm from Bordeaux, yes! I am lost—my son André—without André, I am lost."

Scott thought, Jesus fucked his mother in the ass. Andy's mom is French!

Her son had been working too hard, paying too much attention to his businesses and not enough to his health. He now had three pro shops but in the course of minding his finances had neglected his health. He'd stopped taking his hypertension medications. He had three pro shops but no coverage, which made Scott feel lucky to have coverage through Perry. He didn't feel the sweet pangs of schadenfreude, only fear—not for others, but for himself and his own, far future.

Scott said, "I like Marsha. She seems so devoted, so—"

"Marsha is *merveilleuse*, very marvelous. But I've known her all this time, Marsha."

"And she seems to have a special connection with Andy, which I find very touching."

Whenever he spoke to French people in English he began over-using the intensifier *very*.

She was small and had enormous glasses. Unlike the French Scott had known when he'd lived with Perry in Paris, Madame Sullivan wanted to talk about her personal life, and money.

She said, "No, Marsha I love. But you know, she's very, very wellzy."

"She went to Wellesley?"

"No, she lives on Park Avenue! She has a lot of money, a house out in the Hamptons!"

Scott was ashamed of himself. He'd thought unkind, ungenerous thoughts about Marsha, although actually in the end he'd enjoyed talking to Marsha. Marsha was selfless, a true martyr.

Now he said, "Not to mention, Marsha's here every day."

"Listen, I live in Connecticut. It's not easy getting here with the trains."

She seemed very nice but a little confused about Connecticut's proximity to New York.

He'd been living on the edge so long, he understood when others seemed to be living on their own version of the edge. It was time for him to go. They went back to the room together.

Marsha told Madame Sullivan, "You have to go to Grand Central. It's a simple cab ride."

Scott said, "I'm going out now, too. I'll take her and direct her."

"See? A handsome young escort," said Marsha. "Who could ask for more?"

Scott leaned over Perry's bed and said, "I'll be back in the morning. Okay if I go now?"

"Go," said Perry. He looked comfortable. It was hard to know if he felt lonely.

Scott felt lonely, but the city was beautiful. So much work was being done on New York that it couldn't help being beautiful, continuous rows of greenery. They'd had so much rain, the plants and trees in the parks and along the streets were green and fecund. It was hard to feel bad about life with all this outrageous fecundity. He'd never imagined while watching Woody Allen films as a kid that Manhattan could be such a garden. He liked living here suddenly, after years of resenting its expensiveness and snobbery just as Perry was talking about retiring to a cheaper state like Texas or Florida, but Scott had this pimple under his left nipple that wouldn't go away. He tried not to let Perry see him scratching but it was a warm spring and he'd reach up under his shirt and slick his hand around the sweaty tit-area and feel the bump's itchy persistent hardness.

He made an appointment. Seeing a professional was hard for him. He saw the insurance policy he got through Perry as ballast for Perry's own health problems. Perry was HIV-positive and his complications were not as serious as for other AIDS sufferers, but there were the odd little things, the appointments you had to make at the periodontist, dermatologist, cardiologist, to keep him afloat. You never knew in this age of corner-cutting medicine when you would be told, "We are sorry but we don't see the need for this so you owe us thousands of dollars." And in no other country in the world! Still Scott defended America to angry liberal New Yorkers who laughed at the backward place he'd come from, redneck and racist northern Florida. They were partly right.

As a child he'd been told by both his parents, "You better not get any cavities. I better not hear you need any fillings. You better brush those teeth and floss them and keep them clean."

A cavity would be like a hole in his soul, a dark mark on his white angelic teeth; he'd had a nice set of white teeth people complimented, until he got the braces off—nine fucking cavities.

The dermatologist's was in Chelsea. He'd chosen it from the insurance list to be close so he could go directly from there to the rehab unit to see Perry. He felt guilty about taking the time away from Perry, but Perry encouraged him to go: "You need to get that taken care of, darling."

Perry was never afraid of going to the doctor, throwing off his youthful Christian Science.

The office was what he supposed New Yorkers would feel more comfortable referring to as a "space." It was new and clean and lit like a museum version of a tiki hut, with lots of plants in earthy planters, their soil covered in smooth stones. There was no drywall, only walls of glass with vertical blinds that could be drawn for privacy. He filled out the usual form. He sat there in a stew of thoughts. It was a rare disorder, maybe. He heard a song from the eighties he'd liked.

The doctor was a tiny Central American whose otherwise bald head, with its high healthy pinkish color, boasted a resplendent horseshoe of thick and curly dark hair he kept immaculately and expensively sculpted to the nape and around the ears. He was friendly and said, "Now, Mr. Mason, yes Mr. Scott Mason, I see you have melanoma in the family. Something to stay on top of, obviously. Something to check every year," he went on, nodding at the file. "So tell me . . ."

He had a Queens or a Brooklyn accent, incurious Scott had never learned to distinguish a difference, had never taken the time. Worse, Scott was smiling in amusement and said, "Yes?"

"Tell me why you're here? What're we doing today? Appointment for dermabrasion?"

"I'm fine," said Scott, "except I'm under a lot of stress, which might be why I'm here."

"I'm sorry to hear that. The skin can be a powerful presentation of all kinds of stress."

"That's what I was thinking, exactly. I have this pimple-thing near my left nipple."

"Let's see it. Uh-huh. Yeah. That's nothing to worry about actually. Take off the shirt?"

"Sure."

"When was your last full-body exam?"

"Well, it would have to be two years ago when I had a mole removed from my back."

"And I see you've had others removed in the past. There, *there*. Lots of moles cut off."

"We sort of went into high gear in my family after my dad had his melanoma."

"He made a full recovery?"

The doctor was touching him delicately, palpating but not humming like Santayana—the Argentinian who'd treated him and his father back in Florida when Scott was a teen. There was no plastic surgery at the time mentioned. The moles on Scott's back had been a Big Dipper and Santayana had connected the dots with scars describing the scoops and scalpel lines and stitches. Years to heal over, and he'd consumed vitamin E until they'd faded, the beginning of his faddish relationship with nutritional supplements to which he still clung. Nothing was ever malignant in Scott, but his father's melanomas were a close call, though he was fine until they'd found cancer in his right middle lung lobe and sucked that out in a quick surgery. He'd gone in for a "routine" CT scan for his heart, because of difficulty breathing, and a technician had spotted the capsulized malignancy. Scott had seen his once great-seeming dad dwindled and yellowish and swaddled in his hospital bed, looking not unlike a jaundiced infant, excess chest fluid draining into a bucket.

Scott replied, "We're always on alert. Over the years—"

"Now this," said the doctor, touching the top of his left shoulder, "this is worrying. When was your last full-body exam, two years ago? Did you notice this before? So how long ago?"

"A few months ago," said Scott, remembering the moment in the bathroom. "I never take off my shirt except when I shower, because I'm so vain. I haven't exposed my chest in years."

"You're hilarious," said the doctor. "*Crack me up*. Lie back? Let's see what else . . ."

So all those B vitamins and minerals and antioxidants—Scott was fucking frightened, but then he got this way often, a regular hypochondriac. First it was cancer then it was MS. A friend of his from the bar claimed to go into high dudgeon with his doctor whenever a spot he found on himself turned out benign: "Don't tell me it's benign! I know when I'm dying! This is cancer!"

The doctor touched and looked on with a specially lit scope

strapped to his forehead. The lamp threw a bluish-gray light onto the subject and the area it trained on became a lunar surface.

"Yeah, it's really important for you, someone fair like you, with a family history . . ."

The doctor swept up and down his body, examining from a range of six inches.

"I had a second cousin named Marie. My grandmother found a mole under her bra line."

"Uh-huh?"

"They were getting ready for a wedding. Mamaw said, 'Marie!' Then she died from it."

The doctor tisk-tisked. "Here's another one," touching Scott's right lower abdomen. "It's irregular in shape, color, everything. These are what to look out for. Okay, that's two. For you a yearly full-body exam, the rest of your life. Pull up the hems of your shorts so I can see the legs? Now the bottoms of your feet, take off your sneakers. Now the tushie? Looks good, the rest, but those other two—okay, here's the plan. I'll do a shaving and send those two off for biopsy."

"You're serious," said Scott. "It's that worrying?"

"Shape and color, for starters. Those are two of the warning signs—better to be safe."

When he'd first seen the mole on his left shoulder, standing in front of the big bathroom vanity mirror, it had stood out like a fat juicy period on a sheet of blank paper. Then he looked at it and it seemed small though yes, dark. He'd let himself go in recent years and pledged to return to the gym before he saw anyone about it. The one on his flabby waist he'd never noticed. Most of his exercise he got walking around town in spring and summer and early fall weather. He left the office now, not feeling the excisions because of the Lidocaine local anesthesia. *Crack me up.*

He crossed town and began thinking about Perry's swift progress, the odd miracle of that.

Again the day was beautiful, the sky a clean blue linen he imagined smelling of lavender. He needed to stop thinking in terms of healing plant medicinals—the world was trying to kill all of us. It was nature, nothing to do with God: that part he'd at least been able to cut out mentally.

He'd thought that he could help protect Perry well into his old age. He'd thought.

He stopped thinking about it. The lovely day was an antidote, and he still had so many of his plans. He could pull this one out of the fire, too. He recalled the gallows comedy of *Hannah and Her Sisters*, Woody Allen thinking he had a brain tumor. Teenagers didn't get death. In fact, no one got death, not Perry, not Scott's father, until the curved blade came swinging low for you.

On the ninth floor, he got off the elevator, sanitized his hands with disinfectant foam from the dispenser, one of dozens mounted on the walls everywhere, and arranged his contented face.

"I'm getting out Friday," said Perry, grinning and sitting up straight. He did look fitter.

"Perfect."

"Darling, what's wrong?" said Perry, parodying sudden fright. "Are you all right?"

"Sure. Did they move Andy?"

"No, but they're going to. It's too cold for him. This used to be an MS unit and they kept it cold for some reason having to do with the nerves and muscles. How was your appointment?"

"Not what I expected. The one thing was harmless, but he found two worrying moles."

Perry was back to his cheerful, usual self. He wasn't to be daunted, for either of them.

"Darling, if it's anything, and it isn't, I'll take care of you the way you take care of me."

"I know."

"When are the results?"

"Later next week."

"Oh, surely you don't think it's serious? You had the thing with your dad and he's okay."

"I know."

Watching uncut Woody Allen movies on cable growing up, Scott had wanted a nice view of the Chrysler and Empire State buildings. And of course now he had his two skyscrapers, right outside there, without any idea of what to do with them. What did you do with everything you'd ever wanted and then gotten, and which you might possibly be about to lose?

lack

The dining hall was large and at one end taking over several of the long tables sat the high school kids who'd invaded the campus. They were doing their freewriting exercises. A teacher, or coach he looked more like in his shorts, polo shirt, and sneakers, strolled among the tables and stopped whenever a hand was raised, then knelt whispering his answers to put each kid's mind at ease about their assignment. A barn, practically. I was reminded of nearly thirty years ago when I was in college—the last time I'd been on a meal plan, when I was still the breakfast kind.

At the center were all the stations, the sundae station, the brightly signaged Spice It Up! station, the one where an Asian woman took orders for omelets then went to work with her pan and range of ingredients. It was nine in the morning, but I ignored even the do-it-yourself waffle station where you extruded batter from a dispenser like frozen custard onto a hot waffle iron and waited while deciding what to top your pastry with—peanut butter, say, jam, or dried cranberries.

This was New England, a college tucked between green mountains in a highland full of highly educated people, and cranberries seemed to accompany everything. Here, they were also big on recycling. In my dorm suite, I couldn't find a single trash can to throw wrappings or used Band-Aids in, but there were plastic recycling receptacles everywhere—blue for one kind, green for another, and gray for yet another. My little room was the Puritan-simple usual, scrubbed of all adornment, the mattress on the bed crackling with its waterproof mattress cover under starchy sheets, and the blanket was of a stiff texture you might find in a correctional institution. Outside, just before the rise of another green hill, light the color of baby aspirin flooded in from high industrial lamps. I felt, trying to sleep the previous night, as though I were in a low-end hotel chain placed safely off the interstate. During the day, the school busied itself doing what universities did in the summer off-season, sponsoring self-improvement seminars and workshops, and hosting enormous groups of chattering teenagers from all over. On the dozenth sunny lawn, a discussion group of retirees was ringed Indian-style in the shade of an old maple. Their gray or else bald heads described an archipelago of no doubt hard-lived life stories afloat in a green sea of idealism-planted lawn. A grad student—hunched, his head packed with equations or summer-stipend findings—moped at a jag past them reporting to his research job in the concrete brutalist lab building just beyond. I was only slightly nostalgic. In the dining hall I got a conventional breakfast of eggs and hash browns from an Eastern European woman who bade me please to bring her a plate. I realized I needed to locate plates, utensils, napkins, plastic glasses—everything kept in separate places in this bland utilitarian expanse. Nothing looked particularly appetizing or inviting, but filling up here was an ordinary daily mortification before the day's higher duty of personal mental development. I was here for a purpose, supposedly—and if I haven't already conveyed this, quite happy being there.

A food service worker older than the usual undergraduate sat in a booth away from all the high schoolers eating his breakfast. He wore a dark two-piece uniform and a tight, brimless cap. The cap wrapped around his head as though he were a Western Union messenger or bellhop. He looked at me as I passed, smiling pleasantly. I went back for more coffee or juice that was a syrup you extruded into a glass of water then stirred. Each time I returned to the table, now with more silverware, then with a plate of blueberries and dried cranberries, he smiled around at me.

I'd felt unsexy in my scratchy, crinkly bed the night before, and he was a fast inspiration. I went off in my brain. I was here to abandon one quadrant of it, light up another quadrant of it.

He was used to ambient summer amateurs like me. I romanticized his life thinking it was the stuff of fiction, his quiet lonely life. I was expected to produce something in workshop about two profoundly just-missed souls in just such a soulless scenario. He wore Frankenstein boots. I was here to write in workshop about experience in medias res—us grown-ups' first assignment.

I was trying to sit with different people at every lunch in the University Club, not wanting to be a snob or fall into a known clique. I'd made that mistake in the past whenever I fell into a group situation. All my life I strove to insert myself into a group paradoxically, being insecure, and yet abhorring cliques. I made a joke about it, and a nice young man called Stanley across from me at the table in the Garden Room looked earnestly back at me, forked steak in midair, and said, "Oh, is that how it's pronounced, *clique?*—like it rhymes with geek, or freak?"

The others laughed, either at his not having known, or his choice of rhymes.

He was innocent and looked like a farmer's son, guileless, with cornflower eyes that took everyone in gladly and almost drunkenly. He added, "I thought it was like the sound, *click.*"

The first girl, Meredith, had let him run on a bit. She was very pretty and lithely built and her mouth drooped drolly on either end, disabused of all illusion. Her petulant top lip lifted from the thinner lower one when she spoke in a way that warned of bitchiness as she looked directly at Stanley and said, mournfully, "Yeah, unfortunately he's right about that." Meaning nameless me.

The second girl, Clarissa, was fairer and had her strawberry-blond hair pinned up in back to show off the gentle snowdrift-curving nape of her neck. She was like the quietly witty beauty everyone admired around the punchbowl in a Jane Austen scene, and she said, "*Oui, c'est ça.*"

No one laughed at her perfect pronunciation, which would have spoiled the dry fun.

I could tell none of them remembered my name. Middle-aged, I kept listening, gleaning.

Bombastically, pretentiously, I secretly felt for cute, nerdy Stanley. He'd grown up not on a farm but was the son of a hardware store owner and he'd gone to Dartmouth, I found out. They were all half my age, and trying to ignore that embarrassment I said, "See, when I was in college, Rickie Lee Jones was big, and now to me all these years later everybody starts to sound like her."

I was referring to the hip music, a hip sound track, they played there at lunch every day.

Dully, Meredith said, "Totally." She wrapped her interesting mouth around what she was about to say and rolled her eyes and said, carefully, puffing her lips, bored, "Yep, Cat Power."

It was impressive and lovely watching her lips pop and flap about her consonants.

I'd heard the name of this musical act and said, searchingly, worriedly, "Cat Power?"

"Cat Power," Clarissa assured me, but not looking at me, lifting a forkful of salad.

I'd once thought my generation had invented irony, but theirs had reinvented it virally, a quiet and inexorable epidemic. Cat Power sounded as deliciously depressed as old Rickie Lee.

Stanley smiled gamely. He wasn't going to be daunted or one-upped—he didn't care.

I sliced at my chicken cutlet, which was juicy and I knew tasted good. I said, "It's sort of a four a.m. voice, like she's tired and wants to go to bed but for some reason can't."

Meredith snickered, which I thought meant I was had, I'd just hanged myself in front of her. She drank her ice water with lemon. And Clarissa smiled with ambiguous delight at me.

Meredith put down her cutlery and picked up her paper napkin, dabbed her mouth with it, and said, steadily and forbearingly, "Oh, wait." She did her finger like a metronome tocking out one note (like her mom?). "Wait, it can't be her four a.m. voice, because it's her New York *booze* voice."

No one challenged that it could be both. We snickered and waited, dabbing our mouths.

It was safe to do so, even though I didn't know what the hell Meredith had meant, quite.

Writing was something different for these younger folks but I could not figure out how. They were all clearly invested in it. I'd seen a lot of their generation's films and Meredith and Clarissa squarely fit the *Mean Girls* mode. They were what we used to call Too Cool for School—now, with *girls*.

It was not a John Cheever or Richard Yates enterprise for them. No quarter for realism. I guessed as Americans we were all romantic in some ways. Fame was more important than craft.

Yet fame infected me from an early age. If Salinger was taught in every high school and if he was still famous then something was either going very wrong or very right. Fame was God.

As I got to know them a little more, sharing the lunch table with them often, I heard them talking about mood, how a word put them in mind of a friend's fuck-up, or a parent's maddening habit of being always wrong or misguided—something they'd observed since infancy. They did all seem committed. They talked about their odd dreams in their scratchy, crinkly beds the night before, how dreams could be improved on, to make them even weirder, to say *more* about *them*.

"You know what would be even better? If the bartender already knew about my tattoo!"

I had come here to test my commitment. Literature had a metaphysical power over me.

The workshop I'd chosen to be in was full of younger people, too. But these young folks, all in their twenties, listened to the teacher and took notes and did not seem at all cynical. I tried to hold my tongue, but then again I wanted to be popular. I didn't criticize their work. I pointed out what I loved—and gradually, in workshop at least, I'd become the overenthusiastic nerd that was the exact opposite of the snide, self-assured (but self-loathing) jerk I'd manifested in school.

If I said something nice, after something else nice I'd said, they smiled warmly at me.

"Aw, but that's so lovely," they said, or, "But isn't he great? Let's all take Scott home!"

There was a cute Native American named Toby in my dorm suite. He was working on a memoir about being a gay Navajo. I think he was Navajo, unless he was Hopi. Over coffee one morning he told a Hopi legend but I do think he was Navajo. I don't remember the legend. But I do remember that he was from New Mexico. Wildfires were plaguing the west just then. Toby's boyfriend's mom had just lost her home to one in Colorado Springs. He and I were sitting in the University Club drinking our morning coffee (I offered to buy his coffee because he was a waiter and an undergrad with a partial scholarship and otherwise no means to attend), and on CNN they were showing round-the-clock footage of the fires out west—like the apocalypse, these fires.

"Yeah, shit," he said, his easy, wry consternation a source of attraction for me. "I talked to my boyfriend last night . . . ," and it took a while for him to get out the full story. I hoped that his memoir told the story with a bit less self-interruption, a bit less elliptical fill-in-the-blank.

"What?" I said, smirking expectantly.

"Clay's mom's in Colorado Springs," he said, oversugaring his coffee like the recovering alcoholic I later discovered, from him, that Toby was. "My boyfriend Clay's mom's in that . . ."

He had hipster glasses, which originally had made him seem fierce. He looked smart and menacing. I knew that his memoir would expose everything wrong with white people. It wasn't enough to be gay anymore. You had to be a gay minority, angry on behalf of non-whites and also gays who weren't white. In my twenties, I'd often announced this as just fitting and inevitable.

Now I was just white. I rarely had sex and when I did, it was with one white guy: myself.

". . . and *now* she's coming to fucking *live* with us," Toby finally finished, looking off.

I waited then said, "But do you like Clay's mother?"

"Oh yeah, I love her. I love Reba. Reba's great. But she's going to come *live* with us."

"It'll be all right," I said, perkily sipping my second black coffee. "Don't you think?"

When he smiled, it was dazzle white. He smiled and said, "Little Miss Mary Sunshine!"

I lived in New York and had lost all gift of gab. You had to guard it carefully there. You were always worried about what you'd said and how it would be matched against something you had said earlier, or against someone else's story about you. My partner Perry was somewhat yet not completely famous. His position was tenuous. And he'd recently had a stroke and had gone under the radar and people were wondering if Perry would pull through. Our friend Beau, which was just a nickname for his real name, Robert, was taking care of Perry while I was away for this week, and when I called home everything seemed cozy but temporarily so. Meanwhile, this was my vacation. I'd come stag, so to speak, and did not want to act too knowing or cosmopolitan. I thought about Toby and how far away from life, despite his gayness, he must have felt from me.

"I'm just trying to get everything out of this thing I can," Toby was eventually able to say. "Some of these kids are from big pricey schools, but I'm smarter—my work's better than theirs."

"I'm sure it's a lot more interesting," I said, then I wondered if this didn't sound racist.

"What about you?" he said. "What are you doing here? Heard you have shit going on."

"Well," I said, trying to sound alluring, "my partner had a stroke and this is my vacation. I just meant that some of these people are so young is all."

"How old do you think I am?"

"Twenty-three," I said, adjusting for his gay sensibility. He looked pretty beat-up, rugged and ready for anything, but probably no less than thirty. "Twenty-three or maybe even younger."

"Thirty-one," he said and gave me the smile for the second time. "But it's a good thing. I'm smarter and have more experience, and my writing's better than most of these youngies."

We didn't play the same game about my age, and I said, "But welcome to my vacation."

"Right, and that's cool. Before I came I decided not to do anything I didn't want to."

"Me, too. Although, I have to say, I find myself falling into old please-like-me! patterns."

"Seriously, you, Mr. Popular? Everybody's like, 'What's he think?' But I'm not like that."

I think this was because he'd seen me sitting with the Mean Girls, which suited me fine.

"I'm here to listen and learn," I said, and he nodded and put down his coffee cup, done.

He checked his iPhone and said we'd be late to craft and got up without me.

Craft, in the mornings, was like finger paints but with words. It was fun because nothing was expected of you. Nothing but your twelve hundred dollars and a good collegial attitude was expected of you. There were people there older than me and so I decided to have a good time, as though none of it mattered, which it didn't. I had acted like this in high school and look where it had gotten me: going to a writing workshop in the Berkshires where nothing was expected of me.

After lunch in the University Club I'd call home and usually Beau would pick up.

"Hi, it's me," I said. "What are you guys up to?"

"Well, I walked Perry and that was good. Then we went to lunch for sushi. He's doing well, although I wish he'd walk twice a day. Tonight we're having Tyler and Devon for dinner."

"Those are nice guys," I said and thought of those two precious homosexuals I disliked.

"I understand they're cute, although they're both taken. By each other."

"When it suits. Hello?"

"Oh!" said Beau. "I'm so worried about these wildfires. It just seems so prescient, it just seems so foreboding." He was always reaching for the ten-dollar word, usually a Latinate. "And what is going on with the federal government? What are they doing? I like how it's all about the haves waiting for the next move by the have-nots. We're going into early Roman Empire here."

"How's Perry's diet? Is he eating all the healthy food I left for him in the freezer?"

"More or less. Oh, I miss you! Are you having a good time? Is it like vacation, I hope?"

"It is, but I'm just relieved to hear things are going okay there, too."

Stanley and I just then were crossing paths, and he called out, "Hey, man."

"How's it going?"

"It's cool, man."

Today he was wearing an Izod with the collar flipped up, as though the Mean Girls had gotten to him and were maybe playing a little joke on him, but it was appealing. He walked with longer strides and as we passed he gave me the thumbs-up.

"Who was that?" said Beau.

"One of my classmates."

"Oh! I hope you're having a good time. I hope it's, you know, remunerative for you."

Beau looked like a teenager but was already a professor at Tulane. He'd glided through Yale then Harvard and was now an expert on the influence of Greek drama on Eugene O'Neill—whom he now confessed to hate. Nothing American since 1950 or so was good enough. We'd ceded all power in the world cultural market shortly after winning the Second World War. I would not listen too carefully to his plaints, to use one of his words, because I was postwar, too.

I said, "Miss you."

"Is there anybody up there?" he suddenly said. "Any cuties? Any hotties?"

"Duh, but not who are interested in me."

I no longer wanted to discuss sex with Beau. I'd been in love with him a while ago but it hadn't worked out, and it was better for him to talk about sex with Perry, who'd introduced us.

"Oh!" he said. "Don't tell me it's postindustrial, late-Empire, mid-postmodern malaise."

"Well," I said and—*words* again—laughed. "It just might be."

I got to workshop and sat next to Deepika, who was my age and who taught at the kind of liberal arts college I never could have afforded to attend. I had asked Deepika if her name wasn't Indian (she was pretty with blandly exotic features), and she'd said, "Naw, it's just a name." She never brought up her background, and I guessed that this made her post-postmodern.

Our teacher was a beautiful blonde woman about our age who'd said on the first day that she never wanted to hear in here the phrase, "Grab the reader." She had low affect but when she got going, hitting a sentence she loved, or a reference, she got passionate, saying, "Marvelous!"

All during workshop, in which I wasn't writing, only reading others, commenting in some positive way on their work, and listening, I thought only of drinks later at the University Club.

An earlier evening at the UC, Deepika had said to me, "My job is *unbelievably* bad."

(I'd heard Beau—who pulled in seventy grand a year—say this many, many times.)

I liked when people with job security, especially tenured faculty types, said stuff like this. All literature to me was in the sentence—the well-placed phrase or whatever that drew hushes. I had worked some pretty bad jobs before I met Perry. To me there was romance in this career, the type of which anybody in my family would die to get, making you swoon with boredom without sweating or waking up five days a week before dawn. Literature is a sop to the lazies. It makes you feel good about doing nothing but reading, sitting around committing no compassionate acts, watching your surroundings get dirty and disorderly, getting more and more useless as a "mind."

Deepika said that between committee meetings and grading papers, there was no time for her own writing. She wanted to write a novel about the Tamil Tigers and make them sympathetic for the average disengaged, ignorant American. I nodded at the phrase *Tamil*

Tigers, but Deepika had been mutely seraphic. Today, our teacher told Deepika that her writing was too smart.

The teacher got Deepika in her sights and said, "You know what I mean? Too knowing."

After workshop I sat with Deepika at the bar at the University Club. Each of us ordered a glass of white wine and she said, "And what the fuck does that mean? Too smart, too knowing?"

"I know, right?" I said, imitating the younger ones, thinking of the Mean Girls. "Right?"

I was more interested in whether or not she was related to any Tamil Tigers, but I'd have to wait until her novel came out if it ever did. I wanted to say she needed more dialogue. In real life, Deepika had no shortage of things to say, but her characters did more thinking than acting. I wanted to know not so much about her sexual life as her personal life. She referred to the person she lived with alternately as "partner" and "spouse," but what was the person's gender? Deepika said she was a deep structuralist and that her field straddled political science and philosophy, and that she'd been asking herself a lot of questions lately about the language of our imperialist wars.

"It just seems that we as Americans aren't asking all the tough questions," she said, "you know, about all the hegemonies," and she got me in her sights the way the teacher had done her.

I knew, too, that academics pluralized otherwise singular abstract nouns like hegemony.

I said, "It's so funny that thing you bring up about questions, because not you—you're an academic so it's your job to—but fiction writers, if you read the jacket copy on their books, when the publisher doesn't know what else to say about their own book that's puzzling and dense, they inevitably defer to this question strategy describing their book: 'a novel that mordantly raises questions of postmodern identity.' But all that says to me is they haven't actually read that book, or they have, but they can't make heads or tails out of it. You know?" and I watched her freeze.

"Uh-huh."

I knew I'd insulted her because after all we'd been talking about her fiction all along.

Our barstools were turned toward each other, and we each took a drink and blinked.

"Maybe that's too vague," I said. "I thought she was harsh on you. I like your ideas."

"But I'm too much of an academic."

"Nope," I said, taking a proud next sip. "Not at all." I raised my chin defiantly.

"Then *what*?" she said, and she set her look on me and would not dislodge it.

My mind shuffled for an answer but then a bunch of the other workshoppers came in.

"More later," I said, "but I will tell you what my boyfriend's always telling me . . ."

"What's he always telling you?"

"Well, only," I said, feeling that first grateful glass, "only that you'll make your way."

"Bullshit," she said. "You're a real BS-meister, aren't you? Gift of the Irish gab?"

Perry said, "Do you like your teacher?" and I knew that he was asking if *she* liked *me*. It was important for him to know that others thought I had some talent, too. "And is she terribly nice?"

"Yes, but I get the feeling she doesn't want to play favorites. She's nobody's fool."

"Huh! Beau and I thawed some of the sausage and lentils. It was really delicious."

"Did he make you walk?"

"I could only get to the corner and turn around and hobble staggering back."

We'd been together seventeen years, but things had only begun to get bad in the last two. After a while you wondered. Sex was one thing, love and affection another, and then you were a childish team, a pair of ids afloat in tandem with too much freedom. And then what?

Before the stroke, his doctor had been after him to lose weight for a good while.

I said, "I feel like a lot of this is my fault. If I'd insisted harder, pushed you harder . . ."

"This is my fault, darling. There were plenty of voices, plenty of warning signs."

This was perfunctory, in my mind. As long as he'd been able to have tricks, I was happy. I wasn't going to be responsible for somebody else's sexual contentment—least of all mine.

Soon Perry put Beau on the line and Beau said, "We're having a good time, Boo!"

I wondered if Perry hadn't bought Beau a bottle of gin. Beau sounded less classical now.

Everywhere was happy hour. I was on my way back to the dorm. The University Club's last call was ten-thirty and then there was nothing else to do unless you walked to town, then the walk back to the dorm would be twice as long. I dreamed about sleeping with the teacher. Half-undressed, she faced away, extending her arm, letting her black bra hang, saying, "Nope, fella!"

She wasn't teasing me. Somehow in the dream I knew that she was saying she knew that I wanted to *be* her, not *have* her. Still, when I was waking up on the crackly mattress beneath the stiff, scratchy sheets, I was just getting my face in her tits, her small apricot tits more potent than words. But then I realized where the dream had gone wrong. The teacher never wore a bra. I'd had the dream because I was in love with her male opposite number, Beau, with similar coloring.

I was looking for another place to have breakfast. A hotel in the middle of campus, where Perry and I were originally supposed to stay, resembled my mother's old electric hair-curling appliance she'd gotten one Christmas, but bigger and substituting cement for plastic. The hotel looked self-contained and was about twelve stories tall. It was like something post-Mussolini in Italy, where Perry would prefer to be over anywhere else, but where we couldn't afford to go anymore due to the strong Euro. An international firm had won a competition designing it. Each room's window reminded me of a half-closed eye—from which, in my exhaustion and homesickness, I imagined the heat and steam of my mom's electric curling appliance escaping. The sun was already hot at nine in the morning. I hurried, as though pursued, into the ugly air-conditioned basement café.

I was eating more than usual, as though I were a student, and drinking at the usual rate.

I got scrambled eggs on an english muffin and dispensed myself a coffee. There was no one there from my writing program, in fact no other customers, only a cashier and a line cook. I thought about mid-week afternoon malls when I'd cut my last two high school classes, during the early part of the Reagan administration. My dashed hopes, none of them Reagan's fault. Then I finished my food, grabbed my coffee, and went out. I took a long sweaty walk, skipping craft. I wasn't at all disabused of craft, I'd merely paid for the privilege of choosing to go or not to go.

In one craft class, the teacher, a spoken-word artist, wanted us to access our inner ham or show-off. Her performances were apparently fiercely political, but I was gratified to see that she wasn't beyond appreciating and drawing out our silliest, most superficial selves. She got us into pairs by first getting us into a circle. This was on a patio in the hot sun. We had to jump up and down and shake our limbs and loosen up. Then one by one we ran across the circle and selected a partner and stared at each other. "Now scream, but don't stop looking at each other! Scream!"

We were there to indulge our creative sides; it was the primordial equivalent of jet-skiing in Mykonos. In the mid-eighties not long after Reagan's second election, I would worry that my fucking around had gotten me infected. I flattered myself that when it was clear that I was close to the end, say when I had black tumors all over me, Kaposi sarcoma, I'd fly to Greece wearing dark sunglasses, check into a hotel near the water, and fling myself off a cliff into the deep blue. I wouldn't even need much money for it. I could max out my credit cards getting there. It's not like I was planning to pay the hotel bill. This was how thoughtless and insensitive I was then. I tested negative time and again, however. And then I decided I was going to live and be a writer.

I was just giving myself a narrative, back when the disease was deemed tragic, but Perry had survived it and thrived. He'd put *on* weight, napped when he felt like it, enjoyed life, and I was the midcentury equivalent of a nun out of time. An MTV nun staring at worldly pop icons. I had missed the entire downtown punk orgy because I'd been too wimpy and middle-class about money to risk moving to New York. By the time Perry and I had gotten there after Paris, the city was vacuumed-up, re-cemented, and glassed-over—and the party had moved over to Brooklyn.

I went to the town cemetery and followed a group of schoolchildren who found a plaque on the black iron fence that identified the plot as containing the grave of the Poetess. The stone identified her as no such thing, only gave the dates of her birth and death ("Called Back"). Many of the goodly womenfolk buried there had virtuous first names like Felicity, Hope, or Constance. Perry's nutritionist in New York was called Amity Huhn—and she was strictly food-puritanical.

> Because I could not stop for sex,
> he kindly stopped for me.
> The liv'ry cab held just ourselves
> and Immorality.

Amity Huhn's system was a call to eliminate fried foods and red meat from your diet and replace them with whole grains, lean meats like poultry and fish, and fresh fruit and vegetables—unsurprising stuff. Bread and pasta were an occasional treat, processed sugar was verboten, and when you got a yen for sweets it was better, and more satisfying, to enjoy a modest piece of dark Belgian chocolate over a gooey ultra-fattening pastry. Perry had followed the system for a while, then gotten bored. Amity Huhn had referred him to a daily meal delivery service fitting perfectly into her plan, then when invitations for dinners out picked up, the little prepared plastic boxes had stacked up and gone bad in the fridge. They were replaced by deli cuts and runny cheeses, and I couldn't blame him. If you said you liked cooking you were either a chef or lying. To cook well and nutritiously was hard, athletic work—and Perry had always been the chef in our household.

When people at literary parties asked me how I could have let Perry get so overweight, I (excusing my own indulgences, which were not so evident in a living room just then) told them to imagine a life like Perry's post-AIDS without booze or cigarettes. He'd dropped both vices then moved to Paris, not exactly the most timely of restraints then and there. He'd given them up for sex, in exchange for sex, but I didn't tell them that. I said, what was left but food? If they'd had the curiosity I would have told them for me food was uninteresting. I like smoking and drinking. Sex: who could be bothered at my age to go trolling for it online, the way Perry did routinely?

I left the cemetery and stopped at the ATM for money for drinks following workshop.

At lunch, I got in line for the buffet behind Meredith and Clarissa. As usual there was a nice spread, beef and chicken options, as well as an appetizing vegetarian dish of vegetables and thinly sliced, beige-sauced tofu that might have made Amity Huhn sniff with reserved approval.

On the cover of her bestselling diet book, Amity Huhn was photo-graphed with skillfully chopped, frozen-out dark hair, the face work she'd had done conservatively made-up heaviest on the eyes and lips. She was wearing a dark slimming pants suit and she had a hand cocked on her possibly photoshopped bony hip. She was confident and she commanded you, not without some arch felicity, to get real about your eating. Her practice was on Park Avenue. Her book had an audio edition, while none of Perry's twenty-five books had been recorded for the reading-averse.

"We think we eat sugar," ran her best line (regarding insulin release), "but sugar eats us."

Meredith and Clarissa, both slender and gorgeous, seemed to follow her plan to the letter. They were each enjoying a small cube of fish, generous salad, asparagus, and no rice or pasta.

Meredith said, "Did you meet John? He's a really amazing poet. I mean, he just is."

Clarissa nodded importantly, and I shook the hand of the youngish man standing next to me in line. We all held square plates—square plates meant you were in the presence of an artful cuisine—and I said, "Hi, John. So are you a poet, too?"

Clarissa snickered, saying, "Not just any poet, a poet about the war."

"Which war?"

John laughed quickly and said, countryishly, "That's all right. The Second Gulf War."

"He was a corporal and has amazing things to say," said Meredith. "No, really."

We all sat together. Corporal John said that he'd been in the Marines. He began to break down what all was involved in using artillery. He'd been in a Howitzer unit. I'm not even sure I can say that with confidence. He'd overseen the loading of the Howitzers, big fuckers as he said, and the trick was to decide on the load and the fuse. I'm not conventional for a writer in that I'd write off somebody because they'd been to war. No, in fact his expertise in a field that calls for a lot of training only fascinated me. The literary world is necessarily liberal. *War*, bad. No excuse for being in a war. But I didn't feel that way. I was interested to hear about different fuses. The decision about what fuse to use was made after the range and purpose of the artillery load for the Howitzer was determined, all of it done through computer contact. Legendary Howitzers. It was all a quiet process at first. The unit moved in and set up, say, on the side of the hill. It depended on whether you wanted to knock a hole in a building's wall or smoke people out. Corporal John wasn't cynical. He explained things scientifically. I pictured several of my friends in New York already judging him, turning their backs and walking away with their vodkas or white wines.

Also, I was glad that I wasn't attracted to him, but his were the first words of any interest for me all week. I imagined an entire book of poems told from the Howitzer's point of view.

"The only problem I ever had," he said, "was when the decision was handed down to use white phosphorus. You know white phosphorus?

When it gets on you you can't get it off. It just keeps on burning. Somebody gets hit with it, it doesn't go out until they burn completely up."

"Jesus," said Meredith, "and you're getting that all through infrared field glasses, right?"

"Right," said Clarissa, "through your night-vision goggles, from a safe remove? Jesus."

"Something like that," he said.

I went to workshop, and Deepika said, "How've you been? I saw you having lunch with that John guy, the Marine? God! I got stuck with him at lunch yesterday. He's so—military."

"Well. But how was the sex?" I said. "Good?"

"Fuck you. I was going to tell you—no, I'll tell you anyway. I went home last night and saw on my shelf a book by Perry Knight, *Paris Wanderings*. Damn thing's dedicated to you."

"Most of his friends had died by that point. He didn't have anyone else to dedicate it to."

"Asshole."

After workshop, no one was up at the University Club except Corporal John. We thought that maybe everyone had convened to the library or gone back to the dorm to write assignments.

I said, "Me, I'm looking at this as a vacation. I'm a housewife in search of a vacation."

"I get you."

He told me that he'd had a good workshop. He'd put up a poem the Mean Girls had liked but it wasn't about Howitzers or the military. It was about home, and it was painful to write.

There was something puny and not obviously military about him. His arms were skinny and not very long. His face seemed dwarfed by something congenital, as he drank his big beer.

He said, "My parents divorced when I was in high school. I was a classic military brat. I was in high school and my father came home in uniform and told me. I was the oldest. It freaked me out because I was the next down in rank, so I had to tell the others. Mom like a lot of military moms was classically checked-out. I don't know if you ever saw that movie, based on that book, *The Great Santini*. That was us basically. We moved out with our mom. I was always way more worried about my younger brother Jeremy. He's now a design consultant for Pottery Barn."

"And gay?"

"And gay. He says he wants an older daddy to take care of him. He lives with our dad."

We smiled, although at first this alarmed me: my old heterophobic, antimilitary notions, which I'd thought I'd overcome. They were coming out through a dimly hidden gay wormhole.

"But is your father okay with him being gay and being a designer who wants a daddy?"

"Dad's retired and loosened up quite a bit. He just wants Jeremy to meet someone, too."

"What a great dad."

"But I do write about the old dad, *before*. Actually, it's half of what I write still. Dad's a recovering alcoholic. You might say a re-recovering alcoholic, but he tries. He's a good dad."

We looked at each other and nodded, waiting a bit. Then we decided to get more drinks.

Dinners were on us, and at an Asian bistro in town we sat at a large table. It was the evening before the final one, when there would be farewell workshop drinks and a buffet at the UC.

Toby said, "Well, my father's gone. He worked in a nuclear plant three miles from where I grew up. My brother got leukemia; it was worse to watch than with my mom. She was great."

"Unfuckingbelievable," said Meredith.

Clarissa said, "And now it's just you, all alone?"

"Me and my boyfriend Clay, and now Clay's mom for a while."

Toby seemed a little more resigned to cohabiting with Clay's mom already.

Meredith slid her chopsticks out of their paper sheath like two slender cigarettes.

"What is going on?" said Clarissa. "I'm not apocalyptic or anything, but still."

"What about you guys?" Toby said. "Everybody still have their parents?"

Clarissa replied, "Oh and then some, if you count the stepmom and the stepdad."

"My father's a bartender," said Meredith. "He was supposedly this brilliant logician and was at Stanford for it, then one day he freaked out. My mom is just a frenetic claims adjuster."

"Yeah, insurance," said Toby. "Try that one on for size."

I was the only one ordering a starter and I ate my soup.

"Stan!" said Clarissa. "Where've you been?"

"Yeah, Stan. Tell!"

Stanley was sheepish and said, moving toward the table, "Can I sit with you guys?"

"Are you insane?" Meredith then said, and I moved over a place to make room for Stanley.

"We went to see that movie," he said. "It was all right. John liked it more than I did."

"Where's John?" said Clarissa. "Is he coming, the doof? Should we text him?"

"He said he was going home to do some work. He has to order the poems for his thesis."

"Right," said Clarissa, "because he's going back to Norfolk to *defend* his thesis."

Meredith tightened her puffy mouth, but it wouldn't stow. She raised both eyebrows, put her hand on nerdy Stan's, and looked at him, saying, "What did you think of 'Real Admiral'?"

Always growing up I'd wished that my parents would divorce, but this had not solved any of Corporal John's problems. He was still working his out. By the time my brother and I were in high school my father had stopped hitting us, knocking us against walls, grabbing for his belt and yanking it out of his pants loops to fold it in half and crack it menacingly then wield it and let the hot licks fall senselessly on us wherever. I don't know if our getting bigger and more athletic by then had frightened or intimidated him or if he was tired. The four of us were already starting to dissipate as a unit. My mother and father let us try their beer or wine every time they got a fresh can or glass in their hands. They had stopped flinching and getting bent out of shape because we cussed, which we'd learned in the school hallways in imitation of an outside world they couldn't do anything about. They started cussing and we knew they'd always cussed, probably since high school, too. We loosened up together and laughed a lot, or more than before. We were tense and we unwound under the same roof, and when we got out from the knot of us after my brother and I grew up, the roof just fell in. This had something to do with the fact that, now, I wanted someone much younger and more beautiful than I had ever been to beat my ass and legs with a belt while I was naked and feeling fat and flabby—then bawl me out and remind me I was worthless flesh.

Corporal John had read me "Rear Admiral" that night and now Stanley, wide-eyed, said, "I was blown away. I didn't grow up like that, but I just love John, like my brother! I have to trust what he says. Why wouldn't I? But how could you go through that and ever be the same?"

We waited and then Meredith said, "Well, I guess he's *not* the same."

Clarissa pouted then said, "I'm lucky my dad's an idiot, too self-involved to be violent."

Our meals came and we ate talking about Stanley and John's movie, which sounded idiotic.

Right at the end Deepika came in and said, "Looks like everybody's just getting done."

Everyone was anxious to get to a famous novelist's reading, the last conference biggie.

To Deepika I said, frowning with kindness, "I'll stay, you can order and I'll have coffee."

"You'd do that for me?" said Deepika. "Then let me pay for your coffee."

Later, I called home. Beau had gone straight to bed after his internet-arranged sex date in our neighborhood of Chelsea—Chelsea, where anything could happen. But then you just got used to the possibility of it. The trick—it seemed as you aged—was finding somebody wanting a daddy. Or you could go without. Or you could settle down with somebody who wanted to garden. Whichever way, you didn't have anything up on straight people. You still had to deal with the bodily issues.

"We had a lovely, quiet day," said Perry. "We walked a block and I got tired and we went home. But on the way I had to stop and rest, so we ate lunch at that new vegetarian Indian place. But do you know what I was thinking, besides missing you? I was thinking how horrible it'll be, not knowing when it's the last time I'll be saying hello or good-bye again—how horrible that is."

"You mean hello or good-bye again to me?"

"Well, to anyone—much as I miss you. Saying good-bye to anyone, whomever, on earth."

We said good night and hung up. I turned off my lamp and got into bed and pulled up the covers. In less than a week they'd lost some of their stiffness and starch. Then I thought of older Perry's courage—anyone older's courage. You had to keep going. Then eventually I fell asleep.

avenging angel

Across the inlet, only a few lights burned against the char-black ridge line of East Blue Hill. They were writers and boatbuilders over there—all of them, or nearly all of them, young, happy, and attractive. Their children were blond and played on steep lawns. How those lawns got mowed was a mystery. The summer was coming to a close and bedtime was early. Drive the streets and you'd not meet a lot of oncoming cars, pairs of headlights coming toward you as rare as tropical foliage in Maine, where we were—but then there was nothing to do after say ten p.m. It was a snug community. The days of summer so far north were long, and by the time the dinner dishes were washed, it was time to turn in. Or so my imagination had it. On the deck in front of my little plumbingless cabin, in a Chinese-manufactured adirondack, I had a front-row seat. We were renting the place. We did it every August. We were solitary, each a little bit lonely. My job was to shop and cook and clean, and his was to create. He was paying many thousands of dollars to finish his new novel here, going at quite the clip in his older age. He sat in the main house (it was paces from the cabin where I slept and read and stepped out occasionally onto the deck for a drink of wine and a smoke), and he wrote in the notebooks he'd brought from New York. Every year I was making progress knocking out titles by a different author: Naipaul, DeLillo, Faulkner. I was having trouble concentrating on Faulkner but knew he was obligatory for any Southerner. I was amanuensis, driver, and helpmeet. I typed when necessary. I edited. I proofed whenever a manuscript was ready to go to the publisher. He complained that he was tired, but then the days were so long. We were so far out on Newbury Neck that there was no internet, no cable, only the one TV station coming in, PBS. Each morning after breakfast we'd drive into town, and I'd leave him at a coffee shop before driving to Hannaford, the good supermarket. Before turning the key in the ignition in the downtown public lot I'd check my own email; the signal was that powerful. I had so few messages, but this was his time to unwind and sip a latte and do all his business and mine to listen to the radio. It would not be a good thing in our New York milieu to admit to, but sometimes I'd then drive to Walmart for staples. In Walmart I was a kid again. This was such an agreeably lonely place, Hancock County, rich and poor rubbing up against each other, though apparently not in Walmart, where I saw more evidence of my own people, still buying CDs in the age of downloads, scouring through racks of reduced rock T-shirts, and buying their megaportions of cooking oil, flour, potatoes, white rice. In the twenty-first-century retail warehouse of Walmart I heard one woman say to her husband, "Because I'm *afraid*, Dale," and I was home again. Home again meant sales and bargains. It meant people just making do or thinking in their imaginations apocalyptic thoughts when never was there an apocalypse about to happen. It was Christian and put-upon. It was numberless victimhood. It was frightened, and I still felt some of that ambient fear, although what did I have to fear? Among them I was privileged. I'd gotten an education to do my job, fill the role that I now enjoyed. Enjoyed is a strong word. Strong is masculine and part of me felt emasculated, as did so many of these ovoids, my word for them—a hateful word I know, but said in love because I couldn't put myself above them. I'd been a pear-shaped teen, in a spot. I'd felt I had no future. I'd had some luck and met him. I'd met him in Paris, an accident because I was just there and had written him a fan note, a fan note that had gotten his attention. I was still young then. Whatever little I inherited, I'd gotten young genes. He'd said, "You are the perfect mate for me because you look so young I can indulge my pedophile fantasies, yet I'm not a pedophile." In my family, our hair didn't turn gray quickly. We wrinkled slowly. I had studied English at a state university and could do the job. I'd been doing it for some time. It was a job, but a job that came with some, *many*, pleasures. And I was still the kid, that rock fanboy. I wanted my life to resemble rock and roll and in many senses it did, the freedom, the parties. And then came the silences. They were long and breathed deeply with the quiet act of his writing.

In a pinch, we could be car internet surfers. The Blue Hill library's wireless reached into the parking lot, and we could do a day's errands then park and check our email without going in, though sometimes we went in to look at the books, a more than respectable collection since this area had a history, a sort of WASPy culture, a pedigree. I was trying to finish *The Sound and the Fury* and brought it along no matter what. He had contempt for Faulkner, a soup of the stream-of-consciousness, a mess. I said okay. We didn't always agree. As a teen I'd spent about a third of my life in libraries. Before I got my driver's license I'd had to ride the bus to get there.

Entering any library, I felt my intestines buckle, and then I'd have to go to the men's room, but every time. The smell of the books, the paper, the print, it was galvanic. It made me anxious because I wanted to write and have my words in one or more of those places on the shelves. So I went in and saw all the provocative filth written on, at times carved into, the stall walls, but never did I see any of the promises or come-ons acted on. There was never anyone in there but me. It was a late weekday afternoon, or sometimes a Saturday morning. I went back out to the stacks.

Even now I had this intestinal reaction in libraries. In the Blue Hill library, I wondered if I wouldn't run into one of those literary family men and women camping out in the cool thinking important thoughts and dreaming up characters and plots while their kids combed the aisles. I'd first discovered my lover's books at the Regency Square Branch Library back down in Florida.

He needed to lose weight and I was doing ballet trying to make healthy things taste good. I did not like cooking, which took time away from my reading, my compulsion. I experimented with combinations to season the rote vegetables and lean fish and poultry using ginger and curry, garlic, lemon and lime, rice vinegar, low-sodium Worcestershire, scallions, anything to make the flavor more complicated and thus savory. He was on a salt-restricted diet and the old butter he'd been a fan of, not to mention the bacon and sausage and salami and other cold cuts—all this was forbidden. I had to walk him, too. He wouldn't walk himself because, he said, in his crazy mind there was no goal to that. More and more he cheerfully took my invitations to walk. He was on a cane but trying to do without it. His goals were to finish the novel and walk without the cane.

There were blueberries, dark, musky-sweet, in size somewhere between BBs and pearls. Once a week I made french toast with pure maple syrup piled with the blueberries. When we'd first arrived that month, there were raspberries the size of shirt buttons tasting as intensely raspberry as any artificial "raspberry" flavoring from childhood. It was a challenge trying to gratify him and not make him feel like such a patient. I felt as a parent might, instructing a child through trickery.

We would stop at a roadside stand and buy the produce directly from the farmer, who was better at growing than adding figures. He would have to stop and start all over. A line formed.

Myself, I was getting older and more impatient, too. Intense home care had worn me out.

At a recent New York dinner a female friend had told me, "Understand you're at a special age, and I know because I was there a decade ago. You're at an age where you'll be looked at by different people, younger people, older people, men, women. Boys. Girls. Whether you know it or not you'll be attractive to more people than you've ever felt attractive to before. Enjoy this!"

But in Maine there was so little socializing to help me test her theory about my "appeal."

Really, I would have had to be famous, one of the literati among all the writers here.

On the flight from New York a much younger flight attendant had handed me my coffee and cup of water, and I'd thanked him, smiling, and his responding look had lingered. I was in so many places at once mentally I'd wanted to give him my number. I had a whole scenario worked out. When we landed in Bangor, he announced over the mic, "On behalf of our New York–based crew, I wish you a pleasant stay, or pleasant connection." I thought this was for me and began to wonder if I shouldn't write down my number to press into his hand while deplaning, but I didn't.

And from Bangor, where on earth would you be connecting *to*? Nova Scotia, the Arctic?

The house was surrounded by woods interspersed with vacation homes positioned mostly on the bluffs overlooking the inlet. On a wandering walk alone I'd skirted the property of one of these houses, negotiating the shingle of the sandless beach and scaling the bluff, and found a path I'd never gone down. Suddenly I was in different territory. In five minutes I'd happened upon a broken-down Airstream trailer fronted by a sagging wooden porch. A young couple was sitting on the steps, their baby lying at their feet in its portable plastic cradle. They spotted me from the moment I rounded the gravel bend. He studied me I thought suspiciously, hatefully—until I had passed. She barely regarded me at all but looked down cooing at the child. I didn't look back. I thought of Stephen King's novel *Christine*, grittier and more country-Maine than what the young and beautiful summering writers put out. When they wrote about Maine it was about bourgeois, educated liberals coming to terms with the loss of a child, divorce, or the fight to keep abortions safe and legal. Their characters had nice second homes and reasonable, right-minded spouses.

My first reading compulsion had been Stephen King. Then Salinger, Fitzgerald, Irving. I thought about those early King novels, working-class, Yankee, angry, deterministic. I was down in Florida angry and alone, and I thought that everything in the northeast was like an idyllic New England Updike setting. Chill colorful falls. In Maine the setting shifted between Stephen King and John Updike. At the beginning of the rental's gravel drive were piles of junk and unrecycled trash— loose pyramids of glass and plastic bottles, a rusted-out Jeep, a sagging and leaning travel trailer, broken deck furniture. We later learned that the aged owner of this property, Mr. Grange, redeemed this crap to help fund local scholarships. But we didn't see, from year to year, that the heaps had actually diminished. Mr. Grange collected our recycling once a week—and there were still last summer's wine bottles (from before I'd switched from cheap reds to certain cheap whites).

We called this first length of winding gravel drive our security system. Who, pulling in, no doubt by accident, would have thought anything of value was beyond these Gatsbyesque ash and trash fields, and what would they steal? Laptops full of unprofitable fiction, porn site links?

On my way back, two boys appeared from the woods, suddenly marching when they saw me, their voices dying. They waved, grinning; I waved back. I was salacious and having had an impure adolescence thought their joyfulness smacked of a guilt I could recognize. They were of the right age to remind me of when I was first alive to getting off with a boy; they'd come out of nowhere not following the main path. I had grown up in a north Florida subdivision bordered by the undeveloped woods where I'd had my first adventures. Later, aroused by my crafty younger being, I stood at the kitchen sink, looking out at the inlet debating with myself over combinations of soluble and in-soluble fiber: my fate. Both fibers were necessary to a sound, balanced diet, but too much of either, or heaven forbid both, and you had a meal akin to wood pulp or pond scum on your hands. He anxiously wanted to finish this book but at the same time needed to lose weight. He was used to pigging out toward deadline. Before, I'd satisfy his yens for bacon and sausage, let him eat toast slathered with butter and jam around teatime, midnight snacks of cheese and rice and broiled steak. Now he was cooperating, a compliant heart patient. But I was dreamy, losing the thread. I'd done plenty of odd-job cooking and serving on my way through the wilderness of college and graduate education. A school friend now in AA told me that she'd benefited from her twelve-step program's primary ethos of service. Serving others was not merely therapeutic but it helped restore others' belief in your sincerity. Step Nine—I think it was—had her apologizing to those she'd hurt before getting sober. Ironically, my friend's name was Faith, and before she got sober Faith would meet me at a movie. We'd plan to have dinner afterward as well, but once she said, "Since it'll be so late already after the movie, I was wondering if we could get a drink after it gets out, and you give me the money for a taxi. The subway to East Harlem is dicey so late and I fear for my life, honestly, I'm afraid. You know I'm small, and the chiquitas and mamitas, they can be quite large and intimidating in their packs, and there's been a lot of rape and theft lately in my neighborhood, which *you* can't do anything about of course. I'm so poor. I am a female who is nearly forty and unemployed, though this new temp job could become something when it starts, but for now I can't even afford to get my hair done or buy new clothes. I'm obviously concerned about looking professional and presentable, not to mention trying to meet a man—and how will I ever be able to do that if I can't pay to have my hair colored by experienced professionals? They look at me like I'm special needs, those girls on the train. They think I don't speak Spanish, but I know what they're saying after Bob's and my time in Chile and Argentina when I was still stupid enough to think what people like them needed was a good dose of Marx—what a dope!—and the people on all the buses looked at us like we must be crazy for carrying copies of Noam Chomsky in the station and on the bus—like we had no idea. And we didn't, is the hilarious part. We were typical, guilty, spoiled liberal middle-class kids, with slightly better than-average state university educations, the first in our respective classes, big whoop. And I'm standing there chattled with a giant backpack, four-feet-eleven, and they're towering over me and having the best time thinking I'm ignorant to their insults and hypocritical grins at me. They probably believe I'm a colonialist in their 'hood, an idiot—but you can't be *both*. I mean, aren't colonialists supposedly clever?"

I'd paid for her movie ticket that night, her refreshments, her wine, but not her taxi fare. I stood on the corner and hailed her taxi, and she was tipsy and maybe forgot to ask for the twenty.

"Can I have that twenty?" I can hear her say in her honking Cleveland accent at any other time. She wasn't too shy. Faith was the last in a line of nine children in an Irish Catholic family, and you can imagine how exhausted those parents must have been (Faith was born ten years after the eighth child), trying to respond to the needs of their kids in college or starting high school, all of them experimenting with dope or having adolescent crises. She couldn't act meek or be silent but said what she wanted or needed. But when she was drunk she'd sometimes lose the thread.

I would go months without seeing her then an email would pop into my box or there'd be a message on our answering machine. I'd write or call her back, loath to do it but feeling the tug of obligation. She just always seemed beset. Her problems were romantic—Bob was still trying to get in touch with her from Istanbul and she didn't seem able to cut him off—or else there were everyday practical problems. She got bed bugs, difficult since she had a cat. She got another job and this one at a publishing house—an absolute dream for her—but felt blocked from moving up by the two younger Asian women she said were trying to thwart her progress, always telling her the wrong things to throw her off and edge her out. When I got back from Maine one year there was, however, a sudden burst of sunshine in the form of a long email. She'd gotten sober. She'd been unable to take it anymore. The night before her first meeting, frustrated in her effort to find weed (since her dealer was mad at her for no real reason, it was all a misunderstanding), she had somehow known that when she woke up from her drunken, stoned state, she'd get out of bed and shower and go to the Spanish-language Pentecostal church basement and confess her addictions.

Now when she called and cried she said, "I just need to sit with my feelings. That's what my sponsor would say. I want a child. I'll never meet anyone. I have, like, no fucking money!"

Then I had told her to relax and tried reassuring her that she'd meet someone in AA.

"Really? You think so? But no, you're right—I have *much* to be grateful for. I have an education, I'm intelligent, I've regained my dignity. But in this country, now, in this culture . . ."

Before, the demon had been capitalism, now it was socialism. Now she was proud of her ninety-year-old father, a member of the Greatest Generation because he had fought in World War Two, the one she used to make fun of for his funny old-fashioned beliefs. And though she never made fun of me, more and more I felt like a eunuch, a gay housewife in an imaginary suburb.

"You're unbelievably lucky," she said, "and I'm not saying you have no idea because you work as hard as anyone I know. And it's not because you're a New York homosexual, privileged in the era of gay rights, on the heels of civil rights, which I made my subset in my anthropology major. It's not even that. It's the media. It's the media and the liberal political establishment."

Once I met Faith after one of her meetings, her "Atlantic Meeting," which meant she was among celebrities and artsy ex-drunks who made her feel envious. It was full of writers, theater people, and small-film directors. There she hoped to meet empathetic types who'd read her South America writings. "Not that I'm even counting on it, to be honest. Bunch of flimsy socialists."

I didn't remind her that I probably leaned more in their direction than in hers. They were all outside the Atlantic Meeting smoking, Faith too. "And I hate myself for smoking," she said.

Afterwards we had dinner at a Second Avenue diner that had a reasonably priced menu of salad, entree, side, and bread—a full, home-style spread. I was feeling very optimistic for Faith.

She'd ordered the flounder and things and she was several months into sobriety and said, chewing a roll, bright-eyed, she had gorgeous gray eyes eye-lined just so, "When I think about it, really fucking think about it? I'm just so grateful we ate so well at home, such healthy food. My mom was insistent on it. Whatever her problems were, and they were legion, when we got home every night, there was a nutritious hot meal waiting for us," she said, sounding like a Department of Agriculture propaganda film narrated by a lab-coated scientist-actor. "Such delicious food!"

She had once made fun of the lineup of packages of Birds Eye frozen vegetables on the counter next to the ground beef or split quartered chickens thawing in the sink. "The industrial-agricultural corporate interests in America," she'd said, "is no different, when you think about it, from the military-industrial complex now waging war in Latin America. Eisenhower, Dwight D. fucking Eisenhower, coined the term military-industrial complex. Eisenhower! And yet this son of American wars, the *war-maker*, had been prescient. Not that anyone in post-Nixon America—Jesus Christ, it makes me ill. And shampoo, do you know what the difference between shampoo and soap is? Like one ingredient. I shampoo with Ivory soap—not to be their corporate dupe!"

Way back when, Faith was this little adorable imp with a buzz-cut hairdo. I had instantly fallen for her, wondering if she wasn't a lesbian. She was an Ohio State grad done up in a baby-doll dress, Doc Martens lace-up boots, black tee, and coral lipstick, a feminine firecracker. How she'd hated her parents, the Catholic school she was sent to, her narrow childhood. She'd been "owned" from the get-go, she was a "product." She could deconstruct the whole pathetic deal.

And then, gradually over a couple of decades, then seemingly overnight when I'd gotten the bright, hopeful email, she'd made the swing into the other direction. It was breathtaking.

Her life had been a sketchbook of mistakes—she could admit in the diner, following the Atlantic Meeting. Her notebooks from South America urgently told her, "Make us into a novel! Inform your country!" Only they were not really mistakes. She'd been led through those trials.

"And I really believe this," she said, "that they were a test—in my faith in God—which I never really lost as it turns out. My father, my mother, thank God for them and their example."

She was still fragile and feminine, but also the fierce pixie I'd met in writing workshop. I couldn't count them all, the tightly grasping loves she'd had, and I was the promiscuous gay guy.

You had to go twenty years back to graduate school to see us both, when I was still puny.

I couldn't judge her for leaving the first boyfriend for the second, Bob, who was married. Her hurricane graduate school life—the parties she had in her too-tiny apartment, her late nights arguing with all of the workshop newcomers about the Beats and Bukowski, gulping Pabst Blue Ribbon and smoking menthol lights until she coughed

237

and made no sense. Faith meant what she said, even when she was far gone and next to unintelligible. She had to be carried to bed, or she missed the Monday freshman comp class she was scheduled to teach. We graduated, she took off with Bob to South America. I joined the Peace Corps and ran away to the Middle East and then Eastern Europe. We fell out of touch. And then in New York through a mutual colleague we had gotten back in touch a decade and a half ago, when she was still a bemused leftist, bitter like me.

Already, before 9/11, she was showing some signs. 9/11 and she came unhinged.

"I thank God for Fox News," she said. "No, I thank God for any—*any*—opposing view."

Then it wasn't just the opposing view. It was the right view, the one other networks were afraid to express because it was true. Her mother had died of cancer. Her schizophrenic brother, also. Now she had seven siblings left. Six of them had been trying to talk her into joining AA. I'd long felt queasy around Faith. Her mind was a frantic pendulum, mine a dull, insistent, and heavy bell clapper always gonging on time. She was doing the heavy work, thinking, rethinking.

"But you know what? All this feel-good junk, and I'm serious? This psychotherapeutic mumbo-jumbo, and excuse me for using a cliché, this march-in-line rhetoric, no better than some structuralist, poststructuralist, or semiotic lit-crit claptrap, this weak-kneed, genuflecting-toward-well-meaning, politically correct point of view? It's bullhonkey. I'm sorry but I can't merely fall into pace. I have spent my life yearning towards the truth. I'm an intellectual, and as a professed intellectual, someone who examines the evidence—you know what? Fuck that. I'm a *Catholic*."

Her rough, smoke-cured voice dissolved into a girly foam of rising giggles—the teen who used to throw slumber parties when her upper-middle-aged mother was too tired to host them.

"Well, but Fox News," I said, trying to place Fox on her socialist-activist continuum, still at the stage when I wasn't perceiving her shift, her swing. "Faith, Fox is the fomenting enemy!"

"I know, I know. So who's going to want me?" she said, her pace not letting up. "I want a baby! I want to get married, and yet I'm so over the hill. Do you know how lucky you are?"

"I do, dear." I could hear the bemused condescension in my voice. "No, I do. I really do." But I didn't, quite.

I'd never had to do any of the heavy lifting, I'd never been an activist. I was a *housewife*.

Now she was sober, dividing her salad and main course for a leftovers lunch the next day. She found graceful ways to be blunt. Before, she was a radical-thinking liberal, hoping to make the world a better place. Now she was a conservative hoping to keep the world sane and in its proper place.

I wasn't expecting her to make it personal and suddenly about Perry and me. You didn't try to predict Faith. I hadn't predicted her going into AA, and here she was, all sunshine, lovely.

"I just think you guys would both benefit from AA," she'd said. "You'd both blossom."

"Perry hasn't had a drink or smoke since 1982, he writes a book a year, gets his work done."

"Yeah," she said musingly, "but what it gives back, the program. The system makes you take stock. It makes you catalog and list and in the midst of taking stock you taxonomize your motives and motivations. Are those the same thing?—hard to say! But, it's the kind of question the twelve steps compel you to ask yourself. The hardest part of course is trying not to reach for physical and I'll say sensual coping mechanisms. With Perry, it's food, I guess—right? You examine yourself while sitting with your feelings. See, I already feel better since starting to talk to you."

I seemed to be hearing that she believed her enthusiasm could be that infectious.

"Great." My voice trilled into a chime of exultant exhaustion: "No, but that's great!"

"And for you it's sex, right?"

"I never have sex," I said. "I have an open relationship but never any sex."

"That's what I'm talking about. If you could just sit with your feelings and join AA. My sponsor's about got me convinced to attend Al-Anon meetings, too. You know, from my mom."

Just then I'd wanted to freak and abandon her ass in the diner without paying the check.

"Faith, we have good days and bad days," I said. "That's the long and short of it, okay?"

"Wow, I never thought I'd know you to get so defensive. I mean, when we first met . . ."

"I'm really tired. I just want to say go home, darling, and that I'm the same person . . ."

I paid the check and outside the front door of the diner she smiled and we hugged.

"All right, sir. I have you in my heart, I pray for you, even if you think it does no good."

"That doesn't bother me at all," I said with conciliatory cheer. "It's my Southern idiom."

Later she'd met him, the one whom I'd haplessly and cavalierly promised her she would. I had pictured a Fox News–watching Christian, ideally a Catholic to light candles alongside, but nothing would ever be so simple with Faith. Truth was, I could never stop adoring my Faith.

"You were right, I met a guy," Faith said at lunch. "The only sticky part is he's Hindu. I had trouble telling my dad at first, but he just wants me to be happy, *sane*. He's happy for me!"

"Awesome! And maybe that's why they call them the Greatest Generation."

"I know you hate the Catholic Church," she said. "And that you're anti-Vatican."

"All true. But what's that got to do with your dad, technically? He sounds rather wise."

"It's taken me this long but I've come around to understanding my father's the wisest and most sane person I know. We were arguing about affirmative action, and he said, 'Faith, would I ever tell you to go on welfare when I never in a million years would have—when I *could* have?'"

"He used 'never in a million years'?" I said.

I was in Maine the year before when Faith had called to tell me, "We're engaged, and I'm pregnant!" Nothing Faith ever said could surprise me. "I'm so happy! I'm so in love!"

"What did I tell you?"

"I know, right? Will you come to my wedding? It's in Philadelphia, and it's Hindu."

When she told me the date, I was glad to have something planned so that I could bow out.

"I can't believe what's happening," she'd concluded. "A bountiful basket of blessings!"

There was nothing a gay man could wish for his straight women friends more than some marital bliss. I thought of Faith constantly in Maine, because here was where I'd gotten some of her life's highlights, and anyway there was nothing to do in Maine but listen to the sounds of our thoughts—which was why Perry and I came to Maine. We weren't lashed by the media distractions. We could be peaceful again and work on our friendship, more important than any felicity in bed.

Now I was sitting with my feelings all alone up here, as she'd put it in her program lingo.

I was at the kitchen sink looking out across the inlet after that walk. The night had come on so quickly. He was watching the Olympics in the next room, all the beautifully fit divers, and said, "I don't know, darling, but I've been feeling punk. Tummy aches. Maybe I just shouldn't eat. These meds give me horrible, scalding diarrhea. I'm on the potty all day long practically."

"Do you want me to run off the Neck in the car and grab you some soup?"

"Now, this boy is from North Carolina. I think he's great but he's like in fifth place."

I waited and then called into the next room, "Perry, did you hear my question?"

"I don't know what I want. You know what I want? I want to be sixty again. I remember talking to Hiram Grayson, you remember that guy, poet? A few years ago, I was complaining to him. Maybe he's ten-twelve years older than me. He said, 'I wish I was your age all over. I was your age, I felt great, young. Now everything's going wrong.' Now I know what he means."

With scissors I was snipping kale, trimming it from the tough, chewy stalks to roast, and I did remember Hiram Grayson and his translations of Cavafy. I didn't know if what I was doing I should stop doing or what. The reflective kitchen light made it difficult to look through the plate glass across the inlet, but I leaned in, squinting to peer. I didn't know if my kitchen preparations were about to be wasted, but then a sense of patience came over me. Nutrition was my system of recovery, my religion, but I was starting not to believe even in it. I called, "I remember him."

"Oh, anyway."

"No, go on."

"I dreamed about him saying it again this morning, before I got up—and it felt suicidal."

My reaction was to think of Faith, the well-named, ill-named, second-guessing Faith—it contradicted her name—her second-guessing. Her need to spiritualize and taxonomize and make every-thing into a neat metaphysical bundle, whatever. I put down my scissors and the greens and flicked my hands of their juice and leafy bits. I went in to hug him, half-insensibly.

"Now darling," I began. To lose him was unthinkable, but I thought about it. "Darling."

"I go to bed and think I won't wake up."

"Not waking up and doing something intentionally are two different things."

He laughed, reanimated, and said, "Oh, I know. I was just talking. I can't kill myself!"

I said, "We all think that at times. I'm sorry you have to. Dinner'll be on in fifteen."

My mother would have put me to bed and kissed me, then sat up worrying.

Later that night, a window on the second story of the next house down along the neck, on the other side of the rocky crescent beach, flashed on and off. It would stop for a minute and do it again. The teenagers from my earlier walk: the house was in the direction they'd been headed, tromping through the woods off-trail. Youthful game, one of them trying to get on the nerves of the other and daring him to get pissed off. I remembered the thrill of "haunted houses" as a kid.

There was no plan for who we were. Night was long for us. We'd go to bed separately. I read, which had become my coping strategy. I could live with him as long as we slept separately.

I could see him from the adirondack. His room at the other end of the main house jutted into a field—the front yard, if you were arriving on a boat—of ferns grown high and pine and poplar saplings, and whatever was going on in there was directly in my sight line. He liked to keep the handmade wooden shades rolled up with the chains fastened to hold them in place, the full light of the morning and after-noon coming in to wake him or keep him from napping for too long. He had the overhead recessed lights burning and was reading in bed or sitting at the little desk, where I could see his head through the paned window as he bent into his laptop's screen-glow. Napping too long, when in the past it refreshed him, now depressed and frustrated him. He was losing his life, the remainder of it, he feared, in dribs and drabs. A lot of his Paris friends (who were older, admittedly) had died. People were asking him if once he'd finished the novel he was writing he thought he'd ever write another. I watched him ease up from the desk, pushing on the edge of it with his fists in launching thrusts, one-two, to go to the bathroom, ducking slump-shouldered out of sight, then reenter his snug, pine-paneled sleeping quarters getting ready for bed. He reached up with his right hand to grab the frame of the big picture window you could see the dazzling or somber inlet through, and carefully stepped up onto the platform the bed rested on that was eight inches high. The house had been built by a pair of Buddhist craftsmen in the sixties who'd come to the area with hippies and other alternative types who'd colonized themselves around a famous guru who for all anybody knew had since escaped samsara and the material world, along with its abundant lobsters, and pushed on to nirvana. Everything was tongue-in-groove, or pegged flush. There was glass everywhere and in the solarium at the center of the house the newest owners had scattered the beanbag chairs we didn't use and on the pine walls hung Formica shelving that bore sea-shells and frames of local nature photography. It got too hot in there on the sunnier days to be used as anything but a greenhouse transition zone from his room of slumber and huddled work to the dining room with its oilclothed table and the kitchen. His bathroom had a barrel-shaped tub of tightly fitted cedar planks, no glue or liner. Just out the back door was a shower that cascaded onto always freshly turned bark chips. He bathed outdoors mostly, smelling trees and the ocean. That part of the house was self-contained. For hours, I imagined, he could feel alone in nature.

It had a European washer that cycled forever but was quietly effi-cient and cleaned clothes better than ours at home—and since it fell in his domain, he was in charge of the laundry up here. I was glad, not to relinquish my usual New York workload, but to see him more happily active. I had to walk him and this could be a trial. If it rained, which it did a great deal this year in spates, he might whine and give up, say he wanted to turn back. But he'd put on three pounds in the last week. He'd been away from his previous month of hard physical therapy and was slowing down and getting creakier. The driveway out to the shoreline road was winding and gravel-packed and gave him steady footing. He looked at me, huffing helplessly. I waited pitilessly. He huffed on.

It wasn't in his nature to be sad or depressed or self-pitying for long. He'd been raised in Christian Science, but I wonder if at the end anyone in his family had done anything more than go through that religion as a phase long enough to absorb its basic self-determining optimism. He'd worked hard in physical therapy, sweating from his exertions for the first time on purpose. He'd obeyed his therapists and pushed himself. The harder he worked, the less he complained. When he was done he might be tired but he followed the tenets without sagging defeatedly into laziness.

I'd watched him go from "lame and halt" to hobbling mechanically then to more fluidity. But he had good days and bad days. When people asked about him, I said, "Good and bad days."

When he returned from the bathroom after brushing his teeth or whatever, I watched him pause by the bed, hobble up a step, then, looking down, like a marionette with some of its strings cut, teeter and fall sideways onto it, collapsing, half folding but landing safely before tugging the covers cozily up over him. After dinner earlier he'd said, "Come say good night before you go to bed." "I don't want my violent snoring to wake you up," I said, and he replied, "I don't care."

If I got up first the next morning, I would make the coffee and start the tedious half-hour process of boiling our steel-cut oats. From the fridge I got out the quart-size cardboard basket of blueberries and from the freezer the golden flaxseed meal I would sprinkle over the finished oats and berries and bananas with low-fat Greek yogurt—all while imagining his arteries unclogging.

Still, every once in a while we would drive into town and order the greasy delicious lunch I'd allow him—you couldn't be too strict or you'd have revolt on your hands—and after my fried oysters and his pork chop with sweet potato fries we eased up the hill in the rental car and parked in the library parking lot. The library was prosperous and self-vaunting, many of the cardholders well-known New York authors honoring the organization with readings and benefit appearances. In turn, it celebrated itself on its bulletin boards, which advertised exclusive signings and cocktail gatherings, where you could actually meet seasonal literary celebs and "pick their brains," as one stapled-up flyer crowed. The town generally loved itself in the pages of its weekly publications. It winkingly announced its farmers' markets featuring the organic produce grown here, fruits and vegetables that would make you young again, replant you in mother nature, and remind you how special you were because you were well heeled enough to rub elbows with the entire delightfully casual, liberal, lovable, genius crew. Combination pancake breakfast and book sale with auctions of signed (by their authors!) first editions. Throw a blueberry pie in their face and five dollars'd go to cystic fibrosis, the rheumatoid arthritis center, or literacy among young people with ADHD. Clambake, lobster dinner, hacky-sack tournament—"DOWNEASTERS, come and get involved."

"Downeast" meant we were downwind and east of Boston if you

245

were a leisure sailor—if you were a Kennedy or the author of
Charlotte's Web and *Stuart Little* (who'd summered here).

I doubted that kale figured heavily into the diets of the old WASPy
guard like E. B. White. But kale was now prominent—just as important
an issue as the Iraq War. And at one farmers' market the other week
I'd stopped at a stand and asked what was the difference between the
dark variety of kale and the brighter, juicier-looking one. Kale was
boring kale, I'd once believed. But no.

The man who'd grown it looked healthy and pink. His gray beard
glistened in the Maine sunlight. This was just before the gray overcast
medium-pressure days. He wasn't being tolerant when he tittered, he
was just so high on his own health. And the older couple next to me
listened expectantly when he cheerfully replied, "This darker kale,
she's your choice. Like if you want to make a kale smoothie, that's the
guy you want." He winked at the couple. "Here's your fella."

The man of the couple, bald but gleaming all over, said, "Well, I
was just going to say."

"She's a beauty," said the woman—and we laughed, happily ignorant
of kale's gender.

"It's so full of phytonutrients," the grower broadly announced, "the
choice is obvious."

I believed in the healing power of kale and greens and farm-
fresh produce, God's bounty as expressed in organic agriculture. He
presented only six items on his table, everything lovely. I bought rain-
bow chard, too, and he gave me a free bumper sticker reading, "Get
Your Kale On!"

That night I'd roasted the kale and chard, but everything else had
come from the grocery store, which was no ordinary supermarket.
Upscale supermarkets had stopped designating health food aisles as
such. The one I went to, when I wasn't at Walmart, called their health
food section "Wellness Lifestyle." I wanted to do everything I could to
keep Perry out of the hospital.

I was in the seafood section getting a pound of salmon meditating
on omega oils and their ability to help clear arteries when I saw a
couple of guys coming from dairy, one pushing the cart but both

pivoting their heads trying to remember what they needed. I couldn't recall their names, only their occupations. One was a Brooklyn private school headmaster, the other an architect. It was an effort to decide whether or not I should say hello, but they were headed in my direction.

I waved and the one I'd been attracted to at a party two years before, the one pushing the cart, slowed down and knitted his brows. I waved again and he stopped, looked at me, nodded. I at first read his reaction of "remind-me-again?" vagueness as a kind of admonishment. I recalled their cocoa-colored, surrogate-mom children spinning prettily in the August dusk. I remembered the pride with which the heterosexual, mostly literary couples had included them. We were very, very attractive—gay people—as long as our lives didn't sound perverted or sordid. I acted like a housewife seeing them, pretending to be all about the wild-caught versus the farm-raised salmon but turning toward them, surprised, suddenly uncannily beholden. My mother had led my father away from their hometown to escape the storm of Christian conformity. They'd wanted to dance and drink and not be Baptists. I was a Baptist again. I might as well have been. My parents had watched me get immersion-baptized and were proud, but why? Because it meant I was a part of things, I'd made that anecdotal transition; I was visually and socially whole, until I wasn't again.

We came with a chili I'd spent hours that afternoon assembling with fresh ingredients, including beans I'd soaked overnight and boiled that morning. I was tired from chopping and adding it all at just the right moment. Nor did I resort to using canned tomato sauce or canned tomatoes since it was well known that the linings of the cans combined with the acid of the tomatoes made for a toxic brew—in case anyone asked, and I was sure that these mothers could taste the difference.

While I cooked, the boys in our cove launched their Sunfish, sailing it in nonstop loops.

In the car going over, nervous, I said, "Honey, I don't want you wallflowering, okay?"

"Okay."

Since, but also leading up to, his stroke, in social settings he would hang back unless some nice young person approached, recognizing him. He hadn't gotten his due, was the bottom line.

"I think it's important for you to mingle and talk to folks. It's good for your self-esteem."

Eventually he said, "I will. I promise I'll talk to people and not recede into the scenery."

"Wonderful, darling. Because I just think it's so important for you and your condition."

I was a weird hybrid of my mother and someone else, a gay "aunt" who'd studied group dynamics at Vassar. Mom would never have used a psychological phrase like self-esteem. That would come much later, with Donahue and Oprah. She *would* have used "sociable," but she was also a touch hick-irreverent. She'd have said, "Did you make any new friends, Dingleberry?"

Skip, the private school headmaster, and Barry, the architect, had gotten us invited.

"And you say the architect guy told you he'd just finished my last novel and liked it?"

"As my mother'd say," I said, "'I wouldn't shit you, 'cause you're my favorite turd.'"

"And then cackle," he said. "God, that cackle!"

"*You* didn't grow up with it."

"What's his name, the architect? What kind of architecture?"

"Barry. We didn't talk about it, so you'll have to ask him yourself. We talked about *you*. They were saying they'd heard you'd been ill. Then we exchanged numbers and that was that."

We were headed to the house of the greatest novelist of my generation, whom we had met in New York at a party for him. I'd once reviewed one of his more minor books with a great deal of enthusiasm, and at that New York party I'd identified myself and he'd acted grateful, saying it was one of the smarter reviews and hugging me. We'd exchanged emails but not kept up. It had made me nervous even to think of writing him. I knew he was busy producing large Nabokovian tomes that were funny and that swept the themes of America into big bright piles. He was a dad.

We found the long white wooden fence, after swerving around a black lab in the road, and climbed the steep drive that mounted a lawn-carpeted hill of even, flossy emerald. The view was going to be good. Perry gently and fretfully congratulated me on not getting us killed so far.

The hour was beautiful, and I paused in my mind collecting my thoughts and willpower.

"Let's go home," Perry said.

"Yes, let's."

"But we can't."

"I know."

Perry had been decorated by French literary entities for his service to their patrimony and won prizes all over the world. He was dazzled by runaway youthful success in any country. His climb had been slow, perilous, and demeaning. He'd never starved but he'd free-lanced in squalor for decades and only recently had he begun to surrender to the idea that he was content with what he'd achieved and that it was all relative—probably—anyway. I often had to remind him of this.

We were getting out of the car when he said, "Do you think it's because we fool around?"

"Do I think what's because we fool around?"

"Do you think the reason we don't get invited to things up here is that I write about being promiscuous, and our having other partners? Do you think that impedes you?"

"Yes," I said, flinching a little, "but I don't care. Fuck 'em if they can't take a joke."

"But does that make you mad? Am I getting in the way of your career, writing about it?"

"Not in the least," I said, counting the contacts I *might* have had. "I like my freedom."

"I like it, too. But a funny thing, now that I'm on a cane, they'll probably think . . ."

He looked across at a scenically rail-fenced pasture, high-grown without any animals.

I got out and came around and got his fucking cane out of the back seat. The lobster pot, a tall ironstone vessel, was full near to the top with chili on the floor behind my seat. Just a lady at the covered-dish supper in the fellowship hall after the church service, me and my shitty chili.

I was helping him out of the car when he added, "The old libertine can barely move."

"That's hilarious," I muttered, though how I cared for him. "Here. Grab my hand."

"They probably believe I deserved it, the old lech."

"Don't lose your nerve, Myrna."

The avenging angel in the title of this piece was a goat farmer responsible for making the area's most famous artisanal cheese. It was sold locally but got as far as Boston, and there was a specialty shop in Brooklyn that sold it, too. "Chèvre Chad" it was called. More on him in a bit.

The minute we approached the house there was a carnival of emitted music and lights.

The children of local craftsmen and schoolteachers were tumbling down the grassy slope together with the children of seasonal literary aristocracy, a painterly sight not unworthy of Mary Cassatt, who'd been in the area a century ago. The older kids were up on the terrace sharing fun YouTubes with one another on their iPads and snickering, "Awesome, right? What a moron!"

In another minute I was alone, relieved of the pot, on the patio of the old, large house—a Victorian manor of captains' dreams. This was a perfect world, a Valhalla absolved of cigarette smoking and Jell-O molds. Nearby, a table groaned with salads and fixings, perfect clean meats.

The great writer's wife had nothing to do suddenly, or else she wouldn't have stopped to talk to me. She was drinking a beer and came up to me as though no time had passed since we'd first met at that party years ago in New York, and she said, "We've been so worried.

We'd heard he was ill. But he's getting around fine, right? We just didn't expect you guys to be here."

"Day by day," I said, drinking a matching beer and having decided I'd only drink two.

"He looks great. I need to go in and check on things in a sec. Skip and Barry say hi."

"Oh," I said, suddenly chastened. "Aren't they here?"

"Last night they went to Bar Harbor for lobster and both of them got food poisoning."

It was getting dark and my cell went off in my pocket, vibrating against my right thigh.

It was Faith, I saw from the display. I answered and the writer's wife panicked away.

I went to a corner of the terrace away from the screaming children's voices and answered.

"Hi, it's Faith," I heard punily, and I thought of how Faith, a recent undergrad from Ohio State in cultural anthropology when I'd first met her, would have remarked on all this. I thought of terms like "tribalism" and "reference groups." Back then she could swing a phrase and deploy the nomenclature. "How are you? I hear music. Are you at a party, in Maine? Is it a bad time?"

"Yes, I'm still in Maine," I said, "and yes, at a party. You're *good*, lady."

I thought that, too, she would be envious, the leisurely writer's life. She would make fun of it, but it was what she'd wanted for herself and, as trappings minus kids go, what I'd wanted.

"Is this a bad time?"

"I can move somewhere quieter," I said, stepping onto the immaculate lawn. "Better?"

I thought of her old East Harlem apartment, the drafty box, her crucifix on the wall. But she wasn't living there anymore. She and Rakesh were up in godawful Westchester somewhere.

"It's a bad time, right?" There was a hooty catch in her throat. "Because I hope not."

When we'd spoken a month before, Faith was thrilled with her life and was in love with her baby boy, Matthias, and couldn't be happier living up in Westchester County, she'd said. We were talking a bit more frequently now that she didn't have the distractions of New York to keep her busy, only her daily loads of laundry. She was making her own baby food. Rakesh was still working in the city and she could arrange her days between feeding and diapering Matthias.

"What is it, darling," I said, "not enough for Matthias's college? He eighteen already?"

She laughed. She said, "Rakesh won't take his meds and he's acting crazy, just insane."

"Meds?" I said, and I thought of her sweet-natured, dutiful husband and I stopped.

"He's bipolar, and I guess I never told you about it and he thinks he's Superman and gets into this *thing* and I don't know what to do. He just gets into this thing, this thing I don't *get*."

"Is he there now?" I said, panicking a little.

"No. He's gone off to Costco. We were supposed to go together but he huffed off alone."

"By himself? Will he be all right?"

"I guess so," she said and sniffled. She hiccupped and started to cry and then stopped.

"Are you—should I—? Wait, but is Matthias okay?"

"Matthias is fine. He's my little man, he's so wonderful." And then the little catch in her throat again. I heard her let loose with a series of grief chuckles. "He's my fucking soldier, he's so great. He's right here smiling up at me. *Hi!* He's wonderful. You should come see him when you get back, you'd be shocked how much he's grown! But yeah, Rakesh gets into his thing—"

"Of course I'll come see him and you, the day after we get back, I promise. But—"

She laughed, chuckling and hooting, and said, "You don't have to treat it so urgently. I'm not going to fall apart. But if I could just get Rakesh to come home and cool off, and if we could get to a meeting. He's always better after a meeting, just like me although I never skip mine. He gets sad and angry and resentful, so angry! It's like this burning resentful fire in his eyes, and he gets on the internet, while

I'm busy ironing or what have you, and starts in on me about the Pope, about the Catholic Church. 'Do you *know* what fucking happened in 1455? It's right here!' And I try to tell him about the media, that you can't trust it just because you read it on Wikipedia . . ."

"Why won't he take his medications, if he's got a problem? If it makes him better?"

I was saying the perfunctory thing—what people would ask me. They were holding me accountable, but I had a sometimes noncompliant patient myself, always difficult to explain.

"He doesn't trust it, he said it makes him feel like a zombie, I tell him don't drink coffee! He goes ballistic if he has more than one cup, if he has even one cup. I'll tell you one thing, and you'll probably remember this, I used to diss psychopharmacopeia out of hand, like this was just one more big liberal conspiracy to get us in line with the left-wing world-hegemonic agenda and be zombies! And I still sort of believe that, if you look at other countries around the world, which have faith-based societies and that don't gobble this stuff at a drop of a hat—but I'm a believer in it now. I thank God for these research-based corporations that sincerely do want to help people."

She was chugging her way into the old pressured speech, my shrink had called it. I might as well settle in for the next several minutes because I might not have time to interrupt her.

"I didn't believe but then I had nowhere else to turn, and I prayed on it—then I knew."

I turned toward the little shimmering cove: "I'm glad you've come over to the dark side."

"I don't know what was wrong with me, spotting corporate evil behind every little thing," she said. "I've only told his mom, who keeps saying, 'Faith, Faith! Please don't leave my son!'"

I caught a glimpse of the greatest writer of my generation not looking over. In the time I'd known Faith, he'd probably written a million brilliantly flying, silvery-pinball sentences. He was tall and dark and handsome, the usual, but he was brilliant beyond my capabilities, or my reach. I was a flea to his elephant. I wanted to wrap this up, but then Faith laughed sweet trills.

"When do you think he'll come back?" I said, feeling that she really was getting better.

"You know what? It'll be fine. No kidding. I just needed somebody to talk to for a minute," she said. "I thought if I could just talk to somebody until he got home, and then he could see me getting off the phone and knew I'd had to talk to someone—maybe that'd put the fear of God in him. Okay? Jesus! I'm such a baby! Please go back to your party. I'll be fine. *It'll* be fine."

Where we left off, I promised to call her in a day or two—a pattern with my mother, too.

When I got off a teenage goth girl was standing in front of me, and she said, "Difficult?"

She turned out to be the writer's daughter, and I said, "I remember when you were little."

"Really? How disgusting. That must have been gross. I was such a weird little freak."

"Not. It was at a party for your dad during the summer. You weren't wearing shoes."

"Like I said, gross. Were you as bored as I probably was? Are you bored now?"

She followed me to the kitchen, their beautifully appointed modern country kitchen.

Her mother came back and said, "You know my daughter, Courtney? Your chili's to die for, by the way, divine. I had a taste but there's an intense group lining up for it. Word's good."

I said, "I cooked the beans from scratch last night."

"I could taste that. Courtney's a vegetarian, aren't you, love?"

"That I am. Thanks for mentioning it, Mom. It's so polite to our guest, you big cow."

I remembered this kind of banter with my mother, how we'd tease each other, say hateful things, so that later we could make up and hug and kiss. And I remembered the slow drift away.

"Court, could you go up and tell Dylan and Bowie and Josiah that dinner's on? They are ignoring the grown-ups." The writer's wife turned and said to me, "Playing *Jarhead Desert Kill.*"

"Listen to her," said Courtney, "it's called *Desert Command: Jarhead Kill Shot*."

"Like that makes it any better. Did you notice your partner—or is he your husband—you guys get married yet?—talking to our friend Chad, the goat farmer? And we prided ourselves on thinking Chad was straight. We tried setting him up with Tara the green grocer. Have you tasted her jams, the wild blueberry, natch, being to die for? Tara's the ginger talking to my honey."

"She's gorgeous, but no, I haven't tasted her jams."

"Utterly over the moon for Chad, who thus far has given her not one whit of regard."

"What a great party," I said, "full of attractive, interesting, friendly-looking people."

"But seriously, it's none of my business, and God knows I've already had too much beer and all, but have you guys tied the knot yet? I think it's the duty of every gay couple to marry."

"Really. Why?"

"Don't be vigilant and the bastards win."

"Uh-huh."

"Look at reproductive rights. Already we're twenty years behind where we used to be."

"Which really does suck," I said, as though I was worried. She'd gone to Columbia with Barack Obama and studied political science alongside him, and I added, "You're amazing."

But she didn't appreciate it. I got the feeling that with a husband like hers, the winner of a Pulitzer, she'd expected to be president herself by now; she was grinding her energies down by wasting time talking to me. There were CEOs of major progressive start-ups here, too. I knew my audience with her was about to end, but she was married to the great man. I couldn't unstick.

Chad had long blond ringlets and a child's beautifully startled eyes, and he looked the part of God's chief swordsman in the ultimate desert battle, the Last Days, the Apocalypse, which had been pre-recorded in my young churchgoer's Book of Revelation. He had the plump, narrow, and overall Aryan Cupid's-bow lips throwing into

255

relief the purity of his complexion with their coral, high cheekbones, the works. Dusty-emerald eyes that followed my partner's and, yes (as of late), fiancé's quick glance over at me, but Michael the Archangel didn't cease working the Cupid bow.

"Isn't he hot?" she said finally. "But aren't you jealous? Says he's just a Zen goatherd."

"I've never met a goatherd before."

"Better go over there now," she said and laughed. "We never thought Chad *read*."

"Maybe he doesn't," I said, feeling a twinge of assertiveness. "That wouldn't matter."

"So you are jealous? Sorry. I never should've mixed wine and beer. Never should've crossed genres. You know what Court, my oldest and dearest, did? Stop looking at hot Chad!"

"What did she do?" I said, thinking of my mother at parties around younger men. (Once my mother had to said to me, "Want to know a powerful man, talk to his wife.") I said, "What?"

In my head I heard Mom cackle and wished she'd excuse herself from the party. She was *embarrassing* me. I came back to now, to our hostess, whom I envied and wanted to know more.

"At the beginning of the summer she drives to Walmart in my car without my say-so and applies for a fucking job. At fucking Walmart! Just to spite me, I'm still miserably convinced."

"Uh-huh," I said, wanting another designated-driver-forbidden beer but resisting. People our age never grew up, but talked as though we were still in high school. "And you said no?"

"Are you kidding? I'm not that kind of mom. But what did I ever do to deserve this?"

"Uh-huh," I said with a beery grin, "and so she's been working there all summer?"

"All summer, and says she loves it. Her best friend Rupert has mental retardation."

I nodded, wanting to say that I knew the name-tagged Rupert as a very efficient cashier.

I said, "Where I come from, Walmart's fine. You probably think I'm a sold-out redneck."

"He's actually totally cool and sweet, Rupert. Lives over in Bucksport with his mom, and she's great. Totally working-class. Dances in a titty bar in Bangor, but can you imagine? Me?"

I was more of a cut-out background guest in a party scene in her husband's future biopic, maybe her future biopic, and I nodded and said, "Maybe she'll become a great labor champion."

"Court's decided to be a brain surgeon. If that happens then great, but I love all my kids."

When she'd gone off to tend to her other guests, I felt a gnawing loss I hadn't expected.

More on the avenging angel: Chad was a vegetarian, but as a goat farmer, not vegan—and even so, apologized for not eating what I'd brought. He said he knew the passion it took to make food. He talked passion and he apologized a great deal. He said his mom was Congregationalist. I didn't know where this was going but he said he'd heard from others that my chili was nice and that chili was one of his favorite kid dishes—he'd had a *passion* for his mom's version—and that he was only sorry he couldn't have somehow tasted mine before deciding to convert, as he said.

"The veiled mysteries of the time-space continuum," I said. "The tyranny of gravity."

"Ha ha, and mass, don't forget mass," he said, smiling killingly.

He had his arm around Perry, who'd hung his cane on the step of a side staircase.

Which is how it began, though I hadn't a clue at the time. He accused me of thinking I knew everything, then apologized. I said no apologies were necessary, but he was wrong. The greatest writer of my generation had it wrong in the couple of characters he'd created out of the two of us, my fiancé and me, in a later book. Minor characters. At least he didn't stereotype us, make us lisp or, more impossibly yet, be gross caricatures of dominant top and recessive femme. The evening was also the beginning of my becoming comfortable with the designation *fiancé*.

Perry said, "Chad has his own cheese." His speech had straightened out and cleaned up. For a moment there was no slush or clutter in it. "He wants to take me out on his motorcycle."

I laughed dimly at this idea. But then I wanted him to have fun but worried about Perry's poor balance. He teetered, and leaving a chair or clothes or shoes behind set up future obstacles for himself, and I'd fuss. Sometimes getting into a car, low-slung or not, could be a trial for him.

"Motorcycle," I said, nodding and breathing, careful not to roll my eyes.

But Chad anticipated my objection, watching me, seducing me with his charm—and sex was good for the body and soul. I looked at Perry, who wore an unforgettably hapless grin. He needed this, and I needed to let him have it, was the implication. I knew I'd let him have it, just to have Chad the artisanal cheese maker and goatherd smile at me seductively another moment.

"I have two helmets. I'm an experienced rider. I've been riding for fifteen years."

"Have you been drinking?"

"Not a drop. I only touch the stuff when I'm in the barn tasting my incredible chèvre."

I pictured myself in bed with Chad, my way of approving of Perry going to bed with him. And how odd the gay world was. It was my only mode of vengeance against others' disapproval, more grounds for disapproval, and I said, "Oh, what the fuck," and Chad looked triumphant.

I took the cane, a midcentury model of chrome handled and plugged with gray orthopedic rubber, and suffered them to leave alone together. I opened another beer and listened for the roar of engine on Chad's crotch-rocket. My father had had one and had always called them that. If I had to wait another twenty minutes, lagging behind, whatever. But I felt my sand running out.

I caught sight of the writer, who was suddenly alone and standing at the foot of the stairs, at the other end of the kitchen from the back door I was about to escape through. He lifted a beer at me—and how I would have wished to be invited to join him for just one. His sentences that said so much about me, about us, and could have made an ancient epic of this evening if only my life were his—just for a few minutes . . .

Weakly I saluted him. He saluted me, but with this firm, tight smile I was sure meant he did remember me, and I danced an exit out the door with the cane like a vaudeville showman pumping it side to side, my ham's holy crozier. I didn't look back.

At home, only the master bedroom's lights were on, and I didn't try to muffle my steps. I hung the cane over a coat hook in the entrance and went to the kitchen humming, giddy. My last Pata Negra had been removed from the fridge ("spirited," I thought)—the bottle half-emptied and left next to the sink, where I'd washed the day's dishes and left them to dry in the Buddhists' handmade wooden rack. It was a sour wine, a red I had indulged myself just for nostalgia's sake, but as I lay in the cabin it felt sweet melting and spreading into my thoughts. It wasn't like what the greatest writer of my generation would end up imagining in that scene of his in that excellent and puzzlingly breathless novel about everything, called *Pharaoh's Vipers*. Every novel, I thought ruefully and with some degree of self-mortification, had to be about everything in a way. Right?

It wasn't like death tonight, though I was pleasantly, and even Buddhistically, morbid. It was more of a steady sinking, a slow, comfortable drowning, my head going smeary. I had been to the party, had been invited to the party. I stumbled out for a smoke. Across the inlet and away from the direction of the bedroom where Perry lay with undoubtedly one of the most comely and appealing angels anyone could ever get lucky with, someone might be talking about me. I might be spoken of in terms either damning or reservedly approving. And beyond the inlets and fingers the vessels at sea were sailing or at anchor. Their lonely crews began to dream of mermaids, and flatscreen TVs. They dreamed of those women leading them to the ones they had loved forever.

unsticking

He was chilly and had to pee. He should get up. He was in the tropics (actually the *subtropics*) and he was alone in the rental. The light was bright so it had to be ten a.m. already. Scott went alone to breakfast with the easy self-assuredness of a poet. In New York, he knew a lot of poets, more poets than office workers although many were both. Mentally he saw them in their cubicles, from which they social-networked and posted their screeds of outrage against the rest of the world. If they were president, or less humbly king or emperor, least modestly dictator, first thing they'd do they'd give each poet a living wage, they asserted. Next and almost as noble were the visual artists, and last their novelist friends, even following the filmmakers and dancers, who came after the musicians and the composers. He was glad he hadn't chosen poetry but what he'd chosen was nearly as silly. Whenever people asked, Scott coolly said he was a hausfrau.

One who was more or less happily married. His lover Perry had stopped coming down to Key West so often, needing sex to be within easy reach. In New York, all those Latinos in search of a half-hour daddy. Perry was twenty-five years older than Scott, but with a bottomless libido.

The night before, Scott's trick had said, "So wait, how can you be here a whole month? I mean, what do you do for a living? You some kind of world traveler, rich bitch, financier?"

Sometime in the middle of the night Scott thought his liver belched. Couldn't be good.

Scott really had to stop sleeping around. He'd never been very good at it, and sometimes he knew he was lousy, and inexplicably they'd want to meet up again. He'd buy a lot of drinks, give away a five here or there, try to wrap up the deal or to get it over with, close the book on that little mistake, just make the impending exit—or he'd wake up next to some guy less with regrets than a gloomy amazement. For a few minutes he'd tell himself he still had it. The feeling passed when the conversation got perfunctory. It felt better waking up alone, on his own good time.

Outside, the Polish landscapers' leaf blower went into full whir across the shady deck.

This island was small—and even though it was only for a month a year, before long these little establishments he frequented were exhausted to him. It was a pond, and he was just a trout making its way back to the tributary that had fed him to the stagnant system. Two or three nights a week he'd stay home in this rented cottage and read Kipling, or Saki, or Stevenson. It was not just the feeling of being fucked-out, it might be the weather. Pirate nights here, the moon behind a gauze of ragged clouds, a nor'easter insinuating itself, rain hitting with the force of a monsoon.

He was trying to quit smoking, and lying in bed reading a Penguin classic made him cozy and he wasn't tempted by tobacco. The cessation drug gave him long, tangible dreams involving old friends he hadn't seen in a while or else famous people he'd once met. He was doing the cast members of the dream a service, preparing them meals they enjoyed or hauling their laundry, and the conversations were amusing and frank. Still, by early afternoon he wanted his first cigarette.

The boy and two girls were down from New York, a hen party in southward motion, and at first they didn't seem to notice him. They were laughing and drinking and choogling in place on top of plastic-covered stools. Their voices serrated the bar's air, nasal and whining, near hysterical.

The boy was talking about his roommate in Hell's Kitchen, jubilantly proud, but in a kind of appalled-sounding way. They were all happy to have made it to New York, all of them in their twenties somewhere, and it was exhilarating to them, obviously, to be talking so grown-up. They seemed hardly to have noticed they were on-island, in fact; and the boy said about his roommate, "He's the most chill kid I know, he's *Long Island*. He's a sculptor teaching at FIT, with a gallery already, and he's *my* age!" The boy sipped a pink-slush cocktail and waggled his eyebrows with further mortal astonishment. "He's beautiful, y'all'd be impressed. The kid's *serious* mad-hot."

Boys called girls guys, and everybody of that generation, it seemed, called each other kid.

Once the boy slipped talking about the roommate back in the city and referred to him as a "sculpture." The girls hadn't noticed or were too polite to say something. Really, they all looked like they could still be in high school, but no one ever carded in Key West and there were a lot of runaway-looking teens passing through—real kids, scared but at the same time capable of asking Scott for immorally small sums of money in exchange for whatever sexual favors he might want. He'd talk to them and sometimes take them up on their offers, and next year they'd be gone forever. He hoped that the five dollars he'd handed them while listening to their childhood stories had bought them the cocktail that inspired them to pick up and leave finally, yet from personal experience he knew that's not how it worked. He nodded into their anecdotes of growing-up hell—traumas he had never personally gone through as a boy. They'd order cheap scotch on his dime, laughing at who knew what, something in the backs of their minds they were putting through a compare-and-contrast processing chip, the fishing-boat rape one mentioned, the mother who'd made them into their boyfriend's boy-whore. They'd wink at him, reach over, stroke him down there or pinch his nipple or lift his shirt and bite it and tell him he was one of the nicest guys ever—then for twenty dollars take him to the dark back room and let him go down. Immeasurably un-fathomably sordid pasts, truly badly scripted porn material. But it was happening, and he wasn't trying to stop it.

"Is this not the most amazing bar on the planet?" the first girl said. "I ask you, is it not?"

unsticking

The doors and barred windows of the bar were open to the bright sidewalk that was busy with the cruise-ship daytrippers, the rednecks stopping and looking in and grinning at what they saw, forming the words already to explain it to the folks back home. Every once in a while they entered, dragged by their wives, who announced to the drunks hunched around the rectangle of the front bar they *loved it*, it made them *feel at home*, the more outrageous the better, just like in Alabama before they got hitched when they still knew how to *have fun* for crying out loud. The drag queens came downstairs handing out flyers for the nine and eleven o'clock shows, as tall as Las Vegas showgirls, but with mouths on them, their moth-wing lashes fluttering at these balding and ovoid men and shooting the shit for a moment with the women: "Your man can do *what?*"

The first girl lifted her cosmo in its martini glass and took in the vintage disco, certifiably trashed. She shuddered and a giggle tickled her then she lost her balance and toppled backwards off the stool, landing on her back with a *whomp!* No *crunch*, but her friends fell apart laughing.

The boy and the other girl turned realizing, covering their mouths, and helped her up.

A few minutes later, when Scott came out of the restroom, all three of the kids were gone.

He'd wasted his twenties, attending useless graduate seminars and applying to even more academic programs he'd never had any intentions of entering—doing hard, useless, arcane work.

Scott had never been very realistic. He'd let too many of his years with Perry pass, when he could have made better use of them helping support his lover, waiting tables, doing something out of his lowly, servile skill set, the one that had put bread on the table when he was poor—anything so the uncomplaining Perry could retire at seventy. It seemed the least Scott could do for him. It was the minimum an overworked guy like Perry could ask of a stealthy freeloader from Dixie.

Then again, Perry had indulged him. No one wanted to be lonely. Only the strongest and most determined lived alone, and that's how they died as well. Happier, maybe, but alone.

In Key West, even when he wasn't here, being horny, Perry was with Scott always.

What did you see?" said Perry, and Scott said he hadn't seen much, only the usual tonight. He never wanted to leave when he got started in Key West. It was Shangri-la, Scott's second youth.

After five beers Scott was walking home past palm tree and palm tree. He'd grown up in Florida and the style of some of these houses—concrete-block, flat-roofed—reminded him of the summer evenings when he didn't want to go back inside, and yet it was usually too hot to decide. Sometimes he'd be scamming on another neighborhood kid who wanted sex, too, but sex just did that to you. Perry was talking about the sex he had just had with one Omero. Over the phone, it didn't sound so interesting or all that enticing. It sounded comedy-of-manners, with a computer-dating odor of profile-overload desperation. Over the phone, Scott could smell the silicone gel.

"Omero, *Homer* see, came from the D.R. The Napoleon of sodomy, his profile said. His family are related to Spanish royalty and continental aristocrats," said Perry with a ghastly snort.

It gave Scott peace, that Perry was sexually contented. Perry could never be quite filled-up erotically. He'd come from a time more abject than Scott's, and in Scott's time you still were not supposed to have relations with the same sex. Now it was almost de rigueur even for straight people, a little experimentation before the storm of marriage. "Relations" sounded Biblical. One day the Bible would have no effect on Scott at all. But not yet. Hipsters and young don't-label-me's were still hearing quoted Romans and Corinthians. That night Scott dreamed about a friend from his master's program and his wife. He was serving them a baked salmon with fresh ginger, the secret being to add the ginger toward the end mixed with bottled Asian fish sauce, despite the sodium. In midlife you needed to worry about having a stroke. Those little fuckers were waiting to pounce. Thought you were young but age had been creeping up on you—just ask Perry. He'd just had his first stroke. The fact of the stroke was there in the dream, too, but not Perry. Woody Allen was there, too, saying just before he had sex with Diane Keaton, "I'll get the soy sauce."

The wife, still young and beautiful, still the same as during grad school, was on the other side of the table, not eating but staring across at Scott and, as he deduced in his clean sleep (since dreams imparted the exposition real life couldn't), she reached between her legs playing with her pussy. Meanwhile, the old colleague, still looking good, still stroke-unafflicted, was praising the "Great Williams" of postmodern American literature with his old schoolboy reverence—Gaddis, Gass, and Goyen. Always taking himself too seriously. Then this friend was on his feet in his old black Chuck Taylor sneakers and tight Levi's 501 jeans, gesticulating wildly, singing "Seventy-Six Trombones" like Robert Preston in *Music Man*. Did this mean Scott could have had sex with them way back then? What had he missed about those evenings with them? Or that he was in an eternal-return scenario of never-expired desire, having always wanted to sleep with a boy and his girl, dark and light, giver and taker, himself moving back and forth between both poles?

"Seventy-six trombones!"

No, all it meant was that he wanted a cigarette, and he got up and went to the bathroom in the blue-gray shadows and peed then went out onto the deck in the delicious night and smoked.

The same three kids were two tables away at breakfast, evidently hungover. Few of the items on the kids' plates had been touched at all, but their first bloody marys were drained.

The boy said, "The deal is, I'm not normally comfortable with face-sitting."

"*Gaah*," said the first girl, "I certainly am."

The second girl said, "I myself am a seasoned habituée of that proud li'l practice."

All this youthful irony gleaned from old advertisement bravado and smirk.

"Let me just say," the boy came back, "that this time, actually, it was totally fun and hot?"

They were smoking and from the smell of it Scott got the craving. The city of Key West had been smart never to ban smoking in bars and outdoor restaurants, and here they were outdoors, under lightly flapping red canvas umbrellas. Feature that discussion at the Chamber of Commerce with the mayor and a few city councilmen present: "Your honor, tobacco is our bread and butter."

The waiter, older and disabused, came and forbearingly took their second-round orders.

The second girl had trouble stubbing out her ended cigarette in the table's ashtray and she said, "My mother thinks the only bloody mary worth its weight is a gin one, not a vodka one."

"Amazing," the boy said.

The first girl said, "Amazing, right? Because, lemme just say, what's wrong with vodka?"

"Anyway, that's what my mom says. I'm just. Admittedly, my mom's a freaking loon!"

Moratorium on the word 'amazing.' Also 'impact' as a verb, as well as 'impactful' . . ."

Perry laughed over the phone and said, "Are you resisting returning to New York?"

Scott said, "I don't want to leave. You know how much I miss you, but I prefer it here."

"I don't blame you," Perry said—but only would have said it if he were satisfied, too. He was probably lying down, his voice leisurely and groggy. "I never noticed that about 'amazing.' How'd you get to be so observant?" Perry was always trying to buck Scott up on the intellect front.

Outside, one of the island's many roosters crowed, then it caught fire with the others.

"It's just so overused. It's lost its currency. I could say the same with 'community.' Get two of these chickens together, they're a community, with rights and a common shared history."

Another moment and Perry said, "I can't wait for you to come home."

The wild chickens were protected by law, though locals hated them. He and Perry had to pause while the relay of cock crows subsided. Harsh and rustic, they sounded nearly human.

Before Scott hung up, when the wind rattled the fronds outside his bedroom and Scott lay in the dark, Perry said, "I really had a great time tonight. He was Albanian, and I had no idea."

"Idea about what?" said Scott.

"That in New York, so many Albanians. Apparently they all staff the Italian restaurants."

"Duh."

"You knew that?"

"Haven't you been paying any attention?"

"This one works at an old tacky joint down on Bleecker," said Perry—and then his pause seemed to be telling Scott a profound thing about time, about the illusion of place. Either that or Scott wasn't feeling well. He was losing the illusion of himself, his trace of time slacking up.

Alone with the frond-rattle, he thought, I've eaten nothing today. Nor am I even hungry. And this wasn't right. The island, trying to please you, was out to kill your sorry ass. Sweetly.

He was at Fantasy House getting fucked as he lay on his back, legs splayed in the air. He'd lost weight and his curves and bulges had cinched a bit and he'd felt more appealing and comely.

Fantasy House was an all-male, clothing-optional resort with a pool, wet area, everything. Upstairs, a maze of dark spaces and benches with cushions beneath video monitors playing porn.

Before the sex, this Cedric had said, "I never wear condoms, just saying."

Scott had nodded ungivingly, persisting, and said, "So what do you do for a living?"

"I work in the health industry. I know, funny, right? I'm an unsafe health professional."

"But you don't work in an STD clinic or anything like that, I hope."

"Actually, I'm a respiratory therapist."

"And you don't smoke, I hope."

"I do not. But I do figure, about the condoms, if I have anything then I just have it—and what I have I can't do anything about now, so. It's just my way of thinking. You have a lover?"

"I have a lover."

"*So do I*—and I still think whatever I've got, maybe I can't undo it now. It's my creed."

"It's a position."

"Get up on that table," said Cedric. "I'm going to break my rule, first time in a while."

Afterwards, Cedric's story. Small-town North Carolina upbringing, navy, freedom.

In the night the sound of a full heavy moon groaning as it wheeled above mechanically—slowly, from the dark-blue starry heavens over the Atlantic toward the constellations above the Gulf, full watery and giving a liquid sound, the sky too, all thought and emotions turbidly saline, a solution lapping at his forehead plaintively as he woke to a dry rasp in his throat. Even his bladder rasped with a painful swelling more jagged and scratchier than the coarse grainy shore that was raked by the light foamy fingers of the soft and cool and incursive sea. The subtly calling night-bright sea.

That moon as he'd loped home from Fantasy House the night before was a warm, wet wad of wax, dripping friendly, and his peeing now was a trail of quick oblique razor cuts, killing-hot.

Again the kids—lined up catty-corner from him at the great rectangular bar. They had come in wearing swags of metallic Mardi Gras beads around their necks and were already trashed.

"Oh my God, it's you!" said the first girl. "It's you, right?"

"It's me."

"I'm Branch."

"Nice to meet you, Branch."

"And I'm Durriya."

"Which means diamond."

"Oh my God! That's exactly what it means. Amazing. How did you know?"

"I studied a little Arabic," said Scott. "I was in an Arabic-speaking country for a while."

The boy said, "We have to freaking leave at eight freaking a.m., for fuck's sake."

"You studied Arabic? But oh my God, I love this freaking song. You know what? This song came out when my mother was in high school. How's that for a mind-fuck? I wasn't even born, and my mother was in high school. Is that not a major skull-fuck? I wasn't *alive* . . ."

But Scott had been in college back then, too. The boy caught his eye and smiled.

The boy's name was Shelby. To save time, Scott lied and said he lived here. The boy wanted to talk about New York only. Shelby was from Pennsylvania but vowed he'd never ever go back.

"If I could say," he began quaveringly operatically, by way of a humming, rising prelude, "if I could just say? My life, to be perfectly honest, only got started when I got to New York."

They'd had all the sex they were going to have, and Scott said, "But that's wonderful."

"New York? You know what? New York is, like, for rich people. It's for rich people, or like famous people, or else it's just for like young people. Luckily I'm young, but just barely."

Something tore at Scott and he smiled crookedly and said, "To me, you're very young."

But Shelby was off on a tear, not looking at Scott but refracting himself through others—his peers, his cohort—and this raised his dander: "Are you kidding? Dude, I'm heinous-aged!"

Which Scott thought rather clever if naïve. He was a cute, pretty boy who was wasting it.

Outside the cottage, the night rattled the leaves. The moon was on the wane. Just before it was light he noticed Shelby getting dressed. Scott pretended to sleep. The spectacle of Shelby stealing out, before the stupid older guy faltering in his delirium woke up, weirdly delighted him.

Later he thought about his Paris days with Perry, so much earlier. Sex was gone. But the need was still there. Much older Hélène, Perry's best friend in France, seemed to exemplify this.

"I never said no to a man," she'd said, ironically not long before she'd died. "Never!"

He was remembering this in the hospital, tethered to drips and IVs and monitoring leads, a grotesque of former human shape, a half-mechanical octopus. Sex was this quiet secret, only it was all over the place. You came to it as though secretly, then decided, no, it was quite universal.

And he was sure that he was almost at the end of his Key West tether, almost letting go of its grip, and it made him sad but, just as equally, satisfied and comforted him. He was through.

And then several years passed, not as many as Scott might have wished.

He'd wound down and quit the sex—fatigued, broken some. Perry's visits became less and less frequent. He'd been cheated, were Scott's final bursts of thinking. Once, he'd almost bought the American line of a cumulative, building happiness. Better the French noir sentimentality, though he'd never understood that. He'd watched their friend Hélène dying. She had said near the end, "At least I haven't lost my sense of humor." But Hélène was perhaps the least funny person he'd ever met, though she'd lived an interesting life. Had Scott? Who was Scott? This intubated guy on oxygen? Everything now was a little like that old drunken late-night, early-pee delirium . . .

Hospice had its advantages. If he farted and it turned into shit, he couldn't be blamed. If the bedding was soiled he need only apologize. The memory of sex preoccupied him. Once he'd hoped that his libido would go away. It was like a thirst or hunger attacking him. Eating him up.

He was sharing a room with an older man who had a neurological disorder that made him shout and curse obliquely while at the same time he recalled the summer of 1945, a good year as even Scott believed it must have felt like to the lucky folk who'd just seen a delayed apocalypse.

The man seemed unaware of Scott's presence on the other side of a neatly pleated curtain which he may have taken as a stage curtain, muttering and rehearsing preshow lines to himself.

"For months," the man whose name Scott didn't know called, "full dancing in the streets! Dancing in the streets you've never seen—and believe me, buddy, back then we knew dancing!"

Was Scott his buddy? Each time Scott wondered if the man didn't truly sense him there.

Scott as a boy watching Woody Allen movies on Cinemax when they first got cable could only dream of living in New York one day— the intelligent babble, the backdrop, the being-alive. Even an order of diner french fries had sounded stylish, intellectual, de rigueur. He had come a long way, Scott, and now he was going even farther. Black coffee and fries, intellectual talk, and you're done. Stick a fork in you, you're done. How beautiful the world had been so far and how wonderful the sex, the food, the drink. It was drink and smoke that had brought him here. All of life's pleasures were why he was dying, but in his druggy state he told himself he didn't mind, he did not mind at all. He'd had the dream of New York and he'd had the reality of living here, too. It had been an incredible ride but now it was done. Mom, Dad. Perry? Was Perry still alive? It was not a bad death, overall. But dying here, on the gray East Side, on a dank-looking February day?

It had never occurred to him.